The Pajama Girls of Lambert Square

Also by Rosina Lippi

Tied to the Tracks

Homestead

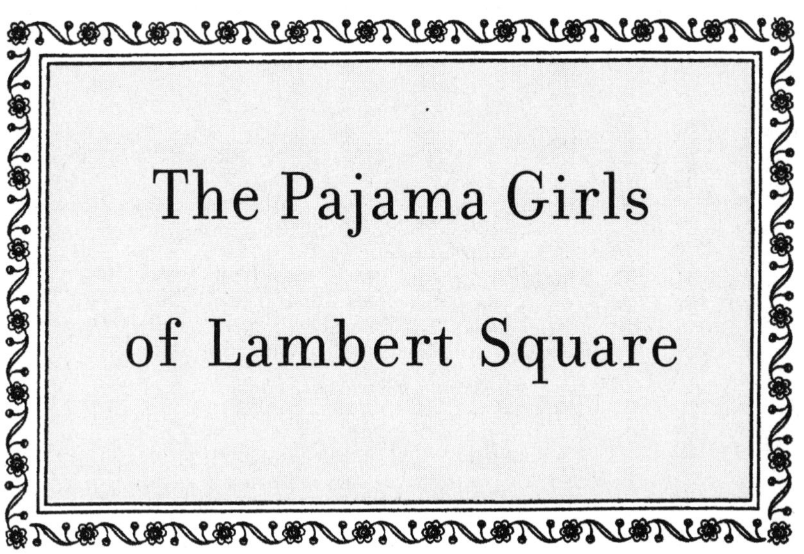

The Pajama Girls of Lambert Square

Rosina Lippi

G. P. Putnam's Sons

New York

G. P. PUTNAM'S SONS
Publishers Since 1838
Published by the Penguin Group
Penguin Group (USA) Inc., 375 Hudson Street, New York, New York 10014, USA • Penguin Group (Canada), 90 Eglinton Avenue East, Suite 700, Toronto, Ontario M4P 2Y3, Canada (a division of Pearson Penguin Canada Inc.) • Penguin Books Ltd, 80 Strand, London WC2R 0RL, England • Penguin Ireland, 25 St Stephen's Green, Dublin 2, Ireland (a division of Penguin Books Ltd) • Penguin Group (Australia), 250 Camberwell Road, Camberwell, Victoria 3124, Australia (a division of Pearson Australia Group Pty Ltd) • Penguin Books India Pvt Ltd, 11 Community Centre, Panchsheel Park, New Delhi–110 017, India • Penguin Group (NZ), 67 Apollo Drive, Rosedale, North Shore 0632, New Zealand (a division of Pearson New Zealand Ltd) • Penguin Books (South Africa) (Pty) Ltd, 24 Sturdee Avenue, Rosebank, Johannesburg 2196, South Africa

Penguin Books Ltd, Registered Offices:
80 Strand, London WC2R 0RL, England

Published simultaneously in Canada

Library of Congress Cataloging-in-Publication Data

Lippi, Rosina, date.
The pajama girls of Lambert Square / Rosina Lippi.
p. cm.
ISBN 978-0-399-15466-9
1. City and town life—South Carolina—Fiction. I. Title.
PS3562.I5795P35 2008 2007038588
813'.54—dc22

Printed in the United States of America
1 3 5 7 9 10 8 6 4 2

Book design by Meighan Cavanaugh

This novel is dedicated to good friends:

Ruth Czirr and Paul Willenborg, who worked hard to keep the Yankee me on the southern straight and narrow,

and

Cheryll Kinsley, who shored me up during the various crises in the year this book was written—only a few of them fictional in nature

A bird may love a fish,

but where will they build a home together?

TEVYE, in *Fiddler on the Roof*

1

Collector's Weekly

May 30, 2004

Small Business for Sale

Scriveners is a specialty shop offering antique and collectible writing instruments with a focus on fountain pens. Large stock of quality paper goods and ephemera. Located in historic Lamb's Corner, South Carolina. Owner retiring. Serious inquiries by U.S. mail only. Robert Lee Cowper, Scriveners, 10 Lambert Square, Lamb's Corner, SC.

2

June 15, 2004

Mr. John A. Dodge
Wordplay Books
270 West Sixth Avenue
Amarillo, TX 79106

Dear Mr. Dodge,

You were the fourth person to answer my newspaper advertisement but only the second to follow the instructions. The fellow who was quicker than you with his response has an illegible signature. I cannot abide a man with a messy hand. From your penmanship it's clear to me you have had a good education, and considerable experience in the world.

I opened Scriveners on September 1, 1973. The shop was located on Main Street until the conversion of the old Lambert Printing Plant was finished and then I moved over there. Scriveners occupies one of two large corner buildings. It consists of three floors: the shop itself, the second level, which I use mostly for sorting stock, and a two bedroom apartment on the top floor, which I have never used.

If you care to call me on the telephone I will answer your questions regarding my stock, the property, and the services we offer. You might also like to get in touch with our mayor, Mrs. Maude Reed-Golden, and with the president of the Lambert Square Merchants' Cooperative, Mrs. Julia Darrow. Before you go to the trouble, a couple things you should know that might change your mind:

1. The first condition of sale, once the buyer and I have agreed on terms, is that both my full-time employees be kept on in their current positions for a period of no less than two years, without reduction in wages or benefits.

2. I have never had a computer and have no computerized inventories, customer lists, or sales history. All that information is kept safely in the mind of one of my clerks.

3. My mother was a Lambert and left me a great deal of money, so that profit has never been my primary concern. In fact, Scriveners has never made any money and operates, as they say, in the red.

Should you wish to open negotiations, I ask that you contact me by return mail or telephone. A courageous man with vision, one who enjoys a challenge and appreciates fine craftsmanship, certainly would.

Yours truly,

Robert Lee Cowper

3

SEPTEMBER 2004

WHEN THE ALARM went off, three of Julia Darrow's four dogs catapulted themselves off the couch to rush the door. Julia, who had fallen asleep in her favorite chair in a jumble of books and blankets, woke more slowly. The fourth and the most relaxed of the dogs was tucked in beside her, and still snoring. Boo was unflappable, which really, Julia had observed many times, was an enviable talent first thing in the morning.

Julia yawned. Gloria, Willie, and Scoot began dancing impatiently, nails clicking on the wood floor like so many castanets. Boo blinked and raised her head at the sound of a light knock.

"Julia?"

"Coming." She pulled herself out of the chair, set Boo down on the floor, and together they padded across the room.

"Monsters," Julia said to the other three. "Ruffians. Mind your manners. Gloria, stop that." She opened the door and they raced out, Scoot disappearing immediately down the stairs with a flick of the tail. Gloria and Willie paused to acknowledge the young girl who stood on the landing. She was here to walk them, and the walk was the thing.

"Bean," Julia said, "I don't pay you enough."

Beatrice Hurt, Bean to friends and family and just about everybody else, was the only child of one of Julia's five employees, and spent most of her free time in the shop when she wasn't in school. She was all knobby elbows and knees and a mass of braids, which stood out not just for their bounty but because they were naturally two shades lighter than the deep molasses of her skin, and the effect set off her bone structure, perfectly symmetrical from the small round chin to the deep-set eyes in the oval of her face. But she was also unusually somber for her age. Her smile, rare as it was, was sweet.

She said, "Mama says you pay me too much as it is. Come on, Boo."

Boo sighed dramatically but when Bean picked her up, she nuzzled and licked the girl's cheek. From the bottom of the stairs came a sharp and impatient bark.

"Scoot," said Bean. "He's gotta go when he's gotta go."

To Bean's retreating back Julia said, "We'll talk about a raise."

IN THE NEW QUIET, JULIA TOOK A MOMENT TO CONTEMPLATE the chair where she had just spent five blissful hours in a dreamless sleep. She had found it at an estate sale in Lake Forest years before, wide and low slung, lavishly cushioned and upholstered in velvet, the fabric as darkly silky and smooth as browned butter. The impression of her heels had made a permanent dip in the ottoman and the nap on the broad arms was worn thin, but she loved the chair for its sturdiness and comfort. The urge to climb back into the nest was strong, but habit was stronger.

Julia had a routine, one she had developed in the first few months after moving to Lamb's Corner, and had refined in the five years since. Coffee and toast, a half hour on the treadmill, a half hour of housework, and a shower before she allowed herself to go down to her office or the shop. She turned on the radio and started her day, making lists in her head as she moved around the four rooms she called home.

Finally Julia stood in the open door of her bedroom closet, considering her choices. These few idle minutes spent breathing in the faint scents of lavender, cotton dried in the open air, crisply ironed linen were her last peaceful ones of the day, and not to be rushed. She ran her hand down a soft flannel sleeve. It would be foolish to indulge such a whim in the early September heat. She would be wearing silk and light cotton for another month at least.

The murmur of voices rose up through the floor, which meant that Julia was running late or somebody else was early. She finger combed her hair, slipped into her workday slippers, and then paused anyway to look over the room. Standing in the doorway she thought, as she always did, of the odd turns of fate that had brought this particular set of bedroom furniture here, to a third-floor apartment in a converted printing plant in a small town in South Carolina. Her own history was almost as odd, but nothing as interesting as the two-hundred-year-old Louis XVI bed of carved plum pudding mahogany with all the matching pieces. It was precious and beautiful and almost priceless, and sometimes Julia dreamed that she was strapped into a harness, dragging all of it, the huge three-door armoire, the bedside tables with their marble tops, the bed itself with its carvings of angels among floral garlands, down a narrow road that reached to the horizon and over the edge of the world.

Julia noted the pillows in their clean white cases, the simple coverlet, the quilt folded at the foot of the bed. Then she closed the door behind her and went to work.

At the bottom of the rear stairs Bean was waiting for her with the dogs. Who flung themselves at Julia in their joy, in their relief, in the vast fury of their unconditional love.

4

TWO YEARS to the day after John Dodge arrived in Amarillo he took off again, this time for Lamb's Corner, South Carolina.

He left behind him a well-run, profitable bookstore in the care of its new owners; he took with him nothing but those personal possessions he could fit into his car, an ability to hold a conversation in Spanish, and a heightened appreciation for Tex-Mex food. It wasn't hard to leave, though he would miss a few people. You couldn't live in a place for two years without making friends, or at least, Dodge didn't care to live like that.

Headed east on I-40 he admitted to himself that he had stayed too long. Amarillo had started to feel like home.

Dodge came to some other conclusions on the long drive cross-country. First, he had had enough of bookstores for a while, and of more intellectual pursuits in general. After this next project—he'd give Scriveners fourteen months, sixteen at the outside—he would look for something very different. As soon as he got settled and things were on track, he'd start the research. Someplace in the north for a change, enough of the red states already. Albany or Seattle or Madison.

His second conclusion was that he was really ready for a dog. A dog would be company on these long drives. The right dog could spend the day with him at work. The right dog was good for business, and even better when it came to early-morning runs. He'd find the nearest shelter once he got settled in Lamb's Corner.

Dodge took his time with the drive. When the urge hit him, he stopped in small towns to see what they had to offer, which businesses were solid and which storefronts empty. Paying attention to the display windows, what was in them, whether anybody stopped to look. He had been studying the body language of shoppers for years. It was all about figuring out what people thought they wanted, and if you approached it just right, actually selling them something they wouldn't feel bad about the next day, and at a profit. He had a head for business, a natural talent for numbers and planning and strategy, but it was reading people that was his true talent, and the part of retail he liked best.

At three or so every day Dodge started looking for a motel, settled in and read late into the night, choosing at random from his pile of books. *South Carolina: A History. The Mind of the South. I'll Take My Stand: The South and the Agrarian Tradition. South Carolina's Civil War. South Carolina: An Economic Profile. A South Carolina Chronology.*

He made notes in the margins of the reports that he had solicited and paid for on the town itself. History, economics, politics. When it came to numbers he didn't like surprises, and never shied away from bad news.

He had books on pens as well. On their history, composition and construction, lore, repair, and the collectors' market. Those books he saved for later, when he could study the two thousand examples he had just bought from Robert Lee Cowper as he read.

. . .

DODGE HAD A ROUTINE WHEN HE ARRIVED IN A NEW PLACE. It was his belief that a town had to be approached slowly, quietly, and with the sure knowledge that you were going to get some things wrong, no matter how much time and research you put in before you ever got there.

He found a motel just outside Lamb's Corner, an independent that had evaded the long reach of the chains and stayed true to its origins: ten two-room cabins that had last been overhauled sometime in the fifties. He checked into Raddie's Café (Hot Biscuits, Country Ham) and Cabins (Television, Air-Conditioning), accepting the key to number three from Raddie himself, and sidestepping questions about where he was headed by asking about the deer racks mounted on the office wall.

Dodge took a shower, stretched out on the nubby bedspread, and called his sister.

"I'm here."

Nora said, "I was wondering about you. Where is *here* again, exactly? Benning or Jackson?"

Dodge settled back on the motel bed and balanced the phone on his belly. Nora was trying to wind him up, but he knew her tricks.

"Benning's way over on the Georgia–Alabama border. I'm a couple few hours from Charleston in one direction the same from Savannah in another."

"And?"

"Fort Jackson is maybe three hours."

"Hooah," said Nora.

"When are you going to stop navigating the country by army base?"

His sister said, "What is it this time, again? Fountain pens?"

"Fountain pens, antique, vintage, and plain old. Paper, stationery, cards, stuff to write on. The good old boy who started the shop back in the seventies wants to travel the world, and I liked the sound of this place. Something a little different for a change."

"You know what would be a little different?" Nora said. "If I could get your niece out of bed without deploying tactical weapons."

They settled in for a long talk. Nora had three kids, two dogs, a clinical therapy practice she shared with her husband, and a big house in Brooklyn.

She was always tense at the start of her weekly conversations with Dodge, and usually calmer at the end, when they went through their standard list of questions.

"The old folks?"

Nora said, "You know, someday you're going to slip and call them that where the Colonel can hear you. Then you'll find out how old he is. I talked to Mom, what, a couple days ago."

"And?"

"The usual."

Dodge decided not to pursue that subject. "The boys?"

"You'll have to explain to me sometime how it is I turned into clearing-house central."

"You're the youngest, you're maternal, and you've been in the same house with the same phone number forever."

Nora grumbled, but she told him what he wanted to know. Dodge's two younger brothers—both of them Army JAG corps lawyers made in the image of their father—had reported in to Nora within the last week. Tom was in Germany and Jimmy at Fort Lewis in Washington.

"You coming for Thanksgiving this year?"

Dodge waited a beat and she said, "Okay, yes. The Colonel will be here."

"I'll see what I can do," Dodge said. "I can't promise you Thanksgiving, but I wouldn't miss Christmas."

"I want you to think about Thanksgiving," Nora said.

"I'm thinking about it."

"Hmmmmm," said Nora.

5

DODGE SPENT his first full day in Lamb's Corner walking around the town but avoiding Lambert Square. He explored the old downtown block for block, counting abandoned stores with soaped windows, taking mental notes of the rest. A laundromat and dry cleaner, an empty space with a sun-faded sign in the window: *Polly and Mister have moved to Lambert Square. Come on by for a cup of coffee*. A repair shop window full of toasters, irons, radios; a drugstore with a sun filter like a thick yellow skin pulled down between the window and the dusty display of boxes and bottles. Aspirin. Gold Bond powder. Alka-Seltzer. A barbershop, a beauty parlor, a pawnshop. The Food Lion's sign needed paint; most of the buildings downtown did, including the one that housed the Moulton County sheriff's office and the volunteer fire department. Two patrol cars out front looked well maintained but long past prime.

The Augusta Lambert Memorial Public Library was small but well kept. Dodge went right by without stopping; librarians were curious types and he wasn't ready for questions.

He paid fifty cents for the *Lamb's Corner Times*, a low-key, small-format four-page paper, more than fifty percent advertisements for back-to-school sales, supplemented by short reports on the city council meeting, a church picnic, new arrivals at the library, changes in the faculty at the grade school, and a half dozen other items of importance to the citizens of Lamb's Corner and nobody else at all.

A starker view of the local economy was to be found in the lobby of the credit union, where a bulletin board was lost beneath many layers of handwritten advertisements. Index cards and half sheets of paper, with telephone numbers carefully printed and then cut into a ruffle, thumbed photos, scribbled notes. Fifteen-year-old cars with a couple hundred thousand miles, must-sell motorboats and double-wides, wedding dresses, quilts, older computers. *Blue Heeler, works cows good. Kittens free to a good home. Coca-Cola puzzle framed as a picture $25 cash.* Guns, ammunition, a bowling ball. *Sears Deep Freeze, 5 years old. Runs real good.* Home beauty parlors, laundry and cleaning and dressmaking services, families looking for good day care that wouldn't break the budget. Church bake sales and a meeting of Al-Anon. The Dorcas House Shelter needed donations of diapers, toys, money. The Moulton County Humane Society was hoping for pet food, chew toys, old towels, and blankets. Dodge made note of the address.

What the bulletin board made clear was that Lambert Square alone couldn't pull the city out of its economic slump.

Dodge went into the chamber of commerce, where a very young receptionist took off his headphones long enough to hand the newcomer the literature he asked for. All stuff he had already.

"So," Dodge asked in a conversational tone. "When does construction start on the Kallsjö plant?"

The kid perked right up. He said, "Nobody knows for sure. Or maybe the mayor knows, but she ain't saying. I'm guessing any day now we'll hear about the groundbreaking. Mary Sue Bushnell, the real estate lady? She's been driving around a lot and not saying much, which if you knew Miz Bushnell, you'd know something's up. My guess is whoever's coming down here to oversee the whole construction business? They'll need places to live. There's some big old fancy houses on the edge of town—" He broke off suddenly and gave Dodge a penetrating look.

"You're not one of them, are you? One of those Kallsjö people, come over from Sweden?"

Dodge, who looked a lot like his grandfather Papadapolous, held up both palms. "No, no. Not me."

"Oh. Good. Well, they're not here yet but they're coming. Papers signed and everything." A startled look came over his face, as though somebody had prodded him with a pin.

"What was I thinking?" he asked himself aloud, and he pulled a photocopy out of a box sitting right on his desk. A newspaper article reproduced on blindingly yellow paper.

"Look here," he said. "The latest news about those Swedes."

Dodge took the sheet and ran his eyes down the article about the change in Lamb's Corner's fortunes, the one that had swayed Dodge's decision to buy out Scriveners:

Lamb's Corner Times

KALLSJÖ PLANS ON SCHEDULE

Moulton County can look forward to greeting a lot of new neighbors sometime in September, when the first wave of Kallsjö executives arrive in town. The Swedish manufacturer of personal and commercial vehicles finalized its purchase of Langtree Plantation six months ago, and soon will begin the construction phase that will bring their North American headquarters and a state-of-the-art assembly plant to our community.

Founded in 1930 by Magnus Gyllensting, Kallsjö's U.S. market share has grown steadily over the last twenty years. Industry analysts attribute Kallsjö's success to its reputation for low-emission, high-fuel-economy vehicles and its investment in research and advanced technologies. Within two years Kallsjö projects the plant will employ 4,500 people.

There has been no official announcement regarding which vehicles will be manufactured here, but some believe the most likely candidates are the two models that sell best in the American market: the Freya, a compact four-door sedan with high safety ratings and excellent gas mileage, and the Thor, a hybrid car famous in the industry for its quirky design, which many pronounced misguided and doomed, but which immediately found a large and appreciative market.

Mayor Maude tells us that she expects Beate Gyllensting, director of North American operations and the great-granddaughter of the company's founder, to be one of the first to arrive, and that her stay in Lamb's Corner will be a lengthy, if not a permanent, one. We encourage our readers to submit questions to be put to Miss Gyllensting when we meet with her soon after her arrival.

"I expect the jobs will be welcome," Dodge said.

"Yes, sir, they surely will be. I'm hoping to get one in the office there myself. Are you thinking of relocating to Lamb's Corner?"

"You never know," Dodge said, and left the kid to think about that.

That afternoon he walked out to the west side of town, through a neighborhood of older houses on streets named after Confederate generals: Ewell, Armistead, Polk, Hill, Pickett, Mosby, Beauregard. The biggest of the houses were clustered on Ewell, many of them built long before air-conditioning or central heating. There were a lot of very old trees: palmettos, tupelos, magnolias and dogwoods, loblolly pines and camellias. A huge live oak with a crown span of a good hundred feet cast deep shade over a Greek Revival behemoth in need of a new roof. The architectural styles ranged from Queen Anne to Craftsman to Spur-of-the-Moment. One small cottage had been painted a bright pink and sat like a playhouse in the middle of a lush garden. Many of the houses had weathered FOR SALE signs bristling with exclamation marks and breathless announcements of lowered prices.

There was what looked to be an empty lot overrun by kudzu, but on second glance Dodge made out the indistinct lines of a small house swallowed up by the vines, like a lump in a snake's belly. It was a disquieting image. The elderly black man who was working in the front garden of the neat house just across the road deserved something better to look at. He seemed to hear Dodge thinking about him, because he looked up and smiled. Touched a knobby old hand to the Atlanta Braves baseball cap and called out.

"Morning, sir. Can I help you find something?"

Dodge walked across to him. "I'm just taking a walk, but thank you."

The old man scratched his chin with his wrist. "Saw you looking at the Abbotts' place. Been on the market three years now. Bet you could get a good price."

"I'm not ready to buy just yet," Dodge said.

"Oh see, I thought maybe you were one of those Swedes come into town early."

Dodge laughed. "You're the second person to say as much to me. Do I look Swedish to you, Mr.—"

"Schmidt. Lamont Schmidt. Would you have guessed me for a German?"

Dodge grinned. "I take your point. I'm John Dodge."

He shook the older man's hand, which was surprisingly small and fine-boned, but strong.

"I'm keeping you from your work. It's a beautiful garden you've got there, even this late in the season."

Lamont Schmidt looked over his shoulder at the rectangle of grass surrounded by flower beds, the neat house of painted brick, and the deep wrap-around porch.

He said, "It's a nice property, yes it is. One of the sweetest little houses in Lamb's Corner. But it ain't mine, Mr. Dodge. I work part-time for a property management company out of Columbia? And they send me by here twice a week or so to see that things are working the way they should, look after the garden. Let me give you my card, in case you decide to buy the Abbott place and settle down right here. You could do worse."

His card was a little soft around the edges, as if it had spent a long time in his shirt pocket. Dodge wished the old man a good day and headed off, feeling good about Lamb's Corner. Comfortable, and at ease with the series of decisions that had brought him here.

He liked the neighborhood with its wide streets and old trees, but there was nothing particularly unusual about it. Every southern town had these neighborhoods. His father had grown up in one just like it. His grandmother Lucy still lived in that house, and told anybody who would listen that she scrubbed her own floors and hung out her own laundry and would do both until she dropped down dead. He'd have to find time to go spend a weekend with his grandmother or he'd never hear the end of it.

Dodge turned a corner and found himself on the edge of what had once been farmland. He walked a quarter mile to a group of outbuildings—a half-collapsed barn, a greenhouse minus its glass, sheds. And a sign done in bright yellows and oranges, its cheery message pockmarked by birdshot: *Welcome to Historic Langtree Plantation.* A stylized map with red rectangles to indicate the locations of the original buildings and fields along the river. Docks and boathouses, the plantation house, destroyed by fire 1970. The slave quarters. Tobacco and cotton sheds. Sugar house. The family cemetery, relocated 1990. Blacksmithy. Wainwright. Bake House. *Tours by appointment, please inquire at the Lamb's Corner Public Library.*

A quarter mile away a fence ran along what must have been the property boundary, dotted with warning signs and neat patches of purple posting paint. On the other side a cluster of maybe two dozen mobile homes on sizable lots, some with small gardens. A few were in poor shape, but Dodge had seen far worse on his drives across the country.

Somewhere in one of the reports he remembered a short paragraph about the agreement Kallsjö had made: they would build a certain amount of low-income housing on the other side of Lamb's Corner. And so in a matter of months the mobile homes would be gone, and an entire automotive manufacturing plant would have risen out of the ground. It would look like another planet.

At the café where he ate his lunch Dodge listened to men in work clothes talking about what was to come, their moods shifting from pragmatic to cynical to philosophical and back again.

It's our past, one of them had said. *It's our history they're paving over.*

An old black man with rheumy eyes had shrugged. *It's food on the table.* And that was the end of the discussion.

6

THE NEXT MORNING Dodge went to sit in Lambert Square before the shops opened.

The plan was to stay right there for as long as he could manage to get away with it. First he had to find a good spot—in this case a well-situated bench in the shade. Then he settled down with an open book in his lap. Sunglasses gave him the freedom to watch the crowd without causing alarm. He meant to look like just another stranger in a place where strangers were welcome, a guy with some money in his pockets, resigned to waiting while his wife or girlfriend or kids shopped.

So his first couple hours in Lambert Square on a very warm morning in early September, Dodge observed. He saw a commercial space put together with care and foresight and imagination. A rectangle of park, lots of trees for shade, a fountain in the middle, and paths that wandered among flower beds. Dodge thought of Lamont Schmidt, and wondered if he'd see him here, watering and weeding. On the far end of the park an elderly man sat on a bench and threw a ball for two very attentive dogs.

The longer redbrick buildings on two sides of the park had been divided into retail shops. The architect had knocked out space for display windows and added dark green canvas awnings. Heavy doors were painted red or yellow or blue. Flower pots flanked windows and spilled over with more color. On the far side of Lambert Square, the two corner buildings stood detached from another redbrick building between them. The fourth side, at Dodge's back, was partially open to River Road and the Chicopee itself, just beyond.

There was a lot of foot traffic. Polly's Café and the bakery had opened hours before, and the outdoor tables were full. People drifted into the square by means of covered walkways that came from the parking structure and went right by Scriveners display windows, which were, Dodge saw with some dismay, filled with boxes. Most of the shoppers were women, many with kids who looked longingly at the park but got dragged indoors anyway. A good proportion of people over fifty and, judging by their clothes and shoes and purses, with some money to spend. Lambert Square was a place where the locals worked, but no doubt most of Lamb's Corner's school shopping was happening fifteen miles away at the Stephensville Kmart or Target, where they got five or six outfits for the price of one of the designer dresses spread out like butterflies in the display window of Jennifer's Rabbit.

The shop in the corner opposite Scriveners seemed to draw a lot of attention. Dodge consulted the map he had picked up outside the information kiosk. *Cocoon: Antique, vintage & quality bedding, linen & sleepwear.* Someplace in one of the reports was a page about Cocoon. All he could recall just now was that the owner was the only non-native of South Carolina. Or had been, until Dodge bought out Robert Lee Cowper.

Mostly Dodge watched Scriveners' front door, which provided him with concrete evidence of what he knew in theory: the shop was in trouble. In an hour exactly two people went in, one of them most likely Lincoln Kay, an older man, tall and concave of chest. Under a bald head his face was long and thin. The other was a woman in pajamas. Bright pink pajamas with some kind of flowery pattern, and matching high-heeled slippers covered with floppy silk roses. Above a face with a pointed chin and wide cheekbones, her hair was short and layered, the kind of cut that would require next to no attention.

Dodge was trying to make sense of the fact that she was wearing pajamas to carry a pile of papers across Lambert Square when he remembered the letter he had in his pocket. It had come along with the last of the paperwork after the sale, written with a fountain pen in Cowper's old-fashioned, tiny script. *As I will be gone by the time you get to Lamb's Corner, here are a few notes to get you started on the right foot. Needless to say this is a somewhat sensitive document and I would appreciate it if it didn't come into public circulation. I would like to come home to Lamb's Corner one day without fear of tar and feathers.*

The older man had written his thoughts on most of his neighbors in Lambert Square. His tone was so forthright and uncensored that Dodge had the idea that he might have been under the influence at the time. Now he skimmed the pages until he found the parts he wanted.

> ***Lincoln Kay.*** A couple few things about Link. First, he knows you can't do without him as he's got every bit of information about the business not to mention the whole inventory locked up in his old bald head. Second, he's a lot smarter than he wants you to know he is. Finally, he's got a heart as soft as pudding, a taste for gossip, and an eye for anything in skirts, though he never married. I suggest you don't depend on Link for news, because when the truth runs up against a good story, he'll sacrifice the truth every time.
>
> ***Julia Darrow.*** Charlie Darrow was the architect who handled the restoration of the old printing plant into what is now Lambert Square. Julia is Charlie's widow. She moved down here from Chicago five years ago, just shortly after Charlie died. Pretty much everybody likes Julia, even those who disapprove of Yankees on general principles. She's the president of the merchants' cooperative, she runs a very profitable business, coordinates a whole network of women who do fine needlework all throughout South Carolina and

Georgia, and she fosters three or four rescue dogs at a time. I don't think the woman ever sleeps. She's right friendly when you run into her on the square, but after hours mostly she keeps to herself. Julia has four full-time employees, all women and all contentious in one way or another. You want to watch out for Exa most especially, as she has never run into a rumor she didn't take to heart. The Cocoon ladies wear pajamas the whole day long, so you'll know them when you see them.

"HOPING FOR A CANCELLATION?"

Dodge started. He turned the letter over in his lap and looked at the old man who had sat down beside him. "Pardon?"

"Mrs. Tindell's." He jerked a thumb over his shoulder to the restaurant behind them. "Lunch at Mrs. Tindell's? You know you need a reservation. Me and Josie here, we've had our reservation for three months."

"It's been five months, dear," said his wife.

They were born and bred southerners, Bob and Josie Beales of Memphis, visiting relatives in Savannah and out on a long day trip. Dodge introduced himself in a way that he hoped would forestall a lot of questions. John Dodge, Brooklyn, New York.

"You don't sound like Brooklyn," said Bob Beales.

"He don't sound like South Carolina, either," said his wife.

"Army brat," said Dodge. "My sister lives in Brooklyn. I use her place as a home base."

It was a gamble. A certain kind of veteran would take this information as an invitation to an hour of war stories. Dodge was relieved to see that Mr. and Mrs. Beales were more concerned about their lunch. Others had begun to assemble in front of the restaurant, mostly couples, some with children.

"I hear the wait for a spot at the dinner table is closer to six months now," Josie Beales told him.

Dodge turned to consider the redbrick building behind him. Once it had been the general manager's residence, and it sat like a squat bulldog where tall cast-iron gates opened onto Chicopee River Road. Now a simple black-and-white sign stuck in a large pot of flowers announced that this was indeed Mrs. Tindell's Restaurant, Reservations Strongly Advised. Below that today's menu had been written in chalk. Bob and Josie would be eating trout fried in cornmeal, corn and red pepper relish, tomatoes, potato croquettes, biscuits, and something called Coronation Butterscotch Pie for dessert.

"I have heard that it's a good place to eat," John Dodge said. "But I'm not here for lunch."

"Then he must be waiting for somebody," Mr. Beales suggested to Mrs. Beales, as if Dodge were a painting to be analyzed for hidden meanings.

She said, "A good-looking man like that, he's waiting for his wife."

"I'm not married," Dodge said.

"Exactly," said Josie Beales. "That's why you're waiting."

IT WAS ONLY THE FIRST OF A SERIES OF UNSETTLING CONVERSAtions that followed one after the other for the rest of the day. The Bealeses had no sooner gone into their lunch at Mrs. Tindell's when two men came out of Swagger's Hook and Hackle and marched right toward Dodge.

It was an interesting pair. The taller of the two was a man who might have been seventy, but was nowhere near calling it quits. This was somebody who worked hard for a living and always had. He wore a leather apron over a collarless shirt, the sleeves rolled up to show muscular forearms, loose trousers of some odd material, and suspenders. He could have stepped out of a time machine from the year 1850, down to the long white hair tied at the nape of his neck with a piece of rawhide. Dodge searched his mind and came up with a name: Joe Don Landry, from Sand Happers Sutlery. Landry's expression was guarded, a little reluctant. His friend was clearly the motivating force in this march across the park.

The smaller man was carefully dressed, with knife pleats in his trousers and shirtsleeves, and a haircut that would have put a marine to shame. He weighed all of 120 pounds and looked like the type who would break into a sweat knocking over an empty trash can, but enjoy himself doing it.

When they were still out of hearing, they stopped to argue a bit and Dodge took the chance to look through Cowper's letter.

> ***Joe Don Landry.*** Joe Don is a good old boy in the best sense. Neighborly, quick to offer help and good with tools. He lives and

breathes the War Between the States. Knows more about it than most history professors, and will try to talk you into joining his Book Club of the Confederacy. He's away quite a bit, attending battle reenactments all over the South. He sells those historical buffs uniforms and boots and swords and such. He also shoes their horses and he's an excellent gunsmith. Jo Don's daughter Sue-Ann owns Charmed, the little jewelry store just across from him on the square. They are good solid folks, friendly, but they know how to mind their own business.

LRoy Swagger owns the Hook and Hackle. LRoy's mama gave him the prettiest name she could think of and spelled it for the nurse the way it sounded to her. To this day I don't think Miss Mae realizes her mistake. LRoy's granddaddy and daddy worked the old printing plant until they shut down and as a result LRoy has never met a Lambert he couldn't figure out how to dislike. He knows everything there is to know about fishing, as long as it involves a fly. LRoy is an award-winning fly tier. Beyond fish he talks football and Jesus and not much else. Married Janie Johnstone when they were both eighteen. Janie was born stone deaf and talks Sign Language with LRoy and their two boys, both married and settled in Columbia. The fact that Janie can't hear LRoy when it gets going is why the marriage has lasted this long, or at least that's how I explain it to myself. Otherwise it's a plain mystery.

Dodge put the letter safely away in his pocket and stood up to greet the men who had resumed their way toward him.

"You must be Mr. Swagger and Mr. Landry. I'm John Dodge." He held out his hand.

"Mister, you've been sitting there now two hours." LRoy Swagger had a surprisingly deep voice, purest South Carolina low country. "We seen you, watching women go by. You tell me why I shouldn't call down to the police station and report a lingerer and pervert, and maybe I'll believe you."

Dodge tried again, putting out his hand to Landry. "John Dodge, I just bought Scriveners. Glad to meet you." Landry shook without hesitation, his pale blue eyes fixed on Dodge in a way that made him glad he hadn't broken any laws lately.

"You got any identification?" Swagger asked.

It took five minutes of an extended introduction and his driver's license before Swagger gave up the idea of calling in the police. He said, "I thought you'd be an older fella, buying Cowper out the way you did, cash straight up. You come from money?"

"Just now I came from Texas," said Dodge. "But I was born in Charlottesville."

Swagger's mouth twitched, as if smiling was something he didn't much approve. "This is no big city, Mr. Dodge—"

"I'd be pleased if you'd call me Dodge. It's what I go by."

Landry cleared his throat. "LRoy, the man is our new neighbor."

"He's a stranger."

"I hope not for long," Dodge said.

Swagger's cheeks worked while he tried to decide whether or not he should be soothed, and then he remembered why he had come over.

"You see that building where my shop is?" He jerked a thumb over his shoulder. "That's the old print foundry. My granddaddy and my daddy worked there. Never missed a day of work, except for when Uncle Sam sent 'em off to war. Joe Don here, his folks helped build the plant some hundred fifty years ago now. Now maybe this place in't what it once was, but it is home, and we look out after one another."

"Good to know," said Dodge. He thought the men would retreat now, having established territorial rights, but it turned out they weren't done with him yet.

"You know anything about the War?" Landry asked. Just *the war*. Wanting to see if Dodge would ask for clarification.

Dodge grinned. "My father is a good old boy Virginia born and raised, and a graduate of West Point. I cut my teeth on the War of Northern Aggression."

Landry's expression relaxed into something like a smile. "I run a little book group," he said. "Maybe you'd be interested."

"Well, sure," Dodge said. "I'd be pleased to hear more about that." And saw he had passed the first test.

Swagger was still scowling. "You fish?"

The next test. Dodge scratched his jaw and stared off into the middle distance. He said, "My daddy took me and my brothers out now and then on a weekend when we were coming up."

There he went, sliding into the local rhythms, his sentences rearranging themselves like flowers turning their faces to the sun. It wasn't so much a talent as a twitch, something he couldn't stop himself from doing even when he made an effort. His sister and brothers had the same habit. What was unusual, and what would have earned him hoots of laughter, was calling Colonel T. R. Dodge of the Army JAG Corps *Daddy*.

"Fly fishing?"

"Is there any other kind?" Dodge said.

Swagger pursed his mouth in a reasonable imitation of a fish. "Come on by anytime," he said. "I'll set you up."

From what Dodge had seen in Swagger's show window, it would cost a minimum of five hundred dollars to put together basic gear. Dodge said, "I'll see what I can do," and LRoy Swagger retreated to rethink his strategy.

He turned his narrow head to Joe Don Landry and said, "Where do you think Mason has got to? I swear I don't know what we pay him for, he provides about as much security as a puppy."

As Landry and Swagger walked away Dodge became aware of the fact that there were people standing in every shop door as far as he could see. There was no hope for it. He got off his bench and set off to introduce himself to his new neighbors.

7

JULIA WAS STANDING at the counter sorting paperwork when Exa Stabley came in from the heat with her cheeks all flushed and her eyes shining.

"Here comes a whopper," said Mayme. "Brace yourself."

This was the way the workday began at Cocoon: the three of them getting ready to open the shop while Exa shared news, gossip, observations, and her philosophy of life. In the first month after they opened, Julia had been at a loss on how to handle Exa, who had been hired not so much for her retail experience as her excellent sewing skills and her connections. She was related to everybody in Lamb's Corner—including Mayme, who was as dark-skinned as Exa was light—and prided herself on getting along with every one of her blood kin. Exa had dozens of stories, and a determination to share them. After a month Julia began to wonder if there wasn't some way to turn her off, or at least down a notch.

"When it comes to Exa Stabley," Mayme said, "here's what you've got to do. Listen to her like you would to a radio station. Sometimes you listen real close, and sometimes you let your mind wander off to more important things. The radio won't take offense, and neither will Exa."

Between Exa, Mayme, and the rest of her female employees providing insight and direction, Julia had eventually learned how things worked in Lamb's Corner with a minimum of missteps.

Now Exa was wound up. "Guess who I just talked to?" She spread out her hands, palms up, and wiggled her fingers.

"John Dodge," said Mayme.

"John Dodge!" Exa beamed. "Who says there are no good-looking single men left? Now maybe he's a little too young for me, but y'all had best get a move on. He won't last long."

"We'll get right on that," Mayme said. "Just as soon as I've got this display case sorted, I'll go on over there and offer him my hand in marriage."

Mayme was divorced and sour on the subject of men in general, something Exa knew but refused to take as the final word on the matter. A woman as beautiful as Mayme Hurt deserved a man, Exa told her to her face. And Bean deserved a daddy. Sooner or later, Exa was sure, she would find the right candidate and then it would just be a matter of getting them in the same room together.

"John Dodge is more your type anyway," Exa said, turning her smile in Julia's direction. Which was code for the fact that she was white and so was John Dodge. Mayme closed her eyes and shook her head at Julia, which meant: *don't bother.*

"I've got those boxes to unpack," Julia said. "Call if you need me."

But Exa was not so easily deterred. She just raised her voice an octave while she told Mayme about the new owner of Scriveners.

"He's just as sweet and polite as he can be." Exa's voice wavered in earnest delight. "Joe Don says he's a good old boy and even LRoy don't have much to complain about. And fine-looking? Dodge don't sound to me like an Italian name, but he's dark. Do you suppose he might be Spanish or maybe even Jewish?" The emphasis on this last proposal was for Julia's sake.

"And something else, he goes by his last name. Says it's a tradition in the family for the firstborn son to be called Dodge? Now personally, I like the name John. And it suits him. John Wayne. John Kennedy—father and son. John Travolta—"

"John Wayne's name wasn't John Wayne," Mayme interrupted.

Exa drew in a shocked breath. "What are you talking about?"

"It's true," Mayme said. "His real name was Marion Morrison. He changed it to get into the movies."

"You are the worst tease," Exa said. "If you think I'm going to believe a big strong man like John Wayne had a girl's name—" She laughed. "You know, it's encouraging when you get into a silly mood. You have to fight that somber streak you got from the Hurt side. Your great-granddaddy Stabley was a cheerful sort."

To Julia's relief this conversation on Mayme's family tree was interrupted by Marnie Lambert, who stopped by most mornings. For a moment Exa got sidetracked in a discussion of Marnie's new skirt and blouse, the fabric and weave and cut and how much it had cost and where it was made and really, the lining hung a little odd and could Exa take care of that for her? It would only need a bit of a minute.

The crisis past, Julia turned her attention to the three large cartons on the worktable. All from her buyer in Italy, six months' worth of her best finds. There was a pleasant shiver of anticipation when a box arrived from Rosa, the thrill that was usually reserved for children on Christmas morning. She adjusted the blade on her penknife and began the delicate business of separating fragile goods from the box they came in.

In the other room Marnie Lambert said, "Well, you are right, Exa. He sure is fine-looking. He's got that rangy build, like a cowboy. And not one of those television cowboys neither, the real ones who work for a living. Or you know what? He could be on one of them recruiting posters for the marines."

"He's got the right haircut for that," said Mayme. "At least he's not trying to hide the fact that his hair is thinning."

"A man who is losing his hair," Exa announced, "is a man with an excess of testosterone."

Mayme snorted. "I swear, we have got to cancel your subscription to *Cosmo*."

Bean came up behind Julia. She said, "I fed the dogs and got them settled upstairs. Can I help with this?"

Julia glanced down at her. "I'll miss you when you start back to school tomorrow."

Bean's mouth pulled down. "Me too you."

The girl listened for a moment to her mother debating Exa and Marnie on the educational value of fashion magazines. Then she said, "I'll take out the trash."

"No, stay," Julia said. "Wait and see what's in this box."

In the front Exa said, "You know Link was all set to hate the man but he never had a chance. Dodge started right away by asking questions, and you know how Link loves to show off that memory of his? If you let him, he'd recite the whole inventory with his eyes closed, like he was telling scripture verses at Sunday school."

Julia peeled away layers of plastic, linen, and archival tissue paper to reveal a bedsheet with a five-inch border of elaborate silk embroidery, white on white. She reached for a fresh pair of white cotton gloves.

"Oh, look," said Bean. She had clasped her hands together tightly to keep herself from touching.

"It is pretty," Julia agreed.

"I can't ever imagine sleeping between sheets like that," said Bean. "Does it feel like heaven?"

"You'd think so, wouldn't you." Julia lifted the sheet out to reveal the next layer. "But these antique linens tend to be fairly heavy and stiff, with all the embroidery. That's why they've survived so long, they were never put to use."

"Like jewelry for the bed?"

Julia grinned at her. "Something like that. Art done with a needle instead of a brush."

"Everybody says my Granny Pearl's quilts are art, but I've got one on my bed and so do all my cousins."

"Your granny's quilts are art," Julia said. "So are your mama's. And I guess someday you'll be making quilts of your own, and maybe you'll bring some of them down here for me to sell. After you make enough for your own grandchildren."

At that Bean wrinkled her nose.

"No interest in quilting?"

"Quilts are fine," Bean said. "But I don't think I'll ever want a husband."

In the front of the shop Exa said, "It's a pure waste, a man like that without a woman on his arm."

At noon Julia took over so Exa could go to the dentist and Mayme could take Bean home for lunch. Help was no farther away than a call to Big Dove and Trixie on the second floor if it came to that, but most likely Julia would be able to handle things on her own.

She liked having the shop to herself now and then. If it was quiet, as it seemed it would be today, she sometimes found a book and sat in one of the three displays that took up the whole front of the shop, each made to look like a section of a bedroom a person would actually want to sleep in. Right now her favorite was the one Exa called country style: one of Mayme's quilts in pale yellow and white, a handwoven butter yellow blanket, and a pile of pillows in perfectly ironed cases, all vintage, all embroidered.

Julia worked hard on putting the display beds together and sometimes she was so successful at making them look inviting that people walked right past the sign that asked them to refrain from reclining. More than once she had had to help a tired shopper up and out, striving for the right combination of gentle admonishment and amusement.

Just a few months after Julia had opened Cocoon, a woman from Atlanta, her arms full of packages, her complexion wan and drawn, had simply thrown herself down across a handmade Belgian lace coverlet that was over a hundred years old. When Julia came over she had held up one manicured hand and a wrist weighed down with a diamond tennis bracelet.

"I will give you a thousand dollars if you let me stay here just like this for fifteen minutes."

Her name was Dorothy Bainbridge, and in the end she allowed Julia to escort her to the divan on the second floor, where the Needlework Girls made her tea and listened to her troubles and admired her very expensive and uncomfortable shoes.

When Dorothy left it was with two sets of hideously expensive Italian sheets and a plump pillow in a Victorian linen case roiling with embroidered silk briar roses. At the door she turned back to Julia with a great smile. "I'll be back," she said. "You can count on it."

Julia always thought of Dorothy when she took the time to sit and look at one of the display beds. She had become a steady customer and something like a friend. Last Christmas she had sent the embroidery sampler that hung on this display wall: *A well-made bed is a wondrous thing.* Julia was considering that statement when John Dodge came in.

8

SHE KNEW HIM from Exa's description and because he could be nobody else, not the way he looked around himself, sizing things up. He paused first to examine the hand-painted vintage saucer that hung on the wall just beside the door. Violets and pansies and in beautiful calligraphy: *If you're smoking in here you'd best be on fire.*

One brow lifted, in admiration or disapproval, and really, Julia didn't care which. He wasn't that good-looking.

He came toward her. She had the sense he missed nothing at all, but what seemed to interest him most were her pajamas: polished cotton scattered with big blowsy roses. Men were usually interested in her pajamas. She tried not to take it personally.

He said, "Haven't seen a living display in a while."

John Dodge had a friendly smile with nothing too personal behind it. A courtesy visit, then. She was the acting head of the merchants' cooperative, and there were still some legal issues to settle. She had heard a lot about John Dodge from Bob Lee Cowper and even more from Exa. One had described a dry businessman of discerning judgment and the other a prince from a fairy tale. In actuality John Dodge struck Julia as a type out of her past. Downtown Chicago was full of men like this one, ambitious and single-minded, brimming with charisma when they wanted something.

She said, "Can I help you?"

He came closer and held out his hand. Julia shook it: big, firm, warm.

"John Dodge. I'm looking for Julia Darrow."

"I'm Julia."

Surprise flickered across his face and was replaced by a smile. "Pajamas part of the marketing?"

"You could say that." Julia pointed with her chin. "The sleepwear section is worth checking out. We carry most of the better-known designers and some up-and-coming ones. Also I have a standing relationship with a few excellent seamstresses who do custom work. Are you in the market for pajamas?"

Too late to take back the opening she had given him, but he didn't even blink.

"I came in to see you in your capacity as head of the merchants' cooperative, but now that you mention it . . ." His eyes moved over the display behind Julia. "I do need sheets. What about that set?"

He jerked his chin at the display bed. Damask sheets of a pale bronze, the subtle woven ivy pattern shining like satin where the sun touched it. The duvet cover's pattern was the exact inverse, one corner folded back to show the detail work on the hem of the top sheet. A light cashmere blanket had been folded over the foot of the bed, in a shade of deep green that complemented the muted bronze of the sheets exactly. A perfectly made bed.

DODGE WATCHED JULIA DARROW RELAX, THE FAINT LINES around her mouth melting away when she talked about the designer, grades of cotton, thread count, hemstitching, and relative value.

There was something very striking about her face, with its sharp chin, high strong cheekbones like small plums tucked under the skin, and a lot of worry lines on her forehead that her bangs didn't quite hide. She had strong brows like wings, a shade darker than her auburn hair, worn severely short in a way that said very clearly that she might own a mirror, but she begrudged the time she had to spend in front of it. And in contrast to every other woman he had seen thus far in Lamb's Corner, she wore no jewelry and no makeup. A woman, Dodge thought, who was making a study of how to hide in plain sight but would never be able to pull that off. At least not as long as she went around in pajamas.

She was saying, "This king-sized set—just the linens, mind you, not the pillows or the duvet or blanket—would come to about two thousand. Of course, there's a discount for members of the cooperative."

She smiled beatifically, which really, Dodge told himself, was an unfair tactic. A sudden smile on the face of a beautiful and anxious woman in pajamas, no wonder she did well in this business.

"And that's reasonable for the market?"

She nodded enthusiastically. "You could triple the cost with some of the bigger name designers. Especially the Italians."

"I'll take it," Dodge said, surprising himself.

She blinked at him. "The sheets?"

"The sheets, the cases, the covers, the . . . what did you call it? Duvet. The whole thing. It looks comfortable, and all I've got up in the apartment is a king-sized bed set still in its plastic. At least I hope I do; I haven't checked to see if everything was delivered."

"But then you'll need more than one set of sheets, won't you?"

They made a pile on the counter that grew into a mountain of bedding. Julia was looking at it critically, her mouth pursed in concentration. Dodge braced himself for the bill.

She said, "You know, you could drive over to the Wal-Mart and get what you need for a lot less money."

Another test. Dodge said, "Even if I did shop at Wal-Mart, do you think I'd be dumb enough to admit it to the president of a small merchants' co-operative?" And he gave her his most sincere smile.

She didn't smile back. "I don't want to coerce you into spending a lot of money."

"I'm not an easy man to coerce," Dodge said. And stopped himself from saying the various things that came to mind. The corner of her mouth twitched as if she wanted to laugh, but instead she folded her arms.

"I'll have all this brought over to your place then. Here comes Mayme. Let me introduce you and then I can give you a short tour, if you'd like."

Mayme Hurt was maybe thirty years old, with a head of short cropped hair that showed off a shapely skull, full cheeks, and a generous mouth. She shook his hand and Dodge recognized a certain type of southern black woman, one who had adopted a particularly formal and professional stance in public. Her posture was almost military, and she wore her tailored dark blue pajamas with such aplomb that she could have walked into any boardroom without raising an eyebrow. He wondered what she looked like when she smiled.

"I'll take Boo up," Julia said.

"Oh, leave her," Mayme said. "She's sleeping so peacefully."

But Julia went over to the wing chair next to the display bed where the dog was still lounging, half asleep. A smallish dog, with kinky black fur and white paws.

Dodge said, "One of your foster dogs?"

Julia looked surprised. "I see the grapevine has already got hold of you.

Yes, she's a foster dog. I've just had her for six months." She paused to rub her knuckles over the sleek black head. "Boo belonged to an old couple who died within a week of each other. I don't know if she'll ever cheer up."

Dodge thought of telling Julia that he had been thinking of getting a dog, and then stopped himself just in time. If he wasn't careful he'd end up buying her entire stock and adopting every dog she had before he got out the door. Instead he followed along as she told him about the business, stopping at one place or another to point something out: antique linens hung on long dowels, large flat drawers of pillowcases edged with lace, stacks of sheets by contemporary designers, and a set of beautiful old shelves that reached to the ceiling filled with pillows and featherbeds and duvets.

"From the original printing plant," Julia said, with obvious pride.

And then there were the pajamas.

"I had no idea," Dodge said, looking through the racks. Pajamas in all configurations, silk and flannel, satin and cotton, in cool colors or hot stripes, some severe in cut and detail and the polar opposite. He spent a moment examining a pair of pajamas in a heavy satin-like fabric, dark blue and covered with embroidered cartoon sheep driving convertibles. He turned over the tag: $175. He was relieved to see that there were many more choices in the thirty-to-fifty-dollar range.

"You really move a lot of the high-end stuff?"

"Mostly through the website," Julia said.

She showed him the classroom in the back where she or one of her employees taught people how to take care of fine linen and lace. The classes were booked months in advance, mostly by the well-to-do who bought their linens from Julia—from places as far away as Seattle and Montreal and San Diego—and then sent their household staff to be trained. It was an odd classroom, in Dodge's experience, nothing more than a few tables and four deep sinks.

"Wait," he said. "Are you telling me I'm spending thousands of dollars on sheets I have to hand wash?"

"Of course not," Julia said. "I can refer you to very good local women who do excellent hand washing. Or if you must you can machine wash modern linens." She said this in a tone that suggested that no sane or reasonable person would do such a thing.

"This is an education," Dodge said. "Carry on."

. . .

JOHN DODGE, JULIA REMINDED HERSELF, WAS A NEW MEMBER of the merchants' cooperative. A colleague, a professional. A polite man who knew a lot about retail and was willing to learn more. She knew for a fact that there was nothing to fear from him, because Bob Lee Cowper was the cautious sort and had paid for an extensive background check. John Dodge, forty years old, unmarried, no bankruptcies or liens, no warrants, no criminal record. Undergraduate and graduate school at Columbia, two years on the stock market before he started this venture of his, acquiring and overhauling small businesses in trouble. No mortgage, no car loans, and he had bought out Bob Lee with a cashier's check. In the last ten years he had lived anywhere between one and two years in six different states: Oregon, Iowa, New Hampshire, Kentucky, Kansas, and Texas.

He said very little about himself, which only added to the dozens of questions lined up in Julia's head.

She knocked on the door of Leo's office, a cubbyhole tucked in under the staircase, and Leo opened it, leaning over from his desk chair. Julia had her usual pang of worry, wondering if she should force Leo into one of the larger spaces on the second floor. But he liked it here, isolated from the otherwise all-female staff, and he used the space well.

"Leo runs the website and auctions and oversees the mail-order part of the business," Julia said. "He's part-time but that's his choice. More than half my business is done through the website."

"No pajamas for Leo," John Dodge said, standing in the doorway.

"Not unless he's working in the front of the store," Julia said. "Which he prefers not to do."

"Which I refuse to do," Leo said. He finally raised his head and focused his gaze on John Dodge.

Dodge drew Leo out with such consummate skill and ease that Julia had to admit that Exa hadn't been exaggerating about him. A man who knew how to talk to strangers and set them at ease. Within five minutes Leo had agreed to meet with Dodge to talk about a computer setup for Scriveners, and Leo's hopes for a wireless network for all of Lambert Square.

She said, "There's another floor, if you'd like to see the rest."

"I thought there were two more floors."

Behind them Leo snorted a short laugh.

Julia threw him an irritated frown. "There's another floor to Cocoon. The top floor is my apartment. I've got workrooms and meeting rooms and an office on the second floor."

"Sure," Dodge said, "I'd like to see it."

Leo's mouth jerked at the corner. "Brave man."

"The rest of the dogs are up there," Julia said.

"I like dogs," Dodge said.

"It's not the dogs I was warning him about," Leo said, and Julia shut the door on him.

AT THE COUNTER THE PHONE RANG AND MAYME PICKED IT UP, one eye on the foot traffic.

A familiar voice said, "May I speak to Julia, please?"

It was a call she had been half expecting for a couple weeks, but Mayme's pulse picked up anyway.

"She's with a customer just now," she said, and was relieved to hear her own voice steady and calm. "May I take a message, Mr. Sigridsson?"

He had an easy laugh. Mayme reminded herself that many things amused Nils Sigridsson.

"Is it Mayme I am speaking to? How are you?"

"I'm well, thank you kindly for inquiring." She glanced over her shoulder, no sign of Julia or anyone else. The only eyes on her were Boo's, somberly reflective. As if a dog could read her mind.

"You have heard I am coming back to Lamb's Corner?"

"Everybody's heard," Mayme said. "It's good news." And then, drawing a deep breath: "The new automotive plant is very good news for the town."

"Och, too bad," he said. "I thought you were looking forward to seeing me again."

He was teasing; that's what he did. A tall, good-looking, single white male with money and a high-ranking job. A foreigner with an accent, who laughed at his own mistakes, who drank like a fish but never seemed to get drunk, who looked into your eyes as if he saw some secret there. Worst of all, a man who was totally ignorant of the way these things worked in the modern-day South. More than that: it was quite obvious to Mayme that he wouldn't care even if she read him a sermon. She could tell him what was appropriate, where the lines were drawn. The local customs, and what it meant for him to be flirting with a black woman. How that would fly.

He had asked her out three times before he gave up, and then he stayed friendly and good-natured. Mayme had begun to wonder if she had misread him, if maybe she had been unfair when he asked Julia out. Julia had refused him until Mayme told her straight out to go on ahead, she had no interest or claim on the Swede. Later she realized that she had been lying to everybody, including herself, but by that time it was too late.

"We'll all be glad to see you," Mayme said. "Did you want me to give Julia a message?"

A small silence. He said, "Have I hurt your feelings?"

She might have said, *Don't flatter yourself*. She would have said just that to any other man.

"Of course not," Mayme said. "I've just got some work to do here."

"Will you have lunch with me someday?"

She barked a laugh. "You were calling for Julia, remember?"

"Because I'm wanting to talk to Julia, this means that you and I can't have lunch together?"

"I didn't say that."

"Good. Then we will have lunch, and soon. Will you be a little glad to see me?"

Mayme closed her eyes. "I can hardly wait," she said. "It's all I've been thinking about since you went away." To herself she said: *Girl, you are too stupid to live. Shake the man off, and be done with it.*

"Oh good," said Nils. "I am looking forward to seeing you, too."

ON THE WAY UP THE STAIRS DODGE ASKED A QUESTION. "SO how long has Leo had a crush on you?"

Julia glanced at him over her shoulder. "I wouldn't say he has a crush. He's just territorial, but he's a good kid at heart."

"All those dire warnings about this tour, that was just posturing."

She hesitated. "Tuesday is the day all the Needlework Girls are here.

That's the name they gave themselves. Older women with expertise in various areas, some of them take on work I have for them—repairing vintage linens, mostly—and some work on their own projects or on custom orders. Leo," said Julia, "has a healthy fear of the Needlework Girls."

There was a volley of laughter from above them, and the hum of sewing machines. A dog barked and another one answered, and then an older woman's voice scolded.

"They scare the hell out of most people, to be honest," Julia said.

"But not you."

She paused with her hand on the door that led into the second-story rooms. "I like difficult old women," she said. "I'm in training to be one myself."

THERE WERE THREE DOGS UPSTAIRS: GLORIA, WHO LOOKED like a cross between a bloodhound and a poodle; Willie, a mutt of indeterminate parentage who was missing an eye and a tail both; and a small dog called Scoot that Julia introduced as part terrier, part papillon, and all India rubber ball.

And the Needlework Girls. Generally Dodge was good with names and faces but this was going to be a challenge. They descended on him with exclamations, questions, and requests, and because he had two loose buttons, it took all of his charm and powers of persuasion to keep his shirt on his back. Julia managed to extract him and he found himself in her office with the door closed and a dog in his lap.

Dodge said, "I see what Leo was trying to say."

"They mean no harm," Julia said. "But then neither does a tornado. Do you want to go over these papers now?"

Sunlight came in the tall window behind the desk and lit her hair so that it blazed with unexpected color, deep reds and golds and a few strands of white. She was so pale that a tracing of blue veins showed at her temples. In this exacting and unforgiving light, she looked like the woman she was, in her mid-thirties, with features a little too off-kilter to be beautiful by current standards. A good face, Dodge decided, one he would have been drawn to anywhere, made all the more interesting by the mysteries attached to it.

"There's a barbecue place I noticed on the other side of town," he said. "Can we do this over dinner?"

Julia Darrow had a whole repertoire of smiles, and he had already begun to differentiate between them. This one said he was not going for barbecue tonight, or not having dinner with her, or both.

She said, "There's no hurry about the paperwork." Her smile had turned brittle with something that Dodge might have called fear, which made no sense that he could see. She moved her chair so that she was in shadow, and he reminded himself of the work there was to do.

"All right, then. Maybe tomorrow." Dodge got up and handed Scoot over. He tried not to see the soulful look the dog sent his way.

9

BACK IN LAMBERT SQUARE Dodge took stock. Now the difficult part, sitting down with an employee he had inherited and had to win over. He pulled out Cowper's notes and found the one he wanted.

> ***Heep (Harold Earl) Epperson*** has been working for me since he finished at the Stephensville Technical College. He studied to be a watchmaker but gave it all up for pens, much to his daddy's disgust. Heep has got a big brother called Weep (Willard Elvis Epperson) who hangs around quite a bit as he has been out of work since the plant closed down. What you need to know about Heep is that he would have liked to buy the shop his own self. And he might have done right well with it, too, because his Caro has got a head for business. As long as you show Heep the respect he deserves as a master craftsman, you two should get along just fine. Also Heep has got an unusual hobby, inventing mixed drinks and improving on the old

ones. As his daddy is a hardshell Baptist you can imagine Heep doesn't have much to do with his folks. You show an appreciation for good liquor and you'll be halfway there with Heep.

IN HIS WORKSHOP AT THE BACK OF SCRIVENERS, HEEP EPPERSON was bent over a loupe examining the nib on a thirty-year-old Parker when Link Kay leaned his head in the door.

"He's coming back from Julia's." Link's long, thin face creased in the vertical folds that were his version of a smile. "Struck dumb, sure as sugar."

"Not every man in the world falls in love with Julia Darrow on sight," said Heep.

"You're just sour," said Link Kay. "Marriage will do that to a man."

"There's not one sour thing about my Caro," Heep said. "Not inside or out."

Link's bald head turned apple red. For a man who thought so much about women, he was easily embarrassed. Heep hated taking advantage, but sometimes it was the only way to get rid of the old man, and he had a lot of work on the table in front of him.

The next person at the door was John Dodge himself. Heep would give his new boss the benefit of the doubt, but he was uneasy. Bob Lee had made sure he'd have his job and salary for at least two years, but if John Dodge had a mind to start from scratch, no doubt he would find a way to force Heep out. He couldn't understand somebody like John Dodge, never settling anywhere for long. How was such a man to be trusted?

Caro wasn't at all worried; just the opposite. She had done her research, and presented it all to Heep over dinner one day. His wife was somebody who was more interested in capital investment and stock market trends than clothes or jewelry, and she looked at the sale of Scriveners like another business transaction, one that might work to their advantage.

To his new employer Heep said, "My wife says if you don't have plans for supper tomorrow, she'd be pleased if you'd eat with us."

"That's good of you," John Dodge said. "I'd like that." His eyes skittered along the long worktable, the neat rows of tools, the labeled cubbyholes and jars that held spare parts, the stack of pen boxes waiting for attention.

"I expect you've got questions," Heep said.

"I do," said Dodge. "But right now I've got to go get settled in the apartment. Can I have a half hour of your time tomorrow morning?"

Heep nodded. "I'm here at seven," he said. "Just yell when you're ready."

In the front of the shop Link had answered the phone and was shouting into it as though it were a tin can on a string. Heep winced. He said, "Link's going a little deaf, but he don't believe it himself. It's getting to be a problem on the phone."

For a moment Dodge listened to the conversation, his head cocked to one side.

"Well now, Mr. Holloway," bellowed Link, "I've been thinking about you, sir. How is that Conklin 40 working out? Is that so? Now that's what we like to hear. Well, good. Yessir, if I can. Why, certainly, we've got most of those Montblanc special editions. Let's see, we've got a Cervantes, a Pope Julius, a Pompadour, though I have to say that the Pompadour feels right awkward to me—what's that? Yessir, we've got a Prince Regent, reconditioned. One previous owner, a good old boy in Los Angeles used to run one of the big university libraries sold us all his pens in the spring of 'ninety-nine. A fine showpiece. I believe the price on that pen is an even three thousand dollars. No, sir, we still don't have one of them what you call websites, but we're under new management and you never know what these young people will get in their heads. In the meantime I can send you a good color photo if you're interested. I'll even put stamps on the envelope."

"The customers like him," Heep said. "He knows everything there is to know about pens and he remembers everything they ever bought and every question they ever asked."

"I can hear that," Dodge said. He thought for a while and then said, "Maybe we'll need more time tomorrow. I want to get your thoughts about a computer setup and a website. I'll find a way to do it that Link can live with, if you're worried."

"I'm not worried," Heep said. "But I'm also glad I'm not you."

DODGE RETRIEVED THE KEY TO THE APARTMENT FROM THE OLD cash register and trotted up the stairs at the back of the shop. At the very top, a helium balloon with WELCOME printed across it had been tied to the doorknob. Dodge braced himself for chaos as he let himself in.

The furniture he had ordered was all there, but the mess he had expected was not. Somebody had done a lot of work and provided him with a sparsely furnished, scrupulously clean apartment with high pressed tin ceilings, varnished hardwood floors, and bookcases built in along the short wall of the parlor.

In the kitchen he found milk, butter, juice, and eggs in the refrigerator, and in the shelves neat rows of jars and boxes and bags. Coffee, tea, bread, and a row of jars with brightly colored labels: *Polly's Pickled Okra. Polly's Mayhaw Jelly. Polly's Piccalilli, South Carolina State Fair Blue Ribbon Winner!* Paper towels and toilet paper in the pantry along with a stacked washer/dryer, a bucket, and some cleaning supplies. The kitchen window looked out over the alley and the shops on Main Street to give him a view of the town and the farmland beyond. In a year's time the view would have changed in favor of big industry, but by that time he would be ready to move on.

The parlor was at the front of the apartment, with four large windows that opened onto Lambert Square. He could just make out a curve of brown-green river through the trees. Dodge stood for a moment looking across the square to the third floor of Cocoon, where blinds had been drawn against the afternoon sun. Julia Darrow's apartment. Best not to start thinking about her at this point when he had a lot to do.

Dodge finished his brief tour, from the bath to the small, completely empty second bedroom to the larger one, where the bed he had ordered from a catalog had been set up and covered with a dust sheet.

On the bedside table was a vase of flowers and a card. *Welcome to Lambert Square. We're glad to have you here. Maude Reed-Golden, Mayor, and the Merchants' Cooperative.*

He had spoken with Lamb's Corner's mayor on the phone three or four times during his negotiations with Cowper and had a good sense of her: charming, disarming, and a formidable administrator and negotiator. He had liked her on the phone, and Cowper's summary had made him laugh out loud:

> ***Maude Reed-Golden.*** Don't you make any mistakes, Mayor Maudie may look like one of them empty-headed models you see on

magazines but she can out-logic and out-argue and plain outmaneuver any man born of woman. You play straight with her and she'll make your life easy. You don't want to think about the other side of that particular coin, son. Believe me. Maude married a man used to be a big-time financial type up there in New York City, worked for some television network. Some folks had their doubts about him settling in Lamb's Corner but he's been here almost ten years and mostly he's turned out harmless. But then it's pretty hard to offend anybody if you never say three words all together at once. He's quiet, is what I'm trying to get across. A man content with his wife and daughters and numbers.

He remembered LRoy Swagger's pinched expression. *We look out for one another.* There was a very complex family dynamic going on, and with that came the question of how small a role he could carve out for himself in it. The front doorbell rang, but before he could get to it, it opened and a small head poked in.

"Anybody home?"

Two older ladies came right in, both of them past seventy and as flexible and lively as teenagers. Both wearing flannel pajamas with broad red stripes and the kind of soft slippers his grandma Lucy wore.

"I don't suppose you recall our names," the shorter one said. "It was that noisy over to Julia's, what with the sewing machines and all of us Needlework Girls carrying on like hens. Me and Big Dove, we're full-time at Cocoon, so you'll be seeing more of us."

Trixie Jameson and Big Dove Porter, both born and raised in Lamb's Corner and no, before Dodge could ask, they were not sisters, no blood kin at all, though folks said they looked so much alike. But the reason for that came in one long breathless sentence: they got their hair done every Friday by a neighbor lady who saved some money by using the same rinse on both of them, and wasn't it a lovely shade?

Dodge admired the pale lavender, tightly permed heads. Neither of them was taller than five feet or weighed more than a hundred pounds, and he was fairly certain that together they could carry him down the stairs and back up again without breaking a sweat, telling stories the whole time.

He was about to ask as delicately as he could what this visit was about when Leo appeared in the doorway with two large baskets, one under each brawny arm.

"We brought the first of your linen," said Trixie.

Big Dove said, "Leo, sugar, put those in the bedroom, would you?"

"You came to make my bed?"

"We came to show you how to make your bed," said Trixie. "Those are fine linens you've invested in, not some rough polyester abomination. Now, you could contract with me to look after your linen. In that case I'd be making your bed once a week."

And so Dodge brought in a chair from the kitchen and sat and watched as the two old ladies transformed the bare mattress into something that looked like an advertisement out of *House & Garden*. They worked as a team, and never stopped talking. They wanted to know whether he cooked for himself, if he liked those fancy coffee drinks or took his the old-fashioned way, if all his belongings were coming by mail, if he had family pictures to put up and didn't photographs just make a place feel like home? Was he going to have a television or maybe he was more of a radio man, whether he liked football or baseball, if he had played himself as a boy, what catalog he had ordered all his things from because Big Dove was thinking about a new sofa and Trixie needed a new kitchen table, and the only place to buy furniture near Lamb's Corner was that cheap fake-wood Wal-Mart stuff made by those poor college students stuck in some Chinese jail for speaking their minds.

"Our Trixie," Big Dove said in a mock whisper. "She has got a crush on that Chinese actor, the one who went flying around in that movie—"

"Yun-Fat," said Trixie.

Dodge made appropriate noises, answered all their questions and finally asked one of his own. "Is this a service you provide to anybody who buys linen?"

Trixie paused to push her glasses up her nose and squinted at him anyway. "Yessir, for anybody who lives within twenty miles of Lamb's Corner. Leo drives us. Last weekend we did the bridal bed for my granddaughter RaeAnn, rose petals and although it's her second marriage and didn't I tell her, it would make more sense to go off and get married quiet someplace and not draw attention to yourself after all that trouble and noise with that ex of hers. But the girl is obstinate, always has been. Won't even listen to the other side of a phonograph record."

"We're done here," said Big Dove. "We'll get out of your hair."

At the door she said, "Are you the kind that takes offense at advice well meant?"

"No, ma'am. I'm happy to hear your advice." Dodge set his face in what he hoped would pass for complete sincerity.

"Well then," said Big Dove, her voice falling to a hoarse whisper. "If you're not partial to folks stopping by to visit, you had best put in a telephone with a message machine. That way a body can leave word and feel like they got across what they need to say, and you don't have to pay any mind at all if you don't care to. My sister Nell and I have been talking at each other that way for three years now. I can't tell you what a relief it's been."

"I don't dislike visitors," Dodge said.

"You will after a week or so of Lamb's Corner," said Trixie. "You've heard the old expression good fences make good neighbors? I'd hold to that, if I were you. That's the reason Julia never invites anybody up to her apartment."

Dodge did a bad job of hiding his surprise, and Big Dove grasped his elbow in one hard hand. She said, "Don't set your sights on our Julia. She's shut up tight as a Chinese puzzle box, nary a seam to be seen."

DODGE SPENT THE NEXT HOUR MOVING HIS THINGS FROM HIS car into the apartment, and trying to make sense of what he had been told, what he had observed, and the gulf between the two. The last thing he did was to unpack his answering machine and plug it in.

10

"ANNABETH TINDELL is the most opinionated, stubborn, bossy woman who ever drew a breath," said Link Kay to Dodge when he came downstairs to the shop just before closing. "But by golly, that dinner bell of hers is always in tune. She'll feed you supper, if you like. It being your first night here and all. A course you'll have to eat in the kitchen, but the food is right tasty anywheres."

Dodge said, "What I'd like to do is to take you out for barbecue. I've got a lot of questions, if you're game."

"Oh, I never say no to a free meal," said Link Kay. "And I got no end of answers. I suppose you'll want to know about your new neighbors."

"What I really want to know about," Dodge said, "is pens."

"Tell you about them, too." Link's smile was as broad as a jack-o'-lantern's and revealed about the same number of gaps in his teeth. "I'd be pleased to teach you every little thing I know."

THEY CLOSED UP AND DROVE ACROSS TOWN TO ADAM'S RIBS, where everybody seemed to know who Dodge was and why he was here. They ate pulled pork and coleslaw, and Dodge spent a couple hours listening to Link Kay talk. He learned a lot, not so much about pens or Lamb's Corner or his neighbors as about Link himself, who turned out to be a lonely old man with a lot of bad habits, chief among them his joy in saying the exact thing everybody was thinking but nobody wanted to hear put into words. But he was a master storyteller.

At one point Dodge said, "You remind me of one of my uncles."

"A handsome devil of uncommon intelligence and charm, I'm sure." Beer loosened an already limber tongue, and unleashed a monologue that lasted through the rest of the meal and the ten minutes it took to drive Link home, a small white clapboard house surrounded by palmettos. As he got out of the car Link hesitated and then leaned over to blast beer fumes in Dodge's direction.

"Thank you kindly for supper," he said. "It's nice to see some young folks still got manners. And now I got two things to say."

Dodge waited while the long face scrunched itself up in thought.

"First, I won't fight you about the computers, and you know why? Because everybody is sure I will, and I don't like to be so predictable. And second, you don't want to be thinking too much about Julia Darrow. She may be a Yankee but she's a tender thing. A real lady, is what I'm saying. And she don't need no more heartbreak, not after the way her husband passed."

"Ah," Dodge said. "People have been hinting all day. She married a local?"

Link looked genuinely surprised. "Charlie Darrow was a Yankee from tip to toe. He was the architect behind the Lambert Square renovation."

Dodge said, "I recall the name now. So how did he die?"

"Heart. Or at least that's the story. Julia showed up here shortly after he passed."

"Go on."

The old man blinked ponderously. "The story is, Charlie didn't go easy, and in the end she had to help him along a bit." He put a long finger to his mouth and whispered around it. "The poor little thing took mercy on *him*, but she don't have a bit to spare for herself."

DODGE LEFT THE CAR IN THE LAMBERT SQUARE PARKING STRUCture and cut through the alley to the back door of Scriveners. He was trudging up the stairs when he found himself face-to-face with an elderly woman in an old-fashioned housedress and apron.

She said, "Why, there you are, Mr. Dodge. I just left your supper upstairs on the table. It's something I always do for new neighbors, you understand. I'm Annabeth Tindell. Joe Bob sends his regards, but he's busy over to the restaurant. I do the cooking and he does the cleaning. It's kept us married these forty years."

Though she stood two steps higher she was still looking up at him, taking stock without apology and not dissatisfied with him, though he was rumpled after a long day, in need of a shave, a shower, and a good night's sleep.

Dodge said what was required of him. "Mrs. Tindell, can I offer you a cup of tea?"

She smiled like a queen bestowing a favor. "Now in't that sweet? I surely would love a cup of tea. And please call me Annabeth."

AT ELEVEN DODGE TOOK A CHANCE AND CALLED HIS SISTER, and got his brother-in-law to start with.

"How're things down there in the Land of Dixie?"

"Interesting," Dodge said.

"Interesting good or interesting bad?"

"I haven't decided yet," Dodge said. "Why don't you come down here, bring the kids, have a look around. See what you think."

Tom was still laughing when Nora got on the line.

She said, "I don't see what's so funny, it's not like every family vacation goes wrong." And: "So tell me."

"It's a wild place," he said. "Maybe I bit off more than I can chew this time."

"Hard to imagine," said Nora. "Give me the big picture."

Dodge thought for a minute. "Today I had something like ten unannounced visitors who just walked into the apartment. Most of them female."

"And what did all these people want from you?"

"Let's see," Dodge said. "Mrs. Tindell brought me supper, Big Dove Porter and Trixie Jameson made my bed, and old Mr. Russell who owns the Tinderbox came by with a pouch of South Carolina's best tobacco—"

"You are *not* going to start to chew."

"Of course not. I'll send it to the Colonel. Now I've lost track. Oh yeah, Hobart and Mae Oglesby from Allied Arts brought me a little handwoven Cherokee rug."

"As a gift?"

"As a gift. They're both full-blooded Cherokee. Apparently Hobart's great-grandma is a clan mother, she lives up near Columbia. And of course everybody has advice, on everything from where to buy underwear to how to clean the bathtub."

"Neighborly."

"That's the word. I lost track of the invitations after the first dozen or so, and I don't remember which ones I accepted. I'm pretty sure I turned down the personalized tour of the Lamb's Corner Funny Money Museum."

Nora gave that particular giggle which meant she had had two glasses of wine with her dinner. She said, "You're making that up."

Dodge settled more comfortably, stretched his legs out and crossed his ankles. He considered telling Nora some hugely entertaining fabrications, but then he didn't really need to.

"That's what the locals call it. You know Lambert Square used to be a printing plant, a family operation? Apparently it all started with John Bedford Lambert, who took up counterfeiting as a hobby. He engraved plates freehand, and he was good at it."

"And his specialty was currency."

"From all over the world. So they set up a little museum in the community center. Now that is an interesting place. A lot of public meeting rooms that anybody can book. They put out a flyer every week. Tomorrow they've got two AA meetings, the Pray for Peace Fellowship, a salsa dancing class, and a meeting of the Elks."

Nora drew in a deep breath and sighed. "I must be coming down with something. It all sounds like fun."

"Lamb's Corner," Dodge said. "Try it, you might like it."

"Enough to settle down?"

Dodge sat up and let out a sigh of his own. "I'd rather not have this conversation again."

"Hmmmm," Nora said. Her therapist hum, Dodge called it. "So give me the downside."

Dodge walked into the kitchen while he tried to answer the question. "The same stuff you run into everywhere. Old lion types who don't want me in their territory. The women who want to marry me off to their daughters or nieces or best friends. Sue-Ann Landry from the jewelry store pretty much nominated herself when I ran into her this morning."

"So who's the front-runner?" Nora kept her voice neutral, but Dodge knew she was smiling.

"There is one name that keeps coming up, but it's always people telling me to steer clear. Nice woman. Lost her husband a couple years ago, spends all her time and energy on her business. And she's good at it."

"Which one is this?"

Dodge described Cocoon, but neglected to mention to his sister how much money he had spent there, or the fact that Julia Darrow had been wearing pajamas when she made the sale.

Nora listened, and then she cut right to the chase. "Asked her out yet?"

That gave Dodge a jolt, but then Nora had always picked up on things that he believed well and truly tucked away. The only defense was to hide his surprise, though he would wonder for days what he had said to give her a heads-up.

"I asked her out, she turned me down. So I took Link—one of the employees I inherited from Cowper—to dinner and he spent a lot of time talking about Julia, too. I guess part of the intrigue is that she's a Yankee."

There was a moment's silence, one that did not bode well. Dodge braced himself.

"Tell me you won't let yourself get tangled up in a situation like that," Nora said.

Dodge thought of Julia sitting in that deep chair in her pink pajamas, the turn of her head, the tentative quality of her smile, and shook his head to dislodge the image before his sister could pluck it out of his mind.

"I don't have to act on every urge."

"Dodge," said Nora, her tone both more serious and softer. "I'm going to repeat that back to you the next time you announce you're ready to move along." There was a pause, and she said, "Tell me about the apartment."

"Big windows, high ceilings, a good view out over the town in two directions. I don't anticipate any problems."

"Hmmmmm," said Nora.

DODGE FELL ASLEEP WITHOUT A PROBLEM AND WOKE IN A PANIC a few hours later when the walls started closing in and the last of the oxygen was gone.

A new place, he told himself as he began his breathing exercises. A new place that would feel like his own in due course. A large, bright apartment with sturdy, unmoving walls, and good ventilation. He drew in cooled air until his lungs were filled, held it for a count of five, let it go. Another ten minutes of that and his pulse was still way high. Dodge got out of bed, pulled on his clothes, and went out.

Lambert Square was well lit at night. Display windows glowed jewel bright; in the park the lampposts that surrounded the fountain threw overlapping circles of soft light. The breeze was warm on his face.

A light burned in the third-floor apartment above Cocoon. Dodge would have noticed, if he had taken the time to look out his own front windows. Maybe Julia Darrow had insomnia; maybe she had company, or work to do, or a good book to read.

Those possibilities were still forefront in his mind when Julia herself came walking toward him out of the shadows. At the same time a small black-and-white form came shooting past her and hurled itself into Dodge's arms.

All four of her dogs were out with her, roaming free among the trees. Dodge rubbed Scoot's head thoroughly and then set him down, and off he went in a blur.

"He needs a lot of exercise," Julia said. The dogs were chasing one another, and her gaze followed them. "They all do, but Scoot is like an overwound clock. I expect that's why his people put him out."

She had exchanged her pajamas for what looked to be an old nightgown and a matching robe, much washed. It was short-sleeved and reached to her knees, and she was barefoot. Dodge wondered if he'd ever see Julia Darrow out of nightclothes and made an effort to put this question aside. He had never been shy with women, but now he found himself fumbling for something to say that would take certain images out of his head.

"You always bring the dogs out this time of night?"

"Usually," Julia said. "They love to run here when it's empty. I clean up after them. Do you mind?"

"Mind?" Dodge turned to look at her. "Why should I?"

She shrugged. "You're not only a new neighbor, you're my only neighbor. I'm just trying to be polite."

Dodge's eyes ran the length of the third floor. "I thought there were four apartments."

"There are," Julia said. "But T.J. and Dan bought a house a year ago and moved in together."

"T.J.?" Dodge said. "T. J. Pepper from the antiques shop?"

"Exa has a nice way of putting it. She told me as long as she's known T.J. he's been sweet on boys. He's been together with Dan Harris—from

Fashionista?—since my second year here. My advice is, never raise the subject in front of Lorna Jean Emerson, or you'll get an earful."

"I'll remember that."

She said, "What are you doing up at three in the morning?"

"New bed," Dodge said. "Nicely made bed, comfortable sheets, but it still takes some getting used to." Which was most but not all of the truth.

Julia looked at him directly. There was something of doubt or indecision there, and then she seemed to come to a conclusion. "Care to set for a while?"

"You're starting to sound like a southerner."

"Really?" Julia said, looking pleased. "Mostly people make fun of the way I talk. Come set."

Dodge hesitated, as awkward as a teenager, and wasn't that stupid. Julia Darrow wasn't even his type; he generally was attracted to women who were more polished, and usually darker of hair and complexion.

She threw him a look over her shoulder, and he gave up and followed her.

JOHN DODGE LOOKED FOR A MOMENT AS IF HE WAS GOING TO refuse her, and then he came ambling along after. He stopped to throw the stick that Gloria dropped at his feet and Julia let herself watch him move. He was tall and well built in a lean and mean way, and Mayme was right, his hair was thinning, but Exa was right, too, it didn't detract from his looks.

Testosterone. Julia snorted gently. So fine, she said to herself. So you're attracted to the man. It's been a while, and hormones are hormones.

He sat down next to her and said, "So tell me about Link Kay and Annabeth Tindell. Some history there?"

Julia coughed a surprised laugh. "You picked up on that already?"

"He always steers the conversation back round to her, one way or another. I have an uncle like him, seventy some years old and still sore about the girl who turned him down."

"You're good at reading people."

"Cowper left me crib notes on everybody I have to work with. Subjects to avoid, background, stuff like that."

One eyebrow lifted. "Confidential information?"

"Not in the business sense," Dodge said. He reached into his shirt pocket and pulled out the letter.

"You can have a look if you like."

Julia hesitated but curiosity won out in the end. She took the page he handed her and read the first paragraph.

> ***Lorna Jean Emerson.*** Lorna Jean owns the bookstore and runs the little Bible museum, which is worth a look. I suppose I should have raised the subject of religion with you before but you are a southerner so I don't suppose Lorna Jean will be much of a surprise. She's the original church lady, except she dresses better. Lorna Jean and her mama sit in the first pew at St. Mary's Episcopal, and you better understand that means something. She staked her claim on Reverend Durant a long time ago and is getting right frustrated at the way he is dragging his feet on the way to the altar. Once she got all the attention she needed by entering beauty pageants, but these days she has to settle for stirring up trouble in Lambert Square. The plain truth is, Lorna Jean is one of those people who is sure she is being shortchanged, by you and me and the good Lord hisself and she's going to fight for what's rightly hers. Namely, everything. I suggest you stay clear of Lorna Jean if you can.

Julia barked a low laugh. "Oh, he is bad."

"But is he wrong?"

"Of course not. Bob Lee is sharp. I suppose he wrote about me, too?"

Dodge said, "You want to see it?"

Julia considered. "Probably not." She studied the page for a moment and then she said something without looking at Dodge, something she might regret but couldn't keep to herself.

"I have the sense that you're a lot like Bob Lee. You're good at seeing beneath the surface."

A smile hovered at the corner of Dodge's mouth and then was gone. His face was dark with beard stubble but his eyes were clear and his gaze alert. He studied her for a moment as if her life story were written on her forehead.

"All I know about you is what other people have told me," he said. "And what I've seen with my own eyes. I discount about eighty percent of the first, and thirty percent of the second."

Julia wished now that she had followed her instincts and changed the subject. She said, "Let me guess, you heard the mercy killing story."

He didn't look surprised or embarrassed or even particularly interested. Any of those things would have been irritating, but this lack of reaction was oddly off-putting in its own way.

"People like a tragedy," Dodge said. "And they like you. If so many people who think so much of you are worried about you, maybe there's a reason."

Gooseflesh rose on Julia's nape and arms, and with that a feeling of acute disorientation and embarrassment, as if she had caught sight of someone spying on her through the bathroom window. That this image was off and inadequate only added to her discomfort. She swallowed hard until she was sure of her voice, and then she said, "Look, I know they mean well. But that particular story is just plain fantasy, courtesy of—" She stopped herself and regrouped. "I have a good life, and I'm generally a very happy person. So, do strangers always open up to you?"

"It's been known to happen," said Dodge. "Listen, I'll tell you something about me, and maybe you'll feel easier." He stuck out his hand and Julia took it automatically, a big hand, calloused for reasons she couldn't imagine.

"Hi, my name is Dodge, and I'm a claustrophobic."

Julia put her free hand to her mouth and hiccupped a laugh. "I'm sorry, it's not funny, but—"

"Sure it's funny," Dodge said. "When I got to the point I could laugh about it, I knew I was really getting better. You ever hear of a closet claustrophobic?"

"But you had to get out of your apartment—"

"I'm a recovering claustrophobic," he said. "I had a relapse."

Julia said, "You could let go of my hand now."

"Oh. Sure."

To fill the odd silence, Julia asked a question she would not have allowed herself even a half hour ago. "Does the claustrophobia have anything to do with—" She paused.

"My nomadic ways? Sure."

"So how long have you been moving around?"

He studied his feet for a minute, as if he had to perform some complex calculation in his head. "I was on the stock market for a couple years," he said. "I started to get bored, and so I sold all my tech stock just before the dot-com bubble burst. That was just dumb luck, no big insight on my part but it seemed like a pretty clear sign. There was somebody I knew from college looking to sell his business in Portland, and that's how it all started. That was, what, ten years ago."

There were questions she might have asked, but discomfort won out over curiosity. And Gloria, big dopey dog that she was, somehow sensed that Julia needed a distraction and came over to drop a stick on the ground in front of them, her whole hind section wagging hopefully. Dodge threw it and Gloria disappeared into the shadows.

Dodge said, "So how did your husband die?"

His tone calm and matter-of-fact. Julia took stock, and found that she could answer.

"We thought he had the flu. Fever, aches, tired all the time, but he just kept popping aspirin and refused to go to the doctor. Then he collapsed on the street outside his office. By the time I got to the hospital he was already out of emergency and in cardiac intensive care. Bacterial endocarditis was the diagnosis, and then heart failure. He died waiting for a transplant."

The old images rose up in her mind, the snow coming down hard in the early dark. Red and blue lights, and the way the paramedics looked at her.

Dodge was saying, "That's just shitty."

"Yes," Julia said. "It was shitty. But he's gone and I'm here. I've got a good life, and work I really like, and friends. And animals."

That should have been the end of it, but Julia had no urge to get up, or to go back to her apartment, or to do anything but sit in the cool night air while the dogs chased one another around trees.

"Tell me about your dogs."

Julia couldn't remember the last time the urge to talk had come over her. Usually she had to force herself to hold up her end of the conversation. As Exa had put it, her chatterbox was busted. But the question was sincere, and so she answered it. She told John Dodge about each of the dogs, how they had been rescued, why they had been brought to her, health and behavior and food issues. Their personalities, each so distinct from the next.

"They need a lot of care," she said. "But I don't mind."

"I've been thinking about getting a dog for a couple years," Dodge said. "Now and then I go have a look at the Humane Society wherever I am, see what they've got in the way of labs and lab mixes. But I've got to say, I like Scoot. He's got a lot of personality."

Julia hesitated, and then said what was required in this situation. "I couldn't let you have Scoot."

Dodge was leaning forward, his forearms on his knees, and his head came up sharp to look at her.

"You going to keep him yourself?"

"No," Julia said. "I'm still looking for the right place for him."

"And I'm not the right place." He was sitting up now.

"No, I'm sorry."

"And how's that?"

She had pushed some button, but she could be firm when it was called for. She said, "You move around every eighteen months or so, one place to the next. Scoot has had a rough time of it; he needs more stability than that."

"He needs somebody who'll stick by him," Dodge said. "I move from place to place, but he'd always go with me."

"I'm sorry," Julia said. "It's not the right situation for Scoot."

Dodge looked at her for a long moment and then let out a short laugh. He shook his head and rubbed a hand over a day's worth of beard stubble.

"I have no wish to offend you," Julia said. "But I'm careful about where I place my dogs."

"Let me ask you this," he said. "When's the last time you did place one?"

Julia felt herself flushing. "I don't see how that's relevant."

"Hmmmm," said John Dodge.

"I owe it to these animals to see that they are well situated with people who can meet their needs."

"Sure," he said. "I can see your reasoning."

But his expression had shifted and closed. Just that quickly the soft hum that had been in the air was gone, and the urge to get home and close her door behind her was irresistible.

"It's late," Dodge said, and Julia wished him a good night, struggling to hide her relief and disappointment, and, most of all, her confusion.

11

This is John Dodge. Please leave a message.

Dodge? John Dodge? This is Trixie. Son, that message of yours makes you sound like a Yankee. I'm calling to say what I forgot this afternoon, and that is, don't go rushing into picking a place to worship. It's a big decision and a fateful one. I would be pleased to advise you, if I can be any help at all.

This is John Dodge. Thank you for calling. Please leave a message.

Dodge this is Big Dove calling, from Cocoon? I wanted to warn you that I gave Marnie from Jennifer's Rabbit your number. I hope that was all right. If you'll pardon my saying so, you might want to think about changing your message? It's a little abrupt, if you take my meaning.

This is John Dodge. Thank you for calling. Sorry to have missed you. Please leave a message.

Hi. This is Marnie Lambert calling? From Jennifer's Rabbit? We met the other day out front of my place. I am calling to invite you to supper Saturday evening. Mama is planning on making her fried chicken which you had better believe is the best in Lamb's Corner. Big Dove mentioned to me that you don't have anything up on your walls, and I've got some nice paintings you might like to borrow. Those bare walls will give you a headache otherwise. Also I want you to know that I am happily married. My husband Harley is serving his country in Afghanistan. I am telling you this so you don't get any wrong-headed ideas.

This is John Dodge. Thank you for calling. Sorry to have missed you. Please leave a message.

Mr. Dodge, this is Bob Lee Cowper calling you from Prague. I've been wondering how your first few days in the shop have been. I will try to catch you downstairs. Oh, and you might want to put a few more pretty words in that message of yours. Friendly is right serious business in South Carolina.

This is John Dodge.

Hello? Hello?

Sorry I'm not here to take your call. Please leave your name and number and I'll get back to you as soon as I can.

Hello? Hello? Yes, Mama, he's picked up but he don't seem to be able to hear me. Bad connection, I guess.

You have reached the answering machine at John Dodge's place. I'm not here to take your call. I'm sorry to have missed you. If you'd be so good as to leave your name and number, I'll get back to you just as quick as I can. Thank you.

John Dodge, this is Lyda Rose Guzman calling, from SugarPuss? You met our boy Leo at Cocoon. Hank stopped by today but you were out, so he left the jade tree I sent by your front door. Plants make a place feel like home, don't you think? Just a little welcome gift. Now I don't know where you worship but if you are interested we would be right pleased to take you along to services on Sunday. Some would call us Deep Water Baptists but I say we are awash in the Glory of the Lord.

You have reached the answering machine at John Dodge's place. I'm not here to take your call. I'm sorry to have missed you. If you'd be so good as to leave your name and number, I'll get back to you just as quick as I can. Thank you.

Mr. Dodge, Bob Lee Cowper here calling again, this time from Hungary. Did you know there's no such place as Budapest? There's two cities, one's Buda, the other's Pest. It's a beautiful place but strange, let me tell you. I am staying across from an Albanian pizza parlor and a Kansas City steak joint.

And today I saw a thousand-year-old hand in a glass box; they took it off some saint and they parade it around for everybody to pray at. I'm glad to see you took my advice about your message to heart. You'll get along just fine in Lamb's Corner, I don't doubt it for one minute.

12

"So TELL US," Exa said the next morning as soon as Julia came downstairs. "How is our new neighbor getting along?"

"Oh, look," Julia said. "Here comes Maude."

Exa threw up her hands in mock disgust. "Well of course, here comes Maude," she said. "Now you'll go off and tell her everything and leave us here wondering."

"I'm not wondering, not me, uhuh," said Mayme, her gaze fixed on the inventory sheet in front of her.

"Exa," Julia said. "There is nothing to tell."

Exa turned and watched the woman coming toward them across the park. It was pretty much impossible not to watch Maude Golden, whose flair for the dramatic had not just survived marriage, motherhood, and a term as mayor, but flourished. She was beautiful and full of energy and she carried herself like a queen. Today she had wound a cobalt, scarlet, and emerald scarf through her dark hair, and she wore a flowing multilayered caftan of the same silk fabric. There was at least ten pounds of silver jewelry around her neck and wrists; you could hear Maude coming from a mile away.

"I swear," Exa said, "I'd like that old girl a whole lot better if she didn't make it so hard to hate her."

This was a classic Exa-ism, one that Julia had to laugh at. She said, "Do you think you could get started with the stock I unpacked yesterday? There's some nice pieces there, but some of it needs special attention."

Exa said, "Just because I'm curious doesn't mean I forget my manners. I know when I'm in the way."

THE FIRST DAYS IN A NEW PLACE WITH A NEW PROJECT WERE guaranteed to bring a steady adrenaline rush, and so Dodge was out of bed with the first vibration of his alarm. Out of bed and ready to be out in the world.

He considered making his own breakfast for all of ten seconds, and then pulled out the Lambert Square guide instead. Mrs. Tindell didn't serve breakfast, but Polly's Café did. Dodge fished Cowper's letter out of yesterday's trousers and sorted through the pages.

> Mister's mama Lila was a legend, and not just in Lamb's Corner. People came from all over to buy her canned goods and sausage. I can still taste her liver pudding. Mister makes it almost as good. Lila was known for her cooking but she also made herself a name as a civil rights worker. You have to imagine the courage it took for her to give birth to a big healthy black baby boy in 1955 and name him Mister, which was as good as spitting in the face of the segregationists. Of which we had plenty back then. Still got more than a few, sorry to say. They came after her, too, but she didn't give a dried apple damn, she stood her ground and lived to a good age and died satisfied. Mister played basketball for Duke until his knees went bad on him. That's where he met and married Polly, and he brought her back to Lamb's Corner so they could open up a café.

Dodge wished now that he had been around to take Cowper's phone calls, not only to thank him for the crib notes but to ask some pointed questions. He took a quick shower, shaved in record time, and went out to see what kind of breakfast Mister and Polly served up.

. . .

JULIA AND MAUDE ATE BREAKFAST AT POLLY'S TWO OR THREE mornings a week. Polly had set aside a regular table for them, tucked back in a corner where they could talk Lambert Square business without being overheard. This morning Polly was ahead of herself; she had already put out their mugs along with toast, butter, and a collection of jam and jelly jars.

She stuck her head out of the kitchen and called to them. "I'll be right there with your plate, Maudie. Mister says to tell y'all he's putting up those plums Jamie Deanne brought from her daddy's trees. Y'all want some?"

With her fists on her hips Maude said, "Poll, you tell that man of yours I'll take whatever he's got left over for me."

When the laughter died down Julia said, "Ever the entertainer."

"I have a reputation to uphold," Maude said. She sat as regally as she walked, her back and long neck in one fluid, straight line. Her bracelets jangled as she reached for the carafe of coffee. "And you would not believe the way my girls go through the stuff. They've got their daddy's sweet tooth."

Maude opened a jar of strawberry jam and picked up a spoon. "What?" she said. "I need the carbs, I have got a hellish day ahead of me. Where is Polly with my food? So how'd it go yesterday?"

"What?"

Maude's mouth contorted. "You are the worst actress, girl. What. John Dodge, his first day."

"If I'm such a bad actress, why do you keep bugging me to try out for your plays?"

"Sugar, I have three girls at home; I am immune to your tricks. Don't try to distract me. Tell me about John Adams Dodge."

"John Adams? How do you know that?"

Maude waved a sticky spoon in the air while she swallowed.

"I talked to him on the phone, didn't I? When he was considering whether or not to buy Bob Lee out. I'll say one thing for him, the man is thorough. So. What did you think of him?"

They paused for Polly, who put a plate in front of Maude. Bacon, eggs, ham, biscuits, red-eye gravy. The idea of such a heavy breakfast made Julia slightly nauseated. She picked up a piece of toast as a compromise, which earned her a sharp look from Polly.

"We were just talking about our new neighbor," Julia said, trying to deflect attention from her eating habits. This time it actually worked. Polly's face brightened.

"What's he like, honey? He han't been in here yet."

"Well," Julia said, "he seems nice enough. I sold him about five thousand dollars' worth of bedding, and he made friends with all the Needlework Girls. Exa's in love."

"Sweet old Exa," said Maude, and the odd thing was, she meant it. Julia had never known anybody like Maude. Whether it was her own absolute self-confidence and satisfaction with her life or simple generosity of spirit, Maude Golden was one of those rare people who could get along with everybody and still get her own way. If you crossed her about something important, she didn't hesitate to bring the full force of her intellect and reasoning powers—both of which were formidable—to bear. But she never belittled anybody's concerns. Which was what made her such a good mayor.

Polly went off to feed somebody else and Julia and Maude settled in. They talked about business while they ate, stopping frequently because people never hesitated to come to Maude with their concerns. One of her favorite stories was how the nurse in the labor and delivery room had used every pause between contractions to make her case for speed bumps along Columbus Street. Maude contended that her youngest daughter's argumentative nature was a direct result.

They were in the middle of a discussion of the agenda for the next meeting of the merchants' cooperative when John Dodge came in, nodded and smiled at Julia, and went right past them to talk to Polly. Then Mister came out of the kitchen, impossibly tall and broad and striking, deep black skin and blinding kitchen whites. The introductions started all over again.

The whole café went quiet while Dodge thanked Mister and Polly for stocking his kitchen cabinets. John Dodge had a good laugh, open and deep and sincere.

"See that?" Maude said. "I'll bet you every pair of shoes I own that Mister has just signed John Dodge up for Wednesday-night poker. Those two are bound to become friends."

"Now wait," Julia said. "How do you know that?"

"The same way I knew you and I were bound to be friends the first time I saw you." Maude lifted her fork and rotated it like an antenna. "A hum in the air. I've read it's got something to do with smell, but I've always thought of it as a sound, that thing that happens sometimes when you meet somebody and things click. Don't you know what I mean?"

Julia did know, but she was rescued from the conversation by John Dodge himself, who came over to the table.

"I'd recognize you anywhere," Maude said, holding out her hand for him to shake. "Sit down, sugar. Had your breakfast?"

Generally when Maude offered a man something he didn't hesitate, but John Dodge looked to Julia before he answered.

She said, "Please do." And saw the way Maude's glance sharpened, her curiosity aroused.

"There," Maude said, putting her hands flat on the table, her beautiful face turning back and forth between them. "Now that's what I call harmonic convergence."

Dodge paused and raised a questioning brow in Julia's direction.

"Just one of Maude's theories," she said. "She's got a million of them."

"Is that so?" Dodge said. "Does she have one to explain why whenever I run into you, you're wearing pajamas?"

Maude produced her biggest, brightest smile. "Now here's a man who gets right down to it. I like that. If you ask Jules she'll tell you it's a marketing tool—"

"Which it is."

Maude grinned. "—and I can't deny that she sells a lot of really expensive pajamas. Can't seem to get enough of them my own self. But that's not the whole story. Sugar, would you pass me the sorghum, please? My first theory," Maude went on, "was that our Julia stayed in pajamas twenty-four/seven because she likes having men follow her around Lambert Square—"

"Hey," said Julia.

"Honey, you know it's true. Don't deny it. But pretty quick I realized that she doesn't take any note of all. The Atlanta Braves could be following her like ducklings after their mama and Julia? She wouldn't blink an eye."

Dodge said, "A woman in pajamas will get most men's attention. Got mine."

"Pardon me," Julia said. "You two do realize I'm sitting right here?"

Maude said, "The sad truth is, our Jules doesn't have a flirtatious bone in her body."

"And there's not a serious one in yours," said Julia, putting out a hand to stop Polly, who was going by with a tray of cups. "Isn't that so?"

Polly jumped right in. "More than two-thirds of the tall tales our Maude tells are usually mostly true." Then she winked at Maude, who was hooting her disagreement, and went on her way.

"So no theory to explain the pajamas," Dodge said to Maude when they stopped laughing.

"Maybe you'll have more luck figuring it out," Maude said. "You look like a man who rises to a challenge."

"Maude—"

"I don't think it's anything very complicated," Dodge interrupted, not even bothering to hide his grin. "Some people can't stay away from booze. My sister is helpless when it comes to chocolate, and my niece never saw a pair of shoes that didn't speak to her. Julia here has a pajama jones."

"Julia," said Julia, "has a business to run. If you'll excuse me, I'll let you get on with this fascinating dissection of my personality on your own."

"MAYBE WE WENT A LITTLE TOO FAR," MAUDE GOLDEN SAID when Julia had left. "Good thing she's not the type to hold a grudge. Would you pass me the coffee?"

It took a minute for them to sort themselves out with the coffee. Then Polly came and Dodge ordered a full breakfast because anything less would be getting off on the wrong foot. Dodge took his time, not just because the coffee was good, but also because it allowed him to collect his thoughts and try to pin down a memory. It hadn't meant much to Dodge to hear that Maude Golden—Maude Reed, most likely at that point—had spent more than a few years as the lead on a soap opera, but as soon as he saw her face, he remembered where he had seen it before.

"About ten years ago," he said, "I was living in Manhattan—"

"Tallulah perfume is what you're thinking about," Maude said. "And me sprawled across Times Square in my underwear. Seems about a million years ago."

"That was a good ad campaign," Dodge said.

The mayor of Lamb's Corner grinned. "In't it sweet of you to say so? Now tell me, are you already booked through to the new year? Because if you can bear some more socializing I'll have you out to supper right away. My Mike would like you."

"I'd be pleased," Dodge said. And it was true; this was one case where he didn't have to manufacture interest.

"Well, good. I'll call you then."

She rose from the table as she was speaking, pulling money from a purse to tuck it under her plate. Then she paused and seemed to be thinking about how best to say something.

"Let me guess," Dodge said. "I should stay away from Julia Darrow because she's fragile and doesn't need any more heartache."

"Hell no," Maude said. "What she needs is somebody to shake her up a bit, and you look like the man for the job to me."

13

DODGE WAS SO BUSY that first full day at Scriveners that he didn't have any time to reflect on Maude Golden or Julia Darrow or anything beyond the shop. He spent the morning in the workshop taking notes on his laptop, stopping to ask questions. It turned out that Heep was a thorough and patient teacher, but the more he talked the more Dodge came to realize how much there was to learn. By noon he had about twenty pages of notes.

"So tell me," Dodge said. "What's your biggest worry?"

Heep blinked at him. "You mean besides losing my job?" He shrugged, looked away, and seemed to think.

"Let me say something here," Dodge interrupted. "I'm not planning on interfering. When I've got good people working with me, I let them get on with it."

"Good," said Heep, and for the first time there was something a little bit like a smile near the surface. He cleared his throat and sent Dodge a sidelong glance. "So we're still on for supper?"

"I was planning on it," Dodge said. "But you haven't answered my question."

Heep tapped his worktable thoughtfully. "It's not a worry, really. Something I would have brought up sooner or later. When you're ready to sell this place and move on, I'm wondering if you'd give me a chance to make an offer before you advertise."

Dodge said, "Sure," and Heep tilted his head in surprise, eyes narrowed.

"Just 'sure'?"

"Why should I mind?" Dodge said. "No reason for us not to do business when the time comes."

"So you really do intend to move on then."

Dodge leaned forward. "You can count on it. Now, how do I get to your place this evening?"

Link stuck his head in the door as Dodge was finishing writing down the directions.

"Delivery at the alley door for you. Computer boxes, it looks like." He sent a pointed look to the laptop in front of Dodge. "How many of them machines do you need, anyway?"

"Three to get started," Dodge told him. "Why don't you come upstairs when Heep is back from lunch, I'll give you a tour."

THERE WAS A WARREN OF ROOMS ON THE SECOND FLOOR BUT only one wasn't piled high with boxes. Dodge claimed it as his office and made adjustments to suit his work habits. By the time Link came upstairs an hour later he had made a good start at getting himself organized.

"I hear you had breakfast with Julia this morning," Link said as he came in the door. And: "Well, look at this. You've been busy."

Dodge said, "I like to get right down to it."

Link stepped back.

"What we're going to do is, we'll get some stock in here from one of those boxes in the other room—"

"I've got things organized," Link interrupted. He sat down, his arms crossed. "I've got a system."

"Sure," Dodge said. "That's why you're going to handle the back-and-forth. Then we'll do this pen by pen. Pull one out, take some digital photos, and then you'll tell me about it. I'm going to be taking notes, and I'll ask questions as they occur to me. Will that work for you?"

Link's mouth quirked and his eyes narrowed. He was a man who knew himself to have been outmaneuvered, but who took this setback in his stride. "Oh, I can talk as long as you care to listen. Or until you have to go to Heep's place for your supper."

"Is there anything going on in this town you don't know about?"

The old man slid until his hips were perched precariously on the edge of the chair. Then he folded his long hands over his belt buckle and smiled.

"Not much. Now, if you'll forgive another word to the wise—"

Dodge braced himself.

"Watch out for blunt force trauma."

"I'll remember that," Dodge said, resisting the urge to ask for the explanation that Link so desperately wanted to provide. "Now, what can you tell me about this pen here?"

Link chewed on his cheek lining for a moment. "That pen," he said. "Now, there's a story."

Dodge opened up his laptop and settled in.

FOR THE REST OF THE DAY JULIA FOUND IT HARD TO STOP THINKING about breakfast, which mostly meant she couldn't keep John Dodge out of her head. The man himself was nowhere to be seen, a relief at first that gave way to vague irritation. If not for Bean, who spent Wednesday evenings with her while Mayme went to her class at the community college, she might have let her curiosity drive her to walking over to Scriveners. To see how things were going, and ask if there was anything she could do. A purely neighborly gesture.

As it was she took Bean to the café for soup and sandwiches and spent an hour talking to Mister and Polly about Lambert Square business.

"Come on, sugar," Polly said. "Tell us about the Swedes. Why ain't they here yet?"

"They're on their way," Julia said, and Polly slapped the table with both palms and sent her husband a triumphant smile. She said, "The same ones as before?"

Julia felt Bean watching her, as curious about this particular point as everyone else. The Swedes had been well liked, even by those who had doubts about Kallsjö and the new assembly plant. Mostly people wondered when they'd start cutting paychecks.

She said, "You'll hear tomorrow anyway. I think there's ten or so executives coming. Including the same three we had before, but this time Oli Söderström is bringing his family."

"I knew it," said Polly. "He bought the Reynolds' place, didn't he?"

"The company bought it, from what I understand," said Julia. "Kallsjö bought six houses on that side of town for their people, and the old Larrabee building on Columbus to use as temporary office space."

"No wonder Mary Sue has been strutting around like she hatched an egg." Polly put back her head and laughed.

Bean said, "How many kids has Mr. Söderström got?"

"I don't know, sweetie," Julia said.

Mister had been watching her with his head tilted slightly to one side, which meant he was about to say something observant and uncomfortable.

"Those were some wild times in Lambert Square when Beate and Nils were renting upstairs. Uhuh, wild times." And he winked at her. Julia resisted the urge to stick out her tongue at him.

"I liked it when they were here," Bean said. "It was fun. Why aren't they coming back? Did they buy houses instead?"

"Some of them will be buying houses, the ones with families. But Beate and Nils would like to come back to Lambert Square. Maude should have talked to you about this already; she was supposed to ask you if you were interested in giving Beate a short-term lease. T.J. has already said he'd be happy to have Nils renting his place."

Polly and Mister exchanged glances that Bean zeroed in on without hesitation.

"Don't you want Beate back?" she asked. "Didn't you like having them here?"

Mister said, "Sugar, we like those Swedes just fine. I'm more than happy to have that Beate living upstairs. That's a fine-looking woman." As he said this he leaned over the table and put a loud kiss on his wife's forehead.

"Shoo, fly." She batted him away, but she was smiling with pleasure.

From the other side of the café there were hoots and catcalls. "You two stop loving each other so much!"

Polly said, "Mister, quit your foolishness and get going. You'll be late."

Bean put her mouth to Julia's ear. "I'm finished. Can we go now?"

JULIA AND BEAN CLIMBED THE STAIRS TO THE SECOND FLOOR OF Cocoon in something less than their usual companionable silence.

"I miss my daddy," Bean said, so quietly that Julia was free to overhear it, if she wanted to.

"I bet you do," she said. "But he's supposed to come for Christmas this year, isn't that right?"

Bean took a deep breath. "I hope so."

There was little to say to comfort the girl. Julia would have liked to make promises, but the truth was that Mayme's ex was less than predictable. He worked on off-shore oil rigs and had a reputation to go along with the lifestyle. And Mayme just got more and more angry at him as time went on, which only made Bean dig in her heels, determined to hold on to her father, no matter how little she saw him.

"Do you miss your family when the holidays come?"

Julia said, "Doesn't everybody?"

AT ELEVEN JULIA WAS MORE AWAKE THAN EVER, AND RESTLESS. She took the dogs downstairs and threw a ball for them until her arm and shoulder ached. It was worth it to see Boo cheer up, rousing herself in pursuit of red rubber.

She loved sitting in Lambert Square park after sunset. The breeze was sweet and cool and the far-off sound of the river soothing. Usually she could fall asleep after a half hour down here, but tonight she only felt jittery.

At midnight there was still no sign of John Dodge. No light in his apartment, either. She had worried at first about him moving into Lambert Square, worried about having to share the park after hours, and here she was wishing for his company. What it would be like when Beate and Nils moved into the two empty apartments, that was a question that kept coming back to her. Everything would change once Kallsjö came to Lamb's Corner, and not just in Lambert Square.

Julia went upstairs and spent an hour answering e-mail and lurking on discussion boards. At one she settled down with a book in her good chair.

Later she couldn't say with any certainty what woke her, but the dogs took immediate advantage by trotting over to the door and looking at her expectantly. Boo stayed behind on the ottoman, snoring peaceably.

"You three will be the end of me," Julia said as they went down the stairs, but she stopped to rub heads before she let them run out into the open. On the bench by the fountain that she favored, she drew her feet up under herself, slung her arms around her knees, and tried not to look at the dark windows on the third floor of Scriveners.

She was just about to ask herself some hard questions when Scoot went flying past, his whole doggy body tense with excitement.

"Ooof," said a male voice in the shadows behind her. And: "Hey, Scoot. Jones, you waiting up for me?"

A deep and vaguely slurred male voice. Julia turned her head and saw Dodge coming toward her with Scoot tucked into the crook of an arm.

What Julia said next was a shock to both of them. "What are you doing out at three in the morning?"

Dodge sat down at the far end of the bench. "Didn't know there was a curfew."

"There isn't. Sorry, I'm just tired."

"S'okay." He put Scoot on the ground and all the dogs stood there looking between him and the red ball Gloria had dropped between his feet. He picked it up and threw it, and the dogs went racing to the other end of the park.

After a moment he said, "Dinner with Caro and Heep and Mister and about a dozen guys. Heep's brother was there, too. Not to mention a whole crowd of Blue Meanies."

Julia pressed a hand to her mouth, but a laugh escaped her anyway. "You didn't."

"My mama," Dodge said, enunciating carefully. "My mama taught me manners. Of course I did."

"So how many Blue Meanies did you drink?"

The ball came back via Scoot, and Dodge threw it again. He ran his free hand over his scalp. "Three?"

"Something tells me it didn't stop there."

Dodge shook his head. "There was a drink called Blunt Force Trauma, I think it was. Link warned me about it, but I didn't realize at the time what he was talking about. Caro said it won some prize."

"Last year in Atlanta. So did you spend the whole evening in Heep's bar being experimented on?"

"Oh no," Dodge said. "There was food, too. And—" His brows knit themselves together. "Poker."

"The Wednesday-night game," Julia said. "You jumped into the deep end."

The dogs were standing in front of Dodge again. He threw the ball. "I had a good time."

"Then you're off on the right foot."

He craned his head around to look at her. "You think so?"

That humming Maude was always talking about was in the air again. Julia said, "It's getting late."

"You're out of practice, Jones," he said. "That pass was a little clumsy."

"I wasn't making a pass," Julia said, flustered. "Just the—" She stopped. He was grinning at her.

"You were just trying to extract yourself before you had to say something nice to me."

Julia swallowed a small hiccup of surprise. "I haven't been nice?"

"You've been perfectly polite."

There was a moment's silence while Julia tried to sort out what he meant, how she felt about what he meant, and what she could possibly say in response. Dodge jumped in before she got very far at all.

"Never mind," he said. "Tomorrow I'll blame this whole conversation on blunt force trauma."

"How did you get back here, anyway?" Julia asked, glad for the change in direction.

"Caro said I was too drunk to walk, so she drove me home. I think I promised her something. Now I remember. Internships."

Julia turned on the bench and pulled her knees up so she could rest her chin on them. "That was bound to happen. You were set up, you realize. Heep poured you full of Blue Meanies and—"

"There was another one called Strip and Run Naked," Dodge interjected. "You know, I don't think alcohol has any effect on Heep at all."

"You're not the first to notice that," Julia said. "So did you keep your clothes on?"

He grinned at her. "As you see. It takes more than a few drinks to separate me from my skivvies."

His grin was disconcerting. Julia felt a very strong urge to giggle, something she clamped down hard. "But you let yourself be talked into one of Caro's schemes. She'll have you coming to her classes and doing independent studies with her students, and in the end she'll turn Scriveners into an extended classroom. Tomorrow you can set things straight."

Dodge blinked at her. "No need. I don't mind giving her students some work, as long as they don't mind spending time with Link."

That broad and not so innocent smile again.

Slowly Julia said, "You're saying that Caro is the one who walked into a trap?"

"I'm saying I see potential for gain on both sides," Dodge corrected her. "And a solution to my Link problem."

"I sense trouble on the horizon."

"Have faith, Jones," Dodge said, and burped softly. "I've got a plan. You want to hear about it?"

"You do remember my name? Because Jones—that's not me."

"Pajama Jones," Dodge said. "That's you all right. You want to hear about my plan or not?"

"A plan to have college coeds drag Link into the technological age? I'm all ears."

Dodge was not very drunk. Not so drunk that he couldn't see that Julia Darrow was opening a door.

She sat there in shortie pajamas, her lower face hidden behind her crossed arms, her knees pressed primly together in stark contrast to bare and very shapely lower legs. The streetlamps brought out the red in her hair, and her eyes seemed very large and dark.

There were rules. He had set them up for himself over the years, and they worked well. When he ignored his rules about the women he could get involved with, trouble generally followed.

He got up and took a deep breath. "Come on, Jones," he said. "I'll make you some coffee." The hesitation on her face made him wonder if he had misread things.

"Or you could make me coffee," he said. "Or we could meet for coffee tomorrow."

Her expression shifted from doubt to decision. "I'm terrible in the kitchen," she said. "You make the coffee, I'll sit and watch you."

JULIA HAD BEEN IN THE APARTMENT BEFORE, BUT NOT SINCE John Dodge moved in. The dogs, less curious than she was, collapsed on the rug and fell asleep before she had made it all the way into the room.

He had bought good, solid furniture, comfortable but without much personality. A ficus tree stood in front of one window and a jade tree in front of the other, probably housewarming gifts from Bo Russell and Mae Oglesby, who spent all summer trying to outdo each other's container gardens. On the coffee table a pile of books, many with bits of paper marking pages. All nonfiction, most of it having to do with South Carolina. A notebook, pencils, a laptop computer, closed. No television or stereo.

From the kitchen Dodge called, "You lost?"

The kitchen was just as utilitarian, a table with two chairs, and a half-empty box of plates and cups and cutlery.

"This apartment is the mirror image of mine," Julia said. "Hard to get lost. I see you travel light."

"That's my motto." He was fiddling with a coffee machine, but he glanced at her over his shoulder. Suddenly he didn't seem so drunk at all, but then Julia watched as he dug a couple aspirin out of a bottle on the counter and downed them.

"So," she said. "What's this plan of yours?"

While he finished with the coffee and poured it he told her. Caro Epperson's interns would have primary responsibility for following Link around and recording whatever he had to say about pens, the business more generally, and particularly customer history. They would also record his phone conversations with customers, one-sided though they would be.

"I've set up a database," Dodge said. He sat down across from her at the kitchen table. "To Link an intern is just a captive audience. I'd guess in three months I'll have most of what's in his head recorded, and I can extract what I need to set up the website and the inventory records."

"So you're paying the interns to listen to Link talk."

Dodge grinned at her. "I did it myself today, five hours nonstop. I'll take a shift now and then to keep Link on his toes."

Julia said, "He does love to tell a story. I have to say, I'm impressed."

Dodge poured milk into his coffee. "I'm good at what I do. As long as it interests me."

And he smiled at her so that her breath hitched and whatever she had meant to say—something witty, something just edgy enough to keep the conversation on its current course—disappeared and she was left with nothing but a familiar and distractingly warm tingle in the pit of her stomach.

SHE HAD AN EXTRAORDINARILY EXPRESSIVE FACE, DODGE thought. He had sent a subtle question, and she had caught it in the solar plexus.

Julia cleared her throat. "And you're modest, too."

"Hey." He put his cup down. "Play to your strengths, that's my approach. Don't you do the same?"

A flutter at the corner of her mouth that might have been an attempt at a smile. There was a sheen of perspiration on her throat, and a creeping of color. Dodge's own interest ratcheted up a notch. He found himself wondering if he was misreading, and decided he was not.

"I think it's time for me to go," Julia said. "It's really too late for this anyway."

"For what?"

The question hung there for a moment, unanswered, and then she was up and moving. Dodge acted without thought, just reached out and caught her wrist. Gently. And stood.

She looked at him, her expression remarkably somber.

"Too late for what?" He stood, keeping hold of her wrist.

Julia looked away sharply, and then back. She raised her face and studied him.

She said, "You're here for what, a year and a half?"

Dodge nodded. "About that."

"And then you're leaving."

"Yes."

"Good," she said. She smelled of some kind of talcum powder without any trace of perfume.

"Why is that good?" Dodge slid his hand up her arm and let it rest on her shoulder.

She closed her eyes briefly. "I'm not interested in a long-term commitment."

"Okay," Dodge said slowly, catching her other hand. "What are you interested in?"

"That's pretty obvious, isn't it?"

"I'm a great believer in getting things out in the open. Disambiguation is my favorite word."

A flicker of something in her eyes, irritation or anger. She said, "If you insist. I'm not looking for a permanent relationship. And I don't date men from Lamb's Corner at all."

She was so close now that he could feel the heat of her, which was enough to rob him of anything he might have thought to say to this proclamation. Instead he slipped an arm around her waist and pulled her up to him and kissed her, a full kiss without hesitation or room for debate.

When he let her go Julia said, "Oh look, my knees have gone all wobbly."

Dodge sat on the edge of the table and pulled her to him so he could support her in the V of his legs and they were face-to-face. He found himself laughing between kisses, his hands moving over her as they warmed to each other. With his thumb he stroked the hollow of her throat. She closed her eyes and breathed very deeply, a woman who enjoyed being touched. Nothing frantic in the way she responded, all her muscles loose, her hands relaxed where they rested on his chest.

He stood, and drew her by the hand into the bedroom.

HER SMOOTH SKIN AND THE COOL, SILKY SHEETS. DODGE SAID, "My God, you feel good."

She pressed herself against him. "And you haven't even got to the best bits."

She moved. Constant, liquid movement all around him until his head swam and so he took her by the shoulders, held her down.

"Time to assume some control," he muttered against her mouth. "See how good I am at puzzle boxes."

"I'm an open book," Julia said, and gasped.

Later he felt as though his skull had been emptied, scraped clean. She lay against his side, ribs heaving, her pale body flushed, her eyes huge and still in her face. A hint of a smile.

He said, "I'm not easily surprised."

She blinked at him, rolled over on her back, and scissored her legs in the tumult of five hundred dollars of rumpled sheets.

"Did you think I've been celibate since my husband died?" Her voice was a little husky, catching in her throat.

He turned on his side to look at her, but she kept her gaze on the ceiling.

"No. Yes. I don't know, I hadn't thought about it in those terms."

She glanced at him, her mouth giving away her doubt. "Sure you did. Everybody wonders about my sex life; it's one of the hot topics around here. So far I've managed to keep things private."

"By not getting involved with anybody local," Dodge said.

"By not getting involved." She turned on her side to face him. "Shocked?"

"Surprised," Dodge said, pulling her closer. "But not displeased. Unless this was . . ." He looked for the right word.

"A one-night stand?"

"It's a reasonable question."

Julia ran a foot up his leg and Dodge, as tired as he was, felt himself stirring in response. She pressed against him and her skin, sweaty even in the cool of the air-conditioning, adhered to his own. She was studying his face as if she had been set an assignment to memorize it. Then she seemed to come to some conclusion, because she smiled.

"No," she said. "Not a one-night stand. But can we take this one night at a time?"

There were questions to ask; Dodge could feel them just under the skin, like the beginning of a burn. That tightening that said it was time to get out of the sun, no matter how fine the weather or promising the day.

It was still dark when Julia got up and pulled her pajamas back on. Dodge cracked an eye and found himself looking at Scoot, who licked his ear with great delicacy.

Dodge wiped his ear and took count: all the dogs on the bed, and Julia out of it.

"Jones."

She looked at him over her shoulder.

"You do know that's not my name, right?"

"Then why did you answer to it?"

Julia made a face and went back to her buttons.

"So are we going to be awkward now?"

She rounded the bed, leaned over, and kissed him. A decent kiss, nothing distant in it and nothing of passion, either.

"See you later."

Dodge wrapped a hand in her pajama top and pulled her close to kiss her back, more thoroughly.

"I'm good at keeping secrets," he said. "If that's what you're worried about."

A line appeared between her brows. "It's not a matter of secrets. It's a matter of privacy."

That she was irritated and offended both was obvious; he had hit a nerve. She seemed to realize it, too, because she produced a forced smile.

"See you later?"

"Hmmmm," Dodge said.

He watched the dogs trot out after her, thought of asking her to leave Scoot behind. Then Dodge rolled over and waited for his mind to stop working so he could go back to sleep.

14

THURSDAY MORNING when Dodge came into the shop at eight, Link was at the front counter with a line of fountain pens spread out before him and an open bottle of India ink. He took one look at Dodge and grimaced.

"Didn't I warn you about those blunt force traumas?"

Dodge said, "You're only young once."

That brought Link up short. He sputtered for a moment and then set his mouth in a studiously grumpy line.

"You know who was in here five minutes ago? Caro. Caro was in here with two of her students." There were bright spots of color high on the old man's cheeks. "Said you needed interns. Said you knew all about it. I told her that must have been the blunt force traumas talking."

"Well, you're right," Dodge said. "I don't need interns, but you do."

Link's left eyelid twitched. "Come again?"

"Those interns are for you. You know how I took notes yesterday when you talked about the pens?"

A cautious nod.

"Well, that's a big job. Three mornings a week and two afternoons, you'll have two interns here working with you. Six of them in all."

"Writing down what I say?" Link's eyelid was still twitching. "On that computer?"

"One of them on the computer, one writing and taking digital photos."

Link tapped the corners of his mouth with thumb and forefinger. "Those two who came in here this morning weren't from Lamb's Corner, but they didn't look downright dull, either." The tone of a man who has stumbled into a good thing and is afraid to take a step for fear of losing it again. Caro had assured Dodge that Link's behavior would be beyond reproach. Dodge found himself hoping she was right.

"Caro will be asking you for your evaluation of each of them," Dodge said, and saw that he had hit the bull's-eye.

"My mama used to say I was a natural-born teacher." He cleared his throat. "Maybe I jumped to conclusions."

"Maybe you did. Did you think I was going to try to replace you with eighteen-year-olds?"

A shrug of one bony shoulder, a grimace, a nod.

Dodge shook his head. "We have a contract, Link. I'm not trying to get around that. So what did you do, chase them away?"

Link snorted. "There's not a man born of woman could scare Caro off when she's got an idea in her head."

"True," said Heep, coming through the door from his workroom. "She'd be the first to admit it."

He winked at Dodge. Heep's whole demeanor had changed, which meant that Dodge had passed some test the night before; whether it had been his willingness to sample Heep's cocktails or the poker game or both was hard to say. Of course, there was a price to winning Heep over. Dodge wondered when the aspirin would kick in.

He was saying, "Caro went over to say hey to Lorna Jean at the bookstore. Her students are at SugarPuss, flirting with Leo."

Dodge looked across the park, empty at this hour. He said, "I've been meaning to stop in the bookstore and say hello."

"No you haven't." Link's equilibrium was coming back fast, along with his knowing grin. "But you've just about run out of excuses."

RIVERVIEW BOOKS WAS THE KIND OF SHOP DODGE NORMALLY avoided. Scented candles, stuffed animals, silk flowers and crystal vases to put them in, gag gifts, china figurines of clowns and kittens all made in China, cards, wrapping paper, plaques to hang on the wall, and someplace in the middle of all that an oasis of bookshelves with a total of no more than a couple hundred books, most all of it nonfiction.

Lorna Jean Emerson was good-looking in a severe, carefully maintained way, with such strict good posture that she might have been wearing a back brace. Nora would have called Lorna Jean Emerson *Madame General,* a title she reserved for a certain type of army wife, the women married to high-ranking officers who assumed a law-and-order, self-control-above-all-else approach to survival. Nylons and high heels no matter the temperature, and all vestiges of personality banished from the range of expressions she bestowed on the public. In comparison her fiancé seemed an easygoing sort. He put down the bits of the display case he was assembling to shake Dodge's hand.

Caro said, "May I introduce you to Reverend Curtis Durant? He's rector over at St. Mary's? But mostly folks just call him Curtis."

Dodge caught the flicker of discomfort that passed over Lorna Jean Emerson's face at this casual infringement on her intended's seriousness of purpose.

"I hope you'll stop by, come Sunday," said Durant. "Our ladies serve up the best covered supper in Lamb's Corner." He patted the small round belly that sat above his belt, and Lorna Jean Emerson's mouth twitched.

"Now, Dodge," Lorna Jean said. "I am so glad you stopped by. Just yesterday we were talking about coming by to welcome you, in't that so, Curtis? But then this business with the Kallsjö people came up, and I got distracted."

"Kallsjö people?" Dodge asked, mostly because he was obliged to.

"Surely you've heard," she said, glancing at Caro. "The two empty apartments across from you have been rented. On a short-term basis. When our charter specifically indicates that while owners may rent—"

"Lorna Jean, darlin," said Curtis Durant. "Maybe this should wait for the meeting?"

She flushed at this interruption but inclined her head. "Very well. Will we see you there, Dodge?"

"Wouldn't miss it for the world," Dodge said.

As soon as they were out the door he said to Caro, "Is there any hope of getting out of that meeting, do you think?"

"Not a chance in hell," Caro told him with a smile.

"So what's the real problem? It can't be the short-term rental thing."

Caro sent him a sidelong glance, and then she did an admirable job of telling him what he needed to know, which was short and not very sweet. Lorna Jean's dislike of the Swedes and efforts to keep them out of Lambert Square had almost nothing to do with their business practices or religious beliefs.

"It's Nils Sigridsson," Caro said. "And dashed hopes."

"Ah." Dodge glanced back at the store and caught sight of Lorna Jean's blond head. "So Curtis wasn't her first choice?"

"She's been keeping company with Curtis Durant for ten years. Lorna Jean thought Nils would help her fix that one way or the other, but Nils never gave her any serious attention. First it was Mayme who turned his head and then when she kept turning him down, he started dating Julia."

They stopped outside SugarPuss. "So Lorna Jean just doesn't want to have to see him every day?" Sidestepping the issue of Julia's dating history, which didn't fool Caro, not for a moment.

She turned to look at him, eyes narrowed. "If Lorna Jean can't have the Swede, then she don't want nobody to have him. Especially not Mayme or Julia." To her student she said: "Margie, you've got foam on your upper lip. You wouldn't show up for an interview in Charleston with foam on your lip, would you? Mr. Dodge deserves the same respect."

The girls were about nineteen, and they looked ill at ease in their suits and high heels. Too much jewelry, too much hair, and way too much perfume, but Dodge could live with all that. While Caro made introductions he caught sight of Leo Guzman standing in the window of SugarPuss looking very pleased. Link might take some winning over, but the interns had Leo's approval.

"I have got to get going, I teach in a half hour," Caro was saying. "Margie, Charlene, good luck. I know Mr. Dodge will get you off to a good start."

There was a quiet moment when Caro had disappeared down the walkway to the parking structure, and then Dodge turned on his broadest, most welcoming smile.

"Coffee?"

They looked at each other, and the taller of the two spoke up. "We've had breakfast, thank you."

"I haven't. We'll call it a breakfast meeting." He gestured to the bakery door. "I hope you've got something to write on, because I need you to take notes."

JULIA WAS WRAPPING A SHEET SET AT THE COUNTER WHEN SHE looked up and saw Dodge crossing Lambert Square park in deep conversation with two young women.

"Will you look at that," Exa said, coming up beside her. "He works fast, don't he?"

A flare of irritation shot up from Julia's stomach into her throat and she swallowed it down again. She said, "Those are interns Caro sent over."

"Interns," said Exa with a huffing laugh. "Is that what they're calling them these days?"

Mayme called over, "Phone for you, Julia."

Julia closed her eyes in relief. If she stayed here she'd end up snapping at Exa, and that would put ideas in her head. The fact that the ideas might be more than just a little true made it all the more important to get away. She took the phone from Mayme with a quick smile.

"Julia Darrow."

Nothing. She raised a brow at Mayme, who inclined her head very slightly in Exa's direction. Mayme to the rescue. Julia mouthed a silent thanks.

Into the dead telephone line she said, "Let me call you back from my office about that, if I may."

MAYME CAME UPSTAIRS AN HOUR LATER AND CLOSED THE office door behind her.

"I think she's got it out of her system," Mayme said. "If you want to come downstairs again."

Julia closed the catalog she had been reading and smiled. "Thanks."

"You look about ready to fall on your face," Mayme said. "A doctor might could give you something mild to help you sleep, you know."

"I'll go up and take a nap this afternoon if things are quiet."

Mayme rotated a shoulder, as though she were loosening up for a pitch. "Dr. Little would made a house call."

Few people were brave enough to talk to Julia about personal matters, but Mayme was one of them. She was so sincere and matter-of-fact that Julia could never take offense. Somehow or another Mayme had turned into more of a friend than an employee, mostly, Julia thought, because they had some things in common. Their marriages had ended in very different ways, but the aftermath was remarkably similar. Except that Mayme had Bean.

"I'll think about it," Julia said. It was all she would do, and they both knew it, but Mayme nodded as if there was some chance things might work out differently this time.

"Oh," she said, turning back from the door. "John Dodge stopped in a few minutes ago. Exa held on to him as long as she could but I think he's gone now. In case you'd rather not run into him."

"I'm not avoiding John Dodge," Julia said, feeling herself begin to flush. "Why would you think I was?"

"Mostly you do avoid people," Mayme said. "Why should he be any different?"

15

DODGE SAT DOWN to read at six. He had no intention of falling asleep, and yet when the phone rang at eight-thirty—a half hour after the scheduled start of the co-op meeting—he woke with some difficulty. There was a crick in his neck from sleeping in a chair, and his head hurt.

Nora said, "Catch you at a bad time?"

Dodge glanced at his watch and then swore. "I'm late for a meeting," he said. "Can I call you back after?"

He didn't stop to comb his hair or look in the mirror; there wasn't time to do anything about what he saw there, anyway. Dodge jogged down the stairs and along the square to the former storehouse that had been renovated into a combination community center, theater, and the Lamb's Corner city hall. There was a light rain falling, and the few people left in the square were hidden under bright red umbrellas emblazoned with white script letters:

Lambert Square in the Rain

Dodge ran up the stairs to the second floor to find the meeting room, his footsteps sounding very loud on the deserted stairs. He stopped to get his bearings and realized he didn't need a map to find where he was going. The doors were open, and the argument was loud.

The agenda for the meeting was still in Dodge's shirt pocket. He pulled it out. Minutes, budget, advertising, holiday season . . . nothing about Kallsjö at all, though that was clearly the subject of discussion. Lorna Jean Emerson and T. J. Pepper were locked in combat over the Swedes, with Mister and Polly standing nearby as backup. Dodge advanced slowly, unsure if he really wanted to walk into the middle of the battle.

". . . my property and I will rent it to whomever I please," T.J. was saying. "For however long I please."

Dodge had met T.J. just a few hours before, when he brought by a houseplant in a Chinese cachepot as a housewarming gift. Something from his shop, T.J. had explained, pointing with his free hand to Lamb's Corner Antiques.

"I thought this might cheer up your place, and I see Big Dove—she's my second cousin on Mama's side? I see she was right, you do need some color."

It looked like a very expensive piece of pottery, and Dodge said so.

"Never you mind," said T.J. He held it up to the light so the colors gleamed. "It is pretty, but it's got a hairline crack. Some would sell it anyway and hope to get away with it." He shot Dodge a sharp glance. "But not me. I'd like you to have it. If you don't mind the little imperfection."

T.J. had struck Dodge as a man comfortable in his own skin, outgoing but with a good dose of healthy wariness. As was only sensible for an openly gay, middle-aged man living in the rural South. That he would be at odds with Lorna Jean Emerson could be no surprise.

Dodge edged forward and got a sense of the room. Thirty or so people, coffee and finger food at the far end, and Maude Golden sitting at a table at the front. She looked more irritated than she did concerned. With her at the table were three other people—a harried-looking middle-aged accountant type studying a pile of printouts, Mayme from Cocoon, who was taking notes, and Julia Darrow. In emerald green silk pajamas that might have come off the set of *Flower Drum Song*.

All day Dodge had been trying to catch a glimpse of Julia, but without any luck. By late afternoon he had admitted to himself that she was avoiding him, and more, that he didn't know if that was a good thing or a bad one. If she had come looking for him he would have been uneasy, but this sense that she was going out of her way to avoid him was worse.

Now there she sat next to Maude Golden, in pajamas. Dodge wondered if she had come through the wet in slippers. Or maybe if she was barefoot. He forced his attention back to the argument.

". . . clearly states in article three—" Lorna Jean Emerson's voice squeaked with righteous indignation.

A man sitting in the first row jumped to his feet. "You know what you can do with your article three!"

Maude Golden was up, too. "Dan, hold it there."

"I think it's time we took a vote," said Mister, unfolding from his chair to his full six and a half feet.

"But article three—"

"Enough," Maude said again, more forcefully.

Heads swiveled back and forth between Maude and Lorna Jean, Dan Harris and T. J. Pepper, Polly and Mister.

Maude said, "Lorna Jean, you've got two choices here. You can give up gracefully or you can go hire a lawyer."

"A lawyer!" LRoy Swagger called out. "Oh Lordy, spare us the lawyers."

"A lawyer," Maude repeated. "You'll have to name us all in the lawsuit. Do you want to drag our business into the courts, Lorna Jean? And while I'm asking questions, are you going to be the one to explain to Nils and Beate why you've gone to such trouble to stop them from renting apartments that are otherwise empty? Apartments that they rented the last time they were in town, let me point out, and on a short-term lease."

Lorna Jean went very still, her head tilted to one side. Her mouth was pressed so hard together that her lips disappeared completely.

It was at that moment Dodge realized that other people had come up to listen and were standing behind him. Two people, as a matter of fact, carrying suitcases and dripping rain. He stepped aside and they moved into the room.

"Oh, please," said the woman. "This I should like to hear."

"I, too," said her companion in a heavier Swedish accent. "I am very interested why Lorna Jean would not want us here. I thought we were all good friends."

. . .

BECAUSE SHE WAS FACING THE AUDIENCE, JULIA NOTICED JOHN Dodge standing in the open door before anyone else. Just what she needed, John Adams Dodge staring at her during Lorna Jean and T.J.'s shouting match. Julia picked up a pen, and started making a to-do list.

1. Ignore JD standing in the door.

Dodge's face and hair were damp, as though he had been sweating. Rain, she reminded herself. It was raining.

Julia put down her pen and glanced at Mike Golden, who was scowling at the screen of his laptop. He probably wasn't even aware of the argument going on. Maude often said she had married a man whose hearing simply turned off in the presence of a balance sheet. And if Mike wasn't listening to Lorna Jean and T.J., he wouldn't take any note of John Dodge. Who was leaning on the door frame now, his arms crossed. His really great arms.

So he was better-looking than she had wanted to admit at first. So there was sexual attraction there. Mutual attraction, consenting adults, full disclosure. The big three. So why had she been feeling all day as if she had done something terminally stupid? She had made it clear what she could and couldn't offer, and he had jumped right in. With enthusiasm.

2. Stay focused.

If Lorna Jean Emerson would ever shut up, Julia told herself, there might be some chance of gathering her thoughts. But Lorna Jean would not shut up, and now Dan Harris was on the verge of losing his temper. It took some doing to get Dan mad, but Lorna Jean was nothing if not determined.

People were popping to their feet all over the room. Julia allowed herself a peek at John Dodge and saw him taking it all in, like a kid in front of a television. Or the monkey cage at the zoo. They amused him, no doubt. He had come to Lamb's Corner to be amused.

3. Don't overanalyze.

Mostly Julia found Lorna Jean irritating and petty, a miserable, morally superior know-it-all, but she had the courage of her convictions and a natural dignity. Maude was working her over, but Lorna Jean stood straight and tall and took it, nary a drop of blood to be seen. And Julia had to admit to herself at least that she admired Lorna Jean for her apparently endless supply of courage. She never shied away from an argument.

Some people seemed to thrive on confrontation. Mister and Polly, Link Kay, Lorna Jean. John Dodge was a fighter, too. He was fast with a comeback and witty, things she had always liked in a man. Things that had seemed important until Charlie came along. Charlie, who loved words but hated arguments, who would retreat into silence in the face of his mother's determination to make something of him and laugh like a loon when he was alone with Julia.

John Dodge was still standing in the doorway. With his damp dark hair and the dimple in his left cheek and that mouth—

Two people came up behind him. Both familiar. Nils Sigridsson, it turned out, was just Dodge's height. Nils had the build of a dedicated marathon runner in a hand-tailored Italian suit, an utterly engaging smile, and the morals of an affectionate alley cat. The other person was Beate Gyllensting, a tiny dark-haired woman in a silk business suit that accentuated a generous figure. Heir to the Kallsjö empire, a formidable negotiator, and, according to Maude, nobody you wanted to turn your back on if your interests ran contrary to her own.

Familiar faces, ones Julia should be glad to see. She had been part of the concerted effort to get Kallsjö to come to Lamb's Corner, after all. Kallsjö would bring in jobs, and jobs were the first priority. In her hurt pride Lorna Jean had forgotten that, but nobody else had.

"I am very interested why Lorna Jean would not want us here," Nils was saying. "I thought we were all good friends?"

"Go on, Lorna Jean," Maude said. "Explain your position to Beate and Nils."

16

AT THREE in the morning Dodge gave up on sleep.

There was a drumming of rain overhead. In the dark bedroom the air was cool and the bed comfortable and just warm enough, and Dodge was widely, completely awake.

He walked out into the parlor and to the windows to watch the rain falling over the park. His gaze kept returning to a line of dark windows where his new neighbors were asleep in their furnished apartments. The Swedes, people called them, or the Kallsjö people. Or even Kallie-Joe, as in when do you think Kallie-Joe will start hiring? Exa Stabley had asked him that, and he had been so charmed by the transliteration that he hadn't corrected her. Whatever you called them, two Swedes interjected into one co-op meeting had brought everything to an abrupt end.

Pretty much everyone had gathered around the newcomers, eager to shake hands and say a few words. Only Lorna Jean and Julia had hung back, their heads bent together as they talked. Not a friendly conversation, even across the room he could tell that. Dodge had seen women fighting like this before, everything held in and nailed down. He hesitated for a minute, telling himself it would be pointless to get involved, and then he was glad to see Lorna Jean pull away and leave.

He caught Julia's gaze. She shrugged, and for a moment Dodge had the odd idea that she wanted to be rescued, standing there alone while everybody else was gathered around the Swedes. But she had made herself clear about public displays of affection or even plain old friendship, and he had agreed.

Dodge had slipped out and walked back to Scriveners, hunch-shouldered in the rain. Polly caught him up just as he was passing her door.

She said, "I wonder if any of that mess made sense to you, Lorna Jean getting all wound up about something as silly as a short-term lease."

Dodge hesitated, but then turned back to Polly. She was a good-looking woman, with sleek dark skin and close-cropped hair that made her eyes seem very large.

He said, "Not so hard to figure out. She got her heart broken and now she doesn't want to have to see the guy every day."

Polly's smile flashed. "There's nothing simple when it comes to Lorna Jean."

Dodge said, "You know, I swore to myself I wouldn't get caught up in the gossip."

"Sugar," Polly said, pressing a hand into his forearm, "I wish you well with that, I truly do."

Of course he was sorry, once he got back to the apartment. He should have waited until Polly told him the rest of the story before he proclaimed his virtue. Unfortunately he had an idea of what she had been going to say.

There was another potted plant sitting in front of Dodge's door. He took it inside, glanced once at the blinking light on his answering machine, and went straight to bed. He was tired enough to sleep right through until morning, he told himself. An order, of sorts, to his subconscious, and one that was duly ignored.

Now he was wide awake. He took a chance and dialed his night-owl sister, who picked up on the first ring.

"Wait," Nora said a few minutes later. "Back up. I'm confused."

"It's not all that complicated," Dodge said. "It's not even very interesting. The Kallsjö people got here, and as much as the work and the boost to the economy are welcome, there will be some bumps along the way."

"Bullshit," Nora said. "It's not about economics at all. You've got a love triangle involving a straightlaced Christian bookstore lady, a wild Swedish industrialist with a polyamorous bent, and a reclusive young widow. I'd call that interesting."

"Okay, now you're embroidering. I didn't say anything about the widow being part of this."

"You said the Swede dumped the bookstore lady for somebody else—"

"That's what I was told."

"—somebody else in Lambert Square."

Dodge closed his eyes briefly and tried to think of something to say that would stop this conversation in its tracks. Because he didn't have an answer, but he did have suspicions pretty close to the scenario his sister was having such fun exploring.

"You're jumping to conclusions."

"What?" Nora said. "The Cocoon woman is celibate?"

Dodge caught a breath, and his sister laughed. "I thought so. This is my prediction, you ready?"

"No," Dodge said. "Not in the least."

"The Cocoon woman ends up with the industrialist—"

"Unlikely," Dodge said.

"Hmmmm," said Nora, and he winced. After a long moment she said, "Watch yourself, will you?"

"I always do."

"No, really watch yourself. No falling in love with a Valkyrie and moving to Sweden."

"Also unlikely," Dodge said, relaxing a little. "Weren't the Valkyries tall and built like linebackers? Beate Gyllensting is about five feet tall. In really expensive, very high heels."

Nora said, "And anyway, I'd much rather see you settled in Lamb's Corner."

You had to admire her doggedness.

"Why this sudden concern with my love life?" Dodge said. "I'm happy as I am. I've got things exactly where I want them."

"And how long will it last this time?" said Nora.

Dodge considered hanging up, but manners won out. That, and the fact that he didn't want to give away so much.

"Why do I let you back me into corners?" Dodge asked.

"That question," said his sister the practicing therapist, "is not so rhetorical as you seem to think it is."

Dodge was standing there with the phone still in his hand when he saw a light go on in Julia's apartment windows. A few minutes later a door opened and her dogs went dashing into Lambert Square park.

17

JULIA OPENED HER UMBRELLA and stepped out into the rain, lecturing herself the whole time about what was reasonable, and what was not.

A reasonable person would hurry the dogs along and get back into the dry and warm. A reasonable person, she told herself, wouldn't be looking up at windows hoping for—what exactly? What was it she wanted?

Julia turned deliberately and headed into the park, whistling for the dogs.

Scoot appeared before her, his whole hind end waggling, and then bounded off into the dark.

"Very funny," Julia called after him. She took off at a slow trot, her yellow rain boots squeaking on the wet grass, and caught up with all the dogs near the fountain. The quartet of panting faces stared up at her, and she found herself smiling in return.

"Reprobates, every one of you." Tails thumped in agreement and Scoot took off again.

"I've got him," called a voice from the shadows. Then John Dodge was there with Scoot sitting jauntily on his arm. Rain was running down Dodge's face, though he didn't seem to notice.

"No umbrella?"

"You looked like you needed some help."

The skin on the back of her neck prickled. "I would have managed. But thanks."

"Share that umbrella, and I'll walk you back to your door."

UNDER OTHER CIRCUMSTANCES DODGE WOULDN'T HAVE BEEN bothered by the rain, but he had the urge to see what she would do if he pushed, and so he did. Shoulder to shoulder under the umbrella, laden down with squirming dogs, Dodge took the opportunity to ask the question she probably least wanted to hear.

"You avoiding me?"

"Of course," Julia said. "I was afraid you'd throw yourself at my feet if you had the chance. I have that effect on men."

"So what you're saying," Dodge went on, "is that I'm an insufferable self-satisfied egomaniac and I should get over myself."

"I don't know you well enough to call you an egomaniac."

"Ouch," said Dodge. "You play rough."

Julia's grin turned into a full smile and then suddenly fled completely. Dodge followed her gaze to Cocoon, where somebody was waiting under the awning, out of the rain. He hadn't stayed around long enough to be introduced, but he recognized Nils Sigridsson.

"You've got company," Dodge said.

Sigridsson called out, "I wondered if you would be down here with the dogs."

Dodge bit back the very childish urge to mock the accent and the singsong rhythm: *voonDAD if you VUD* beee.

"I wasn't expecting him," Julia said in a low voice.

"Looks like he was expecting you," Dodge said. "He's wearing pajamas."

Julia said, "Nils, you didn't get a chance to meet John Dodge earlier. He's the new owner of Scriveners."

Dodge found himself shaking hands with the senior vice president of Kallsjö, a man known not only to Julia but to Scoot, who was yipping in excitement.

"There he is," Sigridsson said. "Scoot, buddy, come to Papa."

Dodge glanced at Julia, who was flushed. Embarrassed or irritated, he thought. Maybe both. He was a little put out himself.

She handed Scoot over, a little reluctantly. "Now isn't this awkward."

Sigridsson laughed. A hearty, apparently genuine laugh. "Are we in competition? If you were hoping to adopt Scoot, I have to tell you, Julia promised him to me."

Julia frowned. "I said you could apply to adopt him if you were to settle in Lamb's Corner."

"You see?" Sigridsson said, rubbing an appreciative Scoot between the ears. "Here I am in Lamb's Corner for good. This is my new home."

"Congratulations," Julia said, but she wasn't smiling.

Dodge said, "I'll leave you two to catch up on old times."

"Not me," Julia said. "I'm going home. Good night."

She walked away from them, the pajama bottoms clinging to her hips and the curve of her buttocks. Chilled as he was, Dodge felt himself stir. At the door she paused and looked back, and Scoot hopped out of Sigridsson's arms and went trotting after her.

Sigridsson said, "She startles like a deer. One wrong move and pffft—" He waved a hand.

Dodge wondered if what he was hearing in Sigridsson's voice was regret or instruction and more: why it bothered him, in either case.

"I'll say good night, too."

"Would you like a drink?" Sigridsson jerked his head upward to the windows of his own apartment. "We are neighbors, after all. And maybe you could fill me in on Julia."

Dodge felt himself bristle in dislike, and wasn't that strange. The guy was nice enough, and it was no sin for him to be interested in Julia. It was perfectly understandable, in fact. Maude Golden hadn't been exaggerating very much when she talked about men following Julia through Lambert Square.

"Another time," Dodge said. "I've got to get some sleep."

UPSTAIRS DODGE GOT A TOWEL OUT OF THE BATHROOM AND rubbed his face and hair dry, shed his wet shirt, brushed his teeth. He was yawning when he walked into the bedroom to find Julia Darrow sitting propped up against his pillows.

"Nils was going to call and I just didn't want to have to deal with him. Do you mind?"

Dodge considered. She looked small in his bed, but there was nothing childlike about Julia Darrow. She filled out her pajama tops as well as she did the bottoms, all curves and shadows. Her hands were curled and at rest on the duvet folded over her lap. The light from the bathroom didn't reach as far as her face, and Dodge could make out very little of her expression.

"I don't mind," Dodge said. His voice came a little rough.

She smiled. "Then why are you standing there covered in gooseflesh?"

Dodge dropped the towel he had wrapped around his waist and climbed under the covers. Julia slid down until she was lying on her side, facing him.

He said, "You feel threatened by Sigridsson?"

Her brow creased, as if she didn't quite recognize the name. "Threatened by Nils? He's harmless."

"Huh," Dodge said, wondering if he could risk asking a few pointed questions. She leaned forward and kissed him, lightly.

"I would be very thankful," she whispered, "if this discussion of Nils could wait until tomorrow."

THE PHONE RANG AT SIX IN THE MORNING AND YANKED DODGE up from a deep sleep. Beside him Julia said, "I should go."

The machine clicked on.

You have reached the answering machine at John Dodge's place. I'm not here to take your call. I'm sorry to have missed you. If you'd be so good as to leave your name and number, I'll get back to you just as quick as I can. Thank you.

Julia giggled. "Call the police," she said. "While you were out Opie snuck in here and recorded a message on your machine." Dodge elbowed her as a familiar voice started its march through the room.

"JD, this is your father. I'm calling to tell you that your brother TJ has been transferred to Fort Irwin and your brother James and his wife are expecting another child. Your mother sends her regards—"

"Dodge, give me that phone."

"Hold on, Sophia, I'm not finished. I am putting something in the mail for you, son. An article I wrote for the *Yale Law Journal*. Sophia, you know I don't like to be—"

"Dodge, this is your mama. Why don't you call for such a long time? I had to get your number from Eleanor. You are my firstborn and I worry about you, running from place to place, wasting your educa—"

The machine cut off. Dodge let the breath he had been holding go in a long whoosh. For a moment he thought Julia had gone back to sleep, and then he realized she was looking at him.

"Your father is very military," she said. "And southern."

"Bred in the bone."

"He called you JD."

"He did."

"Juvenile delinquent?"

"Very astute of you to pick that up. Let's just say that my adolescence was the epitome of rockiness."

"The tension came off of you in a wave. What about your mother?"

"She's a nurse. Retired now."

"She's got an accent."

"Greek," Dodge said.

"Tell me," Julia said, yawning again. "About your names."

Dodge turned on his side to look at her. "My father lives and breathes constitutional law. He named me John Adams Dodge. I've got two brothers, Thomas Jefferson Dodge and James Madison Dodge. I'm the only one who has failed to live up to the name I was given. Hence the JD."

"Because you didn't go to law school, or because you didn't join the army?"

"Both, to start with."

Julia's hair was rumpled, falling over her brow. Dodge resisted the urge to brush it back. If he touched her, they were unlikely to get any more sleep, and she looked tired.

"And your sister?"

"Eleanor Roosevelt Dodge, but everybody calls her Nora. That was my mother's doing."

"So this is a family custom, naming the boys after the founding fathers?" She was intrigued by the idea; he could see the possibilities running through her mind.

"It's worse than that," Dodge said. "My father is Teddy Roosevelt Dodge, and he's got five brothers—"

"Oh no," Julia said, delighted. "Tell me you have an uncle Millard Fillmore or Rutherford Hayes."

"Sorry. But I can offer you John Quincy Adams Dodge, William McKinley Dodge, James Polk Dodge, Harry Truman Dodge—"

"Enough!" Julia laughed. "Who can remember all those names?"

"My mother never can. She calls them all 'brother.'"

Julia's mouth quirked at the corner. "She sounded nice, your mother."

"She is nice," Dodge said. "In her own drill sergeant kind of way. Is it my turn to ask questions now?"

A very slight nod. "You want to know about Nils?"

She slid a hand up his arm and Dodge gave it a pointed look.

"I'm trying to be thoughtful, here," he said. "You're yawning."

"I don't need much sleep. You didn't answer my question, but I'll tell you anyway. I dated Nils for about three weeks, all told. Really he wanted Mayme, but she turned him down. Then he went back to Sweden and that was that. Anything else you want to know?"

Dodge said, "You're in my bed and not in his. What else do I need to know?"

"You don't mind sharing me, huh." It wasn't a question so much as a challenge. One that Dodge felt in his gut.

He said, "There's no right answer to that."

She hiccupped a short laugh. "I hit a nerve."

"You hit what you aimed for."

She thought about that for a minute. "You're right. I apologize. Let me say this straight out, okay? I've got no interest in Nils, beyond friendship. He can be entertaining."

"Is that so?"

Julia flipped over on her back and looked at the ceiling. "What else do you want me to say?"

Dodge thought of all the questions he might ask, the things he had observed about this woman that didn't add up. The one thing he knew for certain was that Julia would disappear for good if he put any of those questions into words at this point.

"Nothing," Dodge said. "Not a thing."

"You're curious," she said, turning on her side. "You're wondering about me."

"Sure I'm curious," Dodge said, and he reached out and pulled her to him.

She flexed under his hands, the silk of her pajamas sliding against skin. Julia drew in a long shivering breath. "I have to be back home by seven."

"Fifty minutes," Dodge said, his fingers tracing the shape of her. "Let's see what we can do with that."

18

FRIDAY NIGHT there was an impromptu party that went off like a rocket. Lit, of course, by the Swedes, who had booked the community center for a meeting and then came pouring out into the square just after the shops closed. There were a dozen or so management types, most of them trailing families. A riot of Swedes wanting to celebrate; who could refuse? Dodge joined in, shook hands and made an attempt to remember names: Gustav, Hadrian, Katrina, Isak, Helena, Manfred, Lotta, Per. He got into an interesting discussion with Odd Åkesson, a man close to seven feet tall and as broad as a refrigerator, who was the architect in charge of the new assembly plant. He had a wife named Anneke and four boys under the age of ten, all of whom promised to be as big as their father.

The Swedes produced a half dozen bottles of akvavit and opened a tab with Polly and Mister for the Southern Baptists who wanted to join in the toasts but who would no more drink hard liquor than they would dance naked in the fountain. The party reached critical mass by the time the streetlights came on—and still no sign of Julia. Light at her apartment windows, light in the second-floor office window, but no Julia.

Dodge was deep in a conversation with somebody called Isak who was the head of human resources when Nils came toward him with Exa Stabley trailing behind. He was brandishing a half-empty bottle of golden-yellow akvavit and gesturing for Dodge's cup.

"Another toast," Nils said. "To new friends." And he glanced over his shoulder toward Cocoon.

Exa caught him by the arm and held out her cup for a refill. Then she held it up in a salute.

"To bold men."

Dodge found himself wondering just how much akvavit Exa had had, and if there was any way to extract her from the party before things got out of hand. Julia would be the logical person to ask, if she ever came out of hiding.

Nils was saying, "Exa, my sweet, my darling. What good fun you are. Elope with me."

And he winked at Dodge while Exa flushed and laughed with delight. She said, "You think I couldn't give you a run for your money?"

"I know you could," he said with utter sincerity. "But if you won't take pity on me, maybe you can tell me—"

"I know," Exa said. She gave Dodge a wink that came straight off a vaudeville stage. "You're looking for Julia. Sorry to say, she's preoccupied these days. But there's plenty of other fine young women around who would be more than pleased—"

"Ah," said Nils. "There she is. Mayme."

In a quieter place, with less alcohol in his system, Dodge thought he might be able to figure out what had just happened. As it was, he followed Nils as he made his way through the crowd brandishing his bottle and talking to everybody. Except Mayme Hurt, who had suddenly disappeared. Nils looked around himself, turned in a circle in one direction and then the other.

"Our Nils," Beate Gyllensting said, coming up to Dodge. "He is a ladies' man."

"You know that's not a compliment, right?"

She shrugged one shoulder. "He takes it as one. Would not you?"

"Are you asking if I'm a ladies' man?"

"I think you are the quiet type, no?"

Dodge grinned down at her. Her eyes were a little wet and her smile a little loose. She reminded him of women he had worked with on Wall Street, the kind who were good at what they did because they worked so hard at it, and then had to work just as hard to relax on the rare occasions they allowed themselves any time off. She was about his age and married to the company she had inherited. They had a lot in common.

"Maybe too quiet for you," Dodge said. In a tone that was meant to be kind.

She blinked at him in surprise. "You think I want you for sex? Americans." She shook her head. "One-track minds."

"I made no such assumption," Dodge said, and hoped his tone was convincing.

She gave him a long and calculating look. "You are a good liar," she said.

"But not good enough. Never mind. We can be drinking buddies, you and me."

Dodge said, "Bring on the akvavit."

AT THREE IN THE MORNING THE PHONE WOKE DODGE OUT OF A very deep, alcohol-enhanced sleep.

"Dodge," said Julia when the recorder clicked on. "I know you're in there. I'm at your kitchen door."

When he opened the door she closed her cell phone with a click and said, "I could have come right in, but I do have some manners."

"So I see," Dodge said, and stood aside to let her in.

She hesitated. "If you've got company—"

"I wouldn't have answered the phone."

She regarded him for a moment. Julia was wearing a ratty terry-cloth robe over a faded nightgown, and she went up on tiptoe to kiss him, a fleeting, hello kind of kiss.

"Caraway," she said, sniffing. "You've been drinking akvavit." She came in, followed by all four of the dogs, who gave him a bleary look before they went off to sleep in the parlor. Even Scoot seemed subdued.

"All of Lambert Square has been drinking akvavit," Dodge said. "Where were you?"

But she had already disappeared into the bedroom, dropping her robe on the floor as she went. Dodge followed her.

He said, "If I believed in vampires, I might be a little worried about you."

"Hmmm?" She half turned toward him, the nightgown already off her shoulders and poised to slide the rest of the way to the floor. "Why are you worried about me?"

There was the question. A bright, self-reliant woman, successful in a business she loved. A little quirky. A little strange. Unapologetic about her sexual appetites, open to suggestion. A woman protective of her own personal space, but with apparently little sense of his.

Which he didn't mind, at the moment at least. The whole situation was odd, but not so odd that he could turn her out of his bed.

"Nothing important," Dodge said, watching the gooseflesh rise along her spine in the chill air. "You should get under the covers."

She slid between the sheets and gave a shiver of contentment. "You're not coming to bed?"

By the time he climbed in, she was already asleep. Dodge turned out the light.

Half asleep, ten minutes or a half hour later, he felt Julia shift and turn toward him. The air was pleasantly cool on his face, and the rest of him was perfectly warm and relaxed.

"I should go back to my place. I'm intruding."

"You're not intruding. You're welcome to stay."

She was silent for a long moment, so long that he wondered if she had fallen back asleep. Then she sat up and put her hands on the coverlet. "It's just that this bed is so comfortable."

"Then stay," Dodge said.

"I can't sleep here forever." Her tone was oddly wistful and uncertain, but she put her head down and drew in a long sighing breath.

At that moment Dodge realized that Julia wasn't really awake at all, that she wasn't talking to him but to herself. Asking hard questions without answers, and telling him more than she ever would have shared in the light of day.

For a long while he stared into the dark and contemplated Julia Darrow, who created perfectly made beds for other people so that they could find the sleep they needed, but could not do the same for herself.

The next morning when Dodge woke, she was gone again.

19

DODGE'S FIRST SATURDAY MORNING at Scriveners was lively in terms of walk-in customers, which was good news. The bad news was that the youngest person through the door was a sixty-year-old retired postal worker with the unusual name of Farmer Holt. Farmer and Link talked a half hour about the Kallsjö people and the new plant and then moved on to local topics including the hernia that had Farmer's father headed for the hospital. After all that he put a dollar and two quarters on the counter and accepted the single ink cartridge offered on the flat of Link's big hand, along with two sheets of writing paper.

Farmer opened the door to leave and stood back to let another man pass. Dodge hadn't seen Lamont Schmidt since his walk around town that first day, and by rights he shouldn't have recognized him at all. Instead of a baseball cap and overalls, he was wearing an ancient but well-preserved dark suit, a crisp white shirt with a red bow tie, and a felt porkpie hat.

"Mr. Schmidt." Dodge stepped forward to offer his hand. "I am happy to see you again, sir."

Link was more than a little surprised to see that Dodge knew Lamont Schmidt, but he took the explanation without a lot of questions and then went to get the box of stationery the old man requested.

"So I see now why you aren't in the market for a house."

Dodge looked around himself. "This is about all I can handle, you're right. I apologize for not being more forthcoming when we talked—"

Mr. Schmidt held up a hand. "No apology needed. A man has got to get his feet under him in a new place first. From what I hear, you are settling right in." And in response to Dodge's raised brow: "I believe you must know my brother Mason, he's one of the security guards."

Mysterious Mason, as Dodge had come to think of him. He had met the man once and never seen him since, though it seemed that Mason had seen Dodge. There was no helping that kind of idle talk in a town this size, after all.

Dodge said, "If I was looking to make an investment, I should have followed your advice and bought a house right then. I'm guessing real estate values will start to climb again soon, with so many new people coming in."

"I hope you're right," said Mr. Schmidt. "I could use the work. There's not many in Lamb's Corner can afford to hire a teenager to mow the lawn, much less a gardener. You keep me in mind now, if you decide to buy a house after all."

When Mr. Schmidt had left, the next two customers were the Gambrel sisters, who had dressed up for this trip into town, including white gloves and straw hats with a variety of small birds perched on broad rims. Ruth and Lila Gambrel were retired taxidermists who had just recently passed the business over to their brother's oldest boy. Now that they were satisfied that their nephew could handle things they had booked a cruise around the world, and they intended to write many postcards.

"There's nothing like a fountain pen to write a postcard," Ruth Gambrel told Dodge. "Would you be interested in something from the Galapagos Islands?"

Lila dug six single dollars and eighty-three cents in dimes and pennies out of her change purse and left the money on the counter along with a large square of gingerbread wrapped in a paper towel imprinted with ducks. In return she put three small boxes of ink cartridges in her purse, along with the receipt Link wrote out by hand.

When they were gone Link said, "We have loyal customers here in Lamb's Corner, we certainly do. I sold Ruth and Lila that pen myself, twenty years ago this fall."

Dodge could tell when Link was looking for an argument, and he also had pretty much figured out that the best way to avoid giving him what he wanted was to find something to agree about, no matter how outrageous the claim.

"That's just the kind of testimonial we'll put on the website," he said.

Link's jaw worked back and forth while he looked for a loophole to drag an argument through. He was drawing in a breath to let loose, when the bell above the door chimed and Nils Sigridsson came in. Dodge was almost glad to see him.

"Now look here," Link said, brightening. "There's a man who knows the value of a quality pen."

Sigridsson took the hand Link offered and shook it forcefully. "Link, my friend. I hope you have good news for me."

Link held on to Sigridsson's hand with both his own. "I do indeed, sir. I do indeed. I tucked her away in a safe place and she's there right now, waiting on you."

"Which pen is this?" Dodge asked.

Link's smile faded a little and he cleared his throat. "I don't think we've got to that box yet. Nils here collects Conway Stewart pens, not so easy to come by—"

His gaze skittered to Sigridsson and then back to Dodge. "How about I bring her by your place after closing?"

"No time like the present," Dodge said, all good cheer. "And I don't believe I've seen a Conway Stewart yet."

"There is nothing funny going on," Sigridsson said when Link had slunk upstairs. "I pay full price."

"Oh, no doubt about that." Dodge leaned back against the wall and folded his arms. "Link is completely trustworthy when it comes to sales. It's his habit of squirreling away pens that I'm trying to get past."

Sigridsson tilted his head to one side and raised his shoulder, as if trying to touch it to his ear. "My English is sometimes . . . holey? Full of holes. Squirreled?"

"He hides pens away like a squirrel hides nuts."

The high forehead smoothed. "Ah. Squirrel is *ekorre*. Yes, I see this about Link."

"Got to know him well during your last stay, did you?"

"Sure. Got to know pretty much everybody in Lambert Square." He grinned. "You must have heard some stories, no?"

Dodge swallowed down his dislike. "I can't say that I have."

"I just want you to know that you needn't worry about me. Julia and I are friends only."

Dodge wondered where in the hell Link was, and if maybe he was standing out of sight listening to all this.

"In case you were concerned," Nils said. "About me."

"Not in the least," Dodge said.

"No bad feelings?"

Dodge suppressed a sigh of irritation. Next the guy would want a hug.

"No bad feelings."

"Good," said the Swede. "I wish you well with your sad insomniac and her pajamas."

20

DODGE WALKED OVER to Cocoon with the intention of asking Julia to join him for lunch. There were some questions, and he had the idea it would go better if he put them to her over a table at Polly's. Nothing earthshaking, he told himself. Just some clarification, a few ground rules.

He found Mayme alone behind the counter, three deep in customers. She waved him on and Dodge headed up the stairs. The big workroom on the second floor was almost empty and very quiet. Trixie and Big Dove were sitting on a sofa under the windows, two old white women with tightly curled bluish hair, and between them the girl called Bean, with coltishly long arms and legs the color of rich coffee and her hair in neat cornrows. They were all knitting, Trixie holding the points of her needles so close to her eyes that Dodge wondered how it was that she had never done herself any harm. The door to Julia's office was closed.

"Oooh, company," Big Dove said with a smile that showed off the full expanse of her bright white dentures. "A gentleman caller."

Trixie used a knitting needle to point to a chair. "Set down, son. Take a load off, as my daddy used to say."

Bean smiled into her lap. She was a shy kid, and watchful.

Dodge sat. "Julia?"

All three of them glanced at the closed door. Trixie said, "She's doing the bookkeeping."

"Don't like to be disturbed," added Big Dove.

"She's got to eat, doesn't she?"

"No she don't," said Bean, glancing at him sideways. "Not when she's bookkeeping."

Big Dove had gone back to her knitting, the needles clicking at high speed. She glanced at Trixie, at Dodge, at the door. She said, "If you're looking for somebody to take to lunch—"

Trixie looked at him over the rims of her reading glasses. "We haven't et yet."

"That's true," said Big Dove. "Have you had your lunch, Bean?"

"No, ma'am," said Bean with a hopeful little grin.

Dodge stood up. "Well then," he said. "Bean, go ask your mama for permission and I'll treat you ladies to lunch."

"You're driving?" Trixie threw a pointed look over her shoulder at Big Dove.

"I hope you are not insinuating anything about my truck," Big Dove said, glaring right back. "It gets you to church right enough on a Sunday." She sniffed. "But I would like a ride in your car, Dodge."

He inclined from the shoulders. "Right this way."

As soon as John Dodge had taken everybody off to lunch, Julia opened her office door and the dogs shot out in the vain hope that they might still catch sight of him. Dodge had a way with dogs, Julia had to admit. He had a way with just about everybody.

The intercom clicked on and Mayme's voice filled the room. "Julia?"

"Right here."

"Julia, I've got Mrs. Travis here from Charleston? She says you put aside a set of sheets for her—"

"Sitting on the long table in the prep room," Julia interrupted.

"Is that you, Julia dear?" A tremulous and very cultured old lady voice floated into the room. A voice completely at odds with the harridan generally known to all the Lambert Square shopkeepers as Mrs. Trouble, but who reminded Julia mostly of the obnoxious Mrs. Van Hopper from *Rebecca*.

"Yes, Mrs. Travis?"

"I thought you'd show me the sheets yourself? I have come all the way from Charleston—"

"Of course, Mrs. Travis. I'll be right down."

There was no help for it, and so Julia left the dogs with some stern words about good behavior, put on her best high-heeled slippers, and went down to the shop, where she found Mrs. Travis was now being entertained by Nils Sigridsson. Mayme rolled her eyes at Julia.

"You know my first husband was a Norwegian," Mrs. Travis was saying to Nils. "But he didn't last long. He couldn't take the heat down here. I hope you're made of sterner stuff."

"I hope so, too," Nils said with a smile that seemed completely genuine.

"Arno was his name, and he was always mooning after home. Finally I told him to take his mournful self back there, and soon after that I met my second husband—"

"Norwegians," Nils said. "They are so emotional."

His interruption was so smooth the old lady didn't even notice that she had been denied the telling of her story. Instead she giggled like a schoolgirl, and Nils winked at Julia over her head.

"Mrs. Travis," Julia said. "You wanted to see those linens?"

"Oh, never mind about that. My driver will come pick them up later." She never even looked at Julia. "Now what I'm going to do," she went right on, "is to get some lunch. Mr. Sigridsson, would you care to join me?"

Nils put a hand over his heart in a gesture of utter disconsolation. Julia caught the quirk at the corner of Mayme's mouth, her antipathy and irritation getting the upper hand. Nils could get under Mayme's skin faster than anybody else, except maybe her ex-husband.

He said, "I am so very sorry to have to decline." He reached out and clasped both of Mrs. Travis's bony old hands. "But I have already accepted an invitation for lunch today."

Julia braced. If he turned to her now she had the option of calling him a liar to his face or going along with the ruse. She hadn't quite decided what to do when she realized he was looking at Mayme.

"Shall we go?"

Mayme was wearing pajamas of a deep pink color that set off her skin so that it glowed like glossy brown satin. And Mayme, who was possibly the most self-possessed individual Julia knew, was unable to meet her eye. More surprising still: Mayme Hurt, who was never at a loss for a quip, couldn't come up with a single sentence. That Mayme had never asked Nils Sigridsson to lunch was a given; what was unclear was why she didn't just say so.

"Maybe she's needed here," said Mrs. Travis to Nils, who kept his gaze on Mayme. "Maybe Julia can't do without her."

Now all attention turned to Julia. She had to sacrifice somebody, that was clear. Either Nils was going to have to sit through lunch with Mrs. Travis and listen to all the stories of her early conquests, or Mayme was going to end up with Nils for an hour.

Mayme Hurt and Nils Sigridsson. The last time he had been in town, Mayme had made it clear that she wasn't interested in him, but something had changed. A thought went through Julia's head: *He's met his match.* And she found herself smiling at Mrs. Travis.

"Things are quiet," Julia said. "Of course Mayme can go to lunch."

WATCHING NILS INTERACT WITH THE WORLD AS THEY WALKED to Polly's was a lesson in itself, and it gave Mayme a little time to gather her thoughts and read herself the riot act. While he stopped to greet everybody, her own attention was divided between the hand he put so lightly on the small of her back and the fact that she was going to lunch with a man she had vowed to steer clear of.

But maybe it would be okay. Mayme proposed this to herself and held on to the idea. Nils Sigridsson was a nice guy. Friendly, outgoing, interested in people, easy to talk to. They would have lunch. They would talk about nothing of any real importance. If he tried to raise the subject of Julia or ask questions about Julia's dating habits, then she, Mayme, would simply step on him. She had lots of experience with such things, after all, and her pink velvet mules had very sharp heels.

The trick was to keep her eyes on her food, on the room, on what was happening outside. Anywhere but on Nils, who was too good-looking. She tried to guilt herself out of her attraction to a bland, white-bread, not-quite-buffoonish Swede, but it wasn't doing her any good.

She was asking herself why she couldn't have a crush on somebody far more suitable and completely safe: Djimon Hounsou, for example, or Don Cheadle. Men she could fantasize about without fear, because neither of them would ever sit across from her in a café, grinning broadly enough to show a piece of spinach caught between incisors.

Nils said, "You know what is your problem?"

"Do tell." Her chest expanding with righteous indignation, filling like a balloon.

"You forget how to have fun. I could show you."

She let out a bark of surprised laughter. "You think?"

"I could," Nils said. "I would like to. The last time I was here—"

"You were busy running after Julia."

He gave her a level look. "Only because you would not have me."

Keeping her gaze even was far harder than she would have thought. "You sure are full of yourself."

"So let me ask you," Nils said, not in the least ruffled. "You want to go to the movies with me this weekend? And dinner, of course. We will talk and laugh and have fun and I will never touch you unless you want me to touch you. We can be just good friends, or maybe we could fall in love. What do you say?"

Right there, right then, Mayme understood that she was out of her depth. Disarmed, charmed in spite of her promises to herself, and in danger of going down for the count.

"NOW, WHAT ARE ALL THOSE CARS?" TRIXIE SAID. SHE CRANED her head to look as Dodge eased into a parking spot.

"They look brand-new," Bean said. "Pretty colors."

Lunch at Moe's with Big Dove and Trixie turned out to be more complex than Dodge had anticipated. Getting the old ladies settled to their satisfaction was a challenge. Bean, entranced by the menu, left the negotiations about drafts and sunlight and views to Dodge to sort out. Once settled she did look up, her expression full of longing.

Dodge said, "I am hungry enough to order one of everything. How about you?"

"This child could outeat a football team all by her lonesome," Dove said.

"Our Bean has got a hollow leg," agreed Trixie.

"Mama says I'm growin," Bean said, looking a little uncertain.

"You'll need a big lunch then," Dodge said, and Trixie winked at him.

"Look at all that traffic," Dove said. "It's like old times."

"In't that pretty? Thank you Jesus." Trixie ran it all together: *Intthat-pretty?* (breath) *Thankyajesus.*

"Yessir," said Dove. "Like the circus was coming to town."

"The circus ain't been to Lamb's Corner since Hector was a pup," Trixie said.

"Hector?" said Bean.

"There's no moss growing on those Kallie-Joe folks, that is for sure."

"Ma'am?" said Bean. "It's not *Kallie-Joe,* it's *kaaahls-yeeeew.*" She leaned forward to touch Big Dove's hand. "Those two little dots? You say that *eeeew.*"

"In't that what I said, sugar?"

"No, ma'am. You said Kallie-Joe."

Trixie said, "She's right, Dove. The way you say it sounds like some old country woman setting on a porch shucking corn."

Dodge laughed at the image, but Big Dove just sniffed.

"This mouth of mine is too old to be wrapping itself around Swedish, and that's the plain truth. What I *could* wrap my mouth around is Moe's special lunch plate. Let's call Lanie over here, get this show on the road."

While they waited for their food Dodge was satisfied to sit quietly and listen to the older ladies talk, but it was clear that they had questions for him. Trixie was especially interested in the long row of shiny new cars outside the building across the way, where Kallsjö had set up its temporary business offices.

She said, "I'm just an old confused lady who only got through the tenth grade, so I'll ask you straight out to explain something to me. Why have they got all those foreign cars lined up like that?"

Dodge caught Bean's expression, which was slightly panicked. She said, "I think they're cute."

"A car in't supposed to be *cute*," Big Dove said. "My daddy, he drove a Ford. Wouldn't even look at no other kind of truck." She cast an uneasy glance out the window. "Them little cars won't be much use out in the county. Those clay roads turn to muck and misery in the rainy season, you need something with some muscle."

"What I was wondering," Trixie went on, "is why bother hauling those little foreign cars all the way down here to Lamb's Corner? It don't make sense."

Big Dove said, "Maybe they're just for show."

"That must be it," Trixie said. "A curiosity to look at, like a two-headed calf. They couldn't mean to build those foreign cars here." She looked directly at Dodge, daring him to contradict her.

They were all looking at him, the two old ladies with a certain hope, and Bean with some degree of sympathy. He cleared his throat and managed a smile. "That model is called the Freya. From what I understand, they do plan to build that very car here at the Lamb's Corner plant."

Trixie's mouth fell open and then shut with a snap. She looked out the window and back at Dodge. "Son," she said, "you must be confused. Those cars are *foreign*. Last I looked, Lamb's Corner, South Carolina, was American."

Big Dove reached over the table and poked Dodge with a forefinger. "You're joshing us."

"No, ma'am," Dodge said. "I'm serious."

Trixie and Big Dove looked at each other. Bean looked at her lap. Dodge looked around for help, but there was none to be found.

"I thought they were going to build Fords or maybe Chryslers," Big Dove said. "Olds-mobiles, even. You've must have got it wrong."

They were looking at him sternly, waiting for him to justify his absurd contention that the Kallsjö company would dare to build an assembly plant in which to manufacture Kallsjö cars. Laughter, Dodge told himself, would be a mistake.

He said, "Things are pretty complicated these days when it comes to cars. If you went out and bought a Buick—"

"That's a *fine* American car," said Trixie. "My uncle Henry had a Buick."

"Most Buicks are made in Canada these days."

Trixie reared back. "No."

"Yes, ma'am, it's true. My sister drives a Mazda. You know where that was built?"

"What is Italy!" Dove hollered, and slapped the table with the palm of her hand.

"Shush," said Trixie. "This ain't *Jeopardy!* we're playing at, Dove. Dodge, those Mazda automobiles are made in Italy, en't that so?"

"Well, no," Dodge said. "Mazda is Japanese."

Big Dove's whole forehead creased itself in half. "Doesn't sound Japanese to me. Sounds Eyetalian."

Trixie said, "Like mazda ball soup."

"Matzo ball soup," Dodge said, trying very hard to keep his voice even, "is Jewish."

The two old ladies exchanged solemn looks that seemed to say they would graciously overlook such an absurd statement, just as they would pretend not to hear him if he passed gas. Trixie cleared her throat. "I never heard of a Jewish car," she said. "Is there such a thing?"

Dodge said, "I truly don't know."

"Well, and why should you?" Big Dove said. "Now, Eyetalian cars. Those little convertibles, those are awful cute."

"Alfa Romeos," said Trixie.

"Like Romeo and Juliet?" Bean asked.

"Not like Romeo and Juliet," said Dodge. He was starting to enjoy himself. "It's RoMAYo, not ROmeo."

"Either way, it's Eyetalian," said Big Dove.

"Yes," Dodge said. "The Alfa Romeo is an Italian car. But if I can get back to my original point, Mazda manufactures their cars in Japan."

"So they are Japanese," Big Dove said. "Well, bless Patsy. Don't nobody remember Pearl Harbor no more?"

"Wait," Dodge said. "It's complicated. Mazda is an American-owned company that makes its cars in Japan. So is my sister's car American or Japanese?"

Trixie smiled nervously. "Dodge, sugar, you're not making any sense. Are you claiming that Americans go to Japan to build cars, and Swedes come here to do the same thing?"

"Yes, ma'am," Dodge said.

Trixie's small mouth pursed. "That's just foolish. Musical chairs for grown-ups. Why would they bother?"

"That's a question I can't answer," Dodge said.

Bean caught sight of something across the street and sat up straight. "Miss Trixie, here come a whole crowd of the Kallsjö people. Why don't we ask them?"

Dodge had never been so glad to see Swedes in his life.

For more than an hour, Julia's attention was taken up by a group of women on a shopping junket from Memphis. They asked a lot of questions and left without buying anything at all. Julia was chalking it all up to karma when the telephone rang.

"Jones," said John Dodge. "What are you up to?"

"Alienating friends," said Julia. "Pissing off customers. Making enemies."

"Busy morning."

"You could say that."

"Had lunch?"

"I'm alone here. Mayme's at lunch, and it's Exa's half day off." There was a lot of noise in the background, raised voices and laughter. "Where are you?"

"Moe's. There's something going on here you should see for yourself."

An elderly couple were looking at a display of antique quilts in the big window. Julia silently implored them to come in.

Dodge was saying, "Trixie and Big Dove have got a tableful of Kallsjö people cornered. Beate Gyllensting is trying to explain why it is Kallsjö can't manufacture Dodge pickup trucks."

Julia found herself smiling into the phone. "Beate can handle herself."

"Oddly enough, she seemed prepared for the question."

There was a hesitation on the other end of the line. "I'll let you go. I have to get back to the shop myself. How about supper?"

Now there was a question inside a question, one she knew was coming. For the past three nights she had found her way to Dodge's bed, coming and going by way of the alley. Last night she had meant to stay home and found herself at his door anyway. She was going to have to offer some kind of explanation, and then find a way to stop herself when her mind turned to John Dodge's bed at two in the morning.

"Sure," Julia said. "Supper would be good."

Mayme came back from lunch with an expression on her face that could only be called inscrutable. She passed Julia on her way to the counter.

Julia couldn't keep the question to herself. "How was it?"

Mayme gave her a withering look. "You threw me to the dogs."

The shop was crowded with customers: a young couple filling out a bridal registry, a half dozen women looking at bedding, a middle-aged man frowning at a rack of women's pajamas, no doubt looking for a gift. It was five minutes before Julia crossed paths with Mayme.

"Was it that bad?"

"To the dogs," Mayme said, and went over to help with the wedding registry.

Julia went to help the man looking at pajamas. He held up a pair of baby dolls in bright purple silk in one hand and extended the other to Julia as he introduced himself.

His name was Rex King, and he wanted a nice present for his wife. Something out of the ordinary. "We've got six grandchildren," he said. "But my old girl has still got her figure."

"If you give me an idea of your price range," Julia said, "I'll show you some things that she might like."

Rex King put the skimpy purple silk back with a resigned sigh.

When Mr. King had been sent off with his gift-wrapped peignoir set and the shop was empty, Julia cornered Mayme.

"So tell me. What did he do?"

"He was polite." Mayme folded her arms tight against her stomach and her mouth into a hard line. When she laughed she passed pretty and got to beautiful in a split second, but this was not one of those times.

"Do you dislike the man on general principles," Julia asked, her irritation coming to the surface quite suddenly, "or is there something specific about him?"

Mayme turned her head suddenly, her expression equal parts surprise and disbelief. "After ten years with my ex, I have got no time for men like Nils. That show he puts on, all that charm and foolishness." Her upper lip curled.

"Sometimes a little foolishness is what you need," Julia said.

Mayme gave a snort, and just that simply it all came together for Julia. The question was, how long Mayme had been keeping her interest in Nils quiet.

She said, "He's a nice guy, you know. Really a good guy at heart." And more slowly, reaching for the right words: "But there's not much more in him than that, I don't think."

"There never is," Mayme said. "And if there was, can you see my mama's face if I brought home a big old blond Swede?"

She had said too much and now she turned away, flustered.

To Mayme's back Julia said, "I never brought him home. Never had him up to the apartment, not once."

A shiver ran down Mayme's back; Julia saw it clearly and understood that she had just handed Mayme something valuable, some kind of assurance that she had been afraid to ask for.

21

BIG DOVE AND TRIXIE were having such a good time with the Swedes that Dodge ended up leaving them at Moe's. He drove back to Lambert Square with Bean riding in the backseat. The kid had warmed to him sometime during lunch—most likely it had something to do with the fact that he had allowed her two desserts—and had a lot to say. She pointed out people on the street and then provided short biographies that would have made Dodge laugh, if he hadn't been worried about hurting her feelings.

"That's Mr. Neugene Pruett," she said. "He raises goats and makes cheese out of the milk and he sells it to restaurants in Charleston for a whole lot of money, but Mama says he has been wearing the same pair of overalls since she was a girl. He's got patches on his patches. He gets his preaching at Calvary Baptist, but his wife—Miss Lithonia?—she goes to Friendship Baptist with us. She's real active in the missionary society, too. Last summer we all went down on a mission trip to Guatemala, and Granny Pearl and Miss Lithonia did all the cooking."

Dodge glanced at her in the mirror. "You've been to Guatemala?"

"Yessir," she said, "I have. And I helped build a church. Dropped a hammer I was carrying over to the work crew and broke my little toe. See there? That's Mr. Lamont Schmidt. He takes care of gardens and such. Mr. Lamont goes to United Methodist, but his wife goes to Calvary. Miss Trixie says that kind of mixed marriage usually goes bust in the first year and it's a praise Jesus miracle they've lasted so long."

"I guess you know everybody in Lamb's Corner," Dodge said.

"Oh, sure," said Bean. "I know everybody and everybody knows me. There's nothing you can do about it, Mama says. But she would come after me for sure if she heard me telling lies."

"So your philosophy," Dodge said, "is that as long as you don't lie, you're on safe ground talking about folks."

"Pretty much," Bean agreed. She grinned at him in the rearview mirror. "The other rule is, you can't give away people's secrets."

"A good rule. You know a lot of secrets?"

She looked out the window. "I know a few."

They stopped at the only red light on Main Street and watched a teenage girl handing out Kallsjö flyers.

"That's Missus Clinkscaler's second youngest. Donna," she said. "She's going for a secretary when she's graduated. Maybe the Swedes will hire her for their office. The Clinkscalers go to Little Creek Baptist to get preached at."

"Huh," said Dodge. "How many Baptist churches are there?"

Bean sat up straight, as though she were performing at a spelling bee. "You mean in Lamb's Corner, or in Moulton County?"

"Um, start with Lamb's Corner."

Her face creased in concentration. "I'll start with my family. Granny Pearl and Mama and me, we go to Friendship Baptist. My grandpa Reed's dead but his folks went to Little Creek. All the Reeds were foot washers. My aunt Dot goes to the AME church; she switched over there after she married a Bagwell. My uncle Lee Ray, he don't go to church at all and Granny Pearl's about worn out praying for him. Then there's Bearing Cross and First Baptist and the Shining Star Missionaries. And a course we got quite a few Methodists and the Episcopalians like Miss Lorna Jean and Mr. Link. There used to be more churches," Bean said, "but then the printing plant closed and the old plantation farm went bust and people started moving away and us Baptists had to scoot closer together." She hesitated. "Mama says you probably don't go to church."

Dodge glanced at her in the rearview mirror. "Wouldn't do much for my popularity if I didn't go to church, would it."

"Not for your eternal soul, neither," Bean said.

Dodge thought for a moment. "Where does Julia go to church?"

Bean looked directly startled. "Miss Julia is a Jew," she said. "There's no place for her to go—" She blushed and dropped her head.

"—except the devil?" Dodge finished for her, and the head popped up again in surprise.

"I've got Southern Baptist cousins," Dodge said. "I have an idea of what kind of talk goes on. But you like Julia?"

"Oh, yessir," Bean said with great seriousness. "Pretty much everybody likes her except the folks who don't like anybody at all and even some of them will nod at her in passing. I can't say there wasn't some worry about her being a Jew and then for a while the missionaries made her life a trial, but now that's all settled, she got them to stop though nobody knows how."

Dodge said, "Well, I'll come to church now and then. What I have done in the past is, I went to a different church every Sunday until I had tried them all."

Bean broke into a big smile. "You'll get fat. All the church ladies will get into a frazzle trying to win you over with homemade pickles and fried chicken and mile-high cakes." She let out a wistful sigh.

"You think I'm up to the challenge?"

"If you don't eat much Saturdays."

They were almost back to Lambert Square, and he decided that he could put a question to Bean.

"So tell me," Dodge said. "How do you think I'm doing? I've been here almost a week, am I off to a good start?"

For a moment he thought she wouldn't answer. Then she took a deep breath and let loose. "I think you're doing pretty good. Better than most folks thought you would. I know Mr. LRoy Swagger lost a bet to his missus about you getting along with Mr. Link but he's always betting her and losing. Miss Jamie Deanne says you talk like a Yankee but you've got manners. Mr. Link was all set on being irksome but he's having a lot of fun making those students of Caro's write down everything he says so you're safe there for now at least. Heep and Mister are going to ask you to go hunting with them when deer season starts and that means you passed the Wednesday night poker test. Most of the ladies in Lambert Square think you're good-looking and they can't understand why you don't have a wife. Miss Lorna Jean says you had one and she ran off because she didn't like all the moving around. Pretty soon one of the Needlework Girls will get up the nerve to ask you about that. Big Dove says if you were a proper Southern Baptist or even Methodist you could have your choice of a dozen fine women, and Miss Trixie says there's more than one way to be close to the Lord and maybe you're a Jew like Miss Julia—"

"You can clear that up for them," Dodge said, and Bean nodded.

"Mr. LRoy will be disappointed that you're not."

"Another bet?"

"Yessir. He doesn't much like you yet but he is slow to warm to new people. Almost as slow as my mama, but she's still mad at my daddy for running off with Rosemary Felton. Mama holds a grudge a long time," Bean said, winding down. "But Miss Julia says a deep wound takes a lot of healing."

Dodge pulled into a parking space and turned to look at Bean, who was looking back at him with a guileless expression, as if she could go on in the same vein for an hour without pause.

"Are they good friends, your mama and Julia?"

The small head bobbed. "Oh, yessir. Real close. Miss Julia has got two best friends, and that would be my mama and Miss Maudie. One for serious and one for foolishness, that's what Miss Maudie says. My mama is the serious one. Big Dove says Mama lost the habit of being happy after Daddy ran off. And Julia—" She paused, and Dodge waited.

"Julia is trying but she hasn't got the hang of happy back since her husband died. Big Dove says she's looking for love in all the wrong places and Miss Trixie says it's time to get past John Travolta in a cowboy hat, and anyway, Julia is a grown woman and can keep company where and when she pleases. I don't understand that part about the cowboy hat but I expect it's some movie. Big Dove and Trixie watch a lot of movies. So does Miss Julia, when it comes to that."

They sat for a minute in the car as the engine ticked down. Dodge said, "So tell me this. How long has it been since Julia has set foot out of Lambert Square?"

Bean went very still. Then she blinked, just once.

Dodge said, "I apologize if I've asked a question you're uncomfortable with. No need to answer."

"That's not it," Bean said. "I was starting to think that nobody would ever notice but me." She leaned forward and lowered her voice. "Never," she said.

"Never?"

"Not once, so far as I know. She came to Lambert Square five years ago and she has never left, not once."

"Not to go to the dentist, or walk down by the river? Take a dog to the vet?"

"No, sir," said Bean. "Not as far as I know. And I been watching close for a good while now."

22

WHEN DODGE came into the shop, Link was helping a customer, his shiny bald head bent down low to look through a magnifying glass at a pen on a velvet pad.

The young woman across from him said, "It's a beautiful pen but I just can't afford—"

"Now here's the boss," Link said. "Let me introduce you."

Her name was Lydia Montgomery, originally of Ogilvie, Georgia, and she was the English teacher at the Moulton County Consolidated High School. She couldn't be more than twenty-five, which made her half the age of the last walk-in customer. Dodge gave her a very sincere smile and she blushed and looked away.

She had come in to buy bottled ink and got caught up in Link's patter. His voice had taken on the cadence of a sermon, a man caught up in his message and bound to share it.

"This Parker 51," he said. "My favorite pen of all time. Went into production in 'forty-one, when I was just a little bit of a boy."

Amazing, Dodge thought, that the cornier Link got, the more effective he was.

"—and you'll find one just like this one here at the Museum of Modern Art in New York City. Why, maybe that one up there in its fancy glass case was made the same day as this one. And you know what? Your handwriting—and you've got a lovely hand, Miss Lydia—will come into its own. Look," he said, and shoved a paper across the counter to Dodge. "I haven't seen such penmanship since Miss Norma Geiger taught Sunday school at Little Creek."

Lydia Montgomery was flushed with embarrassment. "Thank you, Mr. Kay. Really, you are too kind. But two hundred and fifty dollars is a month's rent."

Dodge looked up from the paper where Lydia Montgomery had written nothing more than a shopping list, but in a hand that looked like it had been typeset.

"Nobody teaches penmanship anymore," Link was saying. "I hear complaints all the time how folks can't make hide nor hair out of their kids' writing. It's a pure shame."

Dodge said, "I've got an idea."

SIX O'CLOCK DODGE WAS GETTING READY TO MEET JULIA AT Polly's when the phone rang. He let the machine take it.

"Dodge," Nora said into the machine. "Pick up."

He grabbed the handset and leaned back into the couch. "No hello? No *please*?"

"Hello," Nora said. "You know I hate that message. It doesn't sound anything like you, all aw shucks and pretty please. It's way too Opie for my tastes."

Julia had said almost the same thing, but he kept that to himself. To Nora he said, "You've been in Brooklyn too long. All your southern has been rubbed off. Except when you're talking to the Colonel on the phone; then you sound like Scarlett O'Hara."

"The father-daughter bond," Nora said. "It's like linguistic superglue. So why haven't I heard from you in three days?"

"Busy," Dodge said. "Today I hired an English teacher to teach penmanship classes, part-time. I think it'll take off."

"And you'll sell a lot of pens and ink and paper."

"That's the idea," Dodge said.

"Listen, I didn't call to hear about your newest marketing brainstorm. I called because I am wondering what's going on down there in Lamb's Corner. I feel as though I've missed a couple episodes."

"Well, okay then," Dodge said. "Try this on. There's a Baptist church called the He-Died-for-Your-Sins Predestinarian House of the Almighty with eight members in the congregation."

"One of those good seed bad seed deals? You are or you're not."

"That's it."

"Baptists who don't do missionary work," Nora said. "What will they think up next? Maybe somebody is pulling your leg."

"My sources are reliable. I got an introductory lecture from a little girl called Bean, and a graduate seminar from Link Kay. Do you know the three fundamental gospel truths?"

"Do tell," said Nora.

"Number one is, Jews do not recognize Jesus Christ as the Messiah. Number two is, Protestants do not recognize the Pope as the leader of the Christian church."

"Okay," Nora said slowly. "Number three?"

"Baptists do not recognize each other at the liquor store."

When Nora stopped laughing she said, "Tell me you did not hear that from a little girl called Bean."

"No, that was Link. He's got a million Baptist jokes, apparently. He himself worships with the Episcopalians."

Nora said, "So you've told me a joke, now give me the interesting stuff."

"You want to hear about the history of the Parker 51 pen? Because I spent a good amount of time today learning all about it. I thought I'd give the Colonel one for Christmas."

"When will you figure out that misdirection doesn't work on me?"

"Hope springs eternal." Dodge got up and walked into the kitchen to look down at the alley.

"Give it up, will you? You know you want to tell me."

He took a deep breath. He said, "You ever treat any housebound agoraphobes?"

"Ah," Nora said. And: "The Cocoon lady?"

Dodge laughed out loud. "You could set yourself up as one of those mind readers, get on stage and diagnose from across the room. Sir, there's an Indian head nickel in your left pocket, and you've got a borderline personality disorder with stress-related paranoid ideation and severe dissociative symptoms."

"We all have our little talents," Nora said. "And then there's the name of her shop. Might as well put up a neon sign: *I am agoraphobic*. So what tipped you off?"

"Just a feeling. Then Bean said something and I gave her a little encouragement and it all came out. Apparently Julia hasn't left Lambert Square for five years, but she's got it set up so nobody has even noticed. Or almost nobody. Bean noticed. Maybe some others, but they've circled the wagons around her."

Nora gave him a *Go ahead* hum and Dodge sat down again.

"It's an interesting situation. Every fifth or sixth Sunday she tells people she's going someplace. Atlanta or Charleston. Leaves the dogs with Bean and lets it be known she won't be back until late."

"But Bean is sure she's not actually leaving."

"She thinks Julia hides somewhere in Lambert Square for the day."

After a moment Nora said, "So what are you going to do?"

"I'm not sure. Watch, I guess. For a while at least. Then I'll call you for ideas."

"If you get that far."

"If I get that far," Dodge said, more quietly.

Nora waited, and then she gave up waiting. "You haven't told her."

"I told her," Dodge said. "I gave her my standard I'm-a-recovering-claustrophobic spiel."

"That's not what I meant, and you know it."

"I'll get to it," Dodge said. "When the time is right. So you never said, have you ever treated anybody housebound?"

"Oddly, no," Nora said. "But then it's notoriously hard to get them to come into the office."

"Maybe you'll have to pay a visit," Dodge said. "Make a house call to Lamb's Corner."

Nora said, "You know where I am if you need me."

HALFWAY DOWN THE STAIRS DODGE RAN INTO JULIA, WHO WAS on her way up with a covered plate.

"Annabeth thinks you need feeding," she said.

"And you got the assignment to fatten me up."

"Pretty much."

Dodge made a grab for one of the plates but Julia elbowed him out of her way. "Stand back," she said. "I've got cutlery and I'm not afraid to use it."

The dogs trotted straight for the kitchen, where they stood in front of a particular cabinet and sent Dodge meaningful looks.

"I told you," Julia said to him as he distributed treats. "You give them c-o-o-k-i-e-s, they will never let up asking for more."

Dodge grinned at her. She was wearing pajamas he hadn't seen before, red-striped flannel.

"Less than a week, and I've lost count of how many pairs of pajamas you've got."

She shrugged. "Do you know how many pens you've got?"

"Two thousand three hundred and fifty-nine."

Her jaw dropped and then closed with a click. "You're joking."

He put a hand over his heart. "I never joke about inventory. But in the interest of full disclosure, I have to admit that there are more than that. Maybe a couple dozen Link has got tucked away someplace. The extra specials, he calls them."

Julia set the small table in the kitchen while Dodge leaned against the refrigerator, arms folded, and told her about his day. He was rumpled and his face was dark with beard shadow. He looked good, but it was the kind of good looks that had less to do with body parts—Julia dropped her gaze and tried to concentrate on where to put forks and knives—and more to do with a kind of elemental energy. He almost glowed with it. A natural-born storyteller, Big Dove had pronounced, and Julia couldn't disagree. She found herself laughing more than once while he recounted the lunchtime conversation.

"The best part was Bean," he said.

"She's a good kid," Julia agreed. "'Droll' is the word that comes to mind."

"She's smart. Sees everything."

Was there something in his voice? Julia shot him a glance but saw nothing unusual in his expression.

Dodge was saying, "You know the way Big Dove and Trixie get into a groove, talking?"

"I do indeed."

Dodge went to a cabinet and all four dogs sat up at attention, only to collapse in communal disappointment when he pulled out a bottle of red wine.

"I think Bean must have something close to total recall. You can almost see her tucking away things for later contemplation. At lunch Big Dove mentioned how somebody had been in Lamb's Corner since Hector was a pup—"

Julia took the foil off his plate.

"Thanks. At the time I could see Bean was curious about the expression.

Then this afternoon I heard her talking to Link, asking him what it meant. She recounted a good hunk of the conversation word for word."

"Did Link tell her?"

Dodge paused, his fork over his plate. "He did. Summed up the whole *Iliad* in a paragraph, and made Hector sound like Rambo. I knew he had an imagination, but I had no idea about him being so well-read."

"Well, of course he's well-read," Julia said. "They don't give out Ph.D.'s in art history on a whim."

For once she had surprised him, and Julia couldn't keep from smiling. "You didn't know?"

"Um, no. Link Kay has a Ph.D.?"

"He does. From UVA. He was even a professor for a couple years, at Ogilvie. But he got homesick and he gave it all up to come back to Lamb's Corner. Trixie claims it's something in the water, folks can't stay away."

Julia wished she could take back that bit of editorializing, but Dodge didn't seem to read too much into it.

He said, "I met somebody who went to Ogilvie today. The young woman who teaches English at the high school."

"Lydia Montgomery."

"That's her. Link has taken a liking to her."

"That surprises you?"

"Well, yeah," Dodge said. "It doesn't surprise you?"

Julia studied Dodge's face. He was uncomfortable, but she decided not to let him off the hook.

"Is it Link's age or the fact that Lydia's a big woman that has got you hung up?"

Dodge shrugged. "Both? Neither? Just tell me what you want to say."

Julia gave him a solemn look. "What did you think about Lydia?"

"I liked her. She's smart."

"Oh now, that's code."

"She's not smart?"

"She's brilliant, but if you mention that first—"

"If I talk about her looks first you'll nail me on that and call me sexist. Admit it, Jones, you're trying to paint me into a corner."

There was some tension in him. She had hit a vulnerable spot, and the urge to poke it again was pretty much irresistible.

"So would you date her?"

Dodge grimaced. "She's way too young for me, and by extension, she's too young for Link."

"Maybe she likes older men."

"So you're saying you want me to ask Lydia Montgomery out."

"No. I'm wondering if you would."

"You are a very bad liar, Jones. You don't wonder any such thing, you're just trying to wind me up."

"You cut me to the quick," Julia said.

Dodge took his time opening the wine bottle. He could feel Julia waiting for him to pick up the conversation, wondering if he would evade or advance. This was a new side to her, ready with a fast quip, as light on her feet as a fencing master.

He leaned over to pour her wine and looked her directly in the eye.

"You want to know why I'm not interested in dating Lydia Montgomery? I'll tell you."

He put the bottle down but stayed just where he was. Close enough to kiss her, close enough that she couldn't walk away or even turn away.

"One. She's too young for me. Two. She wouldn't be interested in me. Three. I don't date women that vulnerable. Four. I don't date employees."

He got the reaction he was hoping for. Julia pulled back as far as she could.

"Employee?"

"I hired her to teach penmanship, part-time. I'm going to set up a classroom on the second floor."

"Oh."

"So you're satisfied with my reasoning?"

She jerked a shoulder. "Sure. Of course. Why wouldn't I be?"

"Because I could go on, if you need to hear more."

"I think you should sit down," Julia said. "And eat."

"Five," Dodge said. "I'm not so much drawn to the teacher type. Six."

"Okay." She pushed her chair back so that it squealed, and Dodge sat down and picked up his fork. Pleased with himself and with her and with the entire world, just at that moment.

"So," she said brightly, and took a swallow of wine. "How is this penmanship thing going to work? How much are you going to charge?"

DODGE, WHO WAS USUALLY VERY FORTHCOMING ABOUT BUSINESS matters, let her ask questions and draw him out. Julia watched him forking up corn pudding and it occurred to her that she was being taught a lesson. She had teased; she would be teased, but in his own odd way. This was almost like an oral exam, where she would be judged on her powers of observation.

She said, "So the parents will drop their kids off for a penmanship lesson. But then they'll probably hightail it to Polly's or SugarPuss. How will you make them stick around?"

"No need. They'll pass the display cases on the way in and out. And of course the kids' papers will be up for everybody to see, gold stars and all that. Are you going to eat those collard greens?"

"Pardon?" Julia looked at her plate, which she had hardly touched.

"Collard greens."

"Well, no. I'm not especially fond of them."

"Yankee," Dodge said, and reached over to take them off her plate. His expression went quiet, as though something less pleasant than collard greens had occurred to him.

"What?" Julia asked.

"Lorna Jean Emerson came into the shop today. Said she wanted a present for Curtis, his birthday is coming up."

Julia put down her glass. "A ruse, of course."

He nodded. "She's pretty obvious when she's got something on her mind."

"She wanted to know what you know about Mayme and Nils."

"That wasn't it exactly," Dodge said. "She's already figured out what's going on there, or at least she thinks she has. She was taking a vote, I guess. On how I felt about it."

"And you said?"

"I asked her why she was so interested in the first place and whether she had ever talked to Nils Sigridsson about her crush on him, and how that had gone."

Julia put a hand over her mouth to stifle a guffaw of laughter. "You didn't."

"Maybe not those exact words, but I did. I figured if I refocused the discussion on her, she might forget that we've got a Nubian princess in our midst who is being courted by a Viking."

"And did it work?"

Dodge shrugged. He picked up the bottle and filled Julia's empty glass while he thought. "I think maybe I did divert her, for a little while at least. It occurs to me that there might be a way to put an end to this whole campaign of hers, but I don't know if we could get Curtis Durant to go along with it."

Julia said, "Marrying Lorna Jean off would be a temporary solution, you know that. If Mayme and Nils are serious, they'll have to deal with the color issue one way or the other." She downed half her glass, mostly because she wanted to stop talking before she said things she had on her mind that were best not spoken out loud. The only problem with the plan, she knew it even going in, was that good wine made her talkative.

When Dodge was finished eating and Julia had made an effort to make a dent in her own food, she sat back with a sigh and a small but very articulated burp surfaced without warning. She put her hand over her mouth and giggled.

"Are you drunk?" Dodge asked, leaning back so his chair was balanced on two legs.

She wrinkled her nose at him. "Just a little buzzed. Does that count?"

"Depends." The chair came down with a thump and Dodge slid his hand across the table until his fingers covered hers. Julia let him turn her hand over, and then shivered when his thumb stroked the triangular indentation where palm meets wrist. "How irresistible am I looking to you just now?"

Julia laughed and pulled her hand away, slapped at him. "You are conceited."

"I prefer 'self-assured.' I've got a proposition."

Julia bit down on the urge to giggle. "Yes?"

"How about we go over to SugarPuss for ice cream and then go neck down by the river."

Julia pulled her hand away, picked up their empty plates, and walked to the sink with them.

. . .

DODGE WAITED THIRTY SECONDS. "SO IS THAT A NO TO THE ICE cream?"

She glanced at him over her shoulder. "I like ice cream. I'm not so crazy about mosquitoes."

"Well then, your tax dollars are being well spent. You didn't know that Maude put in one of those power traps by the boat dock?"

He watched the muscles in her back tense, and then he watched as she forced them to relax.

"I forgot about that," she said finally. She put the dishes on the sideboard and then took her time drying her hands.

"Let's just worry about the ice cream to start with," she said. "That work for you?"

He came up behind her and slipped his arms around her waist. With his chin on her shoulder he said, "Six. I'm already dating somebody, and she's as much as I can handle."

Over dinner Julia had proved Nils Sigridsson wrong: it hadn't taken much effort to make her laugh. She had laughed and argued and her whole physical being had seemed to brighten. She had teased and responded to teasing, but then he had pushed—ever so slightly—the idea of going for a walk. Something so simple, but all the good feelings between them had disappeared just that easily.

So he backtracked. Put his arms around her waist and told her the truth, used the D word. They were dating, and he didn't mind who knew about it. And she had responded; he had felt her leaning into him, her willingness to let things flow. As long as he was willing to follow her unspoken rules.

He kissed her temple. "Ice cream," he said. "That's enough of a plan for me right at the moment."

SUGARPUSS DID A LOT OF BUSINESS ON A SATURDAY NIGHT, mostly couples that stopped by when the seven-o'clock showing at the Rose Theater let out. Ten dollars bought admission for two to a movie guaranteed to be at least twenty years old, and a choice between a tub of popcorn with real butter or a coupon for two ice cream cones at SugarPuss.

To Dodge it looked as though most everybody had gone the ice cream route. At the next table Lamont Schmidt and his wife rehashed *Charade,* marveling at the length of Audrey Hepburn's neck and asking each other why it was nobody made movies like that anymore.

"Lambert Square on Friday and Saturday nights is Maude's creation," Julia told Dodge. "It used to be dead down here all weekend."

"Clever Maude," Dodge said.

"She is clever," Julia agreed. "She also knows Lamb's Corner and understands how things work here."

"You don't?"

She studied her ice cream for a moment. "I'm learning. But if you didn't grow up here you'll always be a couple steps behind."

"It's the same in all small towns," Dodge said.

"Yeah? Well, I lived all my life in Chicago until I moved here, so it's been an education."

Dodge stirred his melting ice cream.

"How often do you go home to visit?"

She glanced at him. "It's not easy to get away when you're trying to get a new business off the ground. Not that I need to tell you about that. You had a bookstore in San Antonio, is that right?"

Dodge had to admire the deft way she steered the discussion away from topics that unsettled her. Probably she had a lot of success with it; most people liked to be asked about themselves.

It was a delicate game he was playing, one he wasn't even sure he should get tangled up in. So he took her question at face value and told her about San Antonio, what the bookstore had been like when he took it over, what changes he had made and why, what had worked and what hadn't. The tension that had come to the fore when he asked about Chicago ebbed away, and she was relaxed and caught up in the discussion when Lyda Rose came up to their table.

"Now don't tell me y'all are talking business," Lyda Rose said. "What kind of date is that?"

Julia flushed, started to say something and stopped. Which showed her good sense, in Dodge's estimation. A debate with Lyda Rose on what constituted a date would not be easily won. In the few exchanges Dodge had had with her, he had found Lyda Rose Guzman to be the soul of generosity:

a woman absolutely sure she knew what you needed, and determined to see that you got it.

"Where's Leo tonight?" Dodge asked, and Julia threw him a thankful glance.

Lyda Rose said, "He's out with one of your interns, an O'Connor girl from out in the county?"

"Janet."

"That's her. I have to have a talk with that boy; he's set on running wild. Can I get y'all some coffee or tea? I'm afraid the espresso machine is in a snit and doesn't care to work this evening."

"I should probably get home," Julia said.

"It's not even eight," Lyda Rose said. "But you suit yourselves." She winked at Dodge and hurried off, stopping to talk to customers as she went.

"Lambert Square," Julia said with a rueful smile. "Get your mothering here."

Dodge took a chance. He said, "So let's take that walk by the river." He leaned forward and waggled his eyebrows at her. "Put all this sugar to good use."

Asking about Chicago had put her on alert, but this was worse. Julia flushed, cleared her throat, wiped her mouth with her napkin, picked up her spoon and put it down again. "Not tonight," she said finally. "I'm just too tired."

"Huh," Dodge said. As close to a challenge as he dared, at that moment.

She raised her head and looked at him directly. Unflinching. "Look," she began. "This is hard to say, but let me try. I know I've been coming by a lot at night—"

"No complaints here," Dodge said.

She managed a small smile. "—but I don't want to take advantage. You should be able to have company over without worrying about me waltzing in at two in the morning."

He could have asked her what she meant by company, but that would change the course of the conversation and Dodge didn't want to give up the edge he had.

He said, "So are we finished, then? Is that what you're trying to say?"

"No." She grimaced in irritation, her hands fluttering. "That's not what I meant. Just that I won't intrude on your personal space like that anymore."

Dodge captured one of her hands with his own and held it still. "Say what you mean, would you?"

A muscle in her jaw tightened and then relaxed. "We've known each other less than a week, Dodge. Don't you think this is moving a little fast? I mean, I take responsibility for that, showing up the way I have . . . I just think we should slow things down a little."

Dodge squeezed her hand and then let it go. He looked her directly in the eye and smiled. "So that's a no to a walk down to the river."

And there it was: a bright flash of anger lit up her face and cast all the things she meant to hide into neon brightness. It was a matter of two seconds before she took control and shut him out again, but by then the damage was done.

They understood each other perfectly.

23

LATE AT NIGHT Julia sits in a chair at the bedroom window with needlework in her lap and the dogs asleep at her feet. There is a circle of light and inside the circle, the work in her hands and nothing else.

She is mending a towel that was handwoven some two hundred years ago. The linen is flawless, heavy, sleek to the touch. Jefferson was president when this towel came off the loom. Julia imagines a small farm where the flax was sowed, tended, harvested. All the labor that went into rendering hollow stems into something the women could spin into thread and then weave.

Finally someone sat down with a needle and a spool of turkey red floss to sew the initials along the hem. Maybe her own initials, on one of a dozen towels for her wedding chest, or her son's, to be sent along when he went to take up a job in the city, or even the initials of a stranger, someone with the money to pay for her time. The initials—EEG—occupy Julia's thoughts as she repairs them. Eleanor Evelyn Elizabeth Emma Eva Evangeline, Graham, Gallaway, Grisholm, Green, Grant, Gibson, Guthrie, Golightly.

In the circle of light Julia's hands are foreign, mechanical contraptions covered with skin, with a life and purpose of their own. The needle flashes and pierces the linen stretched taut in the circular frame, and the thread follows it.

There is comfort in this work. It is orderly, and small enough to be contained; she will know when she is finished. Her needle makes its way, tracing the ghost of the original stitches, each as clear and clean as a footprint in new snow.

24

EIGHTEEN DAYS after John Dodge came to Lambert Square, Julia sat down with Maude Golden over breakfast, determined to ask for help, or at least for advice. Except Maude launched right into her newest story of the wonders wrought by Kallsjö.

"Did you see it?" she asked. "It was like one of those May Day parades in Russia, all that heavy machinery rolling down the road? I swear," Maude said, holding up a hand. "I got tears in my eyes. Tears. Over backhoes and front-loaders and *bulldozers*." She gave a tight little shake of her head and then lowered her voice to a whisper. "Do you feel it in the air? Lamb's Corner is risen from the dead."

Julia did feel it, and said so. What she didn't say, couldn't bring herself to say, was how uneasy it all made her. There were protesters who came every day to stand in front of the construction site with their signs, serious people with real concerns about air pollution and groundwater and the loss of farmland, but Julia's discomfort was purely selfish in nature. It was just plain wrong, she told herself, to be unhappy about the fact that so many people were going back to work.

Maude was studying her with her mouth pursed, never a good sign. She said, "You look like you haven't got any sleep at all, girl. What's up?"

Julia considered the little speech she had prepared, the carefully chosen words that would lay out her history with John Dodge. The exact measurements of the corner where she now stood, surrounded by paint she had put down herself, paint still glossily wet and refusing to dry. Maude was waiting, her perfect eyebrows raised to indicate intense interest. Trustworthy, sensible, worldly and wise Maude, the best friend she had.

"John Dodge," Julia said, "is driving me nuts."

Maude put down her coffee cup so hard that the dishes jumped. "Finally. I was starting to think I'd have to tie you to a chair and get out the bamboo slivers. So tell me." She leaned forward and again her voice dropped. "Why are you two fighting?"

"We aren't *fighting*," Julia said, already irritated. "We're . . . negotiating."

A huge smile spread across Maude's face. "My favorite word. So give me some details here. What are we negotiating, exactly?"

Julia drew a deep breath. "I want to be left alone," she said. "And he doesn't."

A frown line appeared between Maude's brows. "Sugar, you are going to have to give me more than that. Are you saying you gave the man his walking papers? When was this?"

"Ten nights ago." Julia closed her eyes and then took a deep breath. "Ten days ago," she said, very clearly.

"That," Maude said with a quick smile, "is what's known as a Freudian slip." She took the last piece of toast and began to butter it. "Do I understand you right? You two got right down to business—don't make a face, if you want help you have to give me the whole story. So you got busy just as soon as he showed his face in Lambert Square—"

"Not the first night," Julia whispered, her head hunched low.

"—and then you backed down. Told him it was all a mistake, let's be friends and all that."

"I never said anything about being friends."

Maude paused, her expression thoughtful. "You were hoping he'd just . . . disappear?"

"I was hoping we could both be adult about this and go about our business."

"Let's back up a second, sugar. Was he bad in bed, was that it?"

Julia folded her hands in front of herself, counted to three.

"I wouldn't have taken him for the selfish kind," Maude was saying. "But then you can never tell until you hit the sheets. Some men talk a good game and then . . . Lordy, Julia, you should see your face. There's no reason to get yourself worked up over a simple question. If you broke off the relationship because you two couldn't—"

"No," Julia interrupted her. "I mean yes. I mean, there was nothing wrong with . . . that. It was good."

"So you kicked a good-looking, smart, funny man with money who knows how to curl your toes—"

"Maude."

"—out of your bed. Why?"

Julia could not bring herself to say that it was not her own bed but his bed she had walked away from, no more than she could answer the completely reasonable question before her. Why had she walked away? Ten days later she could hardly remember what was going through her head at that moment. Something about taking a walk, but could that be right?

"Is he . . . twisted?"

"Maude!"

"What? It's a logical question. Growing up military and all, I could imagine he might have some kinks." She bit her lip, but couldn't keep from smiling.

Julia said, "If I told you the chemistry was wrong, would you be willing to leave it at that?"

"Sugar," Maude said, "you are lying through your teeth, but sure. Let's leave it at that. So what is it you want from the man?"

"That I can answer. What I want is for him to stop pursuing me."

Maude sat back in her chair. "You don't like being courted?"

Julia said, "'Courted' isn't the word that comes to mind. He stops by the shop at least twice a day. He brings coffee. He brings lunch. He brings me articles cut out of the *Economist* and the *Wall Street Journal* and postcards from Bob Lee. Yesterday he spent an hour with Exa learning how to sew on a button. He asked me to come over and see the new classroom on the second floor—"

"In't that a wonder? The man is a marketing genius."

"Yes," Julia said. "He is an evil genius, and he's everywhere. I expect he'll walk through that door any minute. He'll come over here and be just as friendly and sweet as he can be."

Maude looked at her over the rim of her coffee cup. "And this is a problem how exactly?"

"It's a distraction," Julia said. "It's disruptive. He is driving me *nuts*."

"And you're not overreacting one bit."

Julia paused. "I just want my life back. The way it was. Before John Dodge and Kallsjö—" She stopped and shook her head.

Maude took it in her stride. "It is a little crazy, so much changing so fast. Tell me this, have you just told the man to stay away?"

"At least once a day," Julia said. "Yesterday he came upstairs at closing time and invited Big Dove and Trixie out to dinner. So they're getting ready to go and then at the last minute he turns and looks me in the eye and gives me this huge smile—" She paused to demonstrate. "And he says, 'Julia, you care to join us?' "

"The cad," Maude said. "The monster."

"You don't get it," Julia said, with great emphasis. "He keeps asking me out. OUT out. Every day, at least once, and usually in front of somebody."

Maude tapped her knife on the edge of her plate. "Like where?"

"Is that important?"

"I think it is. So do you, or you wouldn't be flushing like a virgin bride on her wedding night."

Julia let out an involuntary squeak of laughter, and Polly turned to look at them from the other side of the café.

"Y'all need more coffee?"

"We're fine!" Maude called back. And to Julia: "Where is it he wants to take you?"

"Bowling," Julia said. "Out for supper. To Heep's for Wednesday night poker and Blue Meanies . . ." Her voice failed her, and she stopped.

"So," Maude said, "he figured you out. In less than a week, too. Took me a couple months."

"There's nothing to figure out," Julia said, and realized she had shredded her napkin into strips. She put it aside carefully. "The problem is simple.

He won't give up. He. Never. Gives. Up. I say no, and he grins and shrugs. Exa," Julia said, "thinks I'm certifiable, turning him down."

"He does have a way with people," Maude agreed.

"That is the understatement of the century," Julia said sourly. "Everybody loves him. Even LRoy likes him, and you know what a trick that is. Lorna Jean is so tickled with the penmanship classes that she's overlooking the fact that he spent his first Sunday with Baptists and the second with Methodists. And Bean—" She drew a deep breath. "Bean thinks Dodge hung the moon. He has got into the habit of going out with her to walk the dogs before school, and she comes back and tells me all about their conversations."

"That might have something to do with Mayme dating Nils," Maude said. "I get the idea Bean doesn't much like him."

"Nils doesn't know the first thing about kids," Julia said. "Bean had him figured out from the start. So did Mayme, for that matter."

"So what the hell is she doing dating him?"

Julia took a moment to swallow some coffee while she considered the best way to answer the question.

"I think she's running some kind of experiment on him," Julia said. "Some behavior modification scheme."

"It's all those psychology classes she's been taking," Maude said. "There's trouble ahead if she's convinced herself she can tame that man."

Julia had spent almost three weeks observing Mayme interact with Nils, but this was the first time she had ever been drawn into a conversation about what she was seeing.

"I know what you mean," she said. "But I have come to the conclusion that Mayme has things under control. And Bean has got Dodge, so she can ignore Nils."

"The scoundrel," said Maude. "Being nice to a little girl."

Julia shook her head. "Bean doesn't need more trouble in her life. She'll get attached and then he'll be off to Utah or Timbuktu or someplace to open a shoe store."

"So it's Bean you're worried about."

"Partly," Julia said, backing down into a moment's silence.

Maude leaned forward. Her eyes moved over Julia's face as if there were clues written there, but her smile was kind and easy.

She said, "So there's a good man in your life. He's kind and thoughtful and he kisses like a god and he wants to take you places, and you didn't know how to handle that so you went and told him you had had your fill and the fun was over. And he shrugged and walked away, but he *keeps coming back*. Worst of all, he's figured out your secret. Is that about it?"

"I don't have a *secret*," Julia said.

"Julia Darrow. You got secrets coming out your eyeballs. You may have most of Lambert Square fooled, but not John Dodge. Now, in't that what you have been trying to say here?"

Julia nodded because she didn't trust her voice.

"Sugar," Maude said, "you do indeed have a problem."

At least business is good.

This was Julia's new mantra, the one that kept her afloat. When she had less than four hours' sleep and John Dodge showed up midmorning, all smiles and easy conversation, and made her laugh. When she heard five different Dodge stories in the course of one afternoon and could not give in to the impulse to shout that she didn't ever want to hear the man's name again, not once, and certainly not in the four walls of her own business where by God she should be able to find a little peace.

At least business is good.

Here it was almost the end of September but people were walking around as though they had just made it through a rough winter, tilting faces up to the sky as if to see what miracle might fall into their laps next. There was thirty percent more foot traffic moving through Lambert Square according to Leo, who liked to keep track of such things when he wasn't busy necking with interns in the alley.

She was going to have to do something about Leo. Exa was turning into a bigger problem, too, simply because she could not keep her curiosity about Mayme and Nils to herself, but for once nobody was willing to speculate with her. Out of respect for Mayme or fear, Julia wasn't sure which. But Exa just wouldn't give up.

She said, "Bean, your mama's smiling a lot lately."

"Just about everybody's smiling these days," Bean said, too smart to be taken in by Exa's tricks. "Well, almost everybody. Those environment kids from the college sure look glum."

"Who would've thought it," Exa said, as easily distracted as ever. "Radicals in Lamb's Corner, carrying signs and all. I bet none of *their* daddies wan't ever out of work."

The upswing in business had to do mostly with the dozen new families who had moved in over the last weeks. In a town of six thousand people it shouldn't have made such a difference, but the Swedes popped up everywhere, in person and in conversation. What kind of furniture they had, what their kids wore to school and what they ate for lunch, what movies they rented from Huey's Gas Station Emporium, how often they went out of town and why.

John Jay Cobb, who put out the newspaper single-handed, had decided that it was his job to make Lamb's Corner acquainted with Kallsjö. He did this by means of interviews with any Swede he could pin down for ten minutes at a time. But instead of satisfying the curiosity of the locals, the short articles and interviews in the *Times* only seemed to raise more questions for contemplation and debate.

Mostly people seemed to like the newcomers. They were friendly and easy to talk to in spite of their accents, and in the end they turned out not to be Catholic, as LRoy Swagger had so gloomily predicted, but Lutheran. Which explained the hard liquor, Big Dove pointed out in a tone that came across as both disappointed and relieved.

Sitting in the workroom with a pile of vintage tablecloths that had come in for consignment, Julia listened to yet another Kallsjö conversation. Another Kallie-Joe conversation, because somehow or another that colorful mispronunciation had not only stuck but spread through the entire town. Julia found herself using it now and then. She was ready to give up that battle as lost, but it did get on Bean's nerves. She was learning schoolyard Swedish from the new kids in her class.

"You got to give them Swedes this much," Trixie said. "The young ones may be some wild, but they turn out all right in the end. Neat housekeepers, and clean." Trixie and Leo had delivered bed linen to three different Swedish households, which established her as the current expert on their domestic habits.

"Now I wouldn't call the young ones *wild*," Big Dove said. She had been working the mangle, and her face was damp and rosy with steam. "Full of life, maybe. And why not. You and me, we weren't no angels before we settled down. Mercy but I could tell some tales on you, Trixie."

Trixie let out a deep chuckle. "We had us some fun, didn't we? You might could take a page from that book," she said, winking at Julia.

Julia looked back to the tablecloth in her lap, the heavy damask in a pattern of mums and winding leaves. The kind of tablecloth you saved for Thanksgiving or a wedding party and then folded away so it could surprise you with how beautiful it was when it came time to bring it out again.

She stood up. "I have got some errands to run."

The two older ladies blinked at her, startled by her rudeness and curious, too, at what had brought it on. Julia felt herself flush with embarrassment.

"Anything I can get for you while I'm out?"

Trixie tilted her head, her mouth pursed. A look passed between her and Big Dove, a whole conversation in a split second.

"As a matter of fact, there is," Trixie said. "My knees are giving me misery today and I'd just as soon not climb any more stairs than strictly necessary." She put a hand on the basket of linen newly laundered and ironed, and gave it a small shove in Julia's direction. "Would you take these up to Dodge's place, sugar? I'd surely appreciate it."

25

JULIA STEPPED OUT into the sunshine and paused. South Carolina's summer held on tooth and nail, the sun so bright on the sheets in the basket that Julia's eyes watered, and she had to squint.

A woman walked by, one arm weighed down by shopping bags and the other pushing a stroller with the undercarriage basket filled to overflowing. The little boy who trailed behind stopped and gaped at Julia, and then he broke into an awkward run.

"Mama," he said. "Mama, that lady is wearing *pajamas* at *lunchtime*. Is she sick?"

Julia stalked off in the opposite direction, shifting the basket so it rode on one hip. It was a beautiful day, she was in perfect health, and business was good. She had nothing to apologize for, and certainly no obligation to explain herself to anyone.

With this thought in her mind, Julia walked into Scriveners, where John Dodge was leaning on the counter in deep conversation with Beate Gyllensting. His whole face was lit up with laughter. They were both laughing. The best of friends, apparently.

"Pardon me," Julia said. "I'm sorry to interrupt." It took all her willpower to keep herself from throwing the basket at Dodge's head.

"No, no." Beate turned, wiping a tear from her cheek with the back of a hand. "No interruption. It's just this postcard from Mr. Cowper."

Dodge held it up. A cathedral, a sky, an unfamiliar city. Beate had retreated and now she was at the door, her hand on the knob.

"I've got to go. Julia, remind Dodge to ask you about Saturday?"

Before the door had closed behind her, Julia had put the basket down on the counter and was backing away.

"Your linen."

"So I see. What do I owe you?"

She composed her expression as best she could, not nearly good enough. "You don't owe me anything. You need to talk to Trixie about what you might owe her, though. Her knees are bothering her today, which is the only reason I'm here."

He was looking at her as if there was nothing out of the ordinary, his expression open and easy. The urge to smack him was almost too much to resist. She took another step backward.

"Wait," Dodge said. "Aren't you supposed to make the bed? I thought that was part of the service."

"That," Julia said between clenched teeth, "is also between you and Trixie."

"And her knees."

Julia felt her mouth twitching at the corner. "You're right," she said, trying for a detached but lofty tone. "I'll take care of it, for Trixie."

She picked up the basket and started around the corner for the stairs, with Dodge right behind her. "I don't need any help," she told him, but then Link was coming down the stairs, his big voice echoing.

He said, "Dodge, what is the matter with you, letting a lady carry a heavy basket like that? Give it over, honey, I'll tote it for you."

"Now aren't you sweet," Julia said, shooting Dodge a look over her shoulder.

"I'll take the basket," Dodge said, and for a moment Julia had the wild idea that he and Link were about to engage in a game of tug-of-war. For once Dodge's sanguine expression was gone, and that put Julia in a much better mood, one that lasted all the way up the stairs, until they were inside his apartment and he closed the door.

"Can't remember the last time I had men fighting over me," Julia said. "You and Link hit a difficult patch?"

Dodge's breath hitched and caught. "Nothing out of the ordinary. He's having a hard time getting comfortable with the penmanship lessons and having kids around."

"Some things," Julia said with a tight smile, "just aren't meant to be."

He laughed at that. "I don't give up that easy, darlin. Surely you noticed that about me."

Julia jerked her chin toward the basket, which was still tucked under his arm. "I can manage on my own from here."

But he followed her into the bedroom and then Dodge looked at Julia across the expanse of his bed. He gave her his friendliest, most sincere smile. The urge to smack him was an itch that would not go away.

"Really," she said. "You are just in the way."

"Let me just help with this much." And he reached for the coverlet.

Maybe silence would do the trick. Julia set to stripping the bed, focusing on the work at hand and refusing to look at John Dodge. And still her mind was racing. Everything was racing, most especially her pulse. It was hard to be betrayed by your own body, but there it was. Dodge and this bed and a closed door, and she had let herself be herded into this situation by two scheming old ladies. If she confronted Trixie she'd get nothing more than a confused smile, and a conversation she didn't want to have. But there were things she wanted to say, oh yes. She rehearsed them to herself while they worked and realized too late that Dodge had grabbed a fresh sheet from the basket and was stretching it across the mattress.

"Hey," Dodge said. "Wake up."

"You really are pushing it, you know that."

Which got her nothing more than another infuriating grin and a flap of the sheet.

She did her part, tucking and smoothing and then walking the sheet down to the other end of the mattress. And there they stood, joined by a bridge of six-hundred-thread-count cotton. Twisted somehow in the middle, and needing to be untangled. Dodge tugged, and for no good reason at all, Julia tugged back.

"I don't have time for games," she said, and pulled harder.

He raised a brow. "I do." And he gave a quick jerk so that Julia landed on her belly on the bed.

She said, "That's no way to treat expensive linens," and scrambled backward off the bed. Her breath was coming fast, and so was his. Julia backed up and Dodge advanced.

"Jones," he said, "it's time we had a little talk."

Julia closed her eyes and when she opened them again he was right there. "This is such a bad idea."

"Liar."

"Really, really bad."

Dodge leaned forward and put a hand on the wall above her head. "We could go to lunch instead. My treat."

"Lunch." His breath was warm on her face, and he was talking about food.

"Lunch," he agreed. "You pick. The meat loaf special at Moe's, or Polly's sandwiches down by the river—"

The only way to shut the man up, Julia decided, was to kiss him. And so she did. Slid her hands up his chest and pulled him down. Kissed him lightly, eyes open, all her senses on high alert. Wondering if he would kiss her back, and hoping that he would.

When it came, his kiss was light and noncommittal. He said, "Your stomach is grumbling."

"I am not hungry," Julia said, irritated now. "But I should get back—"

He kissed her this time but he was still holding most of what he had in reserve, still testing her. Something clenched in Julia's gut, clenched and then clenched harder, and a sound escaped her. It seemed that was what he wanted to hear because he pulled her up against him with one arm around her waist and kissed her the way she wanted to be kissed.

Against her mouth he smiled, pleased with himself and her. Julia found herself smiling back.

"You sure you wouldn't rather have lunch?"

"No more questions."

But he couldn't help himself. He whispered into her hair and mumbled against the curve of her belly, one question after another. *Like this?* and *More?* and *How does this?* She never answered him in words but that didn't seem to matter; he responded as if she had. More and more and more. Rational thought was beyond her, and so Julia gave in, all her frustration rushing up and over and then it was gone, and she found herself sweaty and breathless and satisfied. They were tangled together, arms and legs and sheets damp with sweat, trembling with satisfaction and exhaustion.

Julia said, "I forgot how good you are at this."

Dodge snorted. "No you didn't. You couldn't forget, that's why you let yourself be talked into coming over here."

"Such modesty." She laughed because she couldn't do much else.

"Hey," he said, rubbing his face against her shoulder. "I missed you."

She thought of telling him the truth. That she had missed this room and the bed and the man in the bed. His hands and strength and the smell of him, his sense of humor and his conversation. She should tell him so; it would be the right and generous thing to do, but when she opened her mouth all that came out was a yawn.

He laughed. Pulled the coverlet up over her and tucked her in. "Sleep," he said. "I'll take the sheets back and tell them you went to run some errands."

Then words came, finally, rushing up to fill her mouth and spill out, surprising both of them.

"I don't know what to do," Julia said.

Dodge sat down on the edge of the bed and covered her hand with his. "One step at a time," he said. "Sleep and then we'll talk, okay? Over supper. Hey," he said, his voice dropping low. "Relax. I'll cook."

JULIA SLEPT MOST OF THE AFTERNOON IN DODGE'S PARTIALLY made bed, and then she got into his shower where she tried to sort out what had happened, why it had happened, and how things might be arranged so that it could happen again with minimal damage to her already bruised pride, and more important still, the precarious grasp she had on her privacy.

Really, she told herself, all they needed was a set of ground rules they could both agree to. As intelligent people they could come up with such a list. She would raise the subject over supper.

She put her pajamas back on, made the bed with the fresh but rumpled linen, and went home by way of the back stairs and the alley.

"YOU DID NOT COOK," SAID JULIA. "THAT IS POLLY'S PORK ROAST I smell." She stood in the open back door and cast a doubtful eye over the table. The dogs didn't care who was responsible for the food, but they did hope to get some of it. They sat looking at the table with undisguised longing.

"Polly's pork roast, Polly's mashed potatoes, her black-eyed peas, red cabbage, fried okra, corn bread, and biscuits, too." Dodge gestured toward the table. "Have a seat."

"I can't believe this," Julia said. "Is there anybody you can't wrap around your little finger?"

"Oh sure," Dodge said. "My father, for one. Hand me your plate, I'll serve."

"Did you get dessert, too?"

Dodge forked a huge piece of meat onto her plate. "You do have a sweet tooth."

Julia sat up very straight. "I do not."

"Sure you do," Dodge said. "You just don't let yourself indulge very often." And he winked at her.

"Are we talking about food?"

"We are talking about food," Dodge said. "About cake and ice cream and Annabeth's caramel custard and sugar in your coffee, but most of all, we're talking about chocolate."

Julia narrowed one eye at him while she chewed. Finally she said, "Is this a talent you were born with, or is it the result of long study?"

"Mock if you will," Dodge said, "but I know what I know."

"So what is it I yearn for, in your opinion?"

He took a moment, considering. "Truffles."

Julia waved her fork in the air. "Everybody likes truffles. That's just a reasonable guess."

Dodge held up his hands. "Fine. I stand corrected. Eat your vegetables, Jones, and forget about dessert."

There was a flush of color high on her cheeks, as if she had been drinking. "What I think," Julia said, "is that you like chocolate truffles, and you were hoping I'd keep you company while you binged."

Dodge inclined his head. "An interesting theory. More wine?"

They talked business while they ate and did the dishes, and the whole time Julia cast short glances around the kitchen, her curiosity getting the better of her. Dodge caught her looking and grinned, a superior, self-satisfied grin that itched, but one she could ignore.

Right up until the moment that she opened a cabinet to put the wine-glasses away.

It was a large box. An expensive box, dark pink with a swirl of raised letters across the top: *Chocolates by Gigi*. And, of course, all tied together with a velvet bow the color of cocoa. Julia closed the cabinet door.

"This is what they mean by cutting off your nose to spite your face," Dodge said. He reached around her to open the cabinet, pulled out the box, and thrust it into her hands.

Julia sniffed. "Where did you get them?"

"My brother Jim married a chocolatier. She sends me care packages now and then."

"You have a sister-in-law called Gigi?"

"Actually her name is Waldegunde, but that was too much to put on the box."

"You're making that up."

"Nope. She's from Munich. Her mother is a professor of medieval German literature, which explains the name."

"Dodge," Julia said. She looked him straight in the eye. "You want to sit down and eat a box of truffles? Is that what you're suggesting?"

He took the box out of her hands. In a moment it was open, and he fished out a truffle the size of a walnut, gleaming dark chocolate. Julia opened her mouth to say something complimentary and Dodge stuck the truffle in.

"Take a bite."

Julia closed her eyes and let the flavors slide over her tongue. A sound came from her throat.

"No good?"

She opened her eyes. "That," she said, "was a capitulatory whimper." Julia darted forward to take another bite, and got a smear of chocolate on her cheek in the process.

"I like you like this, Jones," Dodge said, coming in close to lick her cheek clean. "This has definite possibilities."

A HALF HOUR LATER JULIA SAID, "SELF-INDULGENCE HAS TO end somewhere."

Dodge lifted his head. His mouth was smeared with chocolate, and his eyes were unfocused. "Thus spake the queen of self-denial."

Julia heard herself giggle. "Hey. I just ate four huge truffles."

"A good start," Dodge said. "Have another." He fumbled behind himself for the box on the counter, and Julia took the opportunity to slip away. She caught up his free hand and tugged.

"Step away from the chocolate," she said. "Come into the other room, sit with me on the couch."

Dodge cast a last glance at the box of truffles and followed her into the parlor.

"Okay," Julia said. "Now." But when she looked at Dodge she couldn't even remember where she had intended to start. All afternoon she had been constructing talking points in her head, things she needed and wanted to say. Something about Dodge, and this relationship they seemed to be having. Something about boundaries and reasonable accommodations, open communication and privacy.

Dodge didn't seem to mind waiting. He sprawled out on the couch and put his head in her lap, let out a deep and contented sigh. He was studying her, openly and without apology. As if he liked what he saw, and was looking forward to seeing more.

Just that suddenly, all of Julia's uncertainty left her and was replaced by an almost preternatural calm. If she wanted to talk, he would listen, and if she couldn't talk, that would be okay, too.

"I have some conditions," Julia said, her voice coming steady and calm. "If we're going to . . . " She searched for a word. "Keep this up."

Dodge's expression was easy, neutral, and still interested. "Go on," he said. "I'm listening."

"First condition," Julia said. "No questions about Charlie. If I feel like talking about him, I will. Otherwise that subject is off limits."

"Okay," Dodge said. "No questions about Charlie."

"Second condition. Stop asking me to go places. We can see each other here, and only here."

Dodge said, "Define 'here.' "

It took a conscious effort not to grimace. "For the purposes of this discussion, 'here' is Lambert Square."

"Go on."

"Three, you promise me that you really are going to sell Scriveners when you've got it turned around."

"That I can promise without reservation," Dodge said.

"The last condition—this is crucial."

"I'm listening."

"There is nothing *wrong* with me that won't pass with time. Don't suggest therapy or medication or magic crystals or any other miracle cure you read about on the back of a magazine, and don't discuss my . . . habits with anybody else. This is nonnegotiable."

She drew a long, unsteady breath and let it out slowly. Then she forced herself to look him in the eye. It took tremendous effort, but she did it.

Dodge sat up and put an arm around her shoulders, pulled her in closer. "Go on."

"If you agree to all that, I can make some promises of my own. Don't interrupt until I'm done, okay? First of all, I won't stop by without calling first, and I will take no for an answer without complaint. Or questions." She glanced at him to see how he was taking this. "Finally . . ." Her voice wobbled and cracked. "I'm inviting you up to see my apartment. As a gesture."

"A gesture of what?"

She shrugged. "Goodwill."

He said, "That's a big gesture."

"Yes," she said. "It is a big gesture, but it's not an open-ended one. You can't come by unannounced."

Dodge took her face in his hands and kissed her. "You know what this means?"

"Do tell."

"I'm going to have to force-feed you chocolate more often."

ON THE WAY OVER TO HER PLACE, THEY STOPPED TO LET THE dogs run for a few minutes. The evening was cool and damp. Dodge was eager to be back inside, but Julia seemed to be hesitating.

He said, "Do you want me to come around the back way?"

She flushed at that, as if he had insulted her. "Why would I want that?"

This, Dodge realized, was Julia in a fretful mood, unsure of herself, teetering on the edge between flight and fight. "Your privacy is important to you," he said. "And I don't mind."

She turned away, as if she didn't want him to see her expression.

"You think I care what people think of me?"

Yes, Dodge wanted to say. I think you care a lot. But he kept his silence, and after a few minutes some of the tension seemed to drain out of her. Julia whistled softly and Boo came ambling over, huffing a little as she was lifted into Julia's lap.

"So is this the time for me to tell you about my conditions?"

Julia glanced at him. "I thought you'd have a few. Go ahead."

Dodge turned toward her and resisted the urge to touch her. "Are we talking an exclusive relationship here?"

She started. "No. Yes. I don't know. Can we decide that as we go along?"

Dodge moved a little closer and Boo growled at him, a low and empty threat.

"Boo votes no on exclusivity," Dodge said, and Julia gave a small laugh.

"Boo doesn't get a vote."

"So we'll leave that one for now. But I do need answers to a couple more questions."

"That sounds ominous," Julia said.

"I'm not going to ask for the deed to your business, Jones. Relax."

She sat back against the bench. "And if I can't answer?"

"You can answer," Dodge said. "If you want to."

Julia turned her face away for a moment, and then she nodded. "I'll try."

"No discussion of doctors or medication, okay. Clearly you've given this all a lot of thought. So what exactly is it that doesn't need curing?"

He wouldn't have been surprised if she got up and walked away from him without a backward glance, but instead she sat just where she was. A minute passed and then another, and Dodge was aware of the way Boo was watching him, and the lights in Beate's apartment and the lack of lights in Nils's apartment and the fact that the sky was clear and the moon had risen.

Julia cleared her throat. "I am self-protective. I'm cautious, and I don't like to take unnecessary risks. But I am not agoraphobic. Agoraphobia means 'fear of the marketplace' in Greek, which you'd have to agree is not me. I live in the middle of a marketplace, for God's sake. I deal with dozens of people every day. So I don't want to hear any theories about anxiety disorder and agoraphobia. Are you satisfied with that much?"

Dodge inclined his head. "Sure."

Her face was damp with perspiration and her fingers worked Boo's wiry coat. "Anything else?"

"I want to adopt Scoot. Will you let me?"

Scoot had been lying at Dodge's feet, and now he sat up at attention. He looked back and forth between Julia and Dodge, and his tail began to wag. Julia put her face down and rubbed a cheek against Boo's head.

"It's a lot to ask."

"I realize that."

"I'm not sure you do."

A minute passed and another, and Scoot lay back down, his head on his paws.

"Would you consider joint custody?"

Dodge smiled. "Absolutely."

Then Julia stood up. She looked tired and overwhelmed and resolute. "Come on," she said. "We can finish this conversation upstairs."

26

THE FIRST THOUGHT Dodge had, coming into Julia's apartment, was how much work had gone into fitting what must be a whole household of furniture into four rooms. And while he didn't know enough about antiques to be sure, he had the feeling that every piece was very old and quite valuable, with the exception of a well-used velvet couch and matching chair. Boo immediately claimed the ottoman as her own and settled with a contented sigh, while the other dogs made do with the couch.

"I'll be right back." Julia didn't even look at him as she left, most probably, Dodge reasoned, to have an anxiety attack in the privacy of her bathroom. Which might take a while. Dodge walked the perimeter of the parlor, his hands behind his back.

He paused in front of a corner cabinet with beveled glass doors. It was filled with elaborately carved figurines in ivory and jade, most no taller than his little finger. Another glass-fronted cabinet was overburdened with stacks of fragile white china with fine blue scrollwork on the rims, elaborate tea- and coffeepots, serving dishes, platters. A larger, modern cabinet held a wide-screen television and all the associated boxes.

The built-in shelves on the far wall were full of books. Architecture, art, antiques, textiles, business law, accounting. A drop-leaf table flanked by two standing lamps with Tiffany shades, more books in neat piles. There was a laptop computer on the low table between the chair and the couch, along with the largest stand-alone monitor Dodge had ever seen, more books, and a pad of paper with a pencil put across the top at a perfect right angle. Next to it was a shallow box that seemed to be filled with bits of lace.

Julia called from the hallway, "Come into the kitchen, would you?"

The dogs followed happily, jockeying for position as Dodge walked down the short hall. The smaller bedroom had been given over to a treadmill on one side and storage on the other. The main bedroom door was closed.

He called, "Can I have a look?"

At first he thought she hadn't heard him, but then she appeared in the kitchen doorway. The light was at her back and her expression was lost in shadow.

"Sure."

Dodge stayed in the doorway, his hand on the knob. Very aware that Julia was watching him, that this was some kind of test that he might not pass.

Where the parlor had seemed overpopulated, her bedroom was austere in its simplicity. More very old furniture, heavy pieces with ornate carving and gilding. The bed had been made with a simple spread, two immaculate pillows, and a quilt folded at the foot. Nothing personal at all, not even an alarm clock on a bedside table. Dodge closed the door and went into the kitchen, where Julia was putting cups and saucers on a solid and very battered table.

"Let me guess," Dodge said. "From a seventeenth-century French farmhouse."

Julia glanced at him. "Nineteenth. Flemish. Have a seat."

But Dodge stayed where he was while Julia moved around the kitchen making coffee. The open refrigerator revealed blindingly clean shelves, and neat rows of containers. Milk, juice, eggs, butter, covered bowls.

"So," she said, with her back to him.

"So," Dodge echoed.

"You must have something more to say than that."

"You were expecting an appraisal?"

She closed the refrigerator and turned to lean back against it, her wrists crossed at the small of her back. Dodge wondered if she realized how young it made her look to stand like that. If she had any sense of her physical self at that moment, or if she was too busy holding on to her composure to pay attention to anything else.

Julia said, "I guess I was expecting some curiosity."

He smiled. "I'm curious, but I'm not going to press my luck asking you about high-definition televisions and Japanese netsuke."

She lowered her chin to her chest and her arms came around and crossed on her abdomen. When she looked up again, she was smiling. Not a very convincing smile, but a smile.

"It's nice," she said, "that you don't ask a lot of questions."

Dodge didn't respond to that, and he had the sense that she was surprised and maybe a little disappointed. Julia came across the room and sat down on the very edge of her chair, her posture tensed to bolt. "I inherited all this stuff," she said after a while. "The antiques, I mean. There's a lot more of it, in storage in Chicago. Some of it is from my family, but most of it was Charlie's."

Dodge made a sound, one that was meant to convey interest, attention, detachment.

"We had a condo in an old building on the Gold Coast. You know, the twenty-four-hour doorman, a panoramic view of the lake, the whole thing."

"Sounds nice."

She nodded. "It was nice. It was beautiful."

"Miss it?"

"No," Julia said. For a long moment she studied the bottom of her coffee cup, and then she looked up at him.

"Have you ever been in Chicago in January?"

JULIA TALKED. SHE TOLD HIM ABOUT THE WEATHER IN A CITY halfway across the country, the quality of the particular kind of cold that comes off Lake Michigan, the way the city seems to glow on a sunny winter day, so mercilessly bright that people go out in N-3B parkas and sunglasses, like high-mountain hikers. The plain hard work of getting dressed to walk a block to the el stop or the grocery store when the windchill hit twenty below. How layers of clothes suddenly felt like the thinnest silk when a wind came shooting directly off the lake. Julia talked about Chicago in the winter and her face was alive with memories.

The stream of talk began to shift very slightly, a story about trying to navigate an icy sidewalk with arms full of shopping bags; how quickly a clear, bright January afternoon could metamorphose into something very different.

Julia blinked and looked around herself. Let out a small awkward laugh. Stood up suddenly.

"More coffee?"

Dodge held out his cup and made no comment about the flush on her cheeks or the slight tremble in her hands. Instead he told her about a blizzard in Nebraska when he was driving from Memphis to Oregon. By the time he had finished she was calm enough to ask questions.

"What was it in Oregon?"

"A truck stop, near the California border."

She sat down abruptly. "A truck stop?"

"Yup. With a diner and a gift shop. That was a short-term project, only took about six months to turn around."

"Somehow I can't see you slinging hash," Julia said.

Dodge grinned. "I'd like to argue with you, but the truth is, I'm not in a hurry to take on another diner. I'll leave that to Mister and Polly. And Moe."

"Moe came into Cocoon once, right after we opened," Julia said. "He never came back."

"The prices?"

"I don't think he got that far. He said he had gone his whole life so far without seeing Big Dove in her nightgown and he would just as soon have never had the experience."

"I think Big Dove looks great in pajamas," Dodge said. "His loss."

Julia smiled at that. She seemed to be at ease, now that they were actually sitting across from each other at her kitchen table. Dodge had meant it when he told her he wouldn't ask questions, but it was harder than he thought it would be. He wondered if he was really the first person to sit at this table, or if Nils Sigridsson had been allowed this far. He thought of the sterility of the bedroom, and of Julia's insomnia. He remembered her in his own bed, blissfully asleep.

She said, "This is a little awkward, isn't it?"

Dodge picked up her hand from the table. "Not in the least. How about we go put on an old movie and neck on the couch?"

He felt her pulse jump. A flush of color climbed into her face, pleasure and embarrassment. It made him sad for reasons he couldn't put a name to.

A FEW MINUTES AFTER MIDNIGHT DODGE WENT HOME WITHOUT Julia, but with Scoot trotting beside him.

"You should spend some time alone with him," Julia had said at the door. "A trial period."

"Will I get a report card?"

All the playfulness that had been so evident for the last couple hours had left her. She was looking at Scoot with such focus and intensity that Dodge almost called off the whole thing.

"Go on," she said finally. "I'll see you tomorrow."

And so he went home with his new dog—his trial dog, Dodge corrected himself. Wondering what would have to happen for Julia Darrow to take custody away from him, how that would work. Scoot seemed unconcerned about his own future.

When Dodge opened the back door Scoot shot through the kitchen and into the bedroom, where he leaped onto the bed without hesitation. This was a moment to establish who exactly was going to be alpha dog in the household, but Dodge was bone tired and anyway, the phone was ringing. Scoot sat up and gave him an inquisitive look.

"Let's wait for the machine," Dodge said, and Scoot collapsed again.

Nora's voice filled the apartment. The fact that Dodge didn't pick up right away didn't give her even a moment's pause. She launched into a plaintive monologue about the teenage stranger who used to be her first-born son.

Scoot sighed when Dodge picked up the phone.

"Hey. You sound mournful."

"I am mournful. Or I was. It's actually quite therapeutic, talking to your answering machine. Erase that message, will you?"

"Consider it done."

"You sound a little down yourself. What's going on in Lambert Square these days?"

So he told her about the shop. About his ongoing campaign to get Link to reveal the hidey-hole where he kept the most valuable pens; about the addition of two more penmanship classes and Lydia Montgomery, who was working wonders, according to the parents of her students. Many of the mothers who brought in their children had been asking about the possibility of calligraphy, something else Lydia could teach if she could find time in her schedule. He told Nora about his interns, who were generally useful and biddable and curious, and who worked together well with Link and Heep, but not so well with each other.

"It's Leo," Dodge said. "Or maybe I should call him Lotharleo. He's breaking hearts right and left, which, truthfully, wouldn't be any of my business if it weren't for the fact that he's got my interns all turned around."

"Sounds messy."

"You want messy," Dodge said, "I haven't even told you yet about Sigridsson. He's been dating Bean's mother."

Nora had heard a lot about Bean, and she picked up right away on the complexities of the situation.

"Can Bean's mother handle the Swede?"

"Sure," Dodge said. "He can't pull anything over on her, but that doesn't mean she won't get hurt in the end."

"Speaking of romance," Nora said.

"Nothing to report."

There was a short pause. "You always were the worst poker player."

"I didn't say nothing's going on. I said I had nothing to report."

"Aha. Is it your privacy that's the issue, or patient privilege?"

Dodge said, "If I said both, would you leave this alone?"

"Of course not."

"I have to get to bed."

"Dodge."

"Look," Dodge said. "She's a friend. I like her. She's living in a box. If I can help her a little, I'm going to help her."

Nora was quiet, and with that Dodge realized, with great surprise and discomfort, that there were worse things than his little sister's humming at him.

27

FRIDAY NOON Maude showed up unannounced at Julia's office door.

"Lunch?" Julia closed her laptop and sat back in her chair. "What's the occasion?"

"Nothing special," Maude said. "A little girl talk."

Julia accepted the sack Maude handed her. Inside was a peanut butter and jelly sandwich, a bag of carrot sticks, an apple, and a cookie.

"This takes me right back to third grade," Julia said.

"Well, darn," Maude said. She frowned into her own sack. "I guess two of my girls are eating pâté and Camembert on baguettes today."

"I like peanut butter. And I'm touched that you'd go to the trouble to make me a sack lunch. What's the catch?"

"You know me too well," Maude said. "What I want is some information."

Julia's stomach did a little flip, but she held her head up and managed a grim smile. "Rumor mill working overtime?"

"Hell no." Maude waved a carrot stick like a magic wand. "This is me being nosy. You work out your differences with John Dodge?"

Julia took a slug of cold coffee to give herself a minute. The whole time she was aware of Maude's steady gaze.

"We've come to an understanding."

"Is it the kind of understanding that involves sleepovers?"

"It is."

"Oh, good. Are we talking exclusive mining rights?"

Julia inhaled a mouthful of coffee and it took three full minutes until she had stopped coughing.

"I never took you for a prude," Maude said.

"I'm not a prude." Julia wiped her watering eyes. "It's just that your gift for a vivid turn of phrase still takes me by surprise now and then."

Maude grinned out of one side of her mouth. "Why, thank you, sugar. Now how about an answer?"

"We're not exclusive."

Maude narrowed her eyes. "Are you sure?"

"Of course I'm sure. We haven't known each other long enough to talk about exclusivity."

"Well then," Maude said. "You're not worried about him going off to Beate's island house for the weekend? Tell me this isn't coming as a surprise."

"He told me all about it," Julia said. "He's leaving late today and coming back early Monday. Scoot will stay with me while he's gone."

Maude's mouth fell open and then shut with a click. "You let John Dodge have Scoot?"

"On a trial basis," Julia said. "We'll see how it goes."

"Aren't you chock-full of surprises today," Maude said. She narrowed her eyes. "So you're fine with Dodge going off for a weekend with Beate." Maude's teeth, very white and strong, snapped a carrot stick in half.

Julia started to object, and stopped herself. She said, "If that's the way you want to look at it."

A deep frown line appeared between Maude's brows, a sign Julia didn't like at all. She forced herself to take a deep breath, and then she counted to five for good measure. "Look, I made it clear that I don't want to leave Lamb's Corner. Dodge does. If he wants to go to the shore with friends, why should I object?"

Julia liked the calm and reasonable tone she had hit, but it was clear that Maude wasn't buying any.

"Have you completely forgot what happened last time Beate took a houseful of people out to Fripp Island?"

"I don't believe half of those stories," she said. "And if every word was true, it was no worse than the average college dorm party. Personally, I think Lorna Jean made up the whole thing out of pique because Nils didn't invite her along."

Something occurred to Julia and she shot Maude a look. "Who is Nils taking this time?"

"I was wondering if you'd get around to asking," Maude said. "He asked Mayme. Now see, you didn't know that, did you?"

Julia flushed with irritation. "So what exactly is it you think I should be doing? Mayme is a grown woman; I can't exactly lock her in her room because she's running around with a fast boy. And if John Dodge wants to spend a whole weekend drinking and carousing and fornicating with Swedes, there's nothing I can do about that, either. And neither can you."

"That's where you're wrong," Maude said. "Because Mike and me, we're going, too."

Julia sat back. She produced what she trusted was her brightest, most sincere smile. "Is that so. Well, good for you. Hope you have a grand time, don't get arrested if you can help it." She took a very large bite out of her sandwich and began to chew busily.

Maude tapped a finger on the desktop as if she were counting out points she wanted to make, but in the end she just shook her head and began to stuff napkins and plastic bags into her lunch sack.

"Come on," Julia said. "What do you expect me to do?"

"Not a thing," Maude said. She stood up. "You have a nice weekend, sugar."

"I will," Julia said, trying to sound decisive and completely at ease. "Thanks for lunch, Maude."

"You're welcome." Maude paused in the open door. "I am not going to worry about you, not once all weekend."

"That's the most sensible thing you've said today," Julia said. "I hope you mean it."

At closing time Exa said, "Now, that's what I call a good afternoon's trade."

It was true. There was no doubt now that the publicity that came along with the arrival of the Kallsjö people was doing Lambert Square a lot of good. Travelers went out of their way to swing by and have a look at the massive construction site on the far side of town, and then stayed to eat and shop.

"I bet we have a big day tomorrow, too," Exa went on. No doubt she was thinking that the bump up in business would mean a bigger year-end bonus or a raise or both. Something Julia would have to sit down and figure out this weekend. Another thing to put on the list.

"Who'd you get to cover for Mayme tomorrow?"

Julia's head came up. "I thought you were coming in."

"Oh no, sweetie, I can't tomorrow. It's my weekend to do the church flowers. I'm sure I told you that."

"You did tell me," Julia said. "I just forgot. I'll find somebody, don't worry."

"I sure hope you do," Exa said. She pulled out a compact and flipped it open to examine her lipstick. "Otherwise you'll run yourself ragged."

Busy was good, Julia reminded herself as she closed out the cash drawer. Too busy to wonder what was going on in a palace by the sea—that was even better.

From overhead came the sound of dogs at play, nails clicking on the floorboards as they raced back and forth. Gloria and Willie raising Cain. Boo would be watching from the couch, egging them on. Julia hoped that Bean would be willing to work all day Saturday.

Just as soon as she thought of Bean, she saw the little girl walking toward the shop with Leo. Scoot was dancing along behind the two of them, pleased with the world and his place in it. Bean was telling Leo a story that involved big hand motions and an elaborately scrunched-up face, her best imitation of Mrs. Gaylord, who had been teaching music at Lamb's Corner Elementary for forty years. Leo, who must have his own Mrs. Gaylord stories, was an appreciative audience. Bean's face glowed with pleasure.

All Julia's irritation with Leo—and there had been a good deal of it over the past weeks—disappeared. Whatever else his faults, he treated Bean with the right combination of gentle teasing and affection, and that put him in Julia's good graces.

Bean caught sight of Julia and raised a hand to wave. Then she pointed, head cocked at an angle, to the apartment windows.

Julia nodded, and Bean swerved off to get the dogs and take them out. But Leo came to the locked door and stood, palms up, shoulders hunched.

She unlocked it for him.

"Got some work I wanted to finish up." He didn't meet her eye, which was something unusual. If there was a shy bone in Leo's body, this was the first direct evidence.

"On a Friday night?"

Leo looked away and then back at her. "I'm taking a break from women until I figure them out."

Julia hesitated, and then she said what was on her mind.

"We're not all that complicated. I can tell you one thing, I don't know a woman alive who likes to be misled or lied to."

"It's not that easy," Leo said, his brow folding.

"Sure it is," Julia said. "It's that easy, and it's that hard, too."

28

LATE SUNDAY AFTERNOON Julia realized she was exhausted; she had finished everything on her to-do list, and more. Which should have been incredibly uplifting, but instead she felt vaguely hollow and nervous and none of her usual distractions helped in the slightest. No DVD, no book, not even Play Babble, a website she allowed herself only in the most dire of circumstances, could take her mind off the image of the box of chocolate truffles in Dodge's kitchen cabinet.

I am a very disciplined person, she told the dogs. Gloria raised her shaggy head and then dropped it again when it was clear this confession had nothing to do with dog cookies.

On any other day of the week Julia could call the grocery store and have what she wanted delivered. Milk and bread and a jar of mustard and *oh* and *Patty Ann, you know those boxes of chocolate-covered Tootsie Rolls? And I'll take a couple pints of Cherry Garcia while I'm at it.* But Lamb's Corner was not big on Sunday shopping, not even the Food Lion.

Julia took the dogs for a walk in Lambert Square, the air crisply cool but not cold, the dark settling in early. She wore a terry-cloth robe over her pajamas, wool socks, and clogs, and she was perfectly comfortable. Winter in South Carolina, if you could call it winter at all. One of the things she liked best about living here. As she threw a stick for the dogs once and then again and again, she was aware of the darkened windows of the apartments behind her.

Julia realized she had already got used to seeing lights in windows other than her own, and more surprising, that she was comforted by evidence of having neighbors.

When she married Charlie and moved into the apartment on Astor, she had forgotten what it meant to have neighbors. Weeks went by without seeing anybody in the halls or elevator. But that hadn't really mattered; she and Charlie were busy people with professions, and commitments, family and friends.

In Lamb's Corner neighbors meant something, and the term was broadly construed. The first challenge Julia had faced was how to keep her apartment out of bounds and secure her privacy without giving offense. She put couches and comfortable chairs in the big open workroom on the second floor of Cocoon, a coffee urn and a refrigerator and a cookie jar, and she was consistent and firm: no visitors on the third floor. It had taken a while, but eventually the message got across and then the theories started surfacing. She had built a shrine to her dead husband, she had his mummified body sitting in the parlor, she had no furniture at all and slept on the bare floor. She heard these rumors through Exa, who took it on as her personal mission to set all of Lamb's Corner straight and could talk about the provenance of Julia's furniture as though it was her own.

Julia had made friends of T. J. Pepper and Dan Harris while they still lived in Lambert Square, looking after their houseplants when they went out of town, feeding Dan's hugely indolent cat, turning lights on and off. Then they had bought a house together and she was without neighbors again. She had even begun to miss the cat.

Now the Swedes were back and she had Dodge, who hadn't asked her for any help while he was gone, though he had houseplants. A huge old hairy spider plant that Big Dove had brought him and violets on the kitchen windowsill, origins unknown. And the ficus tree, and the jade. Julia found herself worrying, about plants.

Probably one of the church ladies who kept his kitchen stocked with pies and cakes and fudge had claimed the privilege of tending them. Those ladies went to great lengths to keep Dodge in sweets, which was a waste. He might know the value of a very expensive truffle, but otherwise Dodge had little interest in the dessert side of the menu. He often brought the church lady offerings over to Cocoon, as he had done just this past week with an enormous layer cake two inches deep in buttery frosting. Luckily it was a Tuesday and the Needlework Girls were on hand to help eat it, though it got them into an argument about whether or not it was seemly for a strict Baptist like Verna Farmer to be so free with the vanilla.

"I'm a simple man," Dodge had told Julia. "I like the occasional ice cream cone. The elusive crisp but chewy chocolate chip cookie. But this"—he gestured to the disappearing Italian crème cake—"is overstatement."

And still the whole thing pleased him and he didn't try to hide it. "Maybe it is bribery," he admitted. "But if Earlene spends hours in her kitchen over a strawberry rhubarb pie and then puts on her nicest dress to bring it down to Lambert Square just for me, then I am man enough to admit I am honored."

"In case you hadn't noticed," Julia told him, "a lot of women do get dressed up to come into town. Hose and high heels and makeup. Some of them still wear hats and gloves."

"The whole world should wear pajamas?"

"It would certainly simplify things," Julia said.

"You're just jealous," Dodge said. "You've got a sweet tooth and I'm getting all the sugar."

He had made her laugh, another talent of his. She hadn't minded him being gone for the weekend, she realized, but she was looking forward to having him back again.

Julia called to the dogs and went back upstairs to search the Internet for chocolate chip cookie recipes.

It was ten before she was finished, and then Julia stood looking at the plate of cookies, each of them perfectly crisp on the edges and chewy at the center. When Dodge came home tomorrow she'd invite him over for coffee and bring out the cookies. It was something new for her, but Julia had the sense that Dodge wouldn't push the advantage. She could ask him over now and then without him getting ideas. Something she had never had the confidence to try with the few men she had dated over the last years.

Nils Sigridsson had never once been in her apartment, and what a good call that had been.

When she had heard from Maude that Nils was coming back to Lamb's Corner for good, Julia had felt a vague panic, which as it turned out had been unfounded. After a few opening gambits, Nils had given up on the idea of Julia filling the empty spot in his bed and turned all his attention to Mayme. She might have been a little insulted, if at that point she hadn't been spending so much time in John Dodge's bed.

Things were just about perfect at this point. Really, what more could a girl want?

Julia fingered the keys in her pocket. She had found them in an envelope slipped under her door when she came up from the shop, one marked *front* and the other *back*. Dodge's handwriting on the envelope: *Julia, sorry I missed you.* What exactly she was meant to do with the keys, that was unclear. Put them aside in case he locked himself out? Pick up his mail, water his plants? Sleep in his bed? Help herself to truffles?

Sleeping in his bed would be a mistake, that much was clear. But she could water his plants and leave the cookies as a gesture of . . . what? Friendship? Sometimes, Julia reminded herself, a cookie is just a cookie. She'd take the plate over and water his plants. She'd leave him a note, too.

Sorry I missed you.

THE DOGS WERE SOUNDLY ASLEEP AND SO SHE WENT BY HERself, the keys in one hand and a covered plate of cookies in the other. Down the alley, through the rear entrance, up the back stairs, and into the darkened kitchen. It smelled of coffee and apples. She flipped on the lights and went into the parlor, where she found perfectly happy, vaguely damp houseplants, no sign of neglect, not even dust on the leaves.

In the kitchen she left the note by the plate of cookies and then hesitated in front of the cabinet before she opened it.

No sign of truffles, though it seemed there was the faintest scent of chocolate. No truffles in any of the other cabinets or the refrigerator.

Julia peeled back the plastic wrap from the plate of cookies and sat down to eat one while she considered. Tomorrow she could call Godiva or some other ungodly overpriced chocolatier and order whatever she wanted. She'd order pounds of the stuff so she'd never find herself in this position again.

One last time, she got up again and very carefully went through all the cabinets, above and below, through the drawers that were almost all empty save for a few dish towels and sponges and minimal silverware. She hauled a chair over and looked into the cabinets over the refrigerator, where she found an ancient corn popper and a wok that still had a price label on it, yellowed and curling at the edges: $9.99.

Once more through the refrigerator and Julia realized two things: Dodge had eaten the truffles all himself, or he had taken them with him to the party at Beate's beach house. The second thing she realized was that plate of cookies was empty, because she had eaten every one of them in the course of her truffle search.

At the door she stopped and then, slowly, retraced her steps. Through the kitchen to the bedroom door, which she opened.

The bedside lamp was on, and the bedding had been folded back, hotel style. Sitting on top of a pile of pillows was the box of truffles.

IN THE END JULIA TOOK ONE. A SINGLE TRUFFLE ON THE EMPTY plate, and then she left, having established that there were seven left in the box, and she was an adult capable of controlling base urges. And still she was feeling a little lightheaded as she made her way down the stairs and let herself out into the alley. All that sugar, so late at night. A dozen warm cookies felt like a bowling ball settled into her gut. Which served her absolutely right, obsessive-compulsive idiot that she was.

That thought was still in Julia's mind when a car turned into the alley, its headlights pinning her down like a bug as it came to an abrupt stop and a door opened.

"Jones," said John Dodge. "In those striped pajamas you look like a prisoner making a break for freedom."

With his body between her and the headlights, Julia could see him. John Dodge in rumpled clothes, in need of a shave, smiling. He reached out and wiped the corner of her mouth with his thumb, which he showed her: chocolate.

"Found the truffles, I see. Is that the last one?"

Julia wished just then that she had taken them all. She felt herself flush with embarrassment.

"Hey to you, too," she said, and she glanced down at the lone truffle in the middle of the large plate. And: "This is the only one I took."

"It's okay," Dodge said, dipping his head to look her in the eye. "I left the keys so you could go help yourself."

"Very nice of you," Julia said stiffly. "But I only took one."

"I would congratulate you on your admirable self-restraint if not for evidence to the contrary." And very delicately he leaned forward to lick at the other corner of her mouth. As meticulously as a cat, but with a smile that was anything but innocent.

"It's not—"

"Definitely chocolate," he said, and then he kissed her again. Pressed up against the cool steel door, caught in the headlights, he kissed her, and Julia found herself kissing him back. He had come home early and caught her red-handed—doing what? she asked herself—and then the physical fact of him overwhelmed her ability to think.

Finally she muttered, "Not truffles."

"Hmmmm?" He raised his head.

"I made cookies."

"I like cookies," Dodge said, his mouth moving to her ear. "But right now? Not high on my list."

He slipped one arm around her waist and pulled her closer. Julia went willingly enough, though the plate presented a challenge, one that didn't suit Dodge, either.

He said, "This is in the way," and he took the plate from her and dropped it, a perfectly good truffle and piece of Fiestaware worth at least twenty dollars, in pieces on the ground and somehow Julia couldn't be bothered to worry about that, because Dodge was all around, solid and strong, and he was very good at this. A man who knew how to kiss, how to use his hands and body to get her attention and keep it. She could buy truffles by the truckload, but this. This was far harder to come by, and so Julia took what was offered to her, until she realized that she was standing in Dodge's headlights with her pajama top open and her skin was a mass of goose bumps, due only in part to the cool night air. And more than that, Dodge was perfectly happy, right here. If she let him he would strip her to the skin and take her against the wall of her place of business. And that would be a bad idea. She was almost sure of it.

Julia reached for the doorknob and Dodge caught her hand and brought it back to him, put it where it would do him the most good and accelerate the proceedings past the point of no return.

"Inside," Julia said against his mouth.

"That's where I'm headed." He was breathing hard, half laughing.

"No, *inside* inside," Julia said, and this time she reached the knob and turned it, and they were stumbling over the door swell into the stairwell to fall with Dodge turning his hip so she landed on top of him, his hands sliding over naked skin.

Upstairs the dogs began to bark, first a questioning sort of *Is that you?* bark that quickly escalated into full-fledged *Lemme at 'em.*

"The dogs," Julia said, an observation more than a question or a demand, and Dodge said, "Sorry, no time," and her pajama bottoms were gone, a knot of flannel hanging off one foot, and there she was holding on to the banister, feet staggered on the stairs, and then Dodge was there behind her. All of him, no hesitation or apology and not much concern for her comfort but then really, the sound that came from her throat was evidence enough that she was enjoying herself. His hands slid down her abdomen and the nerves along her spine went off all at once, *pop pop pop*, like firecrackers.

Julia put her forehead down on the cool wood of the banister and a sound came up out of her throat.

"That good, eh?" Dodge laughing, his breath on the nape of her neck and the long plane of his abdomen against her back. She opened her mouth to tell him that nobody liked a show-off but the capacity for speech was gone so she flung up a hand to smack him and he ducked his head and put his teeth into the tendon that ran along the curve of her neck. He bit with enough force to make her yelp and then shudder, and keep shuddering, in satisfaction devoid of anything resembling guilt.

IN THE IMMEDIATE AFTERMATH DODGE WAS FINDING IT HARD TO think himself. Breathing required attention. Julia was trying to pull herself back into some kind of order, but the tangle of her pajama trousers defeated her and so she tucked them under her arm and stood there, rumpled and half naked, the striped top hanging off her shoulders.

"That was good."

She sputtered a soft laugh. "That was insane."

"Good insane."

"Oh yeah." She steadied herself with one hand on the banister. "I've got to get up there before they spontaneously combust."

"I'll park the car and come back."

The first hint of hesitation, the vaguest shift in her expression. A struggle that lasted a second or two. She would banish him to his own apartment or invite him up. Dodge found himself holding his breath.

Her attention shifted to the dogs. "Okay." The pale rounds of her buttocks flashed as she ran up the stairs. There's something you don't see every day, Dodge thought. And: what a shame.

Back behind the wheel of his car, Dodge shook his head to clear it and then sat there, a little dizzy, and tried to explain to himself what had just happened. The sight of Julia in his headlights so unexpectedly had been a surprise, but it was the odd mixture of defiance and embarrassment about the chocolate that had tripped his wire. There was something about the way she held her shoulders, the dignified and determined tilt to her head, her iron hold on her dignity and self-control that he found compelling. And then of course the pajamas.

He was still thinking about it when he got back from parking. When he knocked on her kitchen door the dogs set up an instantaneous alarm, and Dodge was thankful that Beate and Nils were still away, nobody to call the police to raise questions about a lot of bumping around in the night and agitated dogs.

A large shape threw itself against the door, and then Julia's voice came. "Gloria! Cut it out."

She opened the door. Her legs still bare, and her pajama top unbuttoned so that hall light picked up the mottled flush on her chest and worse, a darkening bruise on her neck in an oval made by his own teeth. Her hair was standing up in little peaks all over her head. Dodge was about to make a comment about how fetching she looked when Scoot wiggled past her and began his look-at-me dance.

"What are you doing back, anyway?" Julia said. "I thought you weren't coming back until tomorrow morning."

Dodge picked up Scoot and rubbed his head for a moment to gather his thoughts. "You know those female spiders who turn on their mates and eat them after sex?"

Julia's expression went blank and then shifted into something more like embarrassment. She stepped back and held the door open for him.

SHE FED HIM LEFTOVERS AT HER KITCHEN TABLE, THE DOGS watching with that cheerful hopefulness that netted them so many cookies.

"So tell me."

Dodge took a long time to chew and swallow, a stalling tactic. Which was stupid, Julia told herself, because she didn't really care what he had done at Beate's beach house. The details were of no interest at all.

"I'm just wondering if you had a good time."

He glanced at her over the rim of his cup. "Just idle curiosity."

"Exactly."

"You don't care who I slept with."

The corner of Julia's mouth flexed. "Should I?"

"So tell me," Dodge said. "Why is it that Jews always answer a question with a question?"

"That's the worst kind of generalization," Julia said, and Dodge put back his head and laughed. A pleased, companionable laugh.

"What?" Smiling in spite of herself.

"You're busted," he said. His eyes watered when he laughed, and he wiped them with the back of his hand. "You're not Jewish."

She got up to get a glass of water, fidgety now because this was Dodge about to hit a bull's-eye and there was nothing she could do about it short of throwing him out on his ear. And that would be rude.

"You're right, I'm not Jewish, but I let people think I am."

"To avoid the competition for your company at church on Sunday."

"Pretty much," Julia said, and shrugged. "If I told them I was raised Episcopalian it would be like—"

"Gentlemen, start your engines."

"This is NASCAR country. But they don't know what to do with a Jew, so they leave me alone. Mostly."

He was looking at her with an expression she couldn't quite parse.

"Surprised? Disappointed?"

"Neither," Dodge said. "Well, maybe struck a little by your chutzpah. That's Yiddish for audacity."

"I've heard the term," Julia said sourly. And: "Tell me again, how did you decide that I'm not Jewish?"

"You really don't know?"

There was a moment's silence, but not an awkward one. Julia studied the glass of water in her hand, took stock of her physical condition: a pleasant state of sexual exhaustion, all her muscles as pliable as warm taffy. Her mind moving at a faster pace, trying to keep up with John Dodge, whose wit was as dry and sharp at midnight as it was at noon, and that really was insufferable. She yawned.

"Sleepy?" He got up to cross the kitchen and stood in front of her. Put a hand on her shoulder, his touch light and sure and jolting.

"I guess." The urge to lean against him was very strong, but she resisted. Without looking Dodge in the eye she said, "Should I come back to your place with you?"

He didn't tense, but there was something there. Some new alertness in him.

"Sure," Dodge said. "Let's head out."

A half hour later they were in his bed, where Dodge had fallen instantly to sleep. Julia lay there quietly beside him, systematically relaxing her body, hands, wrists, arms, shoulders, feet, ankles, knees, thighs. In college she had often gone to the pool to swim laps just before bed. Swimming had been one of the few things that could calm her to the point of dreamless sleep. She hadn't allowed herself to think about swimming in a long while, but now it was in her head and wouldn't go easily. The memories tumbling over one another crisp and clear, the smell of chlorine in the hot air, the echo of voices. They had gone to Door County every year, she and Charlie, to swim in lakes that were shockingly cold in the hottest days of high summer. As they had done the last August before he got sick, though it had been hard for him to get away. The Lambert Square project required so much of his attention in those last months. In Door County they swam and hiked and went to bed early. The best sleep of her life.

The Atlantic was supposed to be much warmer in August, this far south. You could swim for miles. Julia realized two things, both disturbing in their own ways. First, she didn't know what it was like to swim in the Atlantic and most likely never would. Second, Dodge had evaded her questions about the weekend. She had no more idea now of what went on than she had had before he drove into the alley.

29

EXA SAID, "So how was it? Any police involvement?"

Julia looked up from the computer terminal. Today Exa was wearing satin lounging pajamas of her own design, quite elegant in style and beautifully sewn. Less fortunate was the color, a peculiar shade of avocado. In combination with her own high complexion, the final effect was much like that of a tomato on the vine.

She said, "You know, we really should sit down and talk about putting some of your designs into production. Have you come up with a name for your label yet?"

Exa could manage to look both pleased and irritated in the same moment. The internal struggle between her thirst for gossip and her justifiable pride in her work played out in the way she contorted her mouth, and then the businesswoman won out.

"What do you think of Exa's Teds? Or Exa's Teddies? You know, a play on words? Excited?"

Julia did have some thoughts on labels and marketing and so they talked as they got ready to open. Exa asked good questions and had a solid grasp of the business end of things, but what made the whole subject both memorable and sensitive was the fact that in addition to her sense of style and excellent sewing skills, Exa was color-blind. Julia had first suspected this about two weeks after she started working at Cocoon, and she had asked Big Dove about it.

"Well, of course she's color-blind," Big Dove had said. "Both her folks were and most of her grandparents, too. They got wrote up in one of them medical journals. But you take my advice now, don't you talk to her about it. She's convinced herself she sees color just as good as anybody and telling her otherwise will put her in a pure snit."

So this morning Julia said nothing about color and instead they talked about designers and marketing until ten, when Exa went to unlock the doors and Julia left for her weekly meeting with Leo on the website end of the business. She had just congratulated herself on sidestepping those topics she really didn't want to discuss when Exa called her name and Julia turned back.

"I want you to know that your tricks don't fool me at all, not one bit. You pretend you don't care what went on this weekend out there on the island, but you're just as green with envy as the rest of us what wasn't invited."

Julia prided herself on not rising to Exa's bait, but this time she was caught off guard and she said the first thing that came to mind. "Exa Stabley," she said, "you wouldn't know green if it came up and bit you on your backside."

The strongest urge was to leave and slam the door behind herself before Exa could launch a counterattack, but Julia found, to her considerable surprise, that she was too angry to retreat. She advanced a step.

"Listen," she said to the still sputtering Exa. "I consider you a friend. I admire your designs and I'm happy to talk to you about just about anything, but I'm drawing a line. No more gossip about John Dodge. None. If he goes streaking naked through Atlanta one weekend and it's all over the national news, we will not be talking about that here. Do I make myself clear?"

Exa's whole face twitched and her eyes flashed fire bright. She took in a huge deep breath, much like a child who has set her mind to screaming, and then let it out with a whistle.

"You have," she said. Her mouth worked as she tried to keep herself from saying any more. Julia held her gaze for a moment and then walked to the back room and closed the door behind herself. And waited for a full five minutes while her pulse returned to normal and her hands stopped shaking.

She felt oddly alert and still settled. Easy in her skin in a way she had forgotten about. And most of all, pleased with herself.

DODGE HAD A BUSY WEEK AHEAD OF HIM AND THE DETERMINAtion to focus on the task at hand and see things through. It was what he did, what came easiest to him, from reconciling an argument brewing among the interns on the use of the laptops to making decisions on the website, which Leo was almost ready to launch. Dodge had always had the ability to tune the rest of the world out, and in fact he did meet all the goals he set himself without much struggle. But he couldn't deny that most of the time, his mind was elsewhere.

If you counted up the hours, he wasn't spending all that much time with Julia. On four of the five evenings since the Fripp Island house party he had gone out, sometimes until late. Julia didn't seem to take any note. When he called she came over; when he knocked on her door, she opened it, and seemed glad to see him.

She was resolutely easygoing and cheerful. The perfect girlfriend, who had her own interests and didn't begrudge him his, never asked where he was going but was happy enough to hear if he wanted to tell her. She could be playful and funny or talk politics, business, history. As long as he stayed away from those topics she had forbidden, they got along well. More than well.

But it didn't sit right, and Dodge couldn't stop turning things over in his mind. Julia had seen him off to a wild weekend without a qualm and welcomed him back enthusiastically, and what exactly was wrong with that?

Of course Nora was ready to tell him, the next time she called.

"I'm just amazed," his sister said. "That a guy as perceptive as you are when it comes to other people's anxieties can be so clueless about your own."

Dodge fought the urge to slam down the phone. "Go on," he said. "Tell me the rest."

"It's all too easy," Nora said. "Too comfortable. You can imagine yourself settling down there with your Cocoon widow. Of course you're ready to bolt."

It took a run along the river for Dodge to shake himself free of that conversation. Back in the apartment he fed Scoot. He thought of calling Julia but at the last minute he headed over to the Rose Theater and a screening of *Citizen Kane*. Which was the most boring movie ever made, he didn't care what film critics had to say about it. What Dodge did get for his admission fee was a dark place and just the right amount of background noise.

There was something comforting about sitting in a darkened theater while an old black-and-white movie crackled on the screen. He wasn't the only one who felt that way, because the theater was three-quarters full. Dodge scanned the faces lit up by the reflection of the projected light, and took stock. He recognized one out of seven or eight people. Some of the Kallsjö executives, all of them entranced. But then what could you expect from a nation of people who produced Ingmar Bergman. A few older couples who squinted at the screen and whispered to each other now and then.

Spending an hour and a half in the Rose Theater did wonders for his mood. Dodge found himself thinking about drive-in theaters. Most of them gone now, and that was a shame, just when the technology had advanced to the point that it might be possible to get decent sound piped into the family van without shivering in the night chill. That would be an interesting project. An old drive-in that needed to be restored and updated. He started to make a list in his head of things to look into, places where the old drive-ins might still be standing.

He left the theater before the movie was over, wanting to get home so he could write down some of the ideas about what might turn into his next project. When he had sold Scriveners and was ready to move on. Twelve months from now, or fifteen.

Between now and then he had interesting work, and friends. He had Scoot, and Julia. A pretty woman with a sense of humor, an interest in retail, a head for business. When she had a couple glasses of wine she could do devastating imitations, of Maude and Exa and just about everybody else in Lambert Square. A woman who wasn't shy in bed, and never apologized for what she wanted. Damaged, neurotic, but functional because she had developed some coping mechanisms that countered what could only be described as disabling anxieties.

Who did that sound like? And what was that old saying: Physician, heal thyself.

Well, he was healed. Or mostly healed. Julia was the one who had closed herself up in a castle; when she was ready she'd get herself out again. In the meantime he had a business to build up.

Out in the square Dodge ran into Weep Epperson and some of his friends—George and John Henry and Big Randy, all regulars at the Wednesday night poker games—coming out of Joe Don's monthly book club meeting in the Sutlery. All of them were carrying copies of Shaara's *The Last Full Measure*.

They greeted him like a brother come back after years away, when in fact they had all seen one another just last night.

"Hey," Weep said. "You busy this weekend?"

"Just the usual," Dodge said. "What did you have in mind?"

As it turned out, they had an extra ticket for Saturday's game between the Georgia Bulldogs and Vanderbilt.

"Now it ain't a weekend at a beach house with a bunch of Swedish bathing suit models, but it might could be some fun," said Big Randy. "If you felt like spending a weekend in Atlanta, of course."

Dodge didn't miss the underlying challenge, which would have been clear even if John Henry hadn't thrown a significant glance at the third floor of Cocoon.

"Sure," Dodge said. "Count me in."

30

JUST AFTER CLOSING on Saturday Julia was looking forward to a long soak in the tub and a quiet evening in front of the television when Bean came back from walking the dogs with a determined look on her face. The last time she had looked like that, she had decided to take on her mother on the topic of sleepovers. Mayme didn't like them, but Bean was determined that her mother would get over that, and in the end she had prevailed. Julia braced herself.

"So," Bean said, her rounded chin coming up with a jerk. "Is Dodge going to be away every weekend, do you think?"

"Not you, too," Julia said, her irritation getting the better of her. "Why is everybody so concerned about where Dodge spends his weekends?"

"Aren't you concerned?" Bean asked, her gaze sharpening.

"I am not," Julia said. She leaned back against the counter and drew in a deep breath. "And neither should you be."

"But it's two weekends in a row," Bean said. "Two weekends he went and left you alone. Exa says—" and she stopped.

"Exa says there's something wrong in paradise," Julia finished for her.

"Exa says you two must be fighting. You just got back together and you're already on the outs."

"Exa has got a big imagination," Julia said, and kept the rest of what she was thinking to herself; there was no need to discuss Exa's bad habits with a ten-year-old child.

"So you like him," Bean said. "You aren't mad that he's gone again."

"I do like him," Julia said. "And I'm not mad. He's off watching a football game, which to tell you the truth would only bore me to death. It's his right to go out and have a good time with his friends, Bean. I truly don't mind."

Bean's whole face scrunched itself into a fist. "It doesn't seem right," she said. "Leaving you alone."

"But it is right," Julia said. "And as you well know, I like to be alone. You'll just have to take my word for it, Bean. Everything is fine between me and Dodge."

Mayme brought the subject up again later, in a more direct way.

"I was born forty years too late," she said. "None of this makes any sense to me." And when she saw Julia's color begin to rise: "Never mind! None of my business."

"That's right," Julia said. "Nobody's business but mine."

But her temper was up and wouldn't be ignored. At closing she tried for her best casual tone.

"Mayme?"

"What is it, sugar?"

"Do you know what you're doing with Nils?"

There was a long drawn-out silence, and Julia was about to withdraw the question. Then Mayme cleared her throat. She said, "I thought I was too smart for such foolishness, you know? But I'm not. And he's . . . he's unflappable. Where I see roadblocks he sees some kind of crazy grown-up jungle gym. He's not even scared of Mama. He treats her with complete respect and listens to her preaching at him without ever looking bored. Bean is plain rude to him and he just leaves her room to be mad. And he's smart. That whole goofy happy-go-lucky thing? It's a mask he puts on so people will underestimate him. Not that he told me this, you understand. When I accused him of it he made a joke and changed the subject." She drew a deep breath. "I had him all wrong."

Julia couldn't help smiling. "Should I be worried about you?"

"Sure," Mayme said. "You spot me, I spot you. Maybe we'll get through all this without too much damage."

She meant it as a compliment. They were close friends, women who could count on each other when men couldn't be counted on at all. And that was a good thing in theory but Julia would have preferred a different response. *Nothing to worry about,* for example. Meaningless, but a comfort nonetheless.

"I've got to go out of town tomorrow," Julia said, surprising herself and Mayme, too, by the look on her face. "Could Bean take the dogs for the day?"

Mayme's raised brow brought a flash of memory of herself at seventeen in full rebellion after her mother's death, lying to her father about her weekend plans. He hadn't lifted a brow, or asked a question or even tried to hide his distraction.

"You remind me of my mother sometimes," Julia said.

"Because I look so much like her."

"Absolutely. The mirror image." And then, because she felt the need: "Bean is a lucky kid."

Mayme said, "Flattery will get you just about anywhere. We'll keep the dogs tomorrow. While you're gone."

She held Julia's gaze for so long that she found that her mouth had gone so dry that she couldn't have spoken, even if she had known what to say.

31

THE POLITE THING to do would be to stop at his own apartment and take a shower. Dodge reminded himself of this once Weep had dropped him off in the alley behind Scriveners, his ears still ringing.

"I'm too old for this shit," he said to nobody in particular. He had forgotten what it was like to spend six hours in a car with hungover, crazed football fans, a cold chest full of beer, cheap cigars, and an endless supply of warped hard rock CDs. He sniffed at his armpit and grimaced. Julia would kick him out, and with good reason.

Dodge trudged up the stairs and let himself into the apartment. Dropped his bag on the floor and collapsed on the couch.

He eyed the telephone with its blinking message light, then reached over and stabbed at the playback button and began to strip for his shower while he listened.

You've reached John Dodge's answering machine . . .

John Adams Dodge, this is your mama. I'm calling to tell you that I expect to see you at Thanksgiving, do you hear me? Now your father doesn't know I'm calling you, so keep quiet about it. Let him think you came of your own free will. And I hear that you're dating a nice young woman. I think you should bring her with you Thanksgiving. I promise your father will be on his good behavior.

You've reached John Dodge's answering machine . . .

JD, this is your father calling. I'm asking you not to miss Thanksgiving, for your mother's sake. Don't tell her I made this call.

You've reached John Dodge's answering machine . . .

Dodge, when are you going to change that damn message? Gives me the willies every time. I'm calling to warn you that the Colonel is asking a lot of questions about Thanksgiving and Mama has been e-mailing with Maddie and somehow has the idea that you're dating. Maddie must have been listening in on our calls again. She's grounded until she's thirty in case you were wondering.

You've reached John Dodge's answering machine . . .

Dodge, Bob Lee here again. I'm someplace in Germany, got a room in a bed-and-breakfast with a feather bed like a big old marshmallow, like sleeping under a cloud. These folks are friendly enough but they don't know the first thing about a decent breakfast. I'm calling because I don't think I ever did warn you about Halloween. My advice is, avoid Lorna Jean until you can get the background on the whole mess from Maude.

You've reached John Dodge's answering machine . . .

Dodge, this is Caro? I wanted to talk to you about the intern situation as soon as you're able. It might could wait until the Wednesday night game if you're real busy.

You've reached John Dodge's answering machine . . .

Mr. Dodge, this is Reverend Cal from Friendship Baptist? We were so happy to have you join our congregation last month, we were wondering if you might come by again soon. Don't be a stranger, now.

You've reached John Dodge's answering machine . . .

Dodge, this is Lorna Jean Emerson calling you. I just wanted to let you know about Halloween, in case you haven't had a chance to look at the memo I sent around last week. Please be a darling and have a look at it if you would, and call me back with any questions you might have. Or I'll just drop by to explain the situation.

Dodge erased all the messages, making mental notes to himself: throttle niece, pacify mother, pretend you didn't hear that message from the Colonel, remember to tell Link and Heep about the message from Bob Lee, ask Julia what this Halloween business is all about.

He was about to step into the shower when the phone rang again. Dodge stuck his head out the door to listen. An unfamiliar voice, the tone a little imperious.

You've reached John Dodge's answering machine . . .

This is Bonnie Hamblin calling from Chicago. I believe you are a friend of my stepdaughter Julia's. I will try you again tomorrow at your office number.

The voice stayed with him for the whole time he was in the shower, while he shaved and got dressed and dumped his filthy clothes next to the stacked washer/dryer in the pantry off the kitchen. Finally he went to the phone and played it back again. Then he picked up the phone, checked the caller ID list, and pushed a couple buttons.

A man answered the phone and announced that he had reached the Hamblin residence.

"John Dodge returning Bonnie Hamblin's call."

He waited for a full minute, wondering what he was going to say and why he was even bothering to call. Then the handset was picked up on the other end.

"Mr. Dodge?"

"This is John Dodge."

"Thank you for returning my call—"

"How did you get my name?"

An indrawn breath. A woman who did not like to be interrupted. She said, "Aren't you the new owner of Scriveners?"

"I am, but that doesn't answer my question. How did you get my name and number, and why do you assume I'm a friend of Julia's?"

He kept his tone even. A man with a question that needed to be answered, no animosity and no room for argument, either.

"That's a rather long story, Mr. Dodge."

Dodge said nothing. He heard a clicking sound, as though she were tapping a fingernail on the handset. He waited. It was something he was good at, while she was impatient.

Finally she said, "I apologize if I've offended you. I was just calling because I'm worried about Julia."

"You haven't offended me," Dodge said. "But you haven't answered any of my questions, which raises some suspicions. So I'll say good-bye."

Dodge hung up. Unsettled, a little angry, and mostly curious. On the short walk down his stairs, across the square, and up to Julia's apartment he tried to make sense of the phone call. Julia had talked very little about Charlie, and never about her family. She asked him now and then about the Colonel, and when she did he told the stories that would make her laugh. She had never volunteered any information about her own father, and in fact as far as he knew, she was alone in the world.

Julia had not chosen to talk about her family, and he had the sense she would be unhappy about this phone call he had received. He could tell her now and ruin their Sunday evening, or he could wait until tomorrow.

She didn't answer when he knocked. The dogs weren't there, either, or they would have started barking the minute he put his key into the alley door. He fished his cell phone out of his pocket and dialed, waited until he heard Julia's phone ringing on the other side. It rang and rang, but the answering machine never clicked on.

The first faint shiver of apprehension went up his back.

Standing right there in the hall outside Julia's door, Dodge called Mayme at home. Mayme picked up on the second ring and sounded surprised to hear from him.

"You're back," she said. "Were you wanting Bean to bring Scoot over to you?"

"Bean has Scoot?"

"She's got all the dogs," Mayme said. "Julia went out of town for the day."

Dodge's mouth opened and then shut. "Out of town?"

"That's what she said."

"Did she say where?"

"Don't you know?" Mayme asked.

"I wouldn't ask if I did."

"Huh," Mayme said. "Do you want your dog or not?"

Dodge thought. "I'll wait down in the park. She can bring me all the dogs if she wants to."

"Oh, she'd keep those dogs for her own if it was up to her," Mayme said. "But my mama might could have something to say about that. I'll send her right on over."

"Mayme?"

"Yes?"

Dodge hesitated. "How are you doing?" Not what he had meant to ask, but then those words wouldn't come.

"I'm doing just fine, thank you for asking."

"Good," Dodge said. "I'm glad."

A small silence spun out, and then Mayme sighed. "I don't think you need to worry about her safety, Dodge."

"Oh," he said. "Okay then."

After a moment Mayme said, "You feel free to call me back if that question you're wanting to ask works its way up out of your gullet."

"Sure," Dodge said. "Thanks."

But the truth was, he couldn't ask her about any of the things that were in his head. Not without giving away things that Julia almost certainly wouldn't want broadcasted.

Down in the park he sat on a bench facing the walkway that Bean would come through. He had come out of the shower refreshed and awake, but now he caught himself yawning. His stomach growled.

He heard Bean before he saw her, her voice scolding as the dogs pulled her along. As soon as she came into the square she let the leashes go and all four dogs came running, making tight turns around trees and leaping over bushes and flower beds. Scoot jumped right into his lap and the others crowded around his knees. Even Boo, who had decided finally that somebody as generous with treats as John Dodge deserved at least a minimum of her attention. Dodge rubbed heads and talked to them until Bean caught up and flopped herself on the bench.

"Good thing you called," she said. "Gloria swallowed a whole chicken pot pie Granny Pearl had put aside on the counter for supper. Was she mad?" And she giggled at the idea of a dog getting the best of her grandmother.

Dodge said, "Bean, any idea where Julia is?"

Bean's small face went still, her eyes opened very wide. Then without moving her head she scanned the windows on one side of Lambert Square.

"Nope," she said finally. "She could be anywhere. She's got one of them keys that gets you in every door."

"A master key."

Bean nodded. "Three people have them. Miss Julia because she's president of the merchants' co-op, Miss Maudie because she's mayor and city hall is here, and Abe Landry—Joe Don's oldest boy?—because he's head of the volunteer fire department. But Abe's the main preacher at Eden Baptist and so everybody trusts him. The thing is, Julia could be anywhere," Bean said. "Wherever she is, she won't be back until dark. That's how it always goes. Were you planning on sitting here, waiting to see?"

Dodge realized that he had been thinking of doing just that. Waiting on this bench, where he had a view of all the walkways that came into Lambert Square. Because he was worried about her, there was no sense in pretending he wasn't. Worried and more than a little put out.

"I'd better feed these dogs," he said. "Will you let me pay you for looking after Scoot?"

But Bean was under strict orders from her mother not to accept any money from John Dodge, and so she went off home. Dodge waited a few minutes longer, but finally went up to his place, all four dogs at his heels.

DODGE FELL ASLEEP ON THE COUCH WITH A BOOK OPEN ON HIS chest and the dogs close enough to touch. For a long time it was the kind of half-sleep that kept taking him by surprise, a gentle drifting and bobbing along. And then he let himself go, unable to resist anymore.

He woke suddenly, disoriented, a little alarmed. The dogs were all standing at the door, tails wagging like four tattered flags going double time. Willie put back his head and gave his signature howl that sounded for all the world like a doggy hello.

Dodge sat up and his book slid to the floor. He opened the door just as Julia was reaching the top of the stairs. She was wearing pajamas and her oldest terry-cloth robe, looking a little tousled and very much at ease, her smile open and warm and sincere.

There were some questions he wanted to ask. Dodge knew there were; he had listed them for himself while he ate his solitary dinner and walked the dogs and then sat down with a book. Except none of them came to mind, and so instead he took her by the hand and drew her in, put his arms around her and tucked her up against him.

32

"WAIT," NORA SAID to him the next day. "You're confusing me. You were gone for the weekend."

"I was."

"And Julia was gone for part of the weekend."

"She was."

"And you don't know where she was because, wait. You haven't asked her?"

Dodge considered. It did seem implausible, but then the truth often did. "There was no way to ask that wouldn't have sounded . . ." He paused.

"Concerned? Curious? Oh, I know. Possessive. Did she ask you about your weekend?"

"I volunteered what there was to tell."

Nora hummed into the phone.

"I wish you wouldn't do that," Dodge said. "That hum."

"You think she was punishing you for being away two weekends in a row?"

"No," Dodge said, almost too quickly. And after a pause in which he could hear Nora thinking: "It's not about me, it's about something bigger."

He told his sister about the phone conversation he had had with Julia's stepmother.

"There's some deep shit going on there," Nora said. "How did Julia react when you told her?"

"Um," Dodge said.

"You haven't told her."

"Not yet. This was all yesterday, you know. I'll tell her tonight."

There was a long pause. Nora said, "I'm going to stop asking questions now because, believe it or not, we've got things to talk about besides your disappearing girlfriend."

"That sounds ominous."

Nora was tapping on the phone, not a good sign. She said, "Okay, well. Mama called this afternoon. She says they just found out that the Colonel has to be at Fort Jackson for a week at the end of November—"

"Oh Christ," Dodge said.

"And so Mama decided it made more sense, since they were going to be down there anyway—"

"They want to come here for Thanksgiving."

"They *are* coming there for Thanksgiving," Nora said.

"But there's a message from her on my machine, telling me I had better show up in Brooklyn."

"Clearly you didn't act fast enough so they took things into their own hands. If you had just agreed to come here . . ."

Dodge leaned over and pressed his forehead to his desk. Took a deep breath, and then another one. The idea of his parents in Lambert Square was absurd. That wasn't the way things worked. The system had been in place for more than ten years: he would go wherever they were for his mother's birthday in the spring, and he would see them at Christmas. Christmas in Brooklyn, everybody crowded into Nora's house, kids bouncing off the walls. Too much noise for any real conversation. Neutral territory. His father would use the short time he had to indoctrinate the grandchildren into his worldview. His brothers were there to pick up the slack when the kids went on strike. Generally they got along in that setting; Dodge would even admit to himself that he looked forward to Christmas.

Thanksgiving alone with his parents was a different matter altogether.

Nora was saying, "It's an afternoon, Dodge. They'll go back to base that evening, and you'll survive."

"Okay," Dodge said.

Nora drew in a breath. "Okay?"

"Sure," Dodge said. "You'll be here to remind me of my manners, so I'll be just fine."

"Huh?" Nora at a loss for words. It was almost worth it.

"You heard me."

"You want me to come there?"

"Not just you. All of you. You've been talking about a family vacation, haven't you? So pile the whole crowd into the minivan and haul your rear down here."

"I'd have to talk to Tom . . ." Nora's voice trailed away. She cleared her throat. "You're not going to let this go, are you?"

Dodge said, "I seem to have developed a sudden case of lockjaw."

DODGE SAT AT HIS DESK FOR A LONG TIME TRYING TO COME TO grips with the situation. Then he consulted the Lambert Square directory pinned to his wall, picked up the phone and dialed.

"Mrs. Tindell's."

"Miss Annabeth, this is John Dodge calling."

He settled in for the necessary five minutes of social chat, asking the questions that were required of him. Then he got to it.

"I understand that your Thanksgiving meal is for locals?"

"That's true," Annabeth said. "Folks who can't get away to be with their families, or who don't have much family to start with. Lyda Rose and Hank are going to Memphis to have Thanksgiving with Hank's sister Maebelle, but Leo is staying behind and he's going to eat with us. I'm sure Link will be here again this year, and there are a few others. Would you and Julia like to join us this year?"

Julia. Dodge faltered, and then made some logical jumps that would save him from speaking for her. "Julia usually does come, doesn't she?"

Annabeth assured him that Julia had indeed had her Thanksgiving dinner with them every year since she arrived in Lambert Square.

"Well, fine," Dodge said. "But really I was calling to ask if there might be any more spots available for family."

"Your folks?"

"Yes," Dodge said. "Seven of them."

"Well then, I'll just have to get another bird."

"Is that a yes?"

"Of course," said Annabeth. "Who would turn family away at Thanksgiving?"

"Right," Dodge said. "That would be bad form."

She wanted to know about every one of the seven family members who would be at her table, and so Dodge answered her questions with as much detail and patience as he could muster. He glanced out the window while he was talking and saw Mayme Hurt and Nils Sigridsson in what looked like a very one-sided conversation.

It was an odd sight. A good-looking black woman in bright red silk pajamas advancing on a very tall, very blond Swede in a thousand-dollar business suit, poking him in the chest as she talked. Her head was tilted back so she could look him directly in the eye, her upper body shifting from side to side as she made her points known. Sigridsson had both hands up in the universal gesture of capitulation, but it was doing him no good.

"That's set then," Annabeth said. "I'm looking forward to it. Oh and Dodge? We had a cancellation this evening, if you'd like to come have your supper here. Bring Julia along, I'll see if I can't put some meat on her bones."

Dodge had just put down the phone when there was a soft knock and his door opened.

Maude said, "I was wondering if you were watching." And she went straight to the window and stood there in silence for a few moments before she glanced at Dodge over her shoulder.

"You think he needs rescuing?"

"Not by me."

"A learning experience, then."

Dodge grunted softly.

"You don't like him much," Maude said. "What's that about?"

"He likes to screw with people's heads."

"He's met his match with Mayme. If there's anything to be rescued, she'll bring him around."

"He's what, forty? You think there's a real chance he'll settle down?"

Maude gave a sharp laugh. "Now that's what I call projection."

Dodge had to laugh at himself. "Okay," he said. "Point taken. And I will admit that as odd as it seems, they seem to have a chance. Sigridsson responds to Mayme's no-nonsense style."

"Like a cranky baby settles down if you swaddle it nice and tight," Maude said. "Except it looks like he's gone and done some backsliding."

"I was just thinking the same thing. I wonder what odds LRoy is giving."

Maude's mouth pursed and relaxed, but her attention was on the drama unfolding below them. Dodge's strong instinct was to back out of the whole conversation, but there was little hope of that. Mayme and Nils and how long they would last were the hot topic of the moment.

"It's not so much the black-and-white thing," Trixie had told Dodge. "I just don't think that big old Swede can stand up to our Mayme. There are easier women around for the taking." She sniffed, but whether she disapproved of women who would coddle Sigridsson, or Mayme's tough-love approach, that was unclear.

"The point," Big Dove had said, "is that he likes the way she bosses him. Some men need that."

Dodge was well aware that the two older women really didn't like the idea of Mayme with a lily-white Swede, but knew better than to say such a thing out loud in front of Dodge, whose views on racial matters were still unclear to them.

Bean had raised the subject of her mother's new beau on their early-morning walk with the dogs.

"It's disgusting," she told Dodge. "He falls all over hisself, trying to make Mama smile."

Dodge kept his tone neutral. "Is that so?"

Bean's head bobbed. "Mama, she says the most awfulest things to him and he don't even blink. Just yesterday she told him that if he said seven o'clock he had better mean seven o'clock or she'd shut the door in his face and he could go eat those greasy hamburgers he loves so much all by his lonesome because she had better things to do than wait on a man what didn't have the brains God gave a bug or enough plain courtesy to pick up a phone and explain why he was going to be late." Bean drew in a deep breath and let it go.

"She doesn't like him much then."

Bean was too bright to be led so easily, but she was also very young, and unsettled. "She likes him," she said. "I wish she didn't."

"You don't like him," Dodge said.

Bean shrugged in a way Dodge had come to recognize. She didn't feel comfortable in the conversation, and so he had dropped it. She would bring it up again when she was ready.

Now Dodge said, "Maudie, you stop by to discuss Sigridsson's bad habits?"

"Like I've got time to sit around all afternoon gossiping with you," Maude said, but she winked at him. "Really what I came by for was to talk to you about Halloween."

"Can that wait until tomorrow?" Dodge said. "I've got to go see Julia."

At Cocoon Exa, Trixie, and Big Dove were standing at the windows not even pretending that they weren't watching the drama unfolding in front of them. Julia stayed behind the counter, her gaze fixed resolutely on a newspaper article she had already read three times. Something about Halloween. The annual struggle had begun.

Trixie said, "Go on and smack him a good one, honey. I'm sure he has it coming."

The three of them were cheering Mayme on with such enthusiasm that Julia resisted the urge to stop them. So they didn't know what the fight was about but they took Mayme's side without any idea of what was wrong.

"She's going to back him right into the fountain," Exa said gleefully. "Get that beautiful suit all wet."

"I can't hardly see them anymore," said Big Dove. "Let's go out."

"Now hold it," Julia said. So much for resolutions.

"We're not going to interfere," said Exa, one hand already reaching for the doorknob.

"I'm sure," Julia said. "But there's another quarter hour until we close."

Exa wrinkled her nose. "You are such a Goody Two-Shoes—"

"Too late," said Trixie. "Here comes Mayme now."

And she did come, stalking across the park with her head held high. A woman sure of herself, and satisfied with the justice she had dispensed. Julia hoped she could contain her own curiosity. Somebody had to.

Mayme came in and stood there, looking at each of them in turn. Her eyes flashed with something more like satisfaction than anger.

"Good riddance to bad rubbish, that's what I say," Big Dove volunteered.

"You gave him his walking papers right and proper," added Trixie.

"No she did not," Exa said. "Look at her face."

Mayme drew herself up to her full five feet five inches. She said, "Walking papers? Why would I do that, when I've got him just about where I want him?"

On her way to the back room she let a slow smile break over her face. And if that wasn't enough, she winked at Julia.

"Do you understand what that woman is up to?" Trixie asked Exa.

"She's playing with fire," Exa said. "But it does become her."

33

PEOPLE WAVED AT DODGE as he walked across Lambert Square with Scoot trotting behind him. That specifically southern wave, the one that said *in't it nice to see you* and *won't you stop and pass the time with me* and *how are your folks* and *did you catch the football game on Monday* and *have I got a story to tell you.*

Dodge responded with the little pantomime that said he was on an errand that couldn't wait and was heartbroken not to be able to catch up right this minute. This worked with everybody but Nils Sigridsson, who came straight at Dodge, a guided missile.

"Sorry," Dodge said. "Gotta run."

Sigridsson paid no attention. He said, "Did you see that? Mayme yelling at me?"

Dodge stopped after all while Sigridsson went on.

"You seem to understand women. May I ask you a question?"

"What gives you the idea I understand women?"

Sigridsson was in a bad way, vaguely green around the gills with misery. "Julia gave you Scoot," he said. "You must be doing something to make her trust you."

Dodge was not going to discuss Julia with Nils Sigridsson but before he could say so the real lamentations began.

"Julia was simple, compared to Mayme. There is no room for mistakes in the way Mayme looks at the world."

"What you mean," Dodge said, "is that you break the rules and she doesn't let you get away with it."

"Rules?"

"Come on, Nils. The basic rules of any kind of relationship. How old are you anyway, seventeen? You're as bad as Leo."

"Oh," said Sigridsson. "You mean telling the truth, the whole truth, and nothing but the truth."

Dodge felt himself flush. "You've been watching *Law & Order* again. A woman is not a court of law—"

"Mayme is like a judge."

Dodge drew in a breath. "Then why bother, if she's so much trouble. Break it off and look for greener pastures."

"This is good advice," Nils said. "This is the advice I would be giving to myself a few months ago. But . . ." He paused.

"Ah," Dodge said.

Nils said, "She is like one of the warrior women from the old sagas, you know? The Valkyrie. Strong woman, beautiful in battle. Not like the models." He jerked his head toward the window of Fashionista, where a mannequin with all the shape of an inverted exclamation point was poised in a glittery evening dress. "A real woman. Except the only sword she has is her tongue. Weeks now I take her out and bring her flowers and make compliments, and she likes these things, she laughs when we go out and makes jokes, but then, poof, all of a sudden my laughing Mayme is gone and the Valkyrie is there in her place, breathing fire and wearing a—what do you call it?—charity belt. You know what she has hanging on her wall? Listen. 'A thinking woman sleeps with monsters. / The beak that grips her, she becomes.' Who could stay with a woman who puts such poetry on her wall? And what is this beak, do you know? Something from Freud, maybe?"

"I don't know," Dodge said. "Sounds like a conversation you should have with her directly." He clamped down hard on the impulse to laugh. "You've run into a woman who sees through your bullshit and doesn't swoon when you wink in her direction. You're hooked."

"Hooked," Nils echoed.

"Like a fish on the line."

"Hooked like a fish," Nils said mournfully. "This is a phrase I have avoided all my life, but now I am getting it."

DODGE FORCED HIMSELF TO GREET MAYME AS IF THERE WAS nothing unusual about the day. Then he hightailed it up the stairs for Julia's office, and was relieved to see that the workroom had emptied out, no sign of Trixie or Big Dove.

Julia's door stood open. She was leaning back in her desk chair, slippered feet propped up on the rim of the trash can. Today she was wearing crisply ironed pajamas of some kind of shiny cotton, the pattern straight out of the fifties, pineapples and martini glasses and palm trees, reclining bathing beauties in one-piece suits.

"Hey."

Her distraction gave way to a smile. "Sorry. Concentrating, I didn't hear you."

"Interesting reading?"

"A widower from Macon is offering us his wife's entire collection of quilts and linens. Either he doesn't know the value of the stuff, or we're talking Sears and Goldblatt's."

She put down the letter, and Dodge sat on the edge of the desk. "Where'd he hear about Cocoon?"

Julia shrugged. "Word of mouth, is my guess. Unless he reads the quilting and antique magazines where we advertise. Did you come over to talk business?"

"I was thinking about an early supper," Dodge said. "I'll take you to the restaurant at the end of your universe."

She flushed at that, but she didn't protest. "Annabeth had a cancellation?"

"So she says. What do you think?"

Julia looked out the window in a way he had come to recognize as a ploy to gain the time she needed to word her excuse.

She said, "Would you mind if we just stayed here? I've got leftover pasta upstairs. We could make salad."

Another good sign. He would take them while the getting was good.

THEY WERE HALFWAY THROUGH THE MEAL WHEN HE TOOK A deep breath and plunged in.

"Your stepmother called me yesterday."

The smallest of grimaces flashed over her face and was replaced immediately by what Dodge had come to think of as Julia's back-off expression.

"Bonnie Hamblin," Dodge clarified. "She is your stepmother?"

Julia's mouth contorted. "Among other things." She sent him a nervous glance. "What did she want?"

"I don't know. I asked her how she got my number and she wouldn't say, so I ended the conversation."

Julia stared at her food for so long Dodge started to think she was simply not going to discuss the matter of her stepmother, but then her shoulders flexed and she raised her head. Her voice was very steady, but her hands trembled. She folded her fingers together.

"Bonnie's got spies everywhere. She's good at getting information out of people."

Dodge stopped himself before he could ask any other questions or make even the smallest observation. In the course of a normal friendship—and what they had here was more than that, he could admit that to himself even if Julia could not—it would have been routine interest and even common courtesy to ask questions. *When did your mother die, when did your father remarry, did you ever get along with your stepmother, where does your father fit into all this? And by the way, where were you on Sunday?*

But Julia looked nervous enough to lock herself in a closet so he just got up and went to get the open wine bottle on the counter. He brought it back to the table and held it up in a silent question. She nodded.

As they finished the bottle Julia relaxed and began to talk of other things. If you've got to self-medicate, Dodge thought of saying to her, a nice Shiraz is one of the more pleasant options. Of course, it was also how alcoholics are made. But he kept such observations to himself. Three glasses of wine in one evening didn't qualify her for twenty-eight days in a rehab facility. And she was talking. He wanted her to talk, to get back to a place where she could smile.

She was telling him about the way Mayme's public argument with Sigridsson had played out with the Needlework Girls when the phone rang. Like a magic bell in an old fairy tale, the phone rang and the mood shifted instantaneously from light and playful to dread. Then the machine picked up and Dodge watched Julia's face as she listened to the lack of sound. Someone unsure of what to say, if a message on a machine could possibly serve the purpose required of it. And then that person hung up, decisively. A sharp and distinctly irritated click.

"That was her," Julia said. Her expression was odd. Not so much anger or displeasure as resentment and weariness. She looked at Dodge, her head tilted to one side. "You've never been married."

It wasn't a question, but he answered it anyway. "No."

"My mother-in-law was . . . difficult."

"Many are."

"Bonnie was in a class all her own."

Dodge paused. "I thought Bonnie was your stepmother?"

Julia nodded. "She was. And then Charlie died and the only way for her to cope with her grief was to marry my father. Two wicked witches for the price of one."

She stood up suddenly. "I don't want to talk about this."

"Okay," Dodge said. "What do you want to do?"

"Walk the dogs," Julia said. "Let's go walk the dogs."

THE SUN HAD JUST SET AND THE GATHERING DARK HAD A texture, cool and clinging. Mist was rising off the Chicopee and pouring into Lambert Square like syrup into a glass. The light from the streetlamps around the fountain took on a hazy glow. In the half hour they sat together watching the dogs run, the world drew in around them until they found themselves suspended, almost floating in a globe of deepening fog and diffused light no more than ten feet in diameter.

Sweat broke out on Dodge's face and all along his back and he gave a nervous laugh.

"Now here's a new experience," he said. "Claustrophobia in the open air."

A moment later Julia said, "Is this a companionable silence, or a valiant struggle to fight off panic?"

"On a scale of one to ten, I'm at about a five. Not too bad."

He felt her watching him closely, taking an inventory of his symptoms. When he began tapping on his pressure points her attention sharpened, but she didn't ask about what he was doing, or what it was meant to achieve.

"What happens when you hit ten?"

Dodge continued tapping, something he could do pretty unobtrusively in most situations, but not tonight.

"I haven't had the pleasure of a full-blown level-ten episode more than two or three times, but they are memorable. Pounding heart, palpitations, hyperventilation, tunnel vision, dizziness, depersonalization—"

She glanced at him sharply.

"It's an odd term, you're right. A feeling of being removed from your own body, a separation of consciousness and physical self."

"You read a lot about all this."

In the dim light of the single streetlamp her expression was neutral.

"Sure," Dodge said. "But understanding what's going on and recognizing symptoms isn't any kind of automatic fix, as you can tell from the fact that my hands are cool and damp. They also tingle."

"Interesting," Julia said. Her gaze shifted away and back again. "Any other symptoms?"

"Nausea, when things are really extreme. I think that about covers it. I have never fainted. In a fight-or-flight situation, I tend toward fisticuffs."

She smiled at that, a little uneasily. "And what's with the tapping?"

Dodge said, "It's complicated. If you really want to know I can lend you a book."

Her expression went slack for the smallest part of a second. She said, "How did it . . . When did you . . ." She shook her head. "It's none of my business, sorry."

"Hey." He picked up her hand. "Relax. I don't mind the question. I'm comfortable talking about this, no problem."

. . .

For a long moment he hesitated, and Julia thought she had pushed too hard. He would retreat, and keep his story to himself. Which was perfectly fine. She didn't need to know, really. It was rude to have asked.

Dodge said, "It would be easier to explain if I had some kind of traumatic event to tell you about. Being locked in a closet or caught in a refrigerator as a kid. A bad experience in an elevator, something like that. But it didn't start like that for me."

His tone was easy and Julia found herself relaxing, her interest in the story coming up now so that the sound of his voice worked like a siren song.

"Go on," she said.

"I had my first full-fledged attack about six weeks into my first job after college." His gaze moved to the dogs and stayed there as he talked. "I was sitting in my office waiting for my ten-o'clock appointment and . . . I just lost it. The walls closed in, the air disappeared, and I was gone. Out the door, down ten flights of stairs, and out into the street. I almost got hit by a cab, and by the time I stopped running, I was drenched in sweat. The next day I resigned. So that's how it started. If you want to know how I got a handle on it—"

"There's a book you could lend me," Julia finished for him.

He gave her a half smile.

"It's okay," Julia said. "No offense taken." And the strange thing was, it was true. She wouldn't have tolerated this conversation with anybody else, but John Dodge seemed to understand when to back off.

Julia looked at the dogs sprawled at their feet, and she yawned. "Time to get to bed."

For the first time in many days she went back to her own place, and she slept alone.

Julia dreamed, as she often did, of Charlie. In her dreams he was always healthy and alert, in a hurry to get someplace, his hair rumpled, his tie crooked, and ink on his fingers and cuff. Charlie at a run. She had always been able to keep up with him, but in her dreams he outpaced her.

Where now? she called after him. *Where are you going now?*

He smiled at her over his shoulder, that beautiful smile of his, perfect but for an eyetooth that was slightly off kilter, the smile that telegraphed a warning: *You really want to know? Because the answer won't make you happy.*

When she started to lag she called out for him to stop but Charlie couldn't or wouldn't. He went around a corner and she lost sight of him.

The dream always ended just at that point: Charlie disappearing around the corner. Just out of sight, not really gone. All she had to do was follow him.

With time the dream changed, shifting in the details but one essential stayed the same: Julia lost sight of Charlie and then stood, confused about what she was supposed to do, whether or not she should follow him. What was waiting for her around that corner. Symbolism too obvious to ignore.

This time when he disappeared Julia realized she was standing in front of their apartment building on Astor. The building he had inherited when his father died, where they had lived for all of their married life. Eight rooms with parquet floors and high coved ceilings and a butler's pantry, Rookwood tile fireplaces, heavily carved rosewood lintels over every door.

Julia stood there looking into the lobby, aglow with light and warmth, a huge bouquet of flowers on the table in the middle of the foyer, delphinium and peonies and freesia, gorgeous spring flowers. Such bounty, and in the dead of winter.

SHE WOKE SUDDENLY, SWEAT DRENCHED, BREATHING HARD, dizzy and disoriented.

Depersonalization. The word rose up from her gut and sat in her throat. She lay very still and focused on her breathing, the regular in and out of air, until the pounding of her heart slowed to a more normal rhythm.

In the darkened room she could see next to nothing. Boo was beside her and Julia put a hand on the dog's silky coat, took note of the steady beat of her heart. She climbed out of the velvet chair, and trailing her blanket, Julia went to get the phone.

Dodge picked up immediately. "You okay? You need help?" He sounded fully awake, as if he had been sitting there for hours waiting for her to change her mind, to come sleep in his wide bed with him.

"Just listen," Julia said.

34

Bright sun on new snow. Lake Michigan wears a ruffle of ice all along the shoreline, white and stiff, like an Elizabethan collar. When Julia looks out the window and across the glittering blue and white expanse of the lake, her eyes water in protest and so she retreats, back to the bed where Charlie is propped up, books in his lap, his reading glasses sliding down his nose.

They have known each other since Julia was eighteen, the year Charlie joined her father's architectural firm. She married him right out of college, when she was twenty-one and he was thirty-three. She married him for his quick laugh and his love of word games. For the way he played softball, with such intensity, and for the fact that while he played to win, he was good about losing. She married him because he was self-confident enough to stand up to her father. Because he was nothing like her father. She didn't marry him for his money; she has enough of her own. Nor did she marry him for his apartment, though she loved it from the moment she walked through the door. She married him in spite of his mother, who raised him into a good man and now cannot, will not, let him go.

Charlie has been on the transplant list for two months, but today he's doing well. His breathing, his color, his pulse and blood pressure—Julia keeps track of these things for the few hours every day when they have no nursing care—all good. He doesn't look like somebody with a failing heart; if not for the thin, clear tube that feeds him oxygen, he might be any man spending a lazy Saturday in bed with his wife.

Lollygaggers. Charlie likes the word. He pulls his laptop over to consult his favorite dictionaries and reads the best bits to Julia: a quote from an 1868 edition of The Northern Vindicator *of Estherville, Iowa: "The lascivious lollygagging lumps of licentiousness who disgrace the common decencies of life."*

This earnest longing for vindication in nineteenth-century Iowa is the subject of a longer conversation. There are things she should be doing, of course. Bills to be paid, the checkbook to balance. The sheets are overdue to be changed.

Laundry. Prescriptions to fill, groceries, dry cleaning. Some of these things are not optional, but it's a beautiful clear winter's day. Charlie is forty years old and his time is running out but today he is feeling good. Julia stays just where she is.

When the telephone rings they wait. The phone has become the pistol in a game of Russian roulette. Maybe today Charlie will get a heart. Maybe today Charlie won't be able to wait any longer. The caller ID window announces that the caller is private and does not wish to identify herself. This is most certainly Charlie's mother.

Not now, Charlie tells Julia. Not today.

Julia is relieved to let Bonnie Darrow talk to the answering machine. It is a message like a hundred others she has left since Charlie got sick.

I've been reading about this clinic . . . Have you heard of the specialist in London . . . I hope Julia hasn't gone off and left you alone with a nurse, Charlie . . . When is your next appointment because I'd like to ask the doctor some questions.

She needs so much, and Charlie has so little energy. Usually Julia inserts herself between the two of them, takes the brunt of Bonnie's anxiety and fear for her son. It is all well founded, after all. But today Julia doesn't want to share Charlie or console Bonnie, not even for a minute. The day duty nurse has called in sick and Julia has Charlie to herself. Once they took solitude for granted, but now it must be savored.

Charlie continues to read out loud now and then. They make a shambles of the crossword puzzle. He flips through the television channels, his restlessness rising in waves and then settling, again and again.

Now and then the phone rings and the machine picks up. Charlie's former tennis partner, somebody selling windows, Julia's father wanting Charlie's opinion on some project at the office. He picks up twice, the first time for Denise. The field marshal, Charlie calls her, but affectionately. The night duty nurse is a trim, short black woman who does not tolerate whining or self-pity. Charlie's mission, the one he sets himself whenever she comes through the door, is to make Denise laugh. He almost always does.

Denise calls to ask if she should stop at the store on her way from the bus stop. Julia asks if Denise wouldn't mind picking up Charlie's prescription refills . . .

Denise doesn't mind.

The second call Charlie takes is from Maude Golden in Lamb's Corner. She has news about his last project, a converted printing plant. One retail space is left, one of the larger corner buildings, and with all the new business coming into Lamb's Corner they could certainly keep an architect busy. Charlie winks at Julia, and she's thankful to Maude, a woman she's met only once but liked.

In the later afternoon Charlie falls asleep and Julia lies down next to him on their Louis XVI bed. The apartment is filled with beautiful old antiques and valuable paintings, the things Charlie inherited from his father along with the building itself—but the bedroom furniture is Julia's. She brought it with her when she married Charlie. When she was twenty-two years old and assumed her life would go according to plan.

Julia lets herself follow Charlie down into sleep.

She wakes much later, disoriented, uneasy, and then starts up, fear leaping into her throat. Sleep is the worst time. Asleep he might drift away from her, and she'd have no way to pull him back. But he is awake, his head turned to the windows.

Look, Charlie says. Look at the sky.

While she watches, the light goes all at once, as if someone has pulled a shade down over the sun with a sharp snap of the wrist. The wind rises, and the first snow begins to fall. Julia turns on lights, puts a match to the kindling and paper waiting in the fireplace, gets more blankets, brings Charlie his medication and an early supper.

The local newscast comes on early, so the weather people can announce the obvious: a severe snowstorm that may turn into a blizzard before morning. They predict one, then two, and finally three feet of snow over the weekend. The reality will probably be someplace in the middle. While Julia and Charlie eat soup they watch the airports close. Don't go out, the somber meteorologist tells them, unless you absolutely must.

Julia finds the candles, fills jugs with water, takes a shower. In the bedroom Charlie's mood has shifted. He is quiet, busy with his own thoughts. Maybe he is thinking about skiing, or hockey, or just walking in the snow. The things he now loves from a distance. He is so far lost in his memories that he starts at the ringing of the phone.

Denise is, contrary to expectations, defeated by the weather. No bus, and there is no hope of a taxi. Julia reassures Denise and promises not to forget any of the small rituals that keep her husband's damaged heart going.

In fact, she's not unhappy about this. Tonight she will sleep next to Charlie without anyone nearby. It's true she'll have to go out to the pharmacy, but she's not worried. A ten-minute walk in the snow, it will do her good. On the way home she'll make a snowball, one perfect white globe that she can put into Charlie's hands.

She is dressed and ready to go when Charlie calls. Julia clomps down the hall in her boots and heavy long coat and scarves and hat. In the soft glow of the bedside lamps and the fire, Charlie's color is high, and he looks much as he did the first time she saw him playing softball on a hot July afternoon. A big handsome guy with an easy grin, the new guy in her father's office.

"Special requests?" she asks him from the doorway.

"Oh please," he says, looking around himself at side tables heaped with magazines, newspapers, DVDs and CDs, a tower of books. "What could I possibly need?"

The answer to that is all too clear, so Julia clomps across the room to kiss him on the forehead. "That heart is coming," she says. "I can feel it."

The phone rings and they wait while Bonnie speaks into the machine, her voice brittle and wobbling. Her three-martini voice, as Charlie calls it.

Do they still have power? Heat? Water? What will they do if the elevators go out and Charlie needs to get to the hospital? I wish you had let me bring you home, Bonnie says. You'd be so much more comfortable here, you'd be safer.

Charlie shakes his head at the telephone. To Julia he mouths go. *Afraid that his mother might somehow hear him, right through the electronic wall put up by the answering machine.*

THE DOORMAN IS UNEASY ABOUT JULIA GOING OUT INTO THE storm. Visibility is very bad, the storm is getting worse, the temperature is dropping. When Tim is done pointing out the obvious Julia gives him her most encouraging smile—she's been perfecting this smile for months now—and calms him down. It's two and a half short blocks to the pharmacy. She could walk those blocks in her sleep. Blindfolded. Backward. And Charlie needs his meds.

This last argument is the one Tim can't counter, and so Julia heads out into the snow where the cold air fills her lungs with a one-two punch. She's glad to be out in the open, in the clear cold. And if the going is a little rough, she could use the exercise. The only thing that niggles at her conscience is the lie she told Tim. If she takes the quickest route she will have to walk right past Charlie's boyhood home, where Bonnie still lives with her household staff in Georgian Revival splendor. If she's seen she'll be dragged inside and made to account for herself, what she's doing out, why she's left Charlie with the nurse—she doesn't like to think what Bonnie would say if she knew Denise wasn't there at all—why she didn't simply ask Bonnie's driver to go to the pharmacy. Why she can't accept the help that is Bonnie's responsibility—Bonnie's right*—to give.*

And so Julia takes the slightly longer way, just one more block, and plows through the accumulating snow at a pace only slightly quicker than an old woman with a walker. But Charlie has had an excellent day and the snowfall is beautiful, and tomorrow or the day after there will be a heart. She is sure of it.

The pharmacy is deserted except for a single clerk watching music videos on a tiny television, and a pharmacist Julia hasn't seen before. The woman hands over Charlie's refills without comment or question, and Julia is relieved to be spared a longer conversation. She takes five minutes to get a few things: chocolate, microwave popcorn, an odd little game called Pass the Pigs that doesn't look too complex or taxing, and a couple of the more colorful and inventive newspapers, the ones with bright color photos on the front and ads for miracle weight loss and muscle enhancement on the back. Charlie loves to read these papers out loud.

The walk home takes a little longer than she had expected. The snow is drifting fast and Julia walks with her free hand out, her glove trailing along the buildings she passes. She stumbles over a curb and realizes that there's no distinction now between sidewalk and street in the drifting snow. The cars parked on the side street look like a line of bears hunkered down to hibernate under a long blanket. She squints up at the streetlamp and watches for a moment as snowflakes fall through the hazy yellow sphere of light.

And then she comes around the corner, almost home, and the world is suddenly full of light. Revolving globes of flashing red and blue that magnify the falling snow. Two police cars parked at an angle in front of her building, and the long black limo that belongs to Charlie's mother. As Julia stands there, try-

ing to make sense of what she is seeing, the ambulance comes down the street and stops.

In the elevator, Julia tries to catch her breath. Sweat falls into her eyes and she squints against the sting. The paramedics are in the elevator with her, two young men, confident, healthy. They ask her questions about Charlie and she answers. Later she will remember only one small part of this conversation. How one of the paramedics turned to the other and said, lots of fatalities on the roads tonight, maybe this guy'll get his heart.

And so she gets off the elevator with that thought foremost in her mind, maybe tonight, maybe tonight, maybe tonight. Until she sees the policeman standing outside her open door, the expression on his face. Until she hears Bonnie howling.

no no no no no no no no no

The paramedics rush ahead but Julia follows more slowly. Step by step, she pushes herself forward. Knowing what she will find, what she has to see for herself. Her mind draws the picture: Bonnie flung over the bed in her agony, holding on to the son who has escaped her relentless goodwill, finally, once and for all.

Except it's not exactly like that. The bedroom is full of people, police officers and the paramedics, who are standing idle to one side looking solemn and apologetic. Bonnie is kneeling next to Charlie, who is sprawled across the floor on his back, a fist pressed to his chest. One foot is still tangled in the bedclothes. The sheets are stained and the smell of urine is strong in the air.

Bonnie turns her head and looks at Julia, her face contorted and her eyes wild. She is sixty years old but she could pass for forty-five, a woman who invests great amounts of energy and money in staying young. Bonnie leaps to her feet like the athlete she still is, but Julia finds herself incapable of movement. When her mother-in-law grabs her by both arms, the bag she is still carrying falls to the ground, spilling prescription bottles and candy and games. A newspaper flutters open to a story with a vivid black headline BLIND WOMAN GETS NEW KIDNEY FROM DAD SHE HASN'T SEEN IN YEARS. A headline Charlie will love, one that will make him laugh. The image of Charlie laughing is foremost in Julia's mind, blocking out everything else until Bonnie's hand comes up in a fist to connect with her jaw. Julia goes down, aware of a wash of warm blood over her chin. Bonnie is still screaming.

You should have been here. You should have been with him. You had no right to leave him alone. He died alone, and it's all your fault.

From the floor Bonnie seems seven feet tall, a giant of a woman, a siren calling for blood. Then Julia's father is there, too, both of them towering over her. Snow on the shoulders of his dark cashmere coat, his face red with cold. Bonnie throws herself at Truman Hamblin, shrieking and shaking, her thin form convulsing with grief. His arms come up and close around Bonnie. A perfect circle of comfort and understanding and protection. He turns Bonnie away, and they are lost in the milling crowd of strangers.

Julia studies Charlie. His face is less than a foot from her own. His eyes are open and he looks a little surprised, a little puzzled, or maybe, Julia corrects herself, maybe he still hears his mother's wailing. The things she is saying, the terrible accusations. And then she realizes that what she is seeing on Charlie's face, his beloved and still face, is sadness. Because his mother is right, she has failed him. It's all true, every dark word.

•

DODGE SAT ON THE EDGE OF THE BED IN THE DARKENED ROOM, the phone to his ear. Her voice was cool and detached, a cake of ice tamped down hard over a waking volcano.

"You blame yourself because he died alone."

"Of course I blame myself," Julia said. "He was my husband. He was my responsibility. Everybody blamed me."

"You mean your mother-in-law."

"I mean everybody," Julia said. "But Bonnie was the most straightforward about it. I guess I have to give her that much credit, she didn't whisper behind my back."

There were things Dodge could say, logical, rational things Julia knew already and would not appreciate hearing from him. But she had opened a door, and he couldn't turn away. So he asked her.

"And your father?"

Julia made a sound in her throat that was meant to be a yes. "Isn't that obvious? He married her less than a month later. I don't doubt he would have testified against me if things had got that far."

"Hold up," Dodge said. "Wait. What do you mean, testify?"

Julia recited the rest of the story in a monotone. As if she were recounting a disagreement about a parking ticket or a package gone missing. The accusations, the phone calls Bonnie had made. The detectives waiting for Julia when she came back from making the funeral arrangements. The questions they had asked, first in the apartment and later at the police station. About medications, about wills and insurance. The insinuations.

The way her father had been so distant when she called to ask him if she needed a lawyer, and how to find one. The calls from her own friends, muted and curious at the same time, not putting into words what they wanted to know, if the rumors were true.

The insurance investigator, more to the point, less deferential than the detectives. The blunt questions that should have made her angry but instead just wore her out and down.

"The assholes," Dodge said. "The idiots."

A little huff of laughter from Julia, an indrawn breath. Shock, and surprise. "They were doing their job." More emotion in her voice now, a husk of irritation.

"Bullshit," Dodge said.

There was a short silence, in which he found himself trying to get a grasp on his temper. "Nobody charged you with anything, right?"

"No. The coroner's report made it clear enough what happened. I was on my way out the door to the funeral when the detective called to say I was in the clear and free to travel."

Heat flooded through Dodge, a wash of anger that had no ready or appropriate target, and so he swallowed it down.

"The reason I'm telling you all this," Julia said, "is so you don't get any funny ideas about reuniting me with my family. I have absolutely no interest in seeing either of them ever again, for any reason. I'm asking you to promise me that you won't talk to Bonnie or to my father."

"I can promise you that," Dodge said. "Now do you want to come over here to sleep?"

"No," Julia said. Her tone still cool, her voice a little hoarse. "Not tonight."

For the longest time Dodge's thoughts moved slowly through the story Julia had told. It made him sad and angry, it tired him out and set his pulse racing.

A few things were clear. Julia had spoken up in a calculated effort to get his support. But she had kept back the worst of it, shards of mirror in a clutched hand.

One thing he was sure of, something he had suspected for a while now. Julia had been in her parlor when she called, wrapped in blankets and tucked into her big chair with Boo next to her. That chair was where she slept. She had brought the bed she shared with Charlie all the way to South Carolina, and set it up in a room as cool and impersonal, as untouchable as a museum exhibit.

35

THE THIRD WEEK of October, Dodge got up at sunrise and went for his biweekly run. The first thing he saw when he went out into Lambert Square was a banner that had been strung up across one of the information kiosks.

Eden Baptist Church
presents
THE REVELATION WALK & HELL HOUSE!!
Meet us at the Riverwalk Park boat launch
ALL HALLOWS' EVE (Sunday! Oct 31)
at sunset
BRING YOUR BIBLE

Scoot hopped with excitement while Dodge stretched.

"So what's the deal about Halloween?" Dodge asked, and Scoot ran around him in a circle.

"Okay," Dodge said. "First we run, then you answer questions."

They took off, through the park and then across River Drive, Scoot sticking to Dodge's left side as though he had been magnetized. He was such a good running partner Dodge wondered why he had waited so long.

The path that followed the river was mostly unpaved, a wide worn track that was probably far older than the town. It was shaded and pleasant in most weather, and Dodge usually had it to himself, which made it the quietest part of his day and the best opportunity to think things through.

Lately there had been pretty much one thing on his mind, and that was the story Julia had told him. Not even the idea of his parents showing up for Thanksgiving could top it. Dealing with the Colonel for a day was an irritation, but in the greater scheme of things he had nothing to complain about. His father had never tried to have him arrested for murder, after all.

Nora had called twice, each time coming right out to say she was coming for Thanksgiving, but she wanted it on the record that he, John Adams Dodge, owed her, Eleanor Roosevelt Dodge Bugiardini, big time. A favor of tremendous proportions, which she could call in at any time.

"Give it up," Dodge said. "Now that you've got used to the idea and Tom has signed on, you're looking forward to it."

Nora came right back at him. "I may be looking forward to a Thanksgiving dinner I don't have to cook myself," she said. "But I am not looking forward to a whole day in the car with three teenagers."

"Bullshit," Dodge said. "You love the idea of having them all in the van together where they can't escape. I suggest you confiscate all the iPods and headphones before you take off."

Nora said, "He's been on the wagon twenty years, Dodge. Do you think maybe he deserves another chance?"

It was a question she asked him now and then, and one he never answered. There were more important things to think about. Julia, first and foremost.

It was a week since that late-night phone call, and they hadn't talked about it by the light of day. Whether that was good or bad, there was no way to know. He had lost some perspective when it came to Julia.

Her parents were a different matter. It was amazing, the infinite number of ways people had to mess up their kids. Truman Hamblin didn't interest him as a person, and in fact Dodge wouldn't waste any time wondering about the guy. On the other hand, he *was* interested in Bonnie Hamblin. Or rather, Dodge corrected himself, he was interested in what it was she wanted and why she had called him. Something Julia had never explained. Something he hadn't asked about, either. They were both good at ignoring questions.

On some level he was aware that he was thinking about Truman and Bonnie Hamblin so much because it meant he didn't have to think about Julia. He had half expected Julia to avoid him after that phone call, but the next morning she had knocked on his door and asked if he was going to Polly's for breakfast. Maybe she had been a little quieter than usual that first day, but by evening that was gone, too.

Over the next few days she had talked more and her sense of humor surfaced, a little flip, sometimes edging on caustic. With two glasses of wine she was given to telling jokes and she was actually good at it. Once or twice she mentioned Charlie's name, tossed it casually into conversation in a way that said a great deal about her state of mind.

The best times were late at night when they sat in her apartment or his. Sprawled on the couch, the dogs spread out like lumpy rag rugs around them. They talked about business and movies and books and the friends they had in common. The conversation often turned to Mayme Hurt and Nils Sigridsson, the courtship that had Lambert Square mystified and fascinated, the source of a dozen different wagers that might well bankrupt LRoy Swagger.

"Do you think she really loves him?" Dodge had asked, and Julia took her time answering.

"At first I didn't," Julia said. "At first I thought it was an exercise. To prove to herself that she could do it, that she could tame him."

"And now?"

"She may be caught in her own trap."

"I could beat the guy up," Dodge said.

"What would that accomplish?"

"For Mayme? Probably not much, but it would make me feel better."

"Maybe he's serious about her," Julia said. "He might think it's time to settle down, he's almost forty—" She stopped and gave him a lopsided and apologetic grin. "According to Helen, he's looking at houses, so maybe he really is planning on sticking around. I could see him with Mayme." And: "Stranger things have happened."

At three miles Dodge dropped down to a walk, and Scoot took that as an invitation to chase a squirrel just as two young women came from the other direction, in animated conversation.

"I've finally decided on my Halloween costume."

"Policewoman?"

"Uhuh. But a sexy policewoman. Black boots and a tight blue skirt but no cleavage. Mama would have a fit if I went that far."

"So like a sensual policewoman?"

Dodge coughed into his fist to keep from laughing. Then he called to Scoot and started back home on a shorter route.

"So about Halloween," he said, and Scoot gave him his goofiest doggy grin.

IT WASN'T UNTIL HE SAT DOWN AT POLLY'S AND HAD HIS BACON and eggs in front of him that he got any satisfaction. Mister sat down for five minutes to talk and told him all about it. The hard-core Baptists didn't want their children participating in the pagan ritual known as Halloween. So a couple of the churches got together and set up their own activities, designed to scare everybody, young and old, onto the path of righteousness. When Mister went back into the kitchen, Polly picked up where he had left off.

"Last year's theme was the evil of birth control," Polly said. "Don't know what they've got planned for this year. The thing is, they do what they do and the rest of us do what we do, live and let live." Polly's gaze fixed on the door, where Lorna Jean Emerson was taping a flyer to Polly's window. "Most of us, anyway." She started off and then stopped and came back.

"The whole business is messier this year than usual because Halloween falls on a Sunday. And it's the last Sunday of the month, and Lambert Square is open for business."

Dodge said, "Lorna Jean has been trying to get in touch with me. You think—"

"Almost certainly," Polly said with a glance over her shoulder. "Good luck."

Lorna Jean was coming right toward him. Dodge resigned himself to this conversation and hoped he would find a way to refuse her invitation to the Revelation Walk & Hell House!! without turning her into an enemy. But then she surprised him. Instead she sat at his table and leaned forward to whisper in a voice that could be heard in every corner of the noisy café.

"What you have got to understand," she said, "is that the Eden Baptist folks do good work for the Lord. They keep children off the streets and teach scripture and family values. But the truth is—" She looked around herself and lowered her whisper only slightly. "The truth is, I've prayed and prayed but I just can't see any harm in Halloween, not the way we do it. It was so much fun when I was a girl, getting dressed up and going around the neighborhood with your friends."

And she sat back looking satisfied to have made her point and taken a stand.

"So have a lot of people given up trick-or-treating?"

She lifted a shoulder and held it like that for a couple heartbeats. "I expect they'll have maybe twenty or so families with their kids. A hundred fifty, two hundred people. But I won't be joining them. I still use the decorations my daddy made, and I make cookies to give out—six dozen last year—and I carve a mean pumpkin if I do say so myself."

"So you're not going to open the bookstore Sunday afternoon."

"Oh, I'll open," Lorna Jean said, the businesswoman taking over. "Lots of traffic in the square that day. I'll get somebody to fill in for me."

Which meant she could have her Halloween at home without offending the more conservative of her customers. And make a profit on top of all that. You had to admire Lorna Jean's ability to turn a potentially difficult situation to her own advantage.

"What do you think?"

Dodge put down his coffee cup. "About what?"

"Are you going to be one of the Halloweeners, or not?"

He tried not to wince. "I didn't realize I had to make a choice."

"Why do you think I was telling you all this?" Lorna Jean said, irritated. "I'm hoping we can count on you to keep up the old tradition. Put up some decorations, have candy on hand for the kids who come through in the afternoon."

Lorna Jean was so easily wound up, Dodge couldn't help himself. He said, "I wouldn't want to offend my customer base."

She stood up abruptly. "I hope you'll decide to join us," she said. "I myself will be an angel this year, and Curtis is going to be Martin Luther. You'd make a good Abe Lincoln, tall and lean as you are. A dark suit and a fake beard would do it, and a stovepipe hat. I think I've got one of those I could lend you. Will you think about it?"

Mayor Maude came in as Lorna Jean was leaving, and she sailed straight over to Dodge's table.

"You look thunderstruck," she said, turning over her coffee cup. "Lorna Jean give you her Halloweener speech?"

Dodge nodded. "You could have warned me."

"I tried to, don't you remember? But you had to run off and see your sweetie." And in response to Dodge's blank look: "The day Mayme read Nils the riot act out there in the park?"

"Oh, yeah." Dodge thought about that for a moment. "It's hard being the new guy," he said. "All these decisions to make, sides to take, people to offend. Lorna Jean thinks I'd make a good Abe Lincoln."

Maude's mouth fell open. "Why, that old . . ." Her mouth pursed and then gave in to a smile. "You realize that wan't a compliment? Abe Lincoln in't exactly the favorite president of all times down in these parts. And he was plug ugly."

"In Lorna Jean's estimation," Dodge said.

"Oh, he was ugly all right," Maude said. "Lorna Jean knows how to hit a man where it hurts. For what it's worth, I think you're very good-looking, and I'm not the only one. Polly," she called, and Dodge knew better than to try to stop her.

"What is it, baby?"

"Is John Dodge considered a good-looking man? Because somebody told him today he looks like Abe Lincoln."

Heads turned in their direction, but Dodge managed to keep his expression neutral.

Polly's face split into a wide smile. "She did not."

"Did too."

"Lorna Jean Emerson needs glasses, that's all I can say."

Mae Hobart called out, "I'd go trick-or-treating with you anytime, Dodge. I think you look like a movie star."

While the café-wide discussion of Dodge's looks intensified he leaned toward Maude. "If you've had enough fun at my expense, what advice do you have for me?"

She winked at him. "I think you'd make a fine cowboy or you could go see Don Ray, let him fix you up proper as a Confederate officer. I myself am going to be Marie Antoinette." And she batted her eyelashes at him.

"With a head or without?"

"Don't you wish," Maude said. "We'll have to think up a good costume for you. How do you feel about feathers?"

It was noon before Dodge had time to track down Julia, who was in the middle of what sounded like a difficult phone conversation with a customer. She gestured for him to come into the office as she made encouraging noises into the handset.

"Yes, Mrs. Conway. I do understand. It is clear to you that if you enroll your staff in next week's class—"

Dodge bent over and put his nose to the crook of Julia's neck. She smelled of soap and starched linen and coffee. He kissed the soft spot under her ear and felt her shiver, even as a fist came up and smacked him on the side of the head, hard enough to make him draw in a sharp breath. He grabbed the offending fist and kissed the same spot again, this time using his teeth. Julia wiggled so that her chair squeaked, coughed into the phone, excused herself.

Into her free ear he hissed, "Hang up."

And slid his free hand down to open her buttons, one by one, *pop . . . pop . . . pop*.

"I'll call tomorrow with the details." Julia's voice had gone soft and high. She hung up and turned her swivel chair hard, with the unintended result that Dodge ended up half on her lap.

"You are worse than Scoot," she said, but she was grinning.

"It's the opposable thumbs," Dodge said. "Get me into all kinda trouble."

She kissed him briefly and then with a single neat movement she shoved, and he landed on the floor.

"Talk to me about this later," she said, buttoning her top back up. "Right now I'm hungry."

"So," she said over tuna salad on rye. "What are you going to be, a Weener or a Walker?"

Dodge made a valiant effort not to laugh with food in his mouth. He swallowed. "Do I have to be one or the other?"

She said, "Don't be a pussy."

And then Dodge did laugh. He laughed so hard that people turned to look at them and finally Julia thumped him on the back.

When he could talk again he said, "So what's your costume?"

"You'll have to wait and see," Julia said, examining her sandwich with a frown.

"Maude told me hers."

"No she didn't."

Dodge ran a hand through his hair in frustration. "I was sitting right over there. Maude was sitting across from me. She told me that she was going to come as—"

"Marie Antoinette? She always says that, and she always ends up something else." She grinned at him. A somewhat humorless grin, a little forced.

"I'm just offering my help," Dodge said, trying to get back the playful tone. "If you wanted to bounce any costume ideas off of me."

"You're just wondering what I'll look like out of pajamas." And then she went a very dark shade of pink.

Dodge smirked at her. "That was way too easy, Jones. I can't take advantage of you when you're at a low point."

She flicked her fingers at him. "You worry about your own self, Mr. Lincoln."

Dodge laughed. "Somehow I can't see myself as a Yankee president."

"What do you see yourself as?" Julia asked, her tone suddenly subdued. An undercurrent of anger or pain held in check by good manners. All week he had been waiting for this, and now he found himself at a loss. He met her gaze.

"I've been a lot of things," he said. "Right now I'm a guy eating lunch with the woman he's dating."

And then she looked away. When she looked back again most of the anger had gone.

"Sorry," she said. "I shouldn't take out my mood on you." And then, in a rush: "I'm not damaged, you know. I'm really very well adjusted. People go through far worse than I have, every day, and they carry on."

There it was, put before him in simple words. Turned around and disguised as a challenge, but the basics were there. She had told him the worst things about herself and now she was suffering remorse. Before Dodge could even begin to put together a sentence that would strike the right tone, she leaned forward.

"I came here to start again," she said. "You of all people should understand that. Wanting to start over from scratch."

Her mouth set in a line that was meant to be firm and decisive, but struck him as fraught.

"I do know that feeling," Dodge said. It was the truth, but only the smallest part of the truth. He wanted to say more. He wanted to make a confession of his own: that leaving one place for another was a temporary fix at best.

36

OUTSIDE OF WORK Dodge's social life was complicated and overbooked. Wednesday night poker with Heep and Mister and the Blue Meanies, co-op meetings and more invitations than he could possibly accept to every kind of social gathering ever conceived. When he didn't go running in the morning, he went along with Bean while she walked the dogs.

On top of all that he had got into the habit of playing darts with Leo Guzman, who was besieged by young women and floundering. Not that Dodge could fix any of his problems for him, but he had the distinct impression that the kid appreciated the chance to get away from the emotional sinkhole of his own making.

They were at the Punch House, Lamb's Corner's bar of choice just outside town. Dodge liked the place because it was friendly and well stocked, but most of all he came for the poster that hung over the bar.

It was handwritten with markers of various colors. The Punch House, it announced, had NOTHING to do with fighting. The name was HISTORICAL. The VERY FIRST roadhouse in the area had stood on this spot back in 1824, also called the PUNCH HOUSE. Real punch had TWO bottles of dry Madeira wine, and ONE WHOLE bottle of brandy. Also (in much smaller print) spices and sugar.

Dodge loved the sign for its insistence and strident tone, and for the graffiti that had been scrawled across it: *punch is for pussies.*

Leo was saying: "Julia says women can stand anything but being lied to."

Dodge schooled his expression. "Julia said that? Those exact words?"

Leo shrugged. "Something like that. About women not liking lies."

"That's true of just about everybody," Dodge said. "Or do you like it when people lie to you?"

Leo took some time retrieving his darts, his expression thoughtful. "Sometimes a lie makes things easier on everybody."

"Short term, maybe." Time to push a little. "You going to claim none of the girls you've dated have ever lied to you?"

Now Leo looked distinctly uncomfortable. "Okay, I get your point."

"Hey, Leo!" A chorus of young female voices from the other side of the bar. Dodge recognized the sensual policewoman and her friend, but decided to keep that story to himself.

Leo waved a hand that managed to convey a *hello* and a *I'm in the middle of something, hold off* at the same time.

"Oh look, now he's going to pretend he don't know me," the taller girl announced to the room.

"He don't know you very well, does he," her friend said.

"Oh, he knows me. Don't you, Leo? You know me real good."

A flush crawled up Leo's neck, through the artfully maintained beard stubble. His looks were a big part of his problem, the dark hair and heavy beard taking the edge off what would otherwise be an almost feminine beauty: a full mouth and high cheekbones, bright blue eyes under black brows. It was more than the average twenty-year-old female could resist.

Leo threw a dart that hit the bull's-eye dead center.

"Since you're so interested in the details of my love life, let me ask you a question. How is it you find an excuse to go away every weekend without Julia? Football games, business trips, God knows what all. Anything to get out of town come Saturday."

"Don't forget the State Fair," Dodge said. "I spent almost as much time there as you did."

"So it's okay when you run off to amuse yourself someplace else," he said. "Julia don't mind at all."

"You're looking at this all wrong," Dodge said. "Did it never occur to you that maybe Julia doesn't want to spend her weekends with me?"

"SUGAR, I DON'T WANT TO INTERFERE IN YOUR PERSONAL BUSINESS," Trixie said. And stopped, waiting for permission to go on.

Julia drew in a deep breath and forced a smile, which Trixie took as a green light.

"I'm just confused about your . . . your situation."

"There's nothing confusing about it," Julia said.

"Maybe I'm just old, but I don't understand why your young man would leave town every weekend without you."

Julia said, "It hasn't been every weekend."

"The last three or four," Trixie said. "I know for a fact about the last one, because I saw him in Columbia on the fairgrounds. Sugar, if you don't want the man, why don't you just cut him free?"

That made Julia laugh. "You think I send him away on the weekends because I don't want him around?"

Trixie blinked at her, her gray eyes large and round behind her glasses. "You don't send him away?"

"No, ma'am, I do not."

"Do you ask him to stay?"

"Why would I do that?" Julia asked. "He's got things to do, he does them."

Trixie reared back with her head and tucked her chin down against her chest, much like an offended hen. "I realize things have changed since I was young, but still, don't you worry that he's . . ." She looked around herself and lowered her voice. "Seeing somebody else on the side?"

Julia was amused by the conversation, which was not a new one. She had been cornered by Big Dove, Exa, Polly, and Lorna Jean, all of whom suggested with varying degrees of anger or apology that Dodge was double-dealing, as Exa put it so vividly. Mayme was the only one who didn't push for confidences, but then that was because she didn't want to share any of her own. When Julia brought the subject up of her own accord, Mayme pursed her mouth in a way that made her look a lot like Granny Pearl.

"Let them talk," Mayme said. "They'll believe what they want to believe no matter what you say. Personally, I encourage them whenever I get the chance. If they're all worried about you, that gives them less time to stick their noses in my business."

Julia put both hands over her heart in a gesture that was pure Exa. She said, "We wouldn't worry about you if we didn't love you, sugar."

At least that got a grin from Mayme, but after a long moment's silence her gaze sharpened. She said, "Not you, too."

"Wait a minute," Julia said. "Have I invaded your privacy in any way at all?"

"You don't have to come out and ask, I can see it written all over your face. You want to know what I'm doing with Nils."

"Believe me," Julia said. "I really do not want to know what you're doing with Nils. I have got my own situation to worry about."

"In that case," Mayme said, "what are you doing with John Dodge?"

They giggled like schoolgirls, and then they were laughing so hard that Julia had to sit down and hold her ribs. When the worst had passed, Mayme let out a long trembling breath.

"I can tell you this much: I'm in over my head."

"What a coincidence," Julia said. "Me, too."

Over the next week Dodge took an informal poll about what he had come to think of as the Weener/Walker controversy. Lambert Square was mostly in the Halloweener corner, with a few notable exceptions: LRoy Swagger would be going on the Revelation Walk, while his wife, Jamie Deanne, would stay in Lambert Square, in a costume yet to be decided. Lyda Rose and Hank Guzman would join the walk and close SugarPuss. That would leave Leo—as Robin Hood—to help out wherever he was needed. Dodge managed to keep a straight face at the idea of Leo in tights. Both of the women who clerked for Marnie Lambert would excuse themselves from Lambert Square to join their congregations, but Marnie would open.

Link wouldn't be drawn out, beyond the fact that he would indeed be in costume. "Wait and see," he said with a disconcerting wink.

Julia refused to divulge any information about her own plans.

"But you will be in costume."

She wrinkled her nose at him. "You are the worst nag," she said. "When you've got your own costume sorted out, maybe I'll be a little more forthcoming, but until then? Give it a rest."

Dodge liked Julia like this, when she was playful and a little edgy. He said, "I'll see what I can dig up in Charleston this weekend."

He saw something flicker over her expression, gone before he could figure out what it was. Disappointment? Anger?

She said, "What's in Charleston?"

"Peter Logan, an old college buddy," Dodge said. Which was absolutely true, except he hadn't bothered to call Pete to announce his visit and might not stop by at all.

"Somebody from NYU?" Her tone was deceptively cool.

"Columbia. I went to Columbia, and yes, one of the guys I shared a suite with, senior year."

Julia's gaze was fixed on a pen, carefully taken apart and laid out on a piece of rag. She touched the barrel with one finger and rolled it back and forth. Gathering her thoughts, maybe, trying to put some words together. Then she gave a tight smile and stood up.

"Time to get back to work."

Scoot had been watching this conversation with more than his usual attention. When Julia was gone Dodge patted his lap and the dog jumped into it.

"So what was that about?" he asked. "Is she jealous, do you think? Doesn't want me to go?"

Scoot yawned and scratched his head, as clueless as Dodge but far less concerned.

On Friday morning when Dodge stopped in to talk with Heep about the weekend, he got an earful of gossip.

"Just so you know," Heep said, dragging Dodge out of his thoughts with the four-word red flag that meant he had something to relate that was likely to cause some trouble. "Just so you know, the talk in town is that—"

"I'm going off to see a woman. So I've heard."

Heep gave him a sharp look. "You don't care that people are feeling sorry for Julia? Thinking of her as poorly used?"

"Not if Julia doesn't care," Dodge said. But he flinched, and Heep saw him flinch.

"You spend all your time with one woman Monday through Friday and then disappear all weekend. What are people supposed to think?"

"That I have places to go," Dodge said. "Things to do. People to see."

"People to do, is more like it." Heep's scowl deepened. "Nobody wants to see Julia hurt."

"I've got news for you," Dodge said, his temper getting the best of him. "Julia hurts plenty, and it's got nothing to do with me."

"Fine," Heep said, holding up a hand. "Have it your way."

Five minutes later Dodge went back to the workshop. He said, "Not that it's anybody's business, but I'm not going away on the weekends to see a woman."

"Okay," Heep said, his face relaxing. "Just make sure she knows that."

"Anybody else who needs telling?"

Heep shifted on his stool, discomfited now. "I'll drop a word in the right place."

It made no sense to be angry about gossip, Dodge knew that very well. To overreact would be disastrous, and so he clamped down hard on the things he wanted to say.

Julia did know that he wasn't seeing anybody else, Dodge was pretty sure. To raise the subject would mean another discussion about exclusivity, something Dodge wanted to avoid for the time being. That discussion would only further cloud waters already murky enough to get lost in. He was just convincing himself of that as he threw a few things into a weekend bag when Sigridsson called.

"Dodge," he said. "Glad I caught you. Tomorrow night at seven, I am giving a party. In Sweden today they celebrate *Alla helgons dag*—your All Saint's Day, *ja*? And so we have a party here. And to make it more fun Heep will come with his bitters."

"A bitters dinner," Dodge said. "Doesn't sound very appetizing."

Sigridsson cleared his throat. "You are not eating bitters. Bitters are alcohol."

"I know that," Dodge said. "I was joking."

"Oh," Sigridsson said. "I will never be getting the American sense of humor."

"So about this party of yours . . ."

"A new tradition, the Halloweener party. Will you and Julia come?"

The odd truth was, it was an appealing idea. A Saturday evening around a dinner table with people he liked while Heep mixed his cocktails, and entertained them with trivia about the history of alcohol-based drinks. Swedish meatballs and whatever Swedes liked to eat with them. And for once Julia would be there. Sigridsson drove Dodge nuts, but he probably knew how to throw a party and put people at ease. Dodge had never seen Julia in a situation like that, and he wondered if she'd be able to relax and enjoy herself.

"I'm on my way to Charleston," Dodge said. "But thanks for the invitation. I'll let Julia know."

"You are going away again without her?"

"Nils," Dodge said, "that's a loaded question. There's no right way to answer it. Like asking somebody if he still beats his wife."

"You have a wife?"

"No," Dodge said.

"I'm not surprised, if you beat her."

Dodge pushed out a long sigh. "I have never been married."

"If I were married I should never beat my wife. Why would you suggest such a thing? Are you and Julia getting along? Maybe now I see why you are gone every weekend."

"Listen to me very closely," Dodge said. "I have never been married. I have never beat any woman. Are we clear?"

There was a long pause. "I will ask Mayme about this beating business. Maybe she can explain it to me. You're sure about the party?"

"I'm sure," Dodge said. And wished that were true.

Bean stopped by to get Scoot at five. While Dodge put together a few books and papers, she gave him her perspective on the Halloweener Wars. Her family was divided straight down the middle, Mama and Granny Pearl on the side of the costumes and trick-or-treating, and her aunts determined that this year they would entice her to the Revelation Walk.

"So you're talking bribes?" Dodge asked her.

"Better than Christmas, almost," Bean said.

"And what's your decision this year?"

"Oh, I always let Mama and Gran convince me. It's a lot of fun in Lambert Square on Halloween. Except I most usually have to be whatever Mama and Gran decide, and it's almost always something educational." Her nose wrinkled with distaste.

"What's Julia going to be?"

The question, put so innocently, still aroused Bean's suspicions. "She hasn't told you?"

Dodge shook his head. "That big a secret, huh?"

Bean said, "Are you really going to be Abraham Lincoln?"

It made no sense to complain about the way gossip moved through town, and so Dodge stopped himself from commenting.

"I don't know if I'll be back in time."

Bean drew herself up, real distress in her face. "You can't miss Halloween."

"I'll do my best but I can't make any promises."

Bean studied her shoes for a moment and then looked up at him, a small scowl on her face. "I thought you liked Julia."

Dodge sat down on the edge of his desk. "I do like Julia. What makes you think I don't?"

"You go away every weekend, and she . . . she just works."

"You're the second person to mention this to me today. Does she complain about me going away?"

Bean's scowl deepened. "No. But I thought you were going to help her." The girl glanced around herself and lowered her voice. "With her *problem*."

Dodge considered how much to say, and took a tentative direction. "Let me ask you, Bean. Do you think it would help if I tried to drag Julia out of Lambert Square? Tied her up and put her in the car and drove her someplace?"

Bean considered for a moment, then shook her head. "That would just make her mad, and you don't want to do that."

"Then how do you see me helping her?"

She was ready for this question. She said, "You could talk to her. You know, about . . . about her not going anywhere."

"You think talk would fix things?"

Bean shrugged. "You sure got Link where you want him, and LRoy, too. You're good at talking to people." But there was something in her posture that told Dodge she understood what she was asking for was impossible.

She said, "I looked it up, what's wrong with Miss Julia. You call it a *phobia . . .*" She cast a glance at Dodge to see if he was taking her seriously, and satisfied, she went on. "A phobia is being so afraid of something that you can't control yourself. Like, I'm afraid of the cellar but Granny Pearl lets me take Jimbo—her dog?—down with me, and then I'm fine. So that's not a phobia. Julia could have a hundred dogs and it wouldn't make any difference; she's not putting a foot outside Lambert Square. Granny Pearl's got a phobia, too, but I couldn't find a name for it."

"What's that?" Dodge asked.

"She's afraid of birds."

"Ah. That's called ornithophobia."

Bean hesitated. "How do you know stuff like that?"

"I know a lot of words. So Granny Pearl doesn't like birds."

"Ahuh. Any bird. A sparrow got caught up in her hair when she was a little girl? And ever since she throws a fit if one comes close. Granddaddy was always teasing her about it. One time he brought a canary home, in a cage? And Granny said he could sleep on the porch next to the cage if he liked the darn bird so much. So he gave it away. Are you saying there's no way to help Julia?"

Dodge, entranced as always by Bean's stories, started and then found himself shy a thoughtful answer. "There's no quick or easy way. Not if she doesn't want help."

"But you're trying."

"I'm doing what I can."

Bean narrowed her eyes in a way that made her look exactly like her mother. "If you think running off every weekend and making her jealous is going to help—" She stopped herself.

Dodge said, "I'm not trying to make her jealous. The last thing I want to do"—he saw Bean's expression darken, but he pushed on—"is to make her feel threatened."

"So what's supposed to happen when you go off? She's not supposed to notice? I think you want her to be a little jealous of the fun you have when you go."

"My mistake," Dodge said, "is forgetting that inside your ten-year-old head, you've got the reasoning powers of a professor of philosophy."

"You didn't answer my question," Bean said.

"Okay," Dodge said, flustered now. "I go out of town because I've got something to do somewhere else. But the thought has crossed my mind that it might do her some good. Maybe she'll start thinking about the choices she makes. Whether the sacrifices she makes to feel safe are worth what she has to do without. Do you follow?"

"Sure," Bean said. "And that is a dumb plan. Really, really dumb."

DODGE SPENT ALL DAY SATURDAY IN CHARLESTON UNABLE TO shake the memory of that conversation with Bean. What had he been thinking, letting himself get drawn into that discussion with a ten-year-old kid? There were far more appropriate people to discuss this with, people he was related to. Professionals.

Dumb plan. Really, really dumb plan.

The thing was, he had never actually worked out any plan, not consciously. These days he wasn't even completely sure that Julia needed help. She lived a full life, she functioned well in her business setting and had friends and a variety of interests. So she was agoraphobic. There were worse ways to deal with anxieties, far more self-destructive things she could be doing with all that unresolved anger. So maybe she was living inside a box, but it was a very large, very nice box.

And of course there was the fact that she did disappear, now and then, on a Sunday.

Dodge forced his thoughts to order themselves. The point was, if a person had to live inside a set of predefined boundaries to feel safe . . .

Sitting in his car at a red light in downtown Charleston, Dodge broke into a sweat. His throat went dry. He fumbled for the window and opened it, glad for the mist of rain on his face. Started his breathing exercises, and then realized that the light had changed and the person behind him was bumping the horn in that wake-up-buddy way that would quickly escalate to something more intrusive.

He pulled into the parking lot of a restaurant and got out of the car. When he had his breathing under control he waited another five minutes. Wet and shivering, he got back into the car and started it, turned on the heater. He got the pad of notepaper from the glove compartment and fished around until he found a pen. An old, leaky Bic. A few months ago he wouldn't have taken much notice but his consciousness had been raised. He dove back in and found a pencil, and he wrote a question:

What has changed?

Fifteen minutes later the page was still blank. He wrote another question:

What do you want right at this moment?

Dodge looked out the window at Charleston. It was a great city, and he would enjoy looking around it again. But not right now. Right now he wanted to go back to Lambert Square.

He stared at the first question for another five minutes: *what has changed?* and then he pulled out his cell phone and called Nora, but got his brother-in-law instead.

"She's out shopping," Tom said. "You could try her cell, but she's going to be in a crappy mood. Shoe shopping with a teenager is an endurance exercise. What's up?"

"Just checking in," Dodge said. "Catching up."

"Trouble?"

"Don't hum at me," Dodge said.

"I don't hum. Nora's the one with the therapy hum. I nod, and you're spared that by the disembodied magic of the telephone. So no trouble?"

Dodge took a very deep breath, and Tom waited. Tom, the most patient guy in the world, and one of the most observant.

"Nothing out of the ordinary," Dodge said finally. "For me, that is. Remind me why it was I gave up my practice, would you?"

"To my mind the real question was why you started one to begin with."

"You could have told me that back then."

"I did tell you," Tom said. "Any number of times. All through grad school and beyond."

Odd, how something resolved so long ago could still sting. "Was I that bad?"

"You were very good," Tom said. "You were just too empathetic. You could never maintain enough distance. But you did the right thing; you walked away from it, you tried something else."

"I'm always trying something else. I made a list of everything I've done since I left Wall Street."

"And?"

"Long list."

There was a moment's silence. "Twelve years later, you're starting to regret giving up your practice?"

Dodge put his head back and stared at the ceiling. "Maybe. I don't know. I'm forty years old, you'd think some things would be clear by now."

"Interesting," said Tom. "Any idea why you've gone to the trouble of keeping your accreditation and license up to date?"

Dodge said, "For a clinical therapist, Nora has got a very big mouth."

"For a clinical therapist, your evasive maneuvers are less than subtle."

"As you just pointed out, I'm not a clinical therapist anymore."

"You sure about that?" Tom said.

"What's that supposed to mean?"

"You know what it means," his brother-in-law said. "Every place you land you find somebody who needs help. Last time it was the guy who was still living with his mother at what, fifty? And before that the hypochondriac, what was her name?"

Dodge cleared his throat. "Norma."

"You get my point."

"Yes. No. It's misleading when you say it that way. I make friends, sometimes friends need help."

"True," Tom said. "But it's a matter of degree."

There was a long silence.

"So you want Nora to call you back?"

"I don't think so," Dodge said. "I'll call her tomorrow. Can we keep this conversation between us?"

"What conversation?" Tom said. "And besides, Nora doesn't need any more fodder for her theories."

Dodge paused, considered asking, and managed to resist. "So good. This was a good conversation. I think I've got things under control for the moment at least."

"Let me know how that works out for you," Tom said. "You can give me all the gory details next month when we come down."

Thanksgiving. Dodge had managed to put the idea out of his head for days at a time. In fact, he still hadn't broached the topic with Julia.

"Looking forward to it," Dodge said.

"Really?"

"Okay," Dodge said. "I'm looking forward to some of it."

JULIA HAD JUST ABOUT TALKED HERSELF INTO GOING TO THE dinner party at Nils's when the phone rang. She cast a quick glance at the caller ID: Dodge's cell. Before the machine could pick up, she grabbed the phone and tucked it between ear and shoulder while she ran her free hand through her hair.

"Hey. You got dinner plans?"

"Yes," Julia said, not bothering to hide her irritation. "I am on my way to Nils's place. Who are you suddenly, my social director?"

"I'm your dinner date," Dodge said. "I'll be over just as soon as I've changed."

Julia sat down on the couch and Scoot hopped into her lap immediately, sending Willie a very juvenile smirk. She promptly deposited Scoot on the floor and picked up Willie.

"That's what you get," she told him, "for being a smart-ass."

Scoot snorted his displeasure and put his head on his paws. A little shiver of regret ran down Julia's back; taking out her mood on a dog. Really, what was the matter with her? She patted the couch and Scoot jumped up.

"So he came back early," she told the dogs. "What do you think that's about? Good news or bad news?" But none of them had any insights to share beyond Boo, who produced an extravagant yawn.

. . .

DODGE SHOWED UP AT HER DOOR IN CHINOS AND A WHITE POLO shirt that should have cost him somewhere around two hundred dollars.

"Salvation Army?"

He shrugged. "Goodwill. Or my extended closet, as I like to call it."

His hair still damp from the shower and he was grinning, which meant Julia found herself grinning back, though she had promised herself that the most she would offer was a cool smile.

The dogs were less restrained in their enthusiasm, until he spoke a couple words and they settled down around him, high hopes on each doggy face.

"Here," he said, and shoved a box into Julia's hands so he could fish dog cookies out of his pockets. A box that weighed at least two pounds, and had *River Street Sweets* printed across it.

"You went to Charleston to buy candy?"

He had crouched down to pet the dogs and he glanced up at her. "Among other things. You ready?"

Julia glanced down at herself. She was wearing a black three-piece silk crepe lounging pajama set. The scoop neck, very low, was embroidered with peonies in rose and cream and white. It was beautiful, but Julia rarely got a chance to wear it, simply because it fit her like a silk glove. Even Exa considered it a little too much for the shop.

"Am I pushing the envelope with this?"

Dodge ran a hand down her sleeve. "You'll give Sigridsson a stroke. Let's go."

On the stairs she hesitated and he bumped into her.

"So what are you doing back early?"

Dodge leaned forward and whispered in her ear, "The last time you asked me that question in this stairwell—"

Julia took off down the stairs, laughing in spite of herself. At the bottom he caught up with her, slipped an arm around her waist. "Not happy to see me?"

"Now you're fishing," Julia said.

"Care to bite?"

She pushed him away and let herself be caught up again, and when he kissed her she kissed him back. Then she used her thumb to wipe lipstick from his mouth.

"We're late."

Dodge wagged his head in reluctant agreement. "Maybe we should stay here after all."

"For once I want to go out and you don't?"

He started a little, and then laughed. He was still laughing when they knocked on Nils's door and Mayme answered. She was wearing a pale yellow dress with a plunging neckline that set off the deep color of her skin. A new dress, which was all kinds of significant. In Julia's experience Mayme was very careful with her clothing budget.

"Sugar," Dodge said to Mayme, "you look like a million bucks." His tone was completely sincere.

"Sweet talker," Mayme said, winking at Julia. "You wouldn't be making a pass at me, would you?"

Dodge took Julia's hand, and she was glad of it. She went up on tiptoe and said, "Don't let go, I might get lost."

The look he gave her managed to both comfort and unsettle her. Which was absolutely typical, she reminded herself, of John Dodge.

37

NILS HAD DECORATED for Halloween with all the fervor of a new convert, candles in Styrofoam skulls, fake cobwebs studded with plastic spiders. A paper skeleton on the bathroom door.

Mayme said, "Don't look at me, it was all the Swede's idea."

"If you're going to host parties for Nils, maybe you should be calling the man by his given name," Julia said.

"Which one? The one his mama give him, or the Trixie and Big Dove version?"

Dodge laughed. "And what would that be?"

"Nails," Mayme said shortly. "I swear those two sit up late at night thinking of ways to mangle words. I don't doubt it will stick and he'll be known as Nails from Sweden up and down the seaboard before the year is out."

Julia tried not to laugh, but it was tough going.

"Did you notice?" Dodge said, taking Julia's elbow to steer her away. "She didn't correct you when you said she was hosting this party for Sigridsson."

"I'm too hungry to notice much besides my stomach grumbling," Julia said.

There was a buffet set up in the kitchen, a diversity of foods that must certainly horrify some of the more traditional southerners. Maude was standing very still, frowning at a bowl of something vaguely fishy.

Julia said, "Don't be a wimp."

Maude looked away long enough to give Julia a one-armed hug and kiss Dodge on the cheek.

"Are you daring me?" she said to Julia.

"This is man's work," Dodge said, and put a spoonful on his plate.

Maude said, "You have the stomach of a goat." She watched dubiously as he helped himself to a little of everything, no matter how odd and unrecognizable.

"It's not natural," Maude said. "All this white food."

She trailed along with them back into the parlor, and they sat down in the middle of a conversation half in Swedish and half English.

Maude said, "I didn't know you were back, Beate. How was your trip?"

Julia hadn't realized that Beate had been gone—more than a week, it turned out—but rather than give away her monumental lack of observational skills, she sat back and picked from her plate, aware of Dodge's gaze shifting back and forth and the length of his leg pressed against hers. It was strange to be in a group of people like this and to feel . . . comfortable was the only word that came to mind, but it wasn't quite right. At ease, maybe.

"You've got to eat more than that," Dodge said, nudging her. "Or you won't last long when Heep gets started. Let's go say hello."

Julia didn't often see Heep socially, and while his interest in the complexity of mixed drinks was well known to her from stories, she had never seen him behind a bar in full entertainment mode. There were a couple dozen shot glasses lined up in front of him, and two or three dozen bottles on a table behind him, some with hand-printed labels.

"What is this?" Julia asked Dodge.

"You ever been to a wine tasting?"

"Sure," Julia said. She had a quick memory of her mother-in-law arguing with a sommelier, and the even less expected urge to tell Dodge the story. It involved the whole family's being asked to leave the restaurant in disgrace.

Dodge was saying, "This is the same thing, but with bitters."

"I had no idea," Julia said, and it was true. Whoever gave bitters a thought? Heep did, apparently. He had a dozen kinds, from Trinidad, France, the Czech Republic, Italy, Denmark, Germany, with poetic names like Angostura and Bénédictine, Becherovka and Fernet Branca. Made from alpine flowers, South American tree bark, lemon and orange peel, peaches, herbs. The showpiece was his own recipe. Heep Epperson, who spent his days repairing pens, was passionate about the distillation of bitters.

Everybody had migrated over to stand around while Heep talked and poured, poured and talked.

It made Julia curious. She said, "I wonder what other talents people hide away." She had meant the comment for Dodge, but others turned toward her expectantly and so she went on. "Heep goes home every evening to experiment with bitters, so maybe everybody has a secret passion."

"Like what?" Beate asked.

Julia glanced at Maude and Mike. "Now I may be wrong, but I'd guess that Mike reads *GQ*."

There was a ripple of laughter around the room. Maude leaned against her husband as a cat leans against a favored human and patted his cheek. "She's got your number, sugar."

Mike's mouth quirked at the corner. "So I'm interested in nice clothes. How did you guess?"

"Once upon a time," Julia said, "in a former life, I interned at a very exclusive men's shop on Oak Street in Chicago." And she gave a soft burp that people were kind enough to ignore.

"In his former life my husband was a clotheshorse. That's how we met, at a fashion show," Maude said.

Heep said, "I've got another sample for y'all to taste."

Glasses were passed around and Julia tasted, and then tasted again while Heep talked about the balance of cardamom, caraway, and coriander, the bitter oranges he bought from an organic farmer in Florida, the difficulty of getting just the right grain alcohol. He looked at his wife as he said this and she laughed.

"You are not putting a still in my garage," Caro said. "Or in my basement or within a mile of home."

"I am having a garage," Nils said. "In my new house. A very large garage, and a shed. You could put your still there."

And he cast Mayme a look, one that she took pains not to catch. Maude raised an eyebrow in Julia's direction, that simple flexing of a muscle getting across a rather complex message: *Well now, see, he's been talking to her about living together at the very least, but she's holding out for more and did you have any idea they were so serious?*

Julia lifted a shoulder to signal her own surprise and turned away to keep her discomfort to herself.

The evening went by like that, food and alcohol and the gentle teasing aimed at Mayme and Nils. Julia found herself mesmerized by Heep's patter, a modern-day medicine man discoursing on the history of gin, the invention of the martini, the controversial definition of the perfect Manhattan.

He demonstrated, producing pre-chilled mixing glasses, brandied cherries, crushed ice, a dish of perfect lemon peel curls as if by magic. When the serving platter came to her Julia took the shot glass that was less than a quarter full and sipped, trying to taste the nuances Heep was talking about. But there was no hope for it; she had to give up even pretending. Dry vermouth, sweet vermouth, Italian or French vermouth, the infinite variation on rye, and how each one complemented or clashed with a particular variety of bitters.

"I'm going to host a tasting myself," she said aloud to nobody in particular. "And the only alcohol you'll find there will be at the very center of a chocolate truffle."

. . .

DODGE WAS HAVING A GOOD TIME. INTERESTING PEOPLE TO watch, a corner to watch them from, and somebody was always pressing a glass into his hand. And Julia, Julia was a revelation. She was deep in a very serious conversation about the possibility of a Lambert Square Chocolate Festival, but she never left his side and between them her fingers were laced tightly into his. Her pulse ran high and she was flushed with color.

Just the right amount of alcohol made Julia chatty, and she had reached that point now, her free hand moving in the air as she pulled ideas out of nothingness and constructed plans. Her enthusiasm was infectious, but then the room was full of people who were interested directly or indirectly in retail.

"We'll have to come up with a better name," Maude said.

"Death by Truffle," said Caro.

Julia's nose wrinkled. "That's been done to . . . enough."

"Adventures in Truffles. Truffle Adventures."

"Truffle Madness."

Suggestions came fast and fierce but Maude and Julia took turns batting them away.

"All Things Truffle."

"By Their Truffles You Shall Know Them," shouted Heep.

"Truffle Wars."

"The Caged Bird Sings of Truffles."

There was a sudden silence. Julia turned to Dodge as if she had a question to ask, one of great importance, and then a smile broke over her face.

"Truffle Jones."

"Truffle Jones?" Nils asked Mayme. "Who is this Truffle Jones?"

"LRoy won't like it," Caro said. "Not unless you include truffles with fish sauce on the side."

"Oh, LRoy," Maude said, flapping a hand in dismissal. "South Carolina's answer to Woody Allen."

"Woody Allen?" said Nils over the general laughter. "*Bananas*? *Annie Hall*? That Woody Allen? But he's a genius. And what does it mean to say somebody is neurotic, can you tell me? Because Americans use this word a lot."

There was a sudden silence in the room while people glanced at one another, followed by another roar of laughter.

"What?" Nils said. He turned to Mayme. "What?"

"They're laughing because they can't tell you what it means," Mayme said. "One of those words everybody uses but pretty much nobody can define. Mike? Heep? Julia?"

Hands were put up in surrender.

"See?" Mayme said.

"You give up too easily," Maude said. She turned and looked directly at Dodge. "I'll bet you can tell us what it means."

"Arising from inner conflict," Dodge said. His voice sounded very loud in his own ears, or maybe he had just stumbled into one of those sudden quiet moments common to any group gathering. He felt Julia's gaze on him, and Maude's expression was uncharacteristically inscrutable.

"Is that so?" Nils smiled broadly.

Caro said, "My goodness, Dodge, do you have a whole dictionary tucked into your brain?"

No, Dodge thought of saying. *Just a foot firmly stuck in my mouth.* Instead he said: "Crossword puzzles."

Beate said, "So you mean a person who wants two different things at once, things that conflict with one another, that person is neurotic?"

"That's my understanding," Dodge said. Maude had turned away, and what did that mean?

"Well then," Nils said, "I am neurotic and so is almost everybody. Except Mayme."

Mayme's mouth contorted as if she might disagree.

"And then what is psychotic, if we are all neurotic?" Nils turned to Dodge. "Would psychotic be the right term for LRoy?"

"No," Dodge said. "LRoy is cranky. Psychotic is delusional. Hallucinations, paranoia, disorganized thinking."

"Oh," said Caro. "Boo Radley."

"Here we go," said Heep with a nervous laugh. "*To Kill a Mockingbird* as the source of all knowledge and wisdom."

"But everybody gets the blues now and then," said Beate.

"Boo Radley didn't have the blues," said Caro. "Boo Radley had a daddy who locked him up in a dark house and never let him out. Anybody would go a little crazy, stuck inside for years."

There was a clatter of glassware, and Mayme jumped up, brushing at her dress with a napkin. "Oh now, that was purely dumb."

While people passed napkins and advice on how best to get rid of wine stains, Dodge leaned over to Julia.

He said, "Do you mind if we call it a night? I'm still seeing the road in front of me."

Julia didn't seem to mind at all, but Maude was giving him a look that could have cut diamonds.

THEY STOPPED TO GET THE DOGS AND AFTER A LOOP AROUND the park, trouped upstairs to Dodge's apartment. By that time the chilly night air had chased away Dodge's alcohol buzz and seemed to do the same for Julia. Her color stayed high, but she seemed distracted. Twice Dodge said something and she jerked up out of her thoughts to ask him to repeat himself.

The phone started ringing as he opened the door and he sensed Julia stiffening beside him, a rabbit in the headlights. Her stepmother hadn't tried to reach Dodge after that first time, but clearly it was still on Julia's mind.

Then the machine clicked on and his voice with the long greeting he had let himself be pressured into recording—every day he resolved to change it but never quite managed. And then Nora's voice.

"Dodge, if you're there, pick up. There's another little hitch in the Thanksgiving plans. The Colonel wants us to stop on our way down and pick up Grandma Lucy. I think it should be your decision, as you're the one hosting this shindig."

There was a squawk of outraged teenage voices in the background interlaced with enthusiastic barking.

Nora said, "Oh, damnit. Dodge, I'll call you back tomorrow." And the connection cut off.

Julia fell onto the couch and Willie and Scoot immediately began to jockey for position on her lap. Dodge could feel her getting ready to ask a question, and so he sat down beside her to take the lead and get it over with.

"I've been meaning to tell you," he said. "My family is coming here for Thanksgiving. Nora usually hosts it in Brooklyn but things got complicated."

One brow went up. "So who all is coming?"

"Nora, Tom, her kids, my parents. And apparently also my grandmother."

"And Gigi?" She smiled at him, a little playful now. No sign of anxiety, and what did that mean? Dodge had drunk just enough to ask himself questions that he couldn't answer.

"Not this time," Dodge said. "But I'm sure she'll send a box of truffles. You'll have to fight off my sister and her kids for your fair share. They are merciless when it comes to chocolate."

Julia glanced around the apartment. "And they're all staying . . ."

Dodge shook his head. "Not here. I've already booked them into Raddie's Cabins, and we'll eat at Tindell's. I cleared it with Annabeth."

"Okay," Julia said slowly. "Why do you sound so apologetic?"

"Do I?" Dodge tried to sort through what he was feeling, and why it had taken him so long to raise this subject. When was the last time he had introduced a woman he was dating to his family? He had the uneasy feeling he was blocking out the memory because it hadn't gone well.

"I'll stay out of your way, if that's what has got you worried," Julia said. Her tone easy but something wary in her expression.

"Why would I want that?" Dodge said.

She shrugged. "I get the sense you don't like to share too much information with your family. Or maybe it's just your father."

It was an opening she was offering him. *I'd like to hear about your family if you want to tell me.* Dodge examined his own reactions and found he didn't mind. And with Thanksgiving a few weeks away, it was time to fill her in.

She said, "If I told you that every year at Thanksgiving my grandmother got drunk and propositioned my grandfather at the dinner table, would that help at all?"

"An old lady goosing her husband under the table?" Dodge said. "Small potatoes, Jones. You can't do any better than that?"

Julia said, "Who said it was *her* husband she was goosing? Grandmother Hamblin had a wandering eye, and Grandfather Sutherland looked like

Gary Cooper." She bit her lip in a doomed effort to keep from smiling, and then she leaned forward and kissed the corner of his mouth. She smelled of bitters and anise and chocolate. Dodge rubbed a thumb across her cheekbone and she nuzzled into his hand.

He said, "Speaking of propositions."

A HALF HOUR LATER JULIA SAID, "YOU ARE MERCILESS." AND: "How do you do that? How do you read me like that?"

He grinned at her. Sweat moved in rivulets over his face, down his neck into the mat of hair on his chest. She had the taste of it on her tongue, sharp and sweet.

"Jones," he said, his voice hoarse, "you're an open book."

"It's not attractive, you know." She reached for the sheet and he blocked her hand. Julia gave him her most sincere scowl. "That conceited little grin of yours is not in the least attractive. Like a . . . like a . . ."

"Cat who's got into the cream?"

She batted at his head and he laughed, a full laugh from deep in his chest.

"Conceit," she said.

"And how many times did you come?"

She batted at him again and he caught her wrist, held it away. "Lost count, did you?"

What was left to her but surrender? Julia laughed.

"Oh good," Dodge said. "I thought I was going to have to start all over again."

Julia turned on her side. "Now you are bragging. You couldn't do that again."

"You're right," Dodge said. "When I was seventeen I could have, but these days I need a little more time to recoup."

"Hmmmm." Julia burrowed down into the warmth.

Dodge pulled the covers to rights, tucked and smoothed. She hummed in pleasure and satisfaction, her muscles slackening in the heat of his body.

In the dark he gave a short laugh.

She cracked an eye to look at him. "What?"

"You're humming."

"And?"

"Harmonic convergence," he said. "Maude was right."

Julia said, "Maude usually is. I try not to hold it against her."

HE SHOULD HAVE SLEPT, BUT THE MEMORY OF MAUDE'S EXPRESSION kept rousing him to a state of anxious near-wakefulness. As a result he was sluggish and out of sorts, and his mouth tasted like a poorly maintained sandbox. Sometime in the middle of the night his not-quite-asleep mind had settled on a word for that look on Maude's face: accusatory.

Another word occurred to him: paranoia.

He slipped out before Julia woke and the dogs trailed behind him almost on tiptoe, as if they understood the need for silence. They ran into Bean as soon as he came out of the door.

"You looking for these desperadoes?"

She knelt to put leashes on Gloria and Willie, who didn't have the sense to stay close or out of traffic. The dogs were wiggling with excitement, but Bean's face was somber.

"Everything okay?" Dodge asked.

"I'm running behind," Bean said. "Granny Pearl will skin me if I'm late to church."

"Well then, let's get moving," Dodge said.

They weren't even out of Lambert Square before the real reason for Bean's mood presented itself.

"Did you know that Nail the Swede bought the old Larrabee house? The big one with the wraparound porch and an icehouse?"

When she used that particular nickname for Sigridsson her temper had the upper hand.

"I did hear something about that," Dodge said.

Bean said, "Everything's changing, and I don't like it. Not one bit."

Dodge waited to see if she would say anything more, and then he waited a while longer. He caught her glancing at him now and then, her irritation climbing.

"Why do grown-ups lie?"

"Why do kids lie?" Dodge said.

"That's not an answer," Bean said. "Can't you ever just answer a question?"

Dodge considered. Finally he said, "People lie generally because they're afraid of speaking the truth out loud. Afraid of what will happen if they do."

He considered asking her who had been lying to her, and then realized he didn't particularly want to hear the answer.

"You aren't much help," Bean said finally.

"I'm better at listening than giving advice," Dodge said.

Bean snorted.

"But I will make one suggestion. Have you told your mother how you feel?"

Another sharp, disappointed look. "I can't do that."

"Sure you can," Dodge said. "Here, I'll pretend I'm you and you pretend to be your mama." He cleared his throat. "'Mama, I am feeling uneasy about all the time you're spending with Mr. Sigridsson. I wish he would just go away and leave us alone. He's too tall and he's got fish breath and oh yeah, he's white and everybody is talking about you and I don't like it.'"

Bean coughed a surprised laugh and Scoot turned from examining a bush to see if she might need a small, very sincere dog to come to her rescue.

"Did I get it wrong?" Dodge asked.

"Tall is okay," she said. "But he is way white." And then: "He's married already."

Dodge stopped in his tracks. "Nils Sigridsson is married?"

Bean nodded, her mouth pressed tight together.

"Does your mother know? How do *you* know?"

"Mama don't know," Bean said. "I only know because I . . ." She glanced around. "Because I called his house."

"You called his house."

She nodded, studying her shoes.

"Which house is this?"

"Seventeen Hofors, Gävle." She pronounced the words very carefully, as if she had been tutored.

Dodge schooled his expression. "You looked up his address in Sweden—"

"I knew what town he was from," Bean said. "He told us that. And I found the address on the Internet—"

"And you just, called? What happened?"

"A lady answered. And I said, '*Good day, I am looking for Nils.*' In Swedish, I asked Inge Olsen, she's one of the new Kallsjö kids in my grade?

She taught me how to say it. But maybe I didn't say it right because the lady switched to English right away."

"And she said?"

Bean made a miserable face and raised her voice in imitation. "'I'm sorry, dear, Nils is away.' And I said, '*And to whom am I speaking?*' as polite as I could and she said, '*This is his wife. How can I help you?*'"

All that had come out in a rush. Her mouth was trembling as if she might cry, but mostly she looked angry.

"I knew there was something wrong with him," she said. "I knew he was too good to be true."

Dodge ran a hand over his head. "Bean," he said, "did you ever think that maybe the woman you talked to on the phone was his mother?"

Her eyes widened. "She said, 'I am his wife.'"

"Sure. I bet Nils has a father, and I bet he was named after his father."

She blinked at him. "You think?"

"I think," Dodge said, "that you worked yourself up into a state and you were ready to jump to conclusions."

She crossed her arms. "But it still might be true. It might have been his wife."

"Sure," Dodge said again. He sighed as he pulled his cell phone out of his pocket. "And as you are not going to relax until you know the truth, we'll just take a moment here to get to the bottom of this. What's Nils's telephone number?"

She hesitated for a short moment, and gave it to him. Dodge punched in the numbers. It took five rings for Sigridsson to answer.

"*Ja?*"

"Nils, this is Dodge."

"What time is it?"

"It's time for you to answer a question," Dodge said. He schooled his expression for Bean's sake.

"It's not even seven," Nils said. "It's not even seven, on a Sunday morning."

"That's right," Dodge said. "You ready for a question?"

A very deep sigh on the other end of the phone. "Go ahead."

Dodge crouched down so Bean could listen in with him. "What's your father's name, and what does he do for a living?"

"Nils. He's a captain on a tanker. What is this about?"

"A research project," said Dodge. "One last question. Are you now or have you ever been married?"

"No, never," came Sigridsson's increasingly irritated voice. "Is somebody spreading rumors about me? Is somebody carrying lies to Mayme?"

"Nope," Dodge said. "No rumors, no lies, no worries. Go back to sleep."

He shut the cell phone with a snap and gave Bean a smile.

"See?"

She was chewing on her lower lip. "Are you going to tell Mama?"

"Oh no," Dodge said. "But I think you should. If you're worried enough about all this to go searching around the Internet and calling Sweden, I'd say this is something you need to talk to her about. And, when the phone bill comes in she'll be asking some questions anyway."

Bean bit her lip. "I used Nils's cell phone."

Dodge laughed. "You are far too clever for your own good."

"I don't need to talk to Mama," Bean said, a mulish set to her mouth. "I already know what she'd say." Her whole posture changed as she drew herself up.

" 'Little girl, you know I am not going to send the man away. He's good to us and I love him and he bought a big house and you and me are going to live there with him without Granny Pearl because I'ma marry him just as soon as he ask me. White or purple or polka dot, I don't care what people are saying and neither should you. En't I taught you better than that?' "

Her fear and anger came off her small body in waves. Dodge watched her struggle with all of that, more than half expecting tears or hollering or both. But she was her mother's daughter and she pulled herself together.

He said, "Feel good to let that go?"

She nodded, a little reluctantly.

"So maybe it is time to talk to your mama."

"Maybe," she said. "But there's still you to worry about."

"Me?" Dodge stopped. "What did I do?"

Bean looked away, shrugged.

"Did I say something to hurt your feelings?"

For a moment he thought she might actually answer him, but then she straightened her shoulders as if to shake the urge off. She cast him a sidelong glance.

"So are you a Weener or a Walker?"

Dodge wasn't sure about the change in subject, but her expression was so serious she clearly needed an answer.

"I suppose I'd be a Weener if I had a costume."

"I've got a costume for you."

A vague warning bell went off in Dodge's head, but he ignored it. "You do?"

"Uhuh. But you got to let me dress you up without complaining."

Dodge considered. "That embarrassing, huh?"

"Of course not," Bean said. "It's dignified."

"Do I have to wear a dress?"

"I *said* dignified."

"What about a mask, will there be one of those?"

"No," Bean said. "No mask. But there's a fake beard. And I'm not going to tell you anything more about it. You want it or not?"

Dodge considered. A ten-year-old who came up with a costume for a grown man, one who had a beard. Who could that be but Santa Claus? She was unlikely to have ever heard of Rasputin or Walt Whitman, and she wasn't mean enough to dress him up as Abe Lincoln.

"Okay," he said. "But I want to pay you for your trouble."

A big smile broke out over Bean's face. She fished a roll of small plastic bags out of her pocket and thrust it at him. "You pick up today."

"Oh, you are clever," he said. He took the bags and put them in his own pocket. "So when do I present myself for sacrifice?"

"My house right after church," Bean said. "Granny Pearl will have to help. She's looking forward to it."

"I sense I've walked into a trap," Dodge said.

WHEN JULIA CAME DOWN TO OPEN THE SHOP AT NOON, EXA WAS already installed behind the counter and in costume as an aging southern belle straight out of *Hush . . . Hush, Sweet Charlotte*. In her youth, Exa liked to say, she had often been told that she looked like Bette Davis, and it was time to make the most of that resemblance. No doubt she had been working on her dress for weeks, and spent even longer tracking down exactly the right wig with slightly frowsy, very long sausage curls, iron gray. Heavy eyeliner and lipstick applied with a shaky hand completed the effect.

"I was going to carry around a decapitated head," Exa said in all seriousness. "Or at least a hand. You know, from a mannequin, with blood painted on? But I'm saving that for the after-hours party."

Julia was glad Exa's common sense had won out. Once the shops were closed and the customers had gone home, she could go crazy with props. Now Exa made a tour around Julia, her taffeta skirts rustling as she went.

"My my my," she said, putting the tips of her fingers on her cheeks. "Now, this is your fifth Halloween in Lamb's Corner, in't that right? How many of these beautiful suits do you have?"

Julia felt herself flushing with pleasure and affection for Exa, who could be trying in a dozen different ways, and generous in twice as many.

"I don't know," she said. "Maybe a dozen."

"Alls my mama left me when she passed was a parakeet that plucked itself half naked, a lot of bills, and a box full of dud lottery tickets. And here you are with a dozen vintage couture suits that you don't wear but once a year."

While Exa contemplated the vagaries of fate Julia let her mind wander away. Once the tailored jacket and skirt had fit her exactly and now it was a little loose in the waist and bust, but still Julia felt as if she had been trussed like a turkey bound for the oven. This suit, no matter how beautifully designed and made, could never compete with pajamas when it came to comfort.

And then there were the heels, which she'd have to give up before long. When she had been working as a buyer she had often spent twelve- or fourteen-hour days in two-inch heels and never gave them a thought, but that was a habit she had quickly lost and never mourned.

Exa was saying, "You got your fashion sense from your mama."

"Yes," Julia said. "I did. But you're the one who walks away with the first-place prize every year."

Last year Exa had won for her Scarlett O'Hara costume, a southern-belle extravaganza of drapery weight velvet, with a curtain rod that ran along the back of her shoulders and ended in finials and great golden tassels. "Stole from a Carol Burnett skit," Exa had said. "But I don't think she'll mind."

Exa's gaze fixed on something behind Julia, and she turned to look. The first shoppers were drifting into Lambert Square from the parking structure, many of them herding small groups of children in costumes, impatient kids with empty candy bags clutched to their chests.

Julia said, "Supplies on hand?"

"Ready and waiting," Exa said, and she tossed a miniature Kit Kat.

"We're going to get run off our feet today. You up for it?"

Exa fluttered her fingers. "Never underestimate a psycho-biddy. We do it all."

It was easy to lose track of time when the shop was busy, something Julia liked best about being on the floor. People came in empty-handed and went out with a shopping bag or two to make room for the next customers. Except today it didn't work that way. Today her customers didn't leave, they just lined up along the windows to watch Halloween unfolding.

Julia caught a flash of color at the corner of her eye and turned to see Mayme coming across the park. She was wearing a one-piece black leotard that covered her from ankle to wrist, but attached to her shoulders, hips, and hands were silk wings in hot pink, lime green, and deep purple that fluttered with the breeze. Behind her stalked Nils Sigridsson like an overgrown Boy Scout in khaki shorts, regulation blouse complete with a chest band full of badges, and a large butterfly net over his shoulder.

"By golly," said one of the shoppers, turning to Julia. "Y'all sure do know how to throw a party."

"It itches," Dodge said. He lifted a hand to touch the neatly trimmed white beard and mustache that had been glued to his face, but dropped it again. Bean was giving him one of those looks that came straight from her mother.

She said, "Your tie is crooked."

Dodge stopped to look at his reflection in a display window. It had been years since he had last worn a suit and tie, and certainly never one like this. Circa 1940, it had belonged to Bean's grandfather Lewis and smelled of camphor and mothballs. At first sight of it he had put all his hope in the idea that Granny Pearl wouldn't want him wearing her dead husband's best clothes, but the old lady had been as eager as Bean to see him in it. Unfortunately it was a near-perfect fit.

"Stop fussing," she had told him, hands on hips. Granny Pearl was a force of nature, an old black woman who seemed to be afraid of nothing and nobody. Dodge had stopped fussing, and let Bean and her granny dress him up like a mannequin. Granny Pearl had stood back and clucked with satisfaction.

They had combed some kind of white paste into his hair and then slicked it back with Murray's Pomade. The final touch was a pipe and eyeglasses. Small, round, heavy, black. Bean had put them on him and clapped her hands in delight.

"Great," Dodge said. "Except I can't see much."

"You don't have to wear them all the time," Bean said. "But they are just like the portrait." She had found pictures of Sigmund Freud on the Internet and printed them out to show Dodge. The glasses had come from Trudy's Repair and Trade, a jumble of a secondhand store that had clearly done a lot of business in the weeks coming up to Halloween.

Looking at himself in the mirror, Dodge took comfort from one fact: as much as he looked like the portrait of Freud, he doubted anybody would actually recognize who he was supposed to be. But there was still the question of how Bean had arrived at the idea to start with. It was an interesting choice. A disturbing choice, even, but every time Dodge tried to ask Bean about it, she had something far more crucially important to do in another room. Bean's costume involved a carefully draped sheet, a crown of spray-painted ivy, and a torch made out of wood painted white with a fake flame of tissue paper. She made a short but nonetheless convincing Statue of Liberty.

"Let's go," Bean said to him, shivering with excitement. "Let's go to Lambert Square."

TO BEAN'S DISSATISFACTION, DODGE INSISTED ON GOING straight to Scriveners without first stopping at Cocoon. She might even have stayed to argue with him about it, if Nils hadn't come in right after them looking like an overgrown Boy Scout on a mission.

"Dodge," he said, "I am looking for you all over. What was that phone call this morning?"

Bean slipped away before the last word was out of his mouth.

Luckily he was followed very closely by a crowd of kids holding out their goodie bags. Dodge made *sorry can't talk* gestures and by the time the crisis passed, Sigridsson was telling Link—who had shown up as a solo musketeer—about butterflies in Sweden.

The afternoon went on like that, people coming and going. Dodge kept meaning to leave. He wanted to check his e-mail and his phone messages, he had a few other things to do in the office, and sooner or later, he couldn't pretend to himself, he'd have to walk out the door and over to Cocoon. To see the costume Julia had been so secretive about, and to let himself be seen. The things that made him hesitate were small and distinctively odd—Maude's expression the night before, and then Bean's confession that morning. Something in the air, he might have said, if pushed. A sense that things are moving. Planets realigning. Secrets unearthed, and motivations revealed.

THE NEIGHBORS WHO STOPPED BY WERE FULL OF OPINIONS about his costume.

Bo Russell looked him up and down and came to a conclusion. "You're supposed to be that Einstein fella," he said. "But you might could muss up your hair a bit."

Dodge was still laughing when Sue-Ann Landry came in to tell him he was the spitting image of Robert E. Lee, and why hadn't Dodge gone to see her daddy? Joe Don could have put him into a uniform no trouble at all. Mae Oglesby assumed he was supposed to be Walt Whitman, her favorite poet. One of Polly's part-time waitresses came in with her kids and swore he looked just like Santa Claus in *Miracle on 34th Street,* except with better teeth. At three Mike Golden and his daughters showed up. Mike was dressed like a nineteenth-century schoolteacher, suspenders and knee britches and books under his arm, while the girls looked like mirror images of one another in gingham skirts and braids. They followed him around like ducklings.

"Where's your better half?" Link wanted to know.

"Mama's watching the bookstore for Lorna Jean," one of the girls announced. Dodge could not tell them apart, but he thought it was probably Maya who fixed him with a stern eye and said: "She said we should send you over to talk to her. What did you do to make her mad?"

"What did you do?" Mike echoed, looking sincerely interested. They all looked interested, most especially Link.

Dodge said, "I better go find out."

RIVERVIEW BOOKS WAS THE MOST ELABORATELY DECORATED OF all the stores, a South Carolinian version of Martha Stewart's Halloween. Dodge had to duck a bat that swept at his head on a network of threads as he came through the door.

The woman behind the counter was not Marie Antoinette.

"Those awful bustles and heavy skirts," Maude said, anticipating his question. "They always make me change my mind at the last minute."

"So instead you went for . . ." he prompted, and she glanced up from the bowl of candy she was sorting through and then down at herself. Some kind of bush jacket, khaki trousers, a slouch cap.

"Oh," she said, and grabbed up a very large stuffed toy gorilla from behind the counter. She attached the legs around her waist and the arms around her neck with Velcro pads and then struck a pose.

"Sorry," Dodge said.

"Oh, come on," said Maude. "Dian Fossey?"

"The one who was murdered in her bed."

"Trust a man to remember the bloody part," she said. "I got tired of big skirts and makeup." She narrowed her eyes at him. "How'd you come up with that?"

"Bean," Dodge said. "I lost a bet, sort of."

"I can see that. Interesting choice. I see Granny Pearl had a go at you, too."

"They ganged up on me."

"Poor man," said Maude. "So why do I have this sense you haven't been over to see Julia yet?"

"Maybe because I haven't been."

There was a moment's silence.

"You don't want her to look at you and see Dr. Freud, is that it? Afraid she'll figure some things out you'd rather she didn't know?"

Dodge felt his jaw drop.

"Don't look so surprised," Mayor Maude said. "It's just your bad luck that Bean took such an interest. Didn't it occur to you that while she was looking up things in Sweden she might Google your name, too?"

"Start from the beginning," Dodge said, "and explain to me what you think you know."

There wasn't very much to tell, and Maude could be direct as any Yankee when she needed to.

"From what she told me, she found out about you on some page at the Columbia University website."

"Huh," said Dodge. Maude shot him a sharp look.

"Which is why she brought what she found to me. Wanted to know what clinical psychology was, and what *fud* meant. That was her very charming interpretation of Ph.D., in case you're wondering, Dr. Dodge."

Dodge leaned against the door. "So how long have you—"

Maude shrugged. "Yesterday morning. And no, I haven't said anything to anybody at all. Especially not to Julia. I was waiting."

"Waiting for . . ."

"For my superior intelligence and innate good sense to get the upper hand over the urge to kick your butt to Tupelo."

Dodge stood aside so a family of four children and one harried father could come in to collect their treats. Maude was all smiles and praise until the door closed behind them.

Dodge said, "What did you tell Bean?"

"I said people sometimes study to become one thing and then end up being something else. And that she should talk to you directly about all this."

Her look was direct, her mouth drawn into a small purse full of disapproval.

"I was in practice for all of a month," Dodge said. "It's not something I talk about."

There was a long pause while Maude stared off into the shadows at the back of the bookstore. She was stroking the toy gorilla as if it were a child in need of comfort.

She turned to him suddenly. "Have you ever lied to Julia about this?"

Dodge felt the irritation rising in him. "She's never asked."

"So a lie of omission, is what you're saying."

"What exactly is the problem?" Dodge asked. "Why do you care about what I did ten years ago?"

"I could care less," Maude said. "But Julia will care, and you know it. I do care about Julia."

"And I don't?"

"That remains to be seen."

Dodge plucked at a huge display of feathers that had been dyed purple and pink. He forced himself to breathe deeply and to organize his thoughts.

He said, "How does Julia seem to you lately? Compared to a couple of months ago, say."

"Happy," Maude said. "She seems happy. I'd like for her to stay that way, too. For as long as possible. So maybe you better ask yourself if the good you've done her—because you have, I'm not denying that, you've done her a world of good—is going to survive this secret you've been keeping."

The things that came to mind, the things Dodge wanted to say, would sound defensive. He turned to leave and then hesitated.

"Will Bean—" He stopped.

"Bean won't say anything to Julia," Maude said. "Neither will I. This is your mess to fix."

"Maude," Dodge said, his irritation billowing up and out, "you know I am not out to hurt the woman. Just the opposite."

Her expression softened a little. "Well, good," she said, and summoned up a half smile. "You know I must believe you, because if I didn't I'd have already smacked you so hard you'd be coughing up bones."

JULIA SAID, "THAT'S NOT MUCH OF A COSTUME. WHITE HAIR AND an old suit?"

"There was a beard," Dodge said, rubbing his cheek. "But it was itchy." He looked at Bean directly. "Sorry, kid, but the glue was starting to give me hives."

Bean huffed her disappointment. A surly Statue of Liberty clutching a sagging bag of candy. Julia rubbed Bean's shoulder. "What was he supposed to be?"

Bean shrugged. "It's not important."

Julia gave Dodge a look that meant he had hurt the kid's feelings and should be making amends.

"It was a great costume," Dodge said. "She did a lot of research. Looking things up on the Internet and all. Amazing the stuff you find on the Internet."

Bean shot him a scowl, one that made it clear that she knew they were at an impasse. If she wanted to bring up the subject of Freud, she'd also have to do some talking about her research on Sweden.

"Come on, Bean. Who is he supposed to be?" Julia said.

"Abe Lincoln," Bean said. "What he would have looked like as an old man."

LAMBERT SQUARE WAS PRETTY MUCH DESERTED AS THEY MADE their way across the park to the Old Foundry. Bean trailed behind with her sour mood out for the world to see. Julia wondered what was going on between her and Dodge, because something wasn't right.

"Sounds like the party is well under way," Dodge said beside her.

The windows of the community center were lit up. Julia saw Dan Harris dance by in his Captain Hook costume. There was a rumor that T.J. was going to come as Tinker Bell, which would be very funny and cause a great deal of trouble down the line.

She said to Dodge, "You and I are going to stand out for our excessive—"

"Sobriety? Formality?" He took her hand and tucked it into the crook of his arm. "You look fantastic. Don't worry, Jones. I've got your back."

Julia took a deep breath and held it for a moment, trying to make sense of what she was feeling. A little sleepy after a long day but not tired, at least not so tired that she wasn't looking forward to the Weener Party. A social activity, where she would talk to people she liked and eat more than she should and maybe drink enough to feel lightheaded so that when she danced with Dodge—she had a sense that he could dance, that they would dance very well together—she wouldn't bother with being nervous or self-conscious or embarrassed.

Bean ran ahead and disappeared inside, leaving Julia and Dodge alone at the very edge of the park, opposite the old wrought-iron gates that opened onto River Road. There was a moon, not quite round, half hidden by clouds. And there was a bench. A simple bench like all the benches scattered through the park, but this one placed a little differently. You could sit on this bench and have all of Lambert Square disappear behind you.

Julia watched herself sit down. She felt the cold painted slats of the bench press against her back and thigh. She felt Dodge next to her. Shoulder to shoulder, hip to hip, palm to palm, lower arms and fingers entwined. Looking out toward the river and the park that ran along it they might have been anywhere on a crisp fall night.

"Look," Dodge said. "The Walkers."

At the head of the procession a solemn older man carried a poster, carefully lettered with luminescent paint that caught the candlelight:

No Mask
Can Hide
Your Sin
From God

The procession passed, adults and children with candles, small trembling lights like the rise and fall of fireflies. They went quietly save for an occasional voice. A little boy asking a question, an adult voice, lower, in answer.

Julia started to get up but Dodge squeezed her hand gently and pointed with his chin.

The last person in the procession was a girl of eleven or twelve, caught in the shadows between not-child and not-woman. By candlelight her face glowed, a pearly oval bisected by the line of her brow and mouth. Not pretty, not plain, hardly corporeal, she seemed to be dancing. Small hops and turns that sent her hair flying around her like a veil, she spun in place and then leaped forward. As if she were alone. As if she weren't the last in a long procession, but first in a new one, just imagined.

38

This is John Dodge . . .

Dodge? Son, this is Pastor Honeywell from First Methodist. Do you have plans for Thanksgiving? Because if you don't, my wife and I would love to have you join us after services. You might could bring a guest. Give us a call anytime.

This is John Dodge . . .

This is Trixie, Dodge. You know I'm going to my sister's place in Columbia for Thanksgiving? She's not much of a cook but turkey is an overrated bird anyway, seems to me. Anyway you're welcome to come along and listen to our old-lady gossip if you like. I'm putting this on your answer machine so you don't have to feel embarrassed about saying no.

Julia finished pulling on a sock and looked at Dodge, who was leaning over the phone as he listened to his messages. A coldish Saturday morning, overcast. The kind of day best spent sleeping in front of a fire, with a book in your lap. But it was also the last weekend before Thanksgiving and business would be brisk, orders coming in from all over the country. People who wanted fancy tablecloths and damask napkins for their Thanksgiving tables, but who had waited too long and were looking the possibility of polyester in the face. She did a lot of business around this holiday. It was such a big weekend that Dodge was even sticking around. Not, she reminded herself, that it bothered her when he was gone.

She said, "You haven't told people yet about your family coming?"

He lifted a palm and grinned at her over his shoulder.

Two more invitations to Thanksgiving dinner. Julia chided herself for feeling left out; she had spent her first year here discouraging people from inviting her to anything at all. Then an unfamiliar voice, distinctly New England.

This is John Dodge . . .

Dodge, this is Hannah. Why haven't I heard from you in so long? Never mind, I've got something you won't be able to resist. An old movie theater in Burlington. Built 1919, still has all the original detail work and one of those old-fashioned ticket booths, green marble and scrollwork. Seats three hundred. The original organ is still there though it probably doesn't work. The place has been boarded up more than ten years, trouble with the estate that's just about fixed now. It needs a good deal of work to bring it up to code so the bank will be eager to get rid of it. You remember I showed you Burlington that time? College town on Lake Champlain, tough winters but full of kids who will stand in line to see old French movies on a big screen. And it's not so far from Boston. I have a feeling it's going to go fast. You know where to reach me if you're interested.

Dodge was taking notes furiously, his forearms on the little table that served as a desk. Then he pushed the pause button, but he didn't turn around right away.

Julia's voice sounded thin to her own ears. "That sounds interesting."

"Maybe," Dodge said. "You never know until—"

"Until you've seen it," she finished for him. She cleared her throat. "I didn't realize you started looking for the next project so early. You've been here, what—"

"About three months."

He looked as uncomfortable as a man could look, but whether that was the fact that she had overheard the real estate offer or the familiar tone in the agent's voice, that was unclear.

Dodge said, "See you later?"

A flush ran up her back, surprise and irritation. "Sure. I didn't mean to intrude." She was through the door in a split second, the dogs behind her. Scoot, too, without being called, and Julia's throat closed in some emotion she couldn't put a name to.

Oh, wait: thankfulness. She was thankful to a dog for taking her side in a nonexistent argument. Another wave of emotion, and this time she recognized it for what it was immediately: embarrassment.

"THAT WENT WELL." DODGE WAS TALKING, HE REALIZED IT TOO late, to nobody: Scoot had left with Julia. To be walked, because Bean hadn't showed up, which was something that happened very rarely. He wondered if she had decided to act like a kid for once and sleep in on a Saturday morning. Something he wished now that he had done.

Dodge pushed the play button and the next message started.

This is John Dodge . . .

Mr. Dodge, this is Bean calling. I am calling to say two things. First, Mr. Sigridsson is leaving for Sweden tomorrow because somebody important died and Miss Beate is sending him to take over the main office. Second thing is, it sounds like he won't be coming back. And one more thing: I told you so. Didn't I tell you so?

"Well, shit."

Dodge took his jacket from the hook on the door and headed out. Where exactly he wasn't sure. He couldn't show up at Granny Pearl's at eight on a Saturday morning, and what would he say, anyway? I want to talk to Bean, she's hurting. As if they didn't know. As if he had any role to play beyond that of a casual friend.

Somehow or another he had managed to piss off Julia and fail Bean before he even had any coffee. When had Bean left that message, anyway? Last night, most likely, while he and Julia were sitting in the Rose Theater watching *The Quiet Man*.

Whatever he was going to do, it would have to wait until he had had some food. Dodge headed for Polly's.

HE WAS SITTING DOWN WHEN HE SAW BEATE AND NILS AT A table on the other side of the room. There were papers spread out on the table, coffee cups, cell phones. Dodge's own cell phone began to ring but he ignored it and walked over to the Swedes.

Beate looked frazzled, but she managed a small smile in response to Dodge's nod.

"I hear you're headed back to Sweden, what, today?"

Nils took a moment to swallow the last of his coffee. "Today, *ja*. I have to leave for the airport in an hour."

Beate stood up. "Before you read him a sermon, you should know that he's going away because I send him away. This is a business I am running, you know. Not a dating service." And she stalked off, five feet of aggravated Swedish industrialist, her five-hundred-dollar, three-inch heels tapping an impatient rhythm.

Dodge sat down. They were quiet while Polly poured coffee. Even Polly was quiet, uncharacteristically so. Her mouth was pressed hard together.

"Everybody is hating me now," Nils said.

"I'm not exactly popular right at this moment, either," Dodge said.

"Because I'm leaving," Nils said. "Because I have to go, and I said I'd stay."

"So Mayme is—"

"You know how a woman gets that look, the one that says you're exactly as bad as she knew you'd be?"

Dodge wasn't sure he did know, but he nodded.

"*Ja,* well, that was Mayme last night. It would have been much better if she had yelled."

"So what are you going to do about it?"

Nils lifted a shoulder. "This is what Mayme was asking me. But it is my profession, my life's work. I like what I do and I'm very good at it. Beate needs me in Stockholm, I go to Stockholm."

"And Mayme stays here."

Something flashed in Sigridsson's eyes. He said, "Mayme will not come with me, this I know."

"So you know this without asking," Dodge said. "That's convenient. A great superpower to have, omniscience. Relieves you of so many difficult conversations."

Sigridsson was scowling at him. He used his hands to push himself up and scanned the café, and then he called out.

"*Gustav! Du vet det här engelska ordet* omniscient? *Vad betyder det om han kallar mig för det?*"

There was a brief but noisy conversation at the far table, and then the answer came back in multiple voices.

"*Du är en besserwisser. Han säger att du är ensjälvgod tråkmåns.*"

Sigridsson's eyebrows shot up. "You think I'm a conceited bore?"

Dodge coughed. "No. What I'm trying to say is that you're jumping to conclusions and making decisions for other people—for Mayme—based on those conclusions."

There were many irritating things about Sigridsson, but Dodge liked the fact that he was willing to laugh at himself. Except just now. Just now he looked plain mad.

Dodge wondered if a good astrologist might be able to explain exactly what was going on today in Lambert Square.

"So you think I don't know Mayme?"

"Listen," Dodge said. "You're the one who claimed she wouldn't want to go to Sweden, without ever asking her. My sense is that you're not so sure yourself you'd want her there, not if her daughter and mother are part of the bargain. Am I wrong?"

The broad mouth contorted. Nils looked away and back again. "You have met Pearl? You can imagine her in Stockholm?"

"It's not my imagination we're talking about," Dodge said. He drank the last of his coffee and stood up.

"Have a good trip. Hope to see you back here."

Nils snorted into his empty coffee cup.

As soon as he was out of the café Dodge pulled out his cell phone. Nora had tried to get him, but that could wait. He dialed Cocoon, and got Mayme on the phone first thing.

She said, "How can I help you, Mr. Dodge?"

Not a good sign.

"So, Maymie, darlin," Dodge said. "How're things?"

"Kind of you to ask," Mayme said, her tone sweetly sharp. "I'm very well, thank you."

"And Bean?"

A slight hesitation. "Mama is keeping Bean home today. She's a little under the weather."

"She left me a telephone message," Dodge said.

Another pause, this one slightly longer. "Did she?"

"I'm worried about her."

"She's ten years old," Mayme said. "Children her age don't cope well with disappointment. She'll be fine in a day or two."

"And you? Will you be fine?"

"Of course," she said. "Why wouldn't I be?"

Dodge heard Exa huffing in disbelief, and then he heard the dial tone.

JULIA HOLED HERSELF UP IN HER OFFICE FOR MOST OF THE morning, her mind trained resolutely on her accounts, no room for consideration of telephone messages that were none of her business. When it was finally time for her weekly meeting with Leo, she went down to his cubbyhole and dropped into a chair, ready to be distracted. Leo handed her a sheaf of papers and she spent five minutes running her eyes down columns, trying to concentrate on numbers while Leo played an impromptu drum solo on the corner of his desk.

She glanced up and he stopped abruptly.

"October was good, huh?"

"Very good," Julia said. "I've got a lot of stock coming in but it may not be enough to see us through the holidays."

"So can you give me any more hours? I finished the website for Scriveners, and now Dodge'll only need me like an hour a week. There are some things I could do for your website, speed it up a little bit."

Julia sat back. "You've been working a lot lately."

"Every minute I can," Leo agreed. "Saving up."

Julia said, "That was quick. The website for Dodge, I mean."

Leo turned to his keyboard, tapped out a few words, then tilted his monitor so she could see it.

"Have a look."

Leo was good at what he did, and he knew it. The website was elegant and streamlined, easy to use. Shades of sepia and cream with an occasional splash of strong color. Photographs of the storefront and the counter area, also in sepia. Another photo of Heep in his workshop. Links to schedule a repair estimate, talk to a salesperson, get directions. Leo scrolled through pages of specific pens, each of them with a long description, with links to a glossary of terms. Along one edge a faded, full-length shot of Link talking on the telephone. That photo was a masterstroke, any way you looked at it. Link looked the part of the quirky pen specialist in his suspenders and bow tie, a little worn around the edges.

"Sales more than doubled since it went live," Leo said, with justifiable pride. "Hits are through the roof, and once the forum is up and running—you'd be surprised at how much people can talk about ink and paper—my guess is sales will double again. Not even Link can argue with that."

"But I bet he's sad to lose the interns."

The muscles in Leo's jaw rolled, but he didn't rise to the bait. Julia was a little embarrassed to have been angling that way when really what she was wondering was why Dodge hadn't told her how far along he was with his overhaul. Maybe his mind had been on something else, or better said, somewhere else, due north, on the shores of a lake she would never see. With a woman who had interesting things to show him.

Julia said, "I better get busy."

"Busy is good," Leo said, his gaze wandering back to the computer screen. "Sometimes busy is the only good thing."

Just yesterday Julia would have agreed with Leo. She had been seeing Dodge pretty much every weekday since Halloween. They were comfortable with each other, could talk about almost anything. Or at least, she had believed they could.

"You okay?" Leo was watching her. "You look as though you just bit down on a lemon."

"I'm okay," Julia said. "I've just got a lot on my mind."

"Oh yeah," Leo said. "Mayme and all that."

"All what?" Julia asked, alarmed. And Leo told her.

. . .

MAYME SAID, "I REALLY, REALLY DON'T WANT TO TALK ABOUT this."

She had come into Julia's office reluctantly and stood with her back against the closed door, arms folded tightly across her middle.

"Mayme," Julia said, "I just want to know what's going on so I can ignore the rumors."

Mayme pursed her lips and then pushed out a breath. "What is there to tell? Nils has been transferred back to Stockholm for at least three months, maybe for good."

Julia watched Mayme's expression, but there was no emotion to read there. She had clamped down hard.

"He didn't have a choice?"

"There's always a choice," Mayme said, a hint of bitterness creeping in.

Julia had her doubts in this situation, but her loyalties were to Mayme. She was about to say just that when Mayme jerked and turned, as if she had come to a sudden decision.

She said, "I've only got myself to blame. I let my guard down, I let myself get caught up in his . . . his . . . his . . ." Her voice wavered. "His goddamn cheerful optimistic bullshit. That's a mistake I won't make again. I wish I could handle this the way you do, but it's beyond me."

A pulse jumped in Julia's throat. "What do I handle?"

"Men," Mayme said. "You take what you need and then you say good-bye with a smile, and you mean it."

And she opened the door with a jerk, to find Nils Sigridsson standing there, his fist in the air, ready to knock.

THAT NIGHT OVER SUPPER DODGE SAID, "YOU'VE BEEN QUIET. What's on your mind?"

"Just shop stuff," Julia said. "And Mayme."

There was a longer silence while Dodge worked his way through the bowl of chili and thought about what to say. It was a delicate business, and truth be told, he didn't want any part of it, though he wouldn't relax until he saw Bean for himself and knew she was going to be all right.

"I think he asked Mayme to go to Sweden with him," Julia said. "He came in just before he left for the airport and they spent a half hour in my office, talking."

"Aha," Dodge said. "Well, good."

Julia's gaze shifted from her plate to his face. "Good?"

"Good that he came out and asked her. Isn't it?"

"I'm not sure," Julia said. "Why would Mayme want to move to Vermont?" And then a rush of color moved up her throat. "To Sweden. Don't read anything into that."

"Into what?" Dodge said, and came up with an easy grin. "Did Mayme tell you that she wouldn't want to go to Sweden?"

Julia gave him an impatient look. "It's obvious."

"Really? I'm not sure. Everybody seems to think they know what Mayme wants."

Julia folded her arms. "I can tell you what she doesn't want. To uproot her kid and her mother and move halfway across the world to a place that is ninety-nine point nine percent white. Vermont, Sweden, it's all the same."

Dodge could see that in this particular conversation, retreat was the only real option. He could see also that Julia wasn't going to let him do that. For once she was walking right into a confrontation instead of running away from it.

He said, "Who are you mad at?"

It slowed her down for the space of a heartbeat, and then she came right back at him.

"I hate the way people can't keep their word," she said. "And I hate that expression on your face. Say whatever you've got on your mind, would you? Spit it out."

Dodge took a deep breath. He said, "I'm wondering how it is that I broke my word. Specifically."

She looked him directly in the eye. "Nils says he's come back here for good, and look, he's gone already. You say you'll give Scriveners a year and a half, but three months in you're looking for something else."

Dodge wished at that moment that his phone would ring, that something would interrupt long enough to give him a chance to think through his choices. His very limited choices. Once he wouldn't have hesitated to take advantage of this break in Julia's self-discipline, to edge her toward acknowledging the things she had been hiding from herself. But he wasn't a clinician anymore, and Julia wasn't his patient. She was the woman he was dating. A woman he liked a great deal, one who interested him and made him laugh.

He said, "Listen, Jones. I haven't started looking. I do have long-standing business relationships with commercial real estate brokers in a lot of different places. I get calls three or four times a month about things they think might interest me. Almost always I'm not interested."

"So Hannah is just a real estate broker, and you're not in the least interested in that movie theater. Give it up, Dodge. I saw your expression."

"I'm not interested in Hannah," Dodge said. "But the movie theater is worth looking into. I might buy the place and leave it just as it is until I'm done with Scriveners. But it's not likely."

She turned her head hard to the side, as if she didn't want to see his face, or have him see hers.

"And if I might point out," Dodge said, "Nils didn't want to go, and he'll try to find a way to come back."

"You don't *get* it," Julia said. "He made promises. He bought a house. He wooed Granny Pearl, for God's sake. He made Mayme feel safe and happy when she thought that would never happen, and then he . . ." She broke off and shook herself. "But once they leave, they're gone. How is she ever going to trust him again?"

Dodge drew in a sharp breath and she raised her head to look at him.

He said, "Who exactly are we talking about? It's not Nils or me, is it?"

Julia gave him a look that made Dodge draw back a little. Her face contorted with pain and anger, nothing hidden away, no defenses. Then she stood up, arms crossed, and walked out of her kitchen. Dodge heard the bathroom door close.

Under the table Scoot gave an anxious little whine, echoed immediately by Gloria and Boo. Willie yelped his highest, shrillest bark. All of them looking at him, clumsy brute that he was to have upset the Alpha Woman and made her go away. Lips curled in disgust.

Then something hit the bathroom door so hard that it shuddered, and all the dogs crowded under the table together.

"She throws things when she's mad, huh." Dodge reached down and rubbed Gloria's head. Willie tried to climb into his lap, but Scoot had already put down a claim and wasn't budging. Dodge tucked Willie into the crook of his arm.

Another thump, book-like, followed in quick succession by what Dodge assumed to be the pile of novels she kept next to her bathtub.

"Jones!"

"What!"

"You're scaring the dogs."

The door opened a crack and the dogs raced over to disappear one by one into the bathroom. Then the door closed with a click.

Dodge got up and did the dishes. When they were dried and put away, when he had cleaned the sink and swept the floor and the kitchen was in perfect order, he stood very still and listened. No sound from the bathroom at all.

"I'm going back to my place."

"Good idea." Her voice was hoarse.

"Come over later?"

"I doubt it. I need some time."

But the door opened far enough to let Scoot out, and closed softly behind him.

Dodge was in a thoughtful mood as he walked back to his place. Julia usually held her temper in a headlock, but it had got away from her. Because people couldn't keep their promises. Because Mayme and Bean were hurting. Because there was a movie theater in Vermont that threatened the timetable she used to structure her life. Because she didn't want to deal with the idea of him leaving, just yet. Because Charlie had left her.

There was little comfort he could offer her and no guarantees. The truth was, the timetable she depended on was as fragile as any other sandcastle. If he left for Vermont tomorrow or never, if he stayed in Lambert Square exactly fifteen months and then left as he had planned to do, nothing would feel right.

Scoot trotted beside him, alert as ever. Dodge wished he had as much confidence in where he was going.

JUST TWO MESSAGES ON THE PHONE THIS TIME. HE WOULD HAVE ignored them but a look at caller ID told him Nora was still trying to get in touch. Dodge pushed the button and collapsed on the couch to listen.

This is John Dodge . . .

Uncle Dodge, this is your favorite niece Maddie Bugiardini. Mama says I can come down early on Amtrak if I want to and if you say yes. Because I got suspended from school and she might just have to kill me if I hang around the house. It was a matter of conscience, and I'm not sorry. So I'll be coming into Columbia Sunday evening—the day after tomorrow, two in the afternoon. Unless you call back right away and tell me not to. And that would be really, really disappointing because I need to talk to you. You are my favorite uncle, you know. Though you shouldn't say so in front of the Bugiardini uncles, there might be some backlash. See you the day after tomorrow.

This is John Dodge . . .

Dodge, please let her come. I wouldn't do well in prison. And as I'm sure she didn't tell you why she got suspended, let me fill you in. She wore a Lick Bush Beat Dick *T-shirt over her uniform blouse because they were having a visiting speaker who happened to be a Republican. All this at St. Bart's, let me remind you. You can put her to work scrubbing toilets if you like. In fact, that sounds like a good idea to me.*

He dialed Nora from memory, got a wrong number. Checked caller ID and tried again.

"Finally. You don't answer your cell phone anymore?"

"One of those days. I got Maddie's message. I'm sorry I wasn't here."

"Don't be," Nora said. "Wait until she gets there, then you'll have plenty of room for sorry."

"She's coming anyway?"

"As planned," Nora said, a bit of a satisfied smirk in her tone. "She's all yours until we get there on Wednesday evening."

Dodge hesitated. "You're telling me this is a done deal? She's on the train."

"That's what I'm telling you. She gets into Columbia at two tomorrow afternoon. You did tell her she was welcome anytime."

"So I did," Dodge said. "I'll find some way to keep her busy, I guess."

There was a short silence. Nora said, "I sense some trouble."

"The Swede got called back to Stockholm," Dodge said. "There is some unhappiness. Bean is in hiding."

Nora made all the right sounds while Dodge told her the story, starting back with Bean's furtive phone call to Sweden before Halloween.

"You think he's for real?" Nora said. "He didn't engineer the transfer to escape?"

"I think he's for real," Dodge said. "It's hard to fake that kind of unhappiness."

"You don't sound too cheerful yourself."

"I'm more cheerful than Nils Sigridsson, that much is sure. I had better get going if I'm going to make this place suitable for Maddie."

For some reason, Nora found that especially funny.

IT TOOK A COUPLE HOURS TO CLEAN THE KITCHEN AND BATHroom and put the apartment in order. He found the inflatable mattress in the spare bedroom, the one he had brought with him across the country. The whole time he lectured himself: there was no cause for worry. He could take on a seventeen-year-old for three days. Twice he thought he heard Julia on the stairs, and twice he went to check, only to admit that he was indulging in wishful thinking.

At one he took a shower and debated with himself the whole time whether he should pick up the telephone and see how she was doing.

Three months, minus the ten days she had gone on strike. He had seen her in every kind of mood, high and low, but he had rarely—never, he corrected himself—never seen her truly angry or embarrassed. Julia had a natural dignity; she wore it like a magic cape. Until tonight, and that simple slip of the tongue.

Why would she want to move to Vermont?

The thing to do, Dodge reasoned to himself, was to call as he would any other night. See what she was doing, if he should come over or, more likely, if she wanted to come sleep in his bed.

Except she didn't answer. When the machine picked up, Dodge hung up and went to the window. He could imagine her sitting there in the dark in her crowded parlor, awake. As aware of him as he was of her.

He dialed again, and this time when the machine picked up he left a message.

Jones. Sorry I missed you. See you tomorrow.

SCOOT WOKE DODGE AT SEVEN BY NIPPING AT HIS EAR. A WARNING not to be ignored, so he rolled out of bed, found his jeans, pulled on a sweatshirt, stepped into his shoes, and headed out, Scoot dancing impatiently beside him.

There was a light rain falling, chill enough to make Dodge think about turning back for a jacket. But Scoot didn't hesitate. Scoot didn't care about the rain or how a human being might suffer in the cold; Scoot cared only about the park, and he dashed away before Dodge could call out to stop him.

Up to the day he went off to college, Dodge had started every morning with a cold shower. It was one of the Colonel's many rules for healthy living, and Dodge had given it up immediately and with great satisfaction. Now he dashed back up the stairs and back down again, pulling his hood up as he jogged out into the park.

He whistled for Scoot. Whistled again, picking up his pace. Made a circuit around the fountain calling, and then headed toward River Road, his throat suddenly dry. Early on a Sunday morning there was little traffic and no sign of a small black-and-white dog nosing through the bushes. Dodge broke into a jog and caught a flash of red ahead of him on the path, the smooth curve of an umbrella. He cupped his hands around his mouth and called, and Bean stopped and turned. The dogs broke into a run and came toward him. Scoot front and center.

When Bean came up she said, "He was waiting at Julia's door when I came down. Maybe I shouldn't have let him come."

"No harm done," Dodge said. He used a sleeve to wipe his face, wet with rain and sweat.

They walked along quietly while Dodge's pulse slowed down to something near normal. Bean glanced at him now and then, as if she wanted to say something but didn't know where to start.

Dodge said, "I'm sorry, Bean. I feel like I gave you bad advice about Nils."

She lifted one shoulder in a shrug.

For a moment Dodge was at a loss, trying to remember what he had meant. What had he been trying to accomplish? An intelligent kid who missed her father, who needed a friend. Had he promised her some kind of happy ending?

She said, "It's not anybody's fault. Not even Mr. Sigridsson's. Mama says he didn't want to go but he'd get fired if he didn't. Do you think that's true?"

Dodge drew in a deep breath. "That's what he told me, and I believed him."

Bean said, "Mama used to be mad all the time, you know? And then she wasn't. He made her happy."

Dodge waited, but Bean had said everything she wanted to say. They walked back toward Lambert Square in a companionable silence.

Finally he said, "My niece is coming in late this afternoon. I think you'll like her."

Bean perked up at the idea of a seventeen-year-old from New York City who would be spending a full week in Lambert Square. Her questions tumbled over one another, everything from the color of Maddie's hair to her favorite kind of ice cream and whether she had any tattoos. She was still coming up with questions when they got to the fountain.

"Ask your mama if you can come over after school tomorrow," Dodge said. "Then you can show Maddie all around, ask questions until there's nothing left to know. I'll take the dogs up to Julia, save you the trip."

Bean stopped, her expression blank. "Julia isn't home," she said. "I've got the dogs for the day. You didn't know?"

HE DIDN'T KNOW. JULIA HAD PULLED OFF ONE OF HER SUNDAY disappearances, right under his nose. The first whole weekend Dodge had spent in Lamb's Corner in six weeks, and Julia took off. While he stripped out of his wet clothes and changed, while he fed Scoot and made coffee, he thought it through.

It was really very simple: she felt pushed, and so she ran. No, that wasn't quite right: he pushed, and she ran. The question was, where had she run to?

Dodge finished his coffee, and after a moment's consideration of the time, he picked up the phone and called Mayor Maude to ask her for her master key.

She said, "You haven't come clean yet, have you? Or maybe you have, maybe that's why she's gone into hiding."

Dodge took the master key Maude was holding out. "I was planning on having that conversation last night but Swede the Nailer got in my way."

Her mouth contorted. "Sounds like a rationalization to me. And I'm not so sure this is such a good idea. There's a reason she goes to ground, you know."

Dodge had begun second-guessing himself the minute he got off the phone, and now that the first flush of—what? anger? worry? was gone, he knew she was right. He looked at the key in his hand, and handed it back to her.

"I have to go to Columbia anyway."

Some of the stiffness went out of Maude's face. She said, "I know you're worried about her, but I also know she always comes back. Wherever she is, she's safe, and she'll be back. Now, can I have some of that coffee before I have to go off to church? Because otherwise I'm going to fall asleep and embarrass my girls."

They drank coffee at his kitchen table and kept the talk light. Business trends in Lambert Square. People moving back to town to take up jobs at Kallsjö after years of exile in Columbia or Atlanta. The strain on the infrastructure, and how much of that would be covered by Kallsjö's tax bill. Relatives coming in for Thanksgiving: Mike's father and sister from Manhattan, her own father from Florida, a bevy of aunts and cousins. The Dodge clan. He told her about Maddie and the T-shirt debacle, a story Maude appreciated as she had three strong-willed girls of her own.

"There's no shortage of stubborn females in Lamb's Corner," Dodge agreed. Maude looked down into her coffee cup. They were both thinking about Nils, but the things Dodge wanted to say were for Mayme and Bean. It occurred to him that Maude might be the best way to pass those things along.

He said, "For what it's worth, I think he'll come back if he can. If she'll have him at that point."

Maude's head came up sharply. "Of course she'd have him. The woman is cross-eyed with wanting him back. I should have thought you'd see that for yourself."

"Probably I could," Dodge said, "if I let myself look that close. But I gave that up a long time ago."

"Not all the way, you didn't." Her gaze was unblinking.

"Not all the way," Dodge agreed.

"You seem to know what Nils wants," Maude said. "Do you know what you want for yourself?"

"You mean, other than out of this conversation?" He grinned at her. His best grin, the one that was meant to distract, but Maude would have none of that. She raised a brow and waited.

"I'm not sure I do," he said finally.

"Hmmmm," Maude said.

"You're going to get along with my sister," Dodge said. "You've got a lot in common."

JUST WHEN DODGE WAS THINKING ABOUT LEAVING TO PICK UP his niece he got a phone call from Leo, who wanted to let him know that the Scriveners website had gone down for about a half hour but was up and running again, no data lost. And had he looked at the numbers over the last few days? A big-name columnist had mentioned Scriveners on his web blog and the traffic had tripled within a few hours.

Dodge asked the questions that came to mind, but he had considerable confidence in Leo's work and other things on his mind. As should Leo.

"Nothing better to do on a Sunday afternoon?"

"Not really."

For the fiftieth time that day, Dodge went to the window to look across the square to Julia's apartment. Nothing to see, no signs of life.

He said, "You want to take a ride to Columbia, pick up my niece from the Amtrak station?"

"You've got a niece?"

"She's just the advance party. The whole crowd will be showing up later in the week. So you have time to pick her up?"

"I'd have to borrow your car. Unless you want her on the back of my Harley."

"I'm on my way with the keys," Dodge said. "But just so we understand each other, you get amorous with my niece, I'll have to do some serious damage to that pretty face of yours."

Leo drew in a breath. Not a laugh, exactly, but something he had stopped himself from saying. He cleared his throat. "How will I recognize her?"

"I doubt you'll have much trouble. Look for a leggy, dark-haired Madonna type with a Brooklyn accent."

"Madonna?" Leo said, his voice wavering a little. "Are we talking 1980s pop Madonna?"

"No," Dodge said. "We're talking the Madonna you see in old paintings. If all else fails, her name is Magdalene Bugiardini, but everybody calls her Maddie."

"What are you going to be doing?" Leo asked. "Instead of picking up Maddie-not-Madonna?"

"Company coming," Dodge said. "Shopping to do."

IT WAS A LIE, OF COURSE. THERE WAS PLENTY OF FOOD IN THE apartment and no doubt they would eat a lot of their meals at Polly's anyway. Once Leo had taken off, Dodge took Scoot for a walk. Through the park, around the outer perimeter of Lambert Square, and up and down the halls of the open buildings.

The community center was being used for a meeting of the theater guild, and while Dodge couldn't imagine Julia up on a stage, he slipped into the back to listen to a fairly heated argument about the virtues and demerits of modern playwrights and what was wrong with the tried and true, anyway? You could never go wrong with Tennessee Williams, and lest everybody forget what happened the last time they did a musical . . .

There were at least thirty people, but Dodge knew only a few of them. Link and Joe Don and Miles, one of the security guards who spent most of his time sleeping in the information kiosk. Lydia Montgomery was sitting right next to Maude and taking notes.

He left quietly, before Maude could catch sight of him and decide to draft him into the proceedings. Scoot was waiting for him in the hallway, alert and perfectly still, in spite of the foot traffic. There were a few tourists looking at the enlargements of old photographs, grim-faced men in uniform, startled children on the front porch of the big house at Langtree, men and women in the fields. A half dozen others in front of the funny money exhibit, marveling at the audacity it must have taken to draw an exact duplicate of an 1879 twenty-dollar bill with nothing but pen, ink, ruler, and compass.

Dodge stopped outside the suite of offices that represented the entire city government: finance, tax, parks and recreation, planning, public works, office of the mayor. All handled by three full-time and three part-time employees, half of them elected. He cupped his hands and looked into the shadowy interior beyond the receptionist's desk. Nothing to see, no sign of light or movement. Bean thought this was where Julia came on her Sunday walkabouts. She might be sleeping on the couch in Maude's office, right now. That seemed unlikely to Dodge, given the fact that the building was in such heavy use, but he knocked and waited.

Unless she was hiding out in one of the closed shops, Julia wasn't anywhere in Lambert Square. Wherever she had gone, it had taken her outside her sphere of comfort. Which made Dodge wonder how much he really understood about her at all.

In the commotion of Maddie's arrival a dozen stories had to be told, preferably all at once, the unpacking of enough clothes for a month, books and notebooks, CDs and an assortment of electronic devices, makeup and six different kinds of shampoo, Dodge lost track of time.

Her parents had dubbed her Hurricane Maddie, the kid who walked too early and ran too fast, her mind always racing ahead of the rest of her. At two and a half Dodge had first recognized the wild gleam in Maddie's eye for what it was, on the day he helped her climb to the top of the toddler slide, where she poised, arms outspread, openly contemplating the possibilities of flight. He was glad that she hadn't lost the gleam, but then Dodge also recognized that his sister would see this differently.

Maddie was full of observations, which she presented in a strong and unapologetic Brooklyn accent. Her arrival had coincided with the end of the theater guild meeting and many of them had trooped over to the apartment to welcome Maddie in true southern style, which was not a quick process.

Leo had brought up her luggage, looking a little glassy-eyed after the car trip, but neglected to take the opportunity to escape and had been sitting in a corner ever since. Dodge was relieved to see that Maddie paid Leo no special attention, but he wasn't about to let down his guard, either. When the last of the visitors finally drifted away he decided to get it out of the way.

"So what did you think of Leo?"

"Drop-dead gorgeous," Maddie said. "Killer accent, funny, some sharp edges. A ten, straight up. You should see your face, Uncle Dodge. There's nothing to worry about. I'm not going to embarrass you."

She collapsed on the couch with a blissful Scoot in her lap and crossed her eyes at him. "I really want to meet Julia. I promise not to spill the beans."

"Before we make dinner plans, maybe you can clarify for me what kind of beans we're talking about."

There was a banging in the hall and then the sound of dogs thundering up the stairs. Scoot leaped off Maddie's lap and charged the door.

"I knew this would be fun," Maddie shouted over the barking.

When Dodge opened the door Gloria, Willie, and Boo rushed in around him to greet Scoot. Then Bean's face appeared on the staircase, and just behind her, Julia.

"We hear you got company," Bean said.

Dodge met Julia's gaze over Bean's head. "I do. Come on in and help me put some food on the table, and then we'll eat."

"You know, Uncle Dodge," Maddie said, "four dogs and three females in one small kitchen, things are crowded enough as it is."

"He won't go," Bean said, cutting right through to the heart of what Maddie wanted. "He likes to listen."

Julia came over and put a stack of plates in Dodge's hands. Her own hands were cold to the touch, and her color was high. He took the opportunity to run his thumb over hers and she gave him a small and somewhat disconcerted smile.

On the other side of the kitchen Bean was just finishing up with her personal version of the back story on Nils Sigridsson. She had an eager audience in Maddie, and a more cautious one in Julia. Dodge just wanted to drag Julia off into the parlor to ask her some questions, but instead he found himself seated at the kitchen table passing the shrimp and cheese grits casserole and black-eyed peas, both of which Julia had unearthed from his freezer and defrosted in the microwave.

Maddie was saying, "He sounds like a decent guy. Do you think he wants to marry your mom?"

For some reason Bean looked at Julia.

Julia said, "Nils is, he is decent and kind, and he's been good to your mama."

"Yes, ma'am," Bean said. "But that's not what Maddie asked. Do you think he wants to marry Mama?"

"I have no idea," Julia said. "And really, it's none of my business. Your mama is old enough to make her own decisions."

"Mama say, she got married too young the first time."

Maddie was studying Julia closely. She said, "How old were you—" and broke off at the look Dodge gave her. "What?"

"It's okay," Julia said. "But you have to remember this is South Carolina, you've got to be careful not to offend people."

Bean said, "I don't think she does. You can get away with a lot, being a Yankee and all."

"Except she won't," Dodge said. "Will you, Maddie? You're going to be on your best behavior. No personal questions, no political debates, and absolutely no discussions on religion."

Maddie looked pained. "You're worse than Father Mulvaney. He doesn't like confrontation, either."

"I have some sympathy for poor old Father Mulvaney," Dodge said. "What did he do to deserve an argumentative agnostic as his junior class president?"

Bean frowned. "What's agnostic? Is that some kind of Catholic?"

Maddie never hesitated. She said, "Agnostics are like atheists, but more honest."

Julia hiccupped a laugh and Bean's jaw dropped. "You don't believe in God?"

"An atheist flatly denies the existence of any kind of god." Maddie threw Dodge a meaningful look. "Agnostics think there's not enough evidence to declare one way or the other."

"Oh," said Bean. "So you're sitting on the fence."

Dodge smiled broadly at his niece, and she wrinkled her nose at him. To Bean she said, "You can look at it that way. But really, what it means to me is that I'm willing to acknowledge the limits of human understanding."

"Um, Maddie?" Bean said. "When you meet my Granny Pearl, maybe you shouldn't tell her about all this."

"Probably not," Maddie agreed, and Bean heaved a sigh of relief.

"So," said Julia in a brighter tone. "To answer your question—" and both girls turned to her.

"I was twenty-one when I got married."

"That sounds plenty old enough to me," Bean said.

"Maybe," said Maddie. "But I don't think I'm going to get married at all. I'm going to travel and take lovers and make friends all over the world."

"Like your uncle," Bean said, and Dodge inhaled wrong and coughed so hard that Julia leaned over to thump him on the back. At least she was smiling.

Julia said, "What kind of an uncle is Dodge?" And then feigned an innocent look when he turned to her, incredulous.

Maddie said, "Is that a serious question?" And before Dodge could stop her, she launched right in. "He's that gruff but affectionate uncle, the one who'll tell you when you're being bitchy and then make you laugh about it. We take a vote every year and he always comes out at the top of the uncle list."

"How many uncles do you have?" Bean wanted to know.

"Three on Mom's side." She gestured with her chin to Dodge. "And six on my dad's. They're famous in Brooklyn, the seven Bugiardini brothers."

"And which is the worst uncle?" Bean asked.

"I'll have to swear you to secrecy before I can tell you that," Maddie said, and Bean giggled in delight. Julia was laughing, too. She looked happy and at ease, completely unfazed by the sudden appearance of Dodge's houseguest.

Of course, company meant he couldn't ask her questions about how she had spent her day, Dodge reminded himself. That might have something to do with how very relaxed she seemed.

. . .

WHEN THE DISHES WERE DONE JULIA TOOK MATTERS INTO HER own hands and sent the girls out to walk the dogs. She gave specific instructions to Bean, who was to show Maddie around Lambert Square and the riverfront.

"Will that be long enough?" Maddie asked Dodge in a mock whisper, waggling both eyebrows.

"Mind your manners, Brooklyn."

This experience of Dodge with his niece struck Julia as a little odd, but pleasing.

He said, "I'm sorry to spring Hurricane Maddie on you—"

Before he could point out that he would have warned her about Maddie's imminent arrival *had she been around,* and by the way where had she been? Julia interrupted.

"She's a great kid. And I should have guessed you'd be the cool uncle. I bet you let her have her first sip of beer."

"I am the cool uncle," Dodge agreed.

"She's going to be a great distraction for Bean," Julia said.

"She's going to be in my way," Dodge said, and he moved very suddenly, took Julia by the hands and pinned her up against the door so he could kiss her. She laced her fingers through his and stretched, in pleasure and relief. This they could do. Questions and answers might be too much of a challenge right now, but they could hold on to each other and press hard, so that tomorrow she would feel the imprint of his hands and the weight of his bones, so that the taste of him was as familiar to her and as present as her own smells and tastes.

Dodge broke away and buried his nose in the crook of her neck. His breath was warm and damp on her skin.

"So," Julia said. "Where exactly is Hurricane Maddie going to sleep?"

Another deep sigh. "I set up an inflatable mattress in the second bedroom."

"Sheets?"

"My second set. Would you like to inspect them?" He pressed his forehead against hers. "Please say—"

"No."

A few minutes later Julia pulled away, gasping. "Probably this isn't a good idea."

"I beg to differ," Dodge said. "I've never had a better idea in my life." His hands were very busy, but she caught them and held them away.

"They'll be back early, you know they will."

"Okay," he said, dropping his head. He looked so forlorn that Julia had to bite her lip or laugh out loud. She let go of his hands to touch his face and he grabbed her by the waist and then she was against the wall again, in the middle of a kiss so overwhelming that she didn't even hear the sound of voices on the other side of the door until he let her go.

"Back early," Dodge groaned.

"Told you so."

"I'm coming over later," he said. "As soon as she's asleep."

Julia giggled, she couldn't help herself. "I'll leave the porch light on."

TUESDAY MORNING WHEN JULIA CAME DOWN TO OPEN THE SHOP Exa was waiting, so overfilled with questions that she bounced like a balloon.

"I should know better than to take a Monday off," she said. "Everything good happens on Sunday. So what's she like?"

Mayme caught Julia's eye and grinned. Trixie laughed out loud, her head bent over the pile of pillowcases she was sorting.

"What?" Exa said. "What? Will somebody speak up?"

"She's seventeen," Julia said. "Her parents call her Hurricane Maddie. She got suspended in school for taking a political stance that would probably curl your hair. Does that give you enough of a picture?"

It did not, of course. Exa persisted until she drew out every detail, stopping them now and then to compare other versions of some of the same stories she had heard elsewhere. Because all of Lamb's Corner seemed to be fascinated by Dodge's Yankee niece, which was actually a good thing. Maddie had replaced Nils Sigridsson's quick departure as number one on the gossip hit parade.

Trixie was saying, "I'd adopt the girl tomorrow, take her under my wing and rub off some of that Yankee. Then she'd be about perfect."

"What does your mama think of her?" Exa asked Mayme. "Does Pearl like her?"

Mayme raised a shoulder and let it drop, but she was smiling. "Mama says Miss Maddie is the sweetest, funniest heathen she's ever come across."

"Mercy," Exa said. "Where is she now? I'd like to get a look at this hurricane girl."

Julia went into the workroom with that question in her head. She didn't particularly want to think about Maddie asleep in Dodge's extra room. It made her unreasonably cranky in a way that just couldn't be justified. So she had spent two nights out of Dodge's bed. It was a bad idea anyway, to be so dependent that she couldn't get to sleep in her own apartment. Sooner or later Dodge would be leaving for Vermont or Idaho or someplace else with a winter that didn't bear thinking about, and he'd take his bed with him.

Maddie was a mature seventeen, Dodge had pointed out. Julia spending the night in Dodge's bedroom wouldn't surprise or shock or disappoint her. They had been wound together in a sweaty heap on her couch when he said this, his fingertips running up and down her spine. Under other circumstances Julia would have fallen away into an exhausted sleep, but she was wide awake, all her senses on high alert because wasn't this the place where it would have been absolutely right and logical for her to say, *I have a bed, too, you know. You can sleep over here.*

But she didn't say it and he didn't bring it up. And wasn't that ridiculous of her to wish he would, because she had gone to such trouble to make it clear that she didn't like such questions. Instead of asking, Dodge got dressed and kissed her softly and went back to his place. Where he slept the whole night in complete comfort.

He had stuck to the ground rules but the questions he hadn't asked were still there in Julia's mind, hanging on tooth and nail. Why didn't they sleep in her apartment, in her bedroom, in her bed?

There was an answer, if she could just think of it.

Late at night she had stood in the open bedroom doorway, her mind as starkly blank as the moonlight that fell across the bed. So neatly made, so perfectly composed. Not a wrinkle, not a stain to be seen. The bed she had shared with Charlie for all of her marriage, the white-on-white embroidered quilt they had bought in France on their honeymoon. She thought of turning back the covers and smoothing the sheets, of laying her head on the pillows and sleeping, but in the end she went back to her chair and its jumble of books and blankets and dogs, and she had read for another hour until she fell asleep right where she was.

Now Julia checked in on the Needlework Girls, looked at the various projects and answered questions, listened to stories about grandchildren and recipes and the latest scandals, including one about Leo, who had been seen in Columbia looking in the window of a jewelry store. Then she went back downstairs to the workroom to unpack a large shipment from England. Ten days late, held up by customs. Heavy damask table linen, gorgeous stuff that she could have sold ten times over in the last week. But Thanksgiving was two days off, and all of this would need to be laundered and pressed. Lately everything seemed to be running just a little off sync.

Julia reminded herself to talk to Leo about placing some ads, with Christmas and Hanukkah and Kwanzaa just a month off. Her busiest time of year, right up to five o'clock on Christmas Eve. She drew in a deep breath and recited her mantra: At least business is good.

From the front of the shop a babble of voices, Exa, Marnie, Sue-Ann, Lorna Jean, Trixie, and Big Dove, and in the middle of all that, Maddie. Then she appeared at the door.

"Uncle Dodge sent me over, said you're supposed to put me to work."

Maddie with her beautiful smile and bright eyes, clever and generous to a fault, had come to torture Julia with questions.

To Julia's surprise Maddie was interested in the linens. She wanted to know where they had come from, how Julia knew her buyers, how valuable a dozen perfect napkins might be, who would buy them.

"Do you put stuff like this on your table?" she asked Julia.

"I don't entertain much," Julia said, and tensed waiting for the next question. Sooner or later—Julia had the sense it would be sooner—Maddie would express an interest in seeing Julia's apartment. There was no way to refuse her, or at least no suitable way that Julia could think of. And if Maddie saw the apartment, most likely Dodge's sister would want to see it, too, and then his grandmother and there would be no end to it. She imagined every room overrun with strangers, sitting with coffee in the kitchen, sprawled on the couch with the dogs. Looking in her bathroom cabinet, in her closets, out her windows so that strangers walking through Lambert Square would glance up and see them, a half dozen faces looking out into the world.

But she had underestimated Maddie, who wouldn't be satisfied with half gestures. Helping Julia shake out yet another damask tablecloth, she said, "You're good for Uncle Dodge. He's . . . different."

Some kind of response was required, but all that came out of Julia's mouth was a low hum, a go-ahead-tell-me-more sound.

"He's settled down. I mean, his mood. You know how they call me Hurricane Maddie? Well, everybody says I take after him. Mom says it's why he never got along with Grandpa Dodge. Marching in formation was never going to work for him, and it won't work for me, either. You know how I got suspended?"

Julia admitted that yes, she was familiar with the circumstances that had brought Maddie to Lamb's Corner a half week early.

"Well, Uncle Dodge got thrown out of West Point, not three months into his freshman year. On purpose. It's the big family scandal. Grandpa wouldn't talk to him for years."

Julia found she was interested in spite of her intention to stay neutral. "But he went on to Columbia—"

"That's the thing Grandpa couldn't get over," Maddie said. "Uncle Dodge got himself thrown out of West Point because what he really wanted was to drive Grandpa Dodge crazy and the best way to do that was to go to Columbia and st—" She stopped. "Am I talking too much?"

Julia realized she had been holding her breath. She managed to shake her head. "Not at all. But I have to run upstairs for a minute. Do you want to see my apartment?"

Sometimes, Julia told herself, a quick surrender was the least painless of the options available. More, it seemed the only way to stop Maddie from telling secrets Julia wasn't sure she wanted to hear.

The truth was, she was still out of sorts about the Vermont phone call, and there was Thanksgiving to get through; better not invite disaster.

Maddie loved the apartment, loved the furniture and the antiques and the computer and the television setup.

"Now I understand why Uncle Dodge doesn't have a TV," she said, her eyes running over Julia's DVD collection. "He sits over here and watches yours." She pressed the remote to her chest in something very near ecstasy. It turned out that Maddie planned a career writing for television. There was so much good stuff being made, excellent stories and acting and production values, and she wanted to be a part of it. She was so sincere and so very serious that any impulse Julia might have had to laugh disappeared.

"You don't have to explain to me," Julia said. "I've got a full cable subscription, every channel." Something she wouldn't admit to many people, but this confession got her an enthusiastic hug from Maddie, who wanted to know which were her favorite shows, and what trends she saw as on the upswing, and whether she was one of the people who had lost faith in *The Sopranos,* and if she believed, as Maddie did, that the whole reality television debacle was drawing to a close. And Julia found herself answering all those questions and asking some of her own, until an hour had passed.

"No wonder Uncle Dodge fell in love with you," Maddie said. "You have excellent taste in everything."

In the silence that followed—Julia's head was suddenly hollow, no way to make any kind of coherent sentence—Maddie looked abashed and, for once, truly embarrassed. She bit her lip and stuttered a small apologetic laugh.

"He didn't say that to me," she said. "You shouldn't think he's telling me secrets or anything."

"Secrets," Julia echoed.

Maddie went pale very suddenly and started talking at double her usual speed. "I mean, he doesn't talk to me about you. He's not indiscreet. That's a lesson I really have to learn from him; Mom is always telling me that but it's easy for a therapist, they're trained that way."

Julia sat down. "Therapist." She had turned into a parrot, but she didn't seem to know how to stop.

"My mother is a therapist," Maddie said, twirling her hair between two fingers. "My father is a therapist. I listen to them talk at dinner, we all did, just soaked it up. Really, that's all I meant."

Julia managed a smile. "It's okay. Calm down, Maddie. Make yourself comfortable, watch some television. You can come over to watch anytime, really."

The girl drew in a deep, shuddering breath. Then she sat down and looked at the remote in her hand.

It took all of Julia's concentration, but she pulled her thoughts together. She said, "You haven't met Maude yet, have you. You should talk to her, she was in television for more than ten years. Her husband worked for the network—and between them I think they know everybody in the industry."

Maddie's expression eased. "Really? You think I could talk to them? I wouldn't want to impose; Uncle Dodge is always telling me I'm way too Yankee for Lamb's Corner."

"That wouldn't worry Maude," Julia said. "Ask Bean after she comes home from school; she'll take you over to meet them both. Mike is from Manhattan, one of those guys with a dry sense of humor that goes unappreciated down here. Maudie is very southern. It's one of those cases of opposites attracting."

Julia hesitated with her hand on the door. "I have to get back to work, but you stay as long as you like."

Maddie said, "Really?"

"Really." Julia summoned up the easiest smile she possessed. "Now you've made me wonder, how did your parents meet?"

"Dad and Uncle Dodge were friends in graduate school," Maddie said. "They shared an apartment for like, ever, and Mom came to visit one weekend, but Uncle Dodge had a . . . an exam, and so Dad took her out to dinner. And the rest is history."

"One more thing," Julia said. Her face felt as if it might crack from the effort of smiling. "Can I leave the dogs here with you until Bean comes to walk them?"

Maddie, already mesmerized by the cable guide on the television screen, agreed that she'd be more than happy to help.

BECAUSE IT WAS TUESDAY THERE WAS NO PLACE TO GO WHERE she could be sure of a quiet hour to herself. The second floor was the domain of the Needlework Girls, Big Dove and Trixie were in the workroom with the new shipment of table linen, and the shop was full of people. Really she should go down to help, Mayme and Exa were handling the phones as well as the customers.

But instead Julia stood on the stairs, immobile. Confused about her own confusion. Things seemed so obvious now, she wondered how she had overlooked it all. She remembered Dodge as Freud, and Bean's cranky mood that evening. She had been trying to tell Julia something. Julia wondered if maybe down deep she had suspected or even known, without wanting to know.

Neurosis: arising out of inner conflict.

The lower door opened and Leo started up the stairs, his hands full of CDs. He caught sight of her and stopped.

"I was just going to go update the software on your office Mac," he said. "Should I come back later?"

"No." Julia smiled. Or at least she thought she smiled. Leo looked a little alarmed. She said, "Go ahead. I've got some phone calls to make, so I'll use your office. Can you make sure nobody bothers me until I'm done?"

Leo's brow pulled down in a V. "Sure," he said slowly. "But—"

"You can work in my office all afternoon," Julia said, and slipped past him to run down the stairs.

DODGE SPENT A GOOD PART OF HIS MORNING SITTING WITH Heep in his workshop, going over a list of pens waiting for repair, discussing pricing and standard practices. Before he realized it, it was almost one, but no sign of Maddie. She hadn't shown up for their lunch date. He excused himself and used the desk phone to call up to the apartment.

"No answer?" Heep rolled his eyes. "Teenage girls. She's probably out gabbing with somebody in the square and forgot about the time. We raised twins, double the female trouble."

"But worth it," Dodge said. A shiver of foreboding ran up his spine at the idea of Maddie on the loose.

"Sure," Heep said. "Nothing you wouldn't do for your kids."

At half past two he went looking, which involved stopping to talk to just about everybody. To ask Bo Russell any question was to invite a discourse on the most recent tobacco harvest and the evils of modern medicine. Landry had a new book to recommend, and while he was at it, he invited Dodge to Thanksgiving dinner in case he didn't have anywhere else to go.

Annabeth wanted to talk to him about Thanksgiving, too, whether there was something special she might put out for his family, and how fine her pickled okra was this year, she would put a couple jars away in case they wanted to take some home. And by the way, today would be a good day to come by and settle the bill ahead of time, better to get business out of the way.

Lorna Jean hadn't seen Maddie since just before opening when she stopped by Cocoon, and had Dodge heard this rumor going around that Nils had proposed to Mayme right before he left for Sweden? LRoy was taking bets on whether she'd say yes, which Dodge found distinctly irritating. In spite of his resolution to keep out of all such discussions, he told Lorna Jean just what was on his mind, but the reaction he got did nothing to mollify him.

Lorna Jean put a carefully manicured hand to her throat in horrified fascination. "You think she might really accept him?"

Dodge was so irritated—and worried, he admitted to himself he was worried about a lot of things he could hardly put a name to—that when he ran into Lorna Jean's perpetual fiancé on his way to Cocoon, he stopped and had to put a foot down hard on his temper.

Curtis Durant had been deep in conversation with LRoy and looked up, his brow creased in something that might have been confusion or just plain cluelessness. Right then Dodge's mood got the better of him.

"Curtis," Dodge said. "I've been meaning to ask you. Do you ever intend to marry Lorna Jean? Because she's wore out with worrying about it and the whole business is turning her sour. It wasn't pretty, the way she's fussing over Mayme and Nils. Also you should know that your indecision is the basis of LRoy Swagger's longest-standing wager."

He looked pointedly at LRoy, who was trembling with indignation and flushed with embarrassment.

Curtis sent LRoy a startled look.

"It's true," Dodge said. "If she was mine, I wouldn't like that idea one bit."

Curtis had a small pink mouth that dropped open in surprise, making a perfectly round circle. "People are talking about Lorna Jean and me?"

LRoy was scowling. "Well, of course, Curtis. It's going on ten years."

"Oh," said Curtis Durant.

Dodge shook his head in disgust and walked on, aware that they watched his retreating back. He was all the way to Cocoon before his adrenaline rush had petered out, and then he stood there for a long moment watching Exa wrapping up a purchase while she talked to a customer.

Mayme raised one eyebrow into a perfect right angle that asked him why he was hesitating outside the door.

He went in and walked right up to the counter, aware that a half dozen women were sizing him up and nudging one another, no apologies. The shopping junkets were good for business, but in cases like these not great for his mood.

"Pardon me," he said, forcing himself to speak slowly. "Have you seen Maddie?"

Mayme said, "She was in here when we opened. Then she was back in the workroom with Julia and then she went upstairs." She looked to Exa for confirmation.

"Most likely the Needlework Girls got her caught up in their web." She jerked her head over her shoulder in the direction of the stairs.

"Everything all right?" Mayme asked.

"Fine," Dodge said. "Everything is fine. Where's Julia?"

"Who's Julia?" one of the women whispered behind him.

"Girlfriend, I guess. Looks like he might be in hot water."

Mayme was saying, "Let me ask Leo, he's upstairs working in her office." She picked up the phone and turned her back on them while she talked. When she turned back there was something in her expression that made Dodge's throat tighten.

"She's in Leo's office," she said. "She doesn't want to be disturbed."

"Sugar, you can disturb me anytime."

Dodge refused to look in the direction of the whisper, nodded a barely polite good-bye, and headed for the workroom. Once there he stood staring at Leo's office door, his palms damp. Since the first day here when Julia had showed him around he hadn't been back to this particular spot, and there was a reason. He imagined Julia in that boxy cubicle. Sitting in Leo's desk chair, she could lean back and touch her head to a wall, or reach out in either direction and do the same thing with her hands.

He took out a handkerchief and wiped his brow, felt the small rectangle of his cell phone and pulled that out, too. Hesitated a minute before he walked to the other side of the room, where he dialed Maddie's cell phone. The chances that she had left it back in his apartment, failed to charge it, or simply not turned it on were great, but he dialed anyway and waited three rings.

"Hello?"

"Maddie," he said. "Where the hell are you?"

"Uncle Dodge! I'm watching television in Julia's apartment. She's got a television the size of a—"

He cleared his throat. "You're in Julia's apartment."

"Yeah. She said I could stay as long as I wanted. I guess I lost track of time, huh? We were supposed to have lunch."

She was talking fast, almost breathlessly. He said, "Something going on I should know about?"

"Um," Maddie said. "We were just talking, and Julia asked me how Mom and Dad met and I told her."

Dodge closed his eyes. "How much did you tell her?"

"Not very much, but from the expression on her face I got the idea that she was putting two and two together. You want to throw me out?"

"I'd like to strangle you," Dodge said. "But then life would be very boring."

She let out a sigh of relief. "You're not mad?"

"I'm not happy, but I'm not mad. This is my mess to fix. Can you feed yourself?"

"Sure," Maddie said. "Bean should be coming soon to take the dogs and I'll go with her. Her grandmother likes to feed me."

JULIA OPENED THE DOOR TO LEO'S OFFICE, HER EXPRESSION studiously blank.

"Hey," Dodge said. "What's up?"

She stepped back—as far as she could step back—and pointed to the free chair. Dodge wondered if this was the result of calculation, or if she had forgotten the fact that small enclosed spaces didn't do much for him.

"Can we go somewhere else to talk?"

Julia sat back down in Leo's chair.

"So that's a no." He hesitated a moment and then came in.

"Close the door, would you?"

"I'd rather not."

She shrugged. "Suit yourself." Julia leaned back in her chair and put her fingers over her mouth for a moment, but her gaze never left him.

Dodge said, "I put it off too long. I should have told you before you heard it from somebody else, or figured it out on your own."

It might have been his imagination, but her expression seemed to soften the slightest bit.

She said, "Did Bonnie hire you?"

He jolted. "No."

"My father didn't send you."

"Absolutely not."

"You're sweating."

"I'm sitting in a room the size of a shoe box."

"So the whole claustrophobia thing, that was real."

Dodge took a deep breath. "It is real. Yes. I am on the verge of a panic attack."

"Good," Julia said. "I'd like to watch."

Dodge barked a laugh.

"You've been watching me now for more than three months. Studying me, right? Calling your sister the therapist to consult on treatment for an intractable, housebound agoraphobic?"

"No," Dodge said, shaking his head. Wondering how long he could hold on before the urge to bolt got the best of him.

"You didn't talk to your sister about me."

"Of course I told her about you. We're dating."

"But you are a clinical therapist." Her voice had taken on a rasp, but her tone was unremarkable. As though she were commenting on a new shirt.

"I used to be. A long time ago. I did my internship year and then I lasted for all of a month at my first job. My only job."

"You couldn't stay with it but you didn't give up, either. Not all the way."

He forced himself to wait. There was nothing he could say in self-defense, and plenty that might make things worse.

"The mystery is, why I didn't figure it out sooner." She tilted her head as if she were hearing a voice from far away, her mouth turned down at the corner. "Maude knows, doesn't she. The look she gave you when Nils asked if you could define 'neurotic.'"

"Maude found out that weekend."

"From you?"

"No, not me."

She raised an eyebrow. "You're not going to tell me?"

Dodge closed his eyes. "It was Bean. She went hunting around the Internet, about Nils and me both."

"She dressed you up as Freud, didn't she. And it went right over my head."

A bead of sweat ran down Dodge's face and he wiped it away with the back of a hand.

"So," Julia said. "Now what?"

DODGE LOOKED MISERABLE, WHICH SHOULD HAVE MADE HER feel better but instead Julia found herself tensing with anger.

He said, "Now I apologize at length, but first—"

In one twisting motion he was off the chair and halfway through the door. A matter of steps, but his foot caught the chair leg and she watched as he fell, an awkward tumble that took the chair with him, a dance step gone horribly wrong. No more than three seconds total, ending with his head hitting the edge of the door with a sound like a cleaver hitting meat and bone. Then he was out of sight, all but his legs, which were still caught up in the overturned chair.

By the time Julia managed to extract the chair and climb over him he was pulling himself to a sitting position, both hands pressed to the back of his head. There was blood everywhere, a great sheet of it pouring through his fingers and cascading down his back. Julia slipped in it as she went down on her knees beside him, put her hands over his as if she could stop the flow.

"Well, look at this," Big Dove said, in her most grandmotherly tone. She picked up the first thing that came to hand—a sheet, Julia noted with some part of her mind—and crossed the room to hand it to Julia.

"Gone a gusher." Something like admiration in her voice as Julia pressed the folded sheet to Dodge's split head.

Later Julia would try to remember exactly what had happened next. Maybe she had imagined Dodge laughing before he fainted and fell over into her arms. Maybe she herself had laughed, at the pure absurdity of it all, Dodge in such a hurry to get away from her that he found it necessary to crack his head open. Voices all around, striving for the exact tone that would convey concern but not panic, just the right touch of urgency. Phrases floated through her mind, some of them no doubt the product of her imagination. *That sure put a knot in his tail* and *shit fire and save matches* and *butter my butt and call me a biscuit.* A laugh bubbled up out of her gut and she pressed a bloody hand to her mouth to stop it.

"The ambulance is on the way," Trixie said. "RaeAnn is on duty and you know she's the best paramedic in the county."

"It's just a scalp wound," Julia heard herself saying. How oddly calm she sounded. Hadn't she always been the coolest head in an emergency? When she broke her wrist and her mother fainted, Julia had dialed the phone with her left hand. When the small plane carrying Charlie's father had disappeared over Lake Michigan, everyone had turned to Julia for direction and calm, and she had provided both. Now she adjusted her grip on Dodge's head and his eyes fluttered.

"He'll be just fine," Exa said. "Take more than a bump on the head to put John Dodge off his feed. I bet we could close him up with duct tape and save a trip to the emergency room."

"Don't be foolish," Mayme said. "The man lost consciousness, Exa. He needs to go to the hospital."

Then Maddie was there, kneeling down beside her uncle. She took a good hard look, then she sent a tight-lipped smile in Julia's direction. Finally she sat back on her heels.

"He'll need staples and probably they'll do an MRI, make sure he didn't scramble anything." She saw the way Julia was looking at her. "I've got two brothers and nine uncles, three of them Dodges. You know I have twenty-three first cousins, and every one of them is male?"

Dodge mumbled, "We had a three-day party when she was born."

"See?" said Maddie. "All that male testosterone, everybody crazy about football or rugby or worse." She squeezed Julia's shoulder. "You'll get used to it, Julia. The Dodges all bleed like this."

"Little liar," Dodge said, quite clearly.

"There he is, back already," Mayme said. And from Trixie: "Dodge, you shouldn't talk to your niece that way."

"It's my name," Maddie said. "Bugiardini means 'little liars' in Italian."

Dodge was looking at Julia, his gaze not quite focused.

She said, "You could have just asked for a break in the interrogation."

He raised a hand and she caught it.

Somebody yelled from the alley door, "Ambulance is here."

It went so quickly, Julia felt dizzy herself. She stepped away so the paramedics could work and stood there at a loss. Trixie and Big Dove tried to lead her away but she held them off.

"Where will they take him?"

"County Hospital in Stephensville," Trixie said.

The taller female paramedic spoke directly to Trixie. "Granny, who's going to ride along?"

Maddie raised her hand. "I will." To Julia she said, "You had better change before you come. Maybe Leo can drive you."

Julia looked down at herself. What had been ice blue polished cotton that morning was now an abstract painting. Her face and hands felt tight with drying blood. She would go upstairs to her own apartment and shower and change. And then Leo would come to drive her to the hospital, where she would sit in a waiting room until they came out with test results and told her what had to happen next.

The paramedics had Dodge on a stretcher and were headed for the door. Julia ran to catch up to them and they stopped.

"Dodge."

He was more alert now, his eyes hooded but clear. They had put a neck brace on him. Maddie was on the other side of the stretcher, but he kept his gaze on Julia.

She said, "I can't. I can't. I'm sorry, I can't."

He took her fingers and squeezed.

"'S okay," he said. "I know. At the latest I'll be back tomorrow morning. Look after Scoot for me?"

She watched while they loaded the stretcher into the ambulance and Maddie climbed in. Then she turned and faced the crowd that still stood, watching. Her employees. Her friends. Family, in a way. The only family she had. They had heard that last conversation, every word, but not one of them looked surprised. None of them asked why she wasn't going to the hospital, Julia realized, because they already knew.

They had known all along.

. . .

Mayme was about to lock up when she saw Nils Sigridsson coming across Lambert Square, pulling a suitcase behind him.

She had been so happy to see the end of this day. Five minutes ago she would have told anybody who asked that she was exhausted beyond all experience. Now her heart was jumping up into her throat in a frantic attempt to leave her body entirely.

Less than a week gone, and he was back. Vanilla, whipped cream, wonder of wonder white bread Nils was standing there, grinning his ridiculous grin at her through the glass door.

He said, "Are you not going to open?"

"I'm not sure," she said. A lie, and they both knew it. "What are you doing back here so soon?"

"Thanksgiving," he said. "Day after tomorrow, *ja*? Your favorite holiday."

That was true, but when had she told him such a thing? Her mind went off in search of that small and insignificant piece of information while her hands turned keys and knobs and then he was bending down to kiss her—too tall by far—his skin cold, and then warm to the touch. It was dark outside and the lights in the shop were still on, turning them into a window display designed to offend. Things were some easier these days but on the other hand, she wouldn't be surprised if glass got broken in the middle of the night. She stepped back.

She said, "How long can you stay?"

"A week. Will you take me home and feed me?"

"Mama will have a piece of your hide." She was smiling, she couldn't help it.

"This time I am prepared," Nils said. "I brought her many gifts. And for Bean also. And, for you."

Walking home, he took her hand and tucked it into his pocket with his own. "So," he said. "What is new in Lambert Square?"

So she told him. When she was done he was shaking his head in disbelief.

"A concussion?"

"Just a little one," Mayme said. "And twelve staples. But they wanted him to stay overnight."

"And the niece?"

"There with him. Mike Golden is there, too."

"But not Julia."

"Of course not," Mayme said.

They were quiet for a moment. He said, "John Dodge is a psychiatrist."

"No," Mayme said. "He used to be a therapist. There's a difference."

"But he still lied to her," Nils said. "To everybody."

A flush of irritation spread up Mayme's back. She said, "The only person who has any grounds for complaint is Julia, and even then—" She stopped herself.

"A sin of leaving out," Nils said. "Is that what you were going to say?" And when Mayme didn't answer he said, "How is she?"

His interest was detached and his tone neutral, and Mayme found that she wasn't in the least uneasy to have him ask about Julia. But then he had come back, sooner even than he had promised, and that meant something. Quite a few things, in fact. The first one being that he was here for her.

"She retreated upstairs as soon as the ambulance pulled away," Mayme said. "I doubt we'll see her until late tomorrow."

The grip on her hand tightened and he stepped into the narrow alleyway between the barbershop and the bank. Mayme wondered if she should protest, if she could make him understand how badly it might play if the wrong person walked by and saw them kissing in the alley. Her own people would be scandalized, sure she had lost all her native good sense. But all that left her mind when he kissed her. Because he was back. Because he had kept his word.

39

Mike Golden dropped Dodge and Maddie off in the alley behind Scriveners just before noon on Wednesday. Then he leaned across the front seat to give Dodge one last chance to ask for help.

"You be okay?"

"Aside from the zipper in my scalp and a residual headache, I'm fine. Thanks for the ride. Give Maude my love, will you?"

"I could take Maddie along home with me to meet Maude," Mike said. "If you need some quiet time."

Maddie's smile made it clear that she thought this an excellent idea. She tried to look more serious. "But you might need me to help."

Dodge said a silent prayer of thanks to providence. "I'm going to sleep most of the afternoon. Just be sure you're back here before seven, that's just about when your mom and dad should be rolling in."

"I'll be back at six," Maddie said. "Help you get ready."

Not that such a thing was even theoretically possible, of course. Dodge had already resigned himself to chaos.

Maddie paused, one leg back in the car. "Grandma and Grandpa Dodge?"

"Tomorrow morning," Dodge said, and she blew out a breath of relief.

There was no way to avoid Heep or Link, who had missed the accident itself and now were determined to hear the details from him directly. After his staples had been admired and they had assured him that all was under control in the shop, he extracted himself and headed up to the apartment.

"Fair warning," Link called after him. "Ladies been bringing food by since yesterday. At least ten pounds of banana pudding in your calvinator. I may have to go bonk myself on the head. I'm mighty fond of banana pudding."

The last thing on Dodge's mind was pudding of any kind, but he waved a hand over his head to acknowledge his good fortune. Before he was through his back door he had his cell phone out and was dialing Cocoon. Hoping that Julia would answer, and getting Exa instead.

"Well, John Dodge," she said. "Put you back together, did they? No parts left over?"

"They did. Julia around?"

She drew in a sharp breath, a sound calculated to let him know that his shortcut through social niceties had been noted.

"Julia hasn't come down today," she said. "You might could try the apartment."

Dodge did just that, but the phone rang without the machine ever picking up. So he had some work to do with Julia, and not much time to do it before Lambert Square was overrun by Dodges and Bugiardinis. He took five minutes to change and brush his teeth, and then he headed out by way of the alley. A little lightheaded, a little sore, but nothing extreme.

He had spent most of the morning working things out for himself. Going over that conversation with Julia before he had run into the door. Trying to recall her tone and expression and choice of words. No overt anger, which was not surprising, given Julia's talent for sublimation. If they were going to get past this—and he was determined that they would—she'd have to let herself get mad.

The first thing he saw when he came around the last flight of stairs were two envelopes taped to Julia's back door. One with his name on it, and one with Mayme's.

Dodge stood for a long moment considering all the possibilities, and then he opened the envelope addressed to him. Inside was a key, and a note: *Scoot's with me. I will look after him.*

Dodge knew before he opened the door what he would find. The apartment was empty, no sign of Julia.

MAYME TOOK THE ENVELOPE DODGE HELD OUT TO HER. SHE hesitated for a moment, looking out Julia's office window into Lambert Square. Then she opened it. When she finished reading she passed it back to him.

Julia's handwriting was fairly large, with a distinct swinging rhythm and still tightly controlled. Dodge forced himself to read slowly.

You remember how we talked about you taking over the shop for a few days? I'm sorry I didn't give you more notice, especially with the big holiday sale coming, but I hope you'll be able to jump in. It's your show. I've left a power of attorney on the desk in my office in case anything big comes up. You know all the passwords you'll need. We'll talk about a (retroactive) raise as soon as I get back. You can leave a message on my cell if you need to, but I don't know if I'll be able to check it very often. I'm sure JD will take the other dogs if you ask him. Have a good holiday, and please don't worry about me.

She had called him JD, and what did that mean? A distancing tactic, a pulling away. But not just from him, from everything and everybody. From her business, and from Lambert Square. From her dogs.

This was about something bigger than the things he hadn't told her. He looked at Mayme. "What happened after they took me to the hospital?"

Mayme leaned back against the desk, arms folded and her chin on her chest. When she looked up there was an expression he hadn't seen before. At first it struck him as weariness, and then he realized that Mayme was sad.

"She couldn't go with you."

Dodge held up both palms, asking for more.

Mayme looked away. "She had to say that out loud, in front of all of us. It must have been like being stripped naked. No," she corrected herself. "It was like realizing you've been naked all along and everybody knew it except you."

Dodge cleared his throat. "So the fact that she . . ." He hesitated, reluctant to share the words he had promised Julia he would keep to himself.

Mayme managed a smile. "You're the therapist, you must know the name for what she's got. An irrational fear of leaving home."

"Agoraphobia," Dodge said. "You've known all along?"

The look she shot him was pure disgust. "Do you think we're blind? Julia hasn't accepted an invitation in five years, of course people notice. It took some longer than others," she said. "It's possible LRoy still hasn't picked up on it. But mostly people know, and they leave her be."

"Caro Epperson," Dodge said, "and that Boo Radley business of hers at the party? You spilled your drink on purpose."

Mayme's mouth twitched. "Caro has got a head for business but she's dumb as a post when it comes to reading people. So that's Caro and LRoy who probably never realized Julia's got a problem, but you can believe most of us noticed long ago. Last year I was so worried about her—" She broke off, shifting uncomfortably in place.

"You talked to her stepmother?"

Mayme stepped back in surprise, one hand pressed to her throat. "You are good at reading people."

"Don't worry," Dodge said. "I wouldn't tell her."

"I've regretted it every day since," Mayme said. "You know you've done her a world of good? She's so much better in so many ways."

"Is that so?" Dodge said. "Then where in the hell is she? Do you know where she goes on her Sunday jaunts?"

"No," Mayme said. "I don't know and I don't see any way to find out that wouldn't be the worst kind of invasive. I think we'll just have to sit tight until she comes home. Of course you won't do that, will you? You're going to start nosing around just as soon as you get back to your place."

"Or sooner," Dodge said.

Five minutes later he realized how empty a promise he had made. Dodge had no idea at all where to start looking for Julia, and the only sources of possible information—her computer, her mail, the Rolodex on her desk—were out of bounds. Mayme was right, that would be intrusive. The police did things like that. He wasn't a detective, and he had no reason to suspect that she might hurt herself.

And that, he realized, was why she had taken Scoot with her. A sort of reverse hostage, because she would never do anything to put Scoot in danger, which meant she had to keep herself safe.

He heard himself draw in a long breath and then he let it go.

"You look lost."

Dodge started out of his thoughts to find Nils Sigridsson standing in front of him. Sigridsson's smile was as artless as ever, but when he held out his hand, Dodge shook it.

"A lot on my mind," Dodge said. "I didn't see you. So you came back."

"For the holiday, *ja*. To eat turkey with Mayme and her family."

"Brave man."

"You think?" Nils didn't look very concerned. "Mayme's sisters don't like me but the brother is friendly, and Pearl has come about."

"Come around. A boat comes about, a person comes around."

"Whichever way, she has decided I'm not so bad."

"Oh yeah? How'd you pull that off?"

Sigridsson smiled. "A cardigan from my mother, handmade, and furry slippers, and silver earrings that dangle, she likes this, long earrings, and a big tin of *bondkakor* and *daimkakor* cookies, these are a Swedish specialty and my aunt makes them for her. Pearl was very pleased."

"Bribery," Dodge said. "Stick with the basics. Good strategy."

"Did not work so well with Bean," Sigridsson said. "She talks to you about this?"

"No," Dodge said. "I haven't seen Bean much."

Sigridsson drew in a deep breath and let it out slowly. "It is a challenge, a girl this age."

"You know of an age that's not a challenge?"

"*Ja,* you are right. But then I think they are saying the same of us. You are having some problems of your own, I hear. Julia is okay?"

"I think so," Dodge said, and stopped himself from saying more. Nora was on her way, he reminded himself. Nora and Tom. The three of them would sit down and talk things through and then he'd know where to go from there.

He held out his hand to shake; a Swede couldn't resist a handshake, no matter how many times you offered, and it was a great way to end a conversation.

"Maybe we will see each other tomorrow," Sigridsson said. "The visiting in the afternoon."

"Oh sure," Dodge said. "The visiting. In the afternoon."

The message light was blinking on his answering machine.

Dodge, we are about a half hour, maybe forty minutes out, which means we'll be there early. We picked up Grandma Lucy and Buster Cheney without a problem. She's snoring away in the backseat. I've been trying to get you on the phone for hours, I hope everything is okay. Joe Rocket, stop that. Ben, I swear I will throw your dog out the window if you don't— Where was I? Oh, never mind, we'll see you soon.

Two more messages, and as one of them could possibly be from Julia, Dodge hit the play button.

Dodge, Bob Lee Cowper here. I'm in Paris. Don't like it much, I have to say. The old statues in the museums are a lot more friendly than the folks who live here. And it's been raining, that cold kind of rain that chills you right to the bone. I'm going to change my plans and head south, see if the rest of France is worth looking at. And then maybe Sicily or Greece or someplace where the natives won't show their teeth when a man asks a question in English. And why I was calling, I'm guessing you're going over to Tindell's for your Thanksgiving dinner. You'll have a good meal and laugh a lot, and I'm sorry to say I'm not there with you, but I wish you a good day. Also, there's a custom in Lamb's Corner, people go visiting after Thanksgiving dinner. Most likely you'll have folks stopping by, just so you know.

Bob Lee again, I forgot to say something. I had a look at your new website from one of them cyber cafés, and I have to admit, you pulled it off. It looks real good and even I could figure my way around. But I'm wondering if you're still putting up stock, because there are ten, maybe fifteen pens I don't see listed. The cream of the crop, so to speak. My guess is Link has got them hid away somewheres. If he was to fall down dead tomorrow you might never find them. Here's how you handle it: you go on and ask him about the Waterman 504 Indian Scroll, see how he reacts. That might get the ball rolling. You know, if you had told me I'd miss sparring with that old booger, I'd have laughed in your face. Strange how things creep up on you.

The end-of-message beep coincided exactly with the buzz of the intercom from the shop, and following along from that, Dodge's cell phone began to ring. He hit the intercom button and Link's voice came to him at a full shout.

"You got company on the way up! Say, that sister of yours is mighty pretty. Why'd you go and let her marry an Italian?"

Dodge knew that trying to respond over the intercom was useless; either Link's hearing couldn't cope with the static, or he chose to pretend it did.

"Told her about your little accident this morning, too," Link bellowed. "Didn't want it to come as a shock, seeing her big brother stapled together like a cheap book."

Dodge winced.

"I'm just about to close up. I'll see you tomorrow."

Dodge's phone had stopped ringing and started again. He reached into his pocket, but before he could flip it open there was a huge rumbling on the stairs.

"The Bugiardinis have arrived," he said to Scoot, and then remembered: Scoot was gone, and Julia with him.

THINGS HAD JUST BEGUN TO SETTLE DOWN WHEN MADDIE GOT home, bringing with her Gloria, Willie, and Boo, who weren't happy to find two strange dogs already settled in. There was a tense moment between the two packs, but then Grandma Lucy cut it short by scooping up Willie and depositing him on her lap, where she could rub his head and whisper into one cocked ear.

"We have achieved doggy détente," said Freddy in a broadcast voice.

"Now, Fred, you stop talking foolishness," Grandma Lucy said. "Dogs are sensible creatures, and brighter than most boys I have come across, present company hardly excepted. Certainly dogs are more willing to listen to reason when they hear it, not like some young'uns I could name." She glared at the boys and then smiled at their sister. "In't that so, Maddie? Come on over here and give your great-granny some sugar. Then you can help me up, we got places to go."

Grandma Lucy wanted to see some of Lamb's Corner, and she wanted to see it on the arm of the only female among her thirty-four great-grandchildren. According to family lore, the Dodges produced one female per generation, and as such, Maddie had special privileges and responsibilities.

"Not you," Grandma Lucy said, her cane poking in Dodge's direction. "You stay put. You got a bump on your noggin the size of a goose egg. In fact, all y'all big'uns stay put. I want my great-grandbabies to myself. I might could even buy you kids an ice cream, if you behave. As long as I ain't lost my pocketbook. Where did my pocketbook get to?"

It took five frantic minutes to locate Grandma Lucy's pocketbook and get her out the door, followed by the Bugiardini young—all looking remarkably resigned—and their dogs, looking relieved.

Dodge went straight to the kitchen and pulled out bowls and kibble and a plate of leftover beef from the refrigerator, glad of something to do that gave him a good excuse not to sit down across from his sister at the kitchen table. The dogs were glad, too, and deposited themselves on the floor like a bulwark.

He said, "I'm guessing you drugged Ben and Freddy, that's the only explanation I can come up with. They followed Grandma Lucy out of here like lambs to the slaughter."

Tom snorted a laugh, which earned him a sour look from his wife.

"Grandma got in the van this morning and announced that the great-grandbaby who was nicest to her and Buster Cheney for the duration of the trip would be amply rewarded."

"You didn't try to talk her out of that."

"Of course not," Nora said. "It wouldn't do any good. And it's all your fault anyway, you went and invested her money for her and made her rich and it went to her head. Now, never mind Grandma Lucy. What I want to know is, where is your Julia, and what about Scoot?"

Dodge looked from his sister to her husband and back again. They had on their therapist faces, prepared to hear anything and give away nothing of what they were thinking. Usually he could sidestep them easily enough, but his head hurt and his dog and his girl were both gone and he was ill at ease about a half dozen different things.

"I don't know," he said. "She left Lambert Square early this morning and took Scoot with her."

A moment's silence while Nora digested this. "I thought these one-day disappearances happened on a Sunday."

"They did," Dodge said. "This is new."

"Maybe you better start at the beginning," Tom said.

TALKING SOMETHING THROUGH STEP BY STEP HAD ALWAYS worked well for Dodge; it was his way by nature as well as by training. Such an orderly approach forced him to organize his thoughts and make connections, and usually he came out the other end knowing what he needed to do.

Not this time. This time he looked at his sister and the guy he still considered his best friend, and saw on their faces what he hadn't quite been admitting to himself.

"It wasn't me she was running off from. I get that now."

Tom cleared his throat. "That would be my take."

"The question is, what set her off," Dodge said.

Tom said, "What do you think it was?"

"Oh, please," Nora said. "Can we cut the therapy babble and cut to the chase here? You knew she had some serious issues, you were trying to help her in a kind of left-handed way—"

The phone rang, and they all went quiet while Nora shook her head in mock disgust as the recorded message played. Then a familiar voice, but not the one Dodge was hoping for.

John Dodge, this is Maude. I know you're there. Pick up and tell me what's going on with Julia. I'm about worried out of my head.

"Maude the mayor? Mayor Maude?"

Dodge nodded. He leaned over to the phone that hung on the kitchen wall and picked up.

"So tell me," Maude said.

"I don't have any information. I was gone last night, remember? In the hospital. I talked to her at about seven, to let her know I was fine."

"And how did she seem?" Maude and Nora said in stereo.

"She was relieved," Dodge said. "And maybe a little embarrassed."

"Well, of course she was embarrassed," Maude said, loud enough for Tom to hear her on the other side of the kitchen.

"Everybody standing there, her friends and staff and a half dozen strangers for good measure, and she had to come out and say what she's been trying to keep to herself for five years. Just announce it to the world. Hey, everybody, I'm crazy! I never leave the house! And the worst part, seeing that everybody already knew. Of course she was embarrassed."

"Exactly," Nora said, and Maude said, "Who is that?"

"My sister," Dodge said.

"The other therapist? Let me talk to her."

Dodge handed over the phone.

AT ELEVEN THAT NIGHT THE BUGIARDINIS FINALLY WENT OFF TO Raddie's and left Dodge contemplating the odd situation in which he found himself. He sat for a while looking at the telephone and when he couldn't stand it anymore, he dialed Julia's cell number from memory and tried to organize his thoughts while it rang.

Julia's professional voice was clipped, almost curt: *You've reached Julia Darrow's cell phone. Please leave a message.*

Dodge cleared his throat. "Hey. It's me. You told Mayme you'd try to check your messages but my guess is you will check them, because you'll be worried about the shop and the dogs. I can't give you any specific information about the shop except business looked brisk this afternoon. I can tell you that the dogs are fine. A little disoriented, which probably has something to do with the fact that Nora and her whole tribe rolled into town, Grandma Lucy leading the charge. And they brought their dogs. Gloria has made Buster Cheney her new best friend. Buster Cheney is Lucy's dog. She'll tell you that she added on his last name after she'd had him for a month because he's the dumbest, most stubborn dog she's ever run into but she can't think of a way to get rid of him. Did I mention to you that Grandma Lucy is a lefty? Joe Rocket and Willie butted heads at first but I think they'll be joined at the hip from now on. Boo hid in the bedroom for the first couple hours but then at supper she came out and attached herself to Nora and would you listen to my mouth run?"

Dodge wondered if he should tell her everything, if she would be pleased or unhappy to hear that when the Bugiardinis were getting ready to leave for the night Boo had showed up with her leash in her mouth and dropped it at Nora's feet. In the end Boo got her way, and now Willie and Gloria were in a snit. They were watching Dodge through narrowed eyes as he paced up and down muttering into the phone.

He said, "I'll call again tomorrow about this time, in case you feel like talking."

It wasn't what he really wanted to say, but he was stepping carefully, feeling his way. No questions, no intrusions, nothing she might take as an accusation. He felt the urge to apologize, to explain, to say words that would comfort and soothe, that would make her feel safe again. So she could come back to this place that she had made her own. And to him.

40

THEY WERE on their way out the door to Tindell's, all nine of them, when the telephone rang. Dodge picked it up because it could have been Julia, and even if it wasn't, it gave him a little breathing room.

"Mr. John Dodge?"

"That's me."

"Mr. Dodge, this is Lou at Animal Dreams in Stephensville? I am so sorry to disturb you on Thanksgiving but Julia said I should call you to see if you might be able to help us with a problem."

"You talked to Julia? When?"

A short, vaguely alarmed pause. "Why, not ten minutes ago. She said you're a dog lover and you're real good with the nervous ones."

Dodge kept what he was thinking to himself while the woman explained how Julia had volunteered him to take in a dog. Which meant that she was checking her phone messages, and when it suited her, she'd return them. Which was a good thing, but it rankled more than a little.

They were all looking at him when he hung up, his father wanting to know what was going on and holding back questions only because he had made promises. Dodge wondered how long that would last.

Then Freddy—the most sanguine of teenagers, wise beyond his years—stepped up. He said, "Grandpa, I've been wanting to talk to you about my college plans."

"That is a great kid," Dodge said to his sister as they walked across Lambert Square.

"He wants to be a firefighter," Nora said. "That discussion should keep the Colonel going for most of dinner."

MAYME'S THANKSGIVING WENT SOUR AT ELEVEN O'CLOCK exactly, when the kitchen timer and the telephone rang together. She said a quick prayer for patience as she picked up the phone in one hand and an oven mitt in the other. A vow she was bound to break immediately, if this was another busybody wanting to know if the rumors were true, if Julia Darrow really had run off and left her business to Mayme to manage.

But it was her sister Paulene, who was hosting Thanksgiving dinner this year. There was plenty of noise in the background, a kitchen full of women getting in one another's way.

"Mayme," Paulene said. "Say it ain't so."

FIFTEEN MINUTES LATER BEAN CAME INTO THE KITCHEN AND found her mother trimming the blackened edges off her sweet potato pies.

"Who were you yelling at on the phone?"

"Your aunt Paulene," Mayme said.

Bean had always been a quick child, and she picked up immediately on what Mayme wasn't saying.

"We're not going to dinner?"

"You're still invited," Mayme said, striving to keep her voice even. "I'm still invited, but Nils isn't."

"What did Granny Pearl say?"

"She declined to get involved in the conversation."

"So we're not going."

"You think that would be the right thing to do, leave him behind?"

Bean's face took on the truculent expression she had worn for much of the year after her father had run off. "What are we going to do for Thanksgiving, mac and cheese?" The vaguest hint of tears in her voice.

"You've got to choose," Mayme said. "You can go over to your aunt Paulene's and eat her dry turkey and green Jell-O mold with the peas and carrots, or you can come have your dinner with Nils and me at Tindell's."

If she wasn't so mad at her sister, Mayme might have found something comic about her daughter's expression. Bean loved eating out and she especially loved eating at Annabeth Tindell's place. But it was no small matter, being turned away from the family dinner table because your mama was dating a white man with a funny accent who wasn't even a proper Southern Baptist.

Now Bean stood there waiting for Mayme to make everything right. Force everybody to love one another and be good to one another, so they could all sit down together at Thanksgiving dinner, giggling when Cousin Lonny dunked Paulene's biscuits in his coffee because, as he explained at the top of his voice, if he tried to bite into one straight off, his dentures would shatter for sure.

Mayme cleared her throat to get rid of the tickle, and swore she would not cry. She could be disappointed in her family and angry at her sister, but she would hold that back and salvage what she could of the day for Bean. And for Nils, who had come so far, to be with her.

The doorbell rang.

"He ruins *everything*," Bean said, and flounced off.

"Don't you be rude, little girl," Mayme called after her. "And no pouting, you hear? We are going to have a lovely Thanksgiving dinner."

"Miss Annabeth won't have room for us," Bean shouted down the stairs. "Why do you think she would?"

Mayme was dialing the phone when Nils came in carrying a big bouquet of roses and lilies and freesia, white and pink and deep cherry red, shades to match the color the chill had put into his cheeks. Mayme held up a finger and mouthed the word *wait* at him, and then Annabeth was on the line.

She explained the situation, watching as Nils's smile faded a little with every word.

Annabeth said, "Of course we've got room for you. I'll put you at the table with the Dodges. We'll be saying grace in about twenty minutes, is that enough time?"

"We'll be there quick as we can," Mayme said. Nils slipped an arm around her shoulders and she leaned into him.

"Bean will be very angry," he said. "She will say that I break things."

Mayme drew in a deep breath. "You put things back together, is what you do."

NILS WAS UNUSUALLY QUIET ON THE TEN-MINUTE WALK TO LAMbert Square. It took a lot to offend him, but Paulene had managed just fine. Mayme put her hand in his coat pocket, right out on the public street in the light of day. He smiled down at her and his fingers, warm as toast, curled around her own.

Bean sniffed loudly and skipped on ahead.

"I am sorry to be causing you such troubles," he said. "Do you wish I had stayed away?"

"No," Mayme said, leaning against him a little. She had failings enough, but cowardice was not one of them.

"So who will be eating with us?"

That was when Mayme remembered that John Dodge would be there along with his entire family, but without Julia. Mayme had Nils but didn't have her family. Right at that moment she felt bad for John Dodge. She had the far better deal.

ANNABETH'S WAS MADE UP FOR THE HOLIDAY WITH HER BEST tablecloths and napkins, fairy lights strung around the mantelpiece and huge vases filled with branches of magnolia, holly, and cypress. There were two dozen people milling around, none of them strangers. Bean had already attached herself to John Dodge's niece, and that was a good thing. It might improve her mood, and Maddie was exactly the kind of teenager Mayme hoped Bean might be one day. Sure of herself but respectful, curious about the world and afraid of very little in it.

Maddie made a point of introducing Mayme and Nils to her great-grandmother. Lucy Dodge was a dry twist of an old white woman with clear blue eyes and a button pinned to a dark blue serge dress that must have been new in about 1960. White print on a black background: *W stands for Weasel.*

Mayme bit back a smile but the old lady caught the flicker anyway, held on to Mayme's wrist with one hand while she dug around in a purse the size of a small car with the other. Then she pressed a couple buttons into Mayme's hand, going up on tiptoe to whisper in her ear, "Wear 'em if you dare." And she cast a disapproving look at the hand-lettered sign on the wall. *We have found that the discussion of politics and the appreciation of good food are mutually exclusive.*

"Dodge looks exactly like his father," Nils said to Lucy, while Mayme snuck a look at the buttons. A red W crossed out, IMPEACH in big white letters, and on the last one the entire alphabet with the one, crucial letter missing.

"Except for his coloring. A carbon copy." And Nils laughed a little at his own joke, already getting his mood back.

Miss Lucy said, "They may look alike, but otherwise? Chalk and cheese. I swear I will throttle the one who throws the first punch."

"Punch?" Nils said, looking shocked for once.

Miss Lucy patted his arm. "They'll do it with words. That's part of the problem." She watched Dodge walking across the room to greet Bo Russell, hand extended. "Men and their sons," she said. "I wonder sometimes how the human race survives."

Annabeth rang the bell to call them to table, and they began drifting into the dining room, where Annabeth's help—all of them her granddaughters—were putting the last bowls and platters on the table. The mood was light and Mayme was thinking that maybe this change in plans would be a blessing in disguise. Maybe Paulene had done them a favor without meaning to. She felt Nils's light touch at the small of her back and she took a deep breath just as Dodge turned to look at her.

"Mayme," he said, "I am glad to see you looking so happy."

He didn't look very happy himself, and Mayme found herself feeling sorry for him and more than a little irritated with Julia. But she was clear on her loyalties and so she pulled herself together and gave him what she hoped he would take as a friendly smile.

"I am happy," Mayme said.

Bean had popped up beside her, her whole face contorted into a scowl. She said, "I'm not happy. I'm not one bit happy. Julia hasn't come back, and I'm worried even if y'all aren't."

MAYME HAD TO ADMIRE THE WAY NORA STAGE-MANAGED THE seating with all the aplomb of a diplomat, separating her mother from her grandmother and her brother from their father, pairing the ones who got along and using teenagers as padding where otherwise moods and egos might rub. Through it all Dodge's father was in deep conversation with one of the nephews, a kid who clearly knew how to hold his ground without losing his temper or train of thought.

Nora sat down across from Mayme and blew out a long sigh that made her bangs jump.

"You must be a good therapist," Nils said. "You know how to motivate people."

Nora wrinkled her nose. "This has more to do with survival skills."

"Maybe you could come by my aunt Paulene's house later," Bean said from halfway down the table. Mayme wondered when her sweet little daughter's voice had gone so sharp. The child was angry and she would stay angry for a while, there was no rushing her when she had something to work through.

Bean was saying, "She uninvited us because she doesn't like Nils. Nils," she added, refusing to look in her mother's direction, "is white. And we're not."

There was a small silence in which every set of eyes moved from Mayme to Nils to Bean and back again.

Then Dodge said, "Bean, are you trying to hurt your mama's feelings? Because if you are, you can stop now, you got what you wanted."

"Oh, now he tells me," Colonel Dodge said. "All I had to do was ask, and you'd have given up your rebellious ways."

Dodge's grandmother said, "Theodore Roosevelt Dodge."

"Uh-oh," said Bean.

"Wheeee," said Nora, throwing her hands up. "Here we go."

41

You've reached Julia Darrow's cell phone. Please leave a message.

Hey. It's me. I just got back from picking up your new dog in Stephensville. He's hiding in the closet as we—as I—speak. I doubt you've ever had such a neurotic dog to foster. And yes, I do know what that means and yes, it is a professional opinion.

Sorry. I'm sorry. Long day. Thanksgiving dinner was memorable, but right now I'm doing my best to forget it. My parents have gone back to the base. Nora and Tom and the kids and the dogs are back at the motel. All the dogs, it seemed like a good idea. This new little guy needs some quiet and time to adjust. His name is Jimmy Dean, I forgot to say that.

So, I'm going to bed. To sleep. Talk to you tomorrow.

You've reached Julia Darrow's cell phone. Please leave a message.

I'm going to say what's on my mind, I should have done that to start with. I'll tell you something, I sure would like to straighten this out with you, finish that conversation we started, but I'm not going to spill my guts into a machine. So what I'm going to do is, I'm going to leave one message a day, tell you how the dogs are doing and whatever else important is going on in Lambert Square you should know about. And that's it. Otherwise I'm here. If and when you're ready to talk.

42

Dodge sat in front of his computer facing up to the facts. It was all pretty simple: business was better than he had projected. So good, as a matter of fact, that he was seriously short on high-end stock, the kind of pens that brought collectors to the door.

He closed his computer screen and walked downstairs to the shop, where Link was making a show out of polishing the countertop.

"It's a mystery," he said, as if dropping right into the middle of an ongoing conversation. "I swear kids these days have got more than ten fingers apiece, the way they leave prints around. It used to be a lot easier to keep this place looking good, I'll tell you that. Before these darn penmanship lessons." He looked up at Dodge and unease flickered over his face. "Something you wanted to talk about?"

"Pens," Dodge said.

Link's broad smile wasn't as disarming as it was meant to be. "You're in the right place."

"Let me be specific," Dodge said. "I'd like to see the Waterman 504 Indian Scroll."

He had put off Cowper's suggestion for a long time, but now he saw that he should not have. Link's eyebrows rode up and the corners of his mouth quirked. No wonder he never played cards.

"I wondered when it would come to this," Link said. "Bob Lee tip you off?"

"You mean, did he mention to me that I'm missing a lot of valuable pens from the online inventory?"

"I'll take that as a yes. Hold on."

Link went upstairs whistling to himself. Pure Link, not in the least penitent, now that he had been pinned down and found out.

Heep stuck his head in from the back of the shop. "Hey. You coming for poker tonight?"

Speaking of pinned down. Dodge said, "I'll try."

"Okay," Heep said. He scratched his jawline with a thumbnail. "It's been a while."

"Suppose it has." Dodge wondered where Link had got to. Maybe he had escaped the back way, his pockets bristling with expensive fountain pens.

"Since before Thanksgiving," Heep said. "You picking up where Julia left off, sticking close to home?"

Dodge turned his head sharply in Heep's direction. "What was that?"

Heep shrugged. "You heard me."

Dodge said, "But I'm going to pretend I didn't."

"Fair enough. Let me ask you something different. You made any decision about the pen show?"

It was a reasonable question and it set Dodge's teeth on edge. The biggest pen show of the year was coming up, one Cowper had never missed. He had signed up long ago, and the tickets had arrived in the mail just a few days before. Hotel, air reservations, convention tags, everything ready and waiting. The fact was, two people from Scriveners needed to be there, and Dodge needed to make a decision. Another fact: it would make most sense for Dodge to go. The pen show was in Manhattan, and he could go right on from there to Nora and Tom's for Christmas.

To himself he could admit the truth: the idea filled him with dread. Three days at a crowded convention talking to people about pens when the sorry fact was, four months in and he had had enough of the subject, an all-time record. Even the diner had held its charms for a full eight months.

He said, "If I don't go, would you be interested?"

Heep blinked. "You serious?"

"If I don't go I'll need somebody to take my place."

Heep looked happy for all of thirty seconds, then his face fell. "The girls are coming home for Christmas."

"Okay, then," Dodge said. "Kids come first."

There was a moment's silence while they listened to Link moving around upstairs. A thump, and then another thump.

"You know Link loves the pen show," Heep said.

"Yeah, well. I suppose we'll end up going together and leave the shop to you."

"That's what I've been assuming all along."

Link came down the stairs, a small box cradled in the crook of one arm.

"The treasure chest," Heep said. "I was wondering when you'd have to cough that up."

"So let's have a look," Link said.

Dodge felt the sudden strong need to be someplace else. He said, "Aren't there interns coming in this afternoon?"

"Two of 'em," Link said, stroking the box like a cat.

"So the usual routine then," Dodge said. "Photographs, and you can dictate the history and condition notes. I'll ask Leo to stop by later and see to it they go right up on the website. In fact, I'll go talk to him right now."

For once Link seemed not to have a snappy comment, which was a relief. Heep might have said something, but Dodge walked straight out the door, pausing to whistle. Jimmy Dean catapulted himself from his spot behind the register and came galloping after. He was no bigger than a loaf of bread, with one floppy ear and one that stood straight up, fur like hog bristle, and a nose like a cartoon mouse complete with long white whiskers. A pitifully ugly dog, and utterly devoted to Dodge after three weeks in his company. Dodge had tried sending Jimmy Dean off to be walked with the other dogs, but Bean gave it up as a lost cause; Jimmy Dean had to be carried every step that took him away from Lambert Square, and he whimpered the whole time.

Dodge had arrived in Lamb's Corner thinking about getting one dog. Now he had four or even five, depending on how you counted. Depending on whether Julia Darrow ever came back home, and brought Scoot with her.

He should have stopped to put on a jacket, something he always thought of when he was halfway across the park. Mid-December and the temperatures hovered in the low fifties. Last night it had got down to thirty-five, and this morning LRoy was taking bets on snowfall before the year was out. Most years they had no snow at all, which made the whole thing much more of a topic for discussion. That, and the upcoming holiday.

A few snowflakes would fit right into the holiday extravaganza that was now Lambert Square. Whole trees covered with tiny white lights, so that in the deep of night they seemed like something out of a fairy tale. Everywhere you looked, decorations and lights.

Bah, Dodge muttered under his breath. Humbug.

At Cocoon he nearly bumped into the mail carrier, the only man in

Lamb's Corner who could be counted on to be crankier than Dodge was feeling just now. Most of the year he was just taciturn, but in the month of December he was likely to growl if you addressed him directly. Dodge thought it probably had something to do with the fact that his mama had named him Rudolf, and childhood teasing about reindeer and red noses. In any case, he felt a certain affinity to the old man, and nodded to him as they passed.

There were a half dozen customers in Cocoon, all women who turned and looked at Dodge. From behind the counter Mayme waved him over, her expression uncharacteristically fraught. Exa was busy with a customer, which was one piece of luck. He wasn't in the mood for one of her lectures on patience and grace. Dodge picked up Jimmy Dean and tucked him under his arm.

"I have got to talk to you," Mayme said, her voice low. "Just let me call Big Dove in from the workroom to help out here."

"I came by to talk to Leo," Dodge said.

"You can do that, too," Mayme said. "But this is important." And then in response to his sharpened gaze: "No word from Julia. At least not directly."

"Fine," Dodge said. "I'll wait for you in her office."

On the second floor he was accosted immediately by Gloria, Willie, and Boo, who resented the fact that they spent their days here without Julia or Dodge, and further resented the fact that they weren't allowed downstairs to be with Big Dove and Trixie in the workroom while there were so many people in the shop. He took a few minutes to rub heads and thump backs and finally he gave in and fished dog cookies out of his pockets. They followed him into Julia's office.

It was really more Mayme's office now. Still neat and organized, but the smell of Julia's perfume was pretty much gone, and her coffee cup was missing. Dodge sat down behind the desk and the pile of mail sitting there waiting for Mayme's attention. Nothing unusual, no postcards, no sign of Julia's handwriting. Bank statements, vendors, utilities, freight, delivery, cleaning services, accounting, property management. He nudged the pile and it cascaded across the desk. Letters from France, Italy, Ireland, Japan. She had been talking about trying some Japanese textiles in the shop, maybe she had already found a buyer.

He wondered where Mayme was. Probably got caught up with a customer, somebody wanting Julia who needed to be placated and made content with not-Julia. Good trick if you could pull it off.

Get a grip. It was something he told himself quite often these days, but with decreasing success. You'd think he was a seventeen-year-old who got dumped, the way he was mooning around. Making a laughingstock of himself for a woman who had clearly decided she didn't need his help or want his company.

Mayme was doing just fine without Julia; she had the shop to run, a million details to manage.

Something odd about the mail, he realized now. Dodge ran his gaze over the envelopes again and wondered if he should just give up, admit to himself that . . .

He picked up an envelope. Columbia Property Management. Why did Julia need a property management company? Grounds maintenance for Lambert Square was handled by Lamont Schmidt. Who, Dodge reminded himself, worked for a property management company on the side. That had to be the explanation.

Except it didn't feel right.

Mayme was standing in the door. She said, "Something interesting?" Her tone light, but her gaze sharp. Because he was looking through Julia's mail, which really, he should know better.

He came around the desk and handed Mayme the envelope. "Open this."

She blinked at him. "Pardon me?"

"Open it, please. I've just got a hunch. Would you open it?"

Mayme looked from the envelope to Dodge and back again. "Property management. What's that about?"

"My question exactly," Dodge said. "If you won't open it, I'll have to."

She walked over to the window as she ran her finger under the flap and took out the single sheet of paper. Looked at it for a moment, her eyes skimming the page. Then she turned back toward Dodge and read aloud.

"For regularly scheduled maintenance, 136 Armistead Street, Lamb's Corner. And a note at the bottom: please let us know when you'd like us to start up again with the weekly check-ins. Thank you for your continued business."

Dodge drew in a deep breath and dropped his chin to his chest, trying to make sense of it.

"Armistead Street," Mayme was saying. "That's over on the west side of town, near the house Nils bought. Julia doesn't have any property over there."

"Sure she does," Dodge said. "And I'll bet if we went over there now, she'd answer the door."

Mayme stared at him. "You think—"

"It's the only logical explanation. Where else has she been going the past five years on odd Sundays?"

"I can't hardly believe it," Mayme said.

"Then let's find out for sure. I'll give you a call in an hour."

Her head came up with a snap. "You don't want to do that, Dodge. If she is there, you don't want to spring that kind of surprise on her."

"I beg to differ," Dodge said. "That's exactly what I want to do."

He turned toward the door and stopped. "What was it you wanted to talk to me about?"

Mayme leaned back against the wall, her arms crossed, and studied her feet for a moment. When she looked up, he could see how much this was costing her, and so Dodge forced himself to close the door and come back into the room.

"Go on," he said. "I'm listening."

Mayme crossed to the desk and picked up a manila envelope. She handed it to Dodge, and he glanced inside. Air Sabina ticket envelopes, three of them.

"From Nils?"

She nodded. "First class. They came on Monday, and I just can't decide what to do. I've left messages for Julia but she hasn't got back to me."

"Slow down," Dodge said. "Back up."

Mayme nodded. "Nils sent tickets for us to come spend Christmas with him and his family. In Sweden. Mama, too, and she's actually willing to come." A smile twitched at the corner of Mayme's mouth. "I think it was the first-class part that won her over. She even called a travel agent in Charleston to see if the tickets were real, and what they would cost. She was shocked when she found out. I was shocked myself. She said, I guess that big old dumb Swede is in love with you after all."

Dodge said, "And you don't feel like you can leave the shop. When's the flight?"

"Day after tomorrow. He arranged for a Kallsjö car to take us to the airport."

"Sounds like he thought of everything," Dodge said. "You haven't told Bean yet."

"How could I?" Mayme said. "I don't even know if we can go. Believe me, I'd like to tell her especially as her shitheel of a father just canceled his Christmas visit. It might cheer her up to have something fun to look forward to. I do want to go, but I can't just walk away . . ." She gestured around herself. Then she glanced down at the envelope still in her hand.

"I'm at a loss," she said.

"Well, I'm not," Dodge said. "Hold tight, I'll be back."

DODGE CROSSED THE MAILMAN'S PATH AGAIN ON HIS WAY BACK to Scriveners. He stopped right in front of him and the old man squinted up, his thin mouth pursed in irritation. Rudolf had a cold, which made his eyes water and turned his nose an unfortunate shade of red. He had a sour grin that showed off his dentures to poor advantage.

"Now what have you got there. Is that supposed to be a dog?" He grinned down at Jimmy Dean, who promptly placed himself between Dodge's legs for protection.

Dodge said, "One thirty-six Armistead Street."

"What about it?"

"Cross street?"

"Ewell."

"You know who lives there?"

"I deliver mail on this side of town. That's why I'm standing here, wasting my time talking to you in the first place."

"You know Lamb's Corner backwards and forwards," Dodge said. "Or is your memory going?"

"Don't be such a wiseass." Another, longer sniff and Rudolf fumbled a handkerchief out of his pocket. "I know the house. Built in aught-nine by Jack Smithbeck, a typesetter at the printing plant. Had enough kids to bait a trot line, did Jack. His granddaughter Ellie was the last to live in the house;

she passed on to the other side in 'ninety-six. Never married. What people don't realize, you can't leave a house sit empty for long, it will fall right to pieces. An empty house will pine, just like a lonely dog. But then some Yankee bought it as a vacation home, paid a fortune to get it renovated."

"When was that?"

Rudolf frowned. "Maybe six years ago. I don't know the man who bought it. He shows up once in a blue moon and let's just say, he ain't on borrowing terms with his neighbors. In fact, I doubt anybody has ever seed his face."

Dodge had never heard Rudolf say so many words all at once. He had pushed some button.

"You thinking of buying a house?" Rudolf said. "Wanting to move out of Lambert Square?"

"No," Dodge said. "I like Lambert Square, I'm not ready to go anywhere."

Which was, he realized as he ran upstairs to get a jacket, the strangest truth of all.

FOR ALL HIS QUIRKS, JIMMY DEAN HAD BEEN THOROUGHLY trained and heeled beautifully. He trotted alongside Dodge on the walk across Lamb's Corner, his small, oddly shaped head turning from side to side as he took in the sights. A cat crossed the street and he tensed, and then gave a small sigh—another lost opportunity—and picked up his pace.

Dodge realized it would be good if he could sort some things out for himself before he got where he was going. To Julia's house. In his gut he was sure of that much: Julia kept a secret house in Lamb's Corner. A hidey-hole, as Grandma Lucy would have called it.

Lucy had called twice since Thanksgiving to ask about Julia, if she had come back and had Dodge had a chance to ask her about Willie and Gloria? Because Lucy wanted to adopt them both. Willie reminded her of the dog she had as a girl, long before she met her husband, and Gloria, well. Gloria and Willie couldn't be separated, after all, and Buster Cheney needed company.

Dodge promised her he would ask Julia at the first opportunity, and then he assured his sister of the same thing about Boo. Now he glanced down at

Jimmy Dean, who wouldn't miss any of the other three dogs as long as Dodge stuck around.

And there it was, the issue that was really bothering him. The idea of sticking around. Maybe he had got tired of pens sooner than he expected, but he wasn't tired of Lamb's Corner or of Lambert Square, either. How much of that had to do with Julia was another question that needed an answer.

He turned down Ewell Street, nodded a greeting to a young mother pushing a stroller with a hugely fat baby, round red cheeks and a frizz of hair peeking out of a knit cap. A woman came out on a porch and Dodge recognized her: one of the Swedes, but which one? He couldn't keep them all straight. Quite a few of the houses in this neighborhood had sold to Swedes. The sound of hammers and drills was a constant, old houses being brought up to code, roofs replaced, porches shored up and enclosed. In September everything had seemed slightly ragged around the edges. Slowly that was changing, the neighborhood coming awake after a long sleep. Cutouts of giant snowflakes taped to window glass, Christmas trees in parlor windows, bikes on porches, washing hung up in the cold December air. One thing that wasn't changing so fast: most of the cars parked along the curbs were older models, Ford and Chrysler pickups that had been put to hard use. The few Kallsjö cars he saw were almost certainly the property of Kallsjö executives.

It was a bad habit he had, concentrating on unimportant details to avoid the hard stuff. Such as the fact that he was now standing at the corner of Armistead and Ewell.

Dodge took his bearings. On all four corners huge old Victorians on big lots, one of them for sale, one that needed to be pulled down, two that looked to be occupied. In the middle of the block was a double lot with a neat fence, the house set far back enough that it couldn't be seen from this angle. Dodge had been down this street before, and stopped right at that gate to talk to Lamont Schmidt. Who kept an eye on the property, and tended the lawn and garden.

Jimmy Dean was looking up at Dodge, perfectly patient, the very picture of unconditional love.

"Want to go meet Julia?"

The stubby tail wagged three times: yes no yes.

The street was lined with trees, and it would have been easy enough to keep out of sight by standing behind one of them. Dodge thought about that, about taking a few minutes to observe before he made himself known, and then rejected the idea. He was too nervous for games.

He stood across the street looking at the house that Jack Smithbeck had built for his many children in 1909. Painted brick, shutters, a tile roof, a screened porch. Some winding woody plant climbing up a trellis, the kind that bloomed purple in the spring, the name he could never remember. The back half of the property was surrounded by a sturdy fence a good seven feet high that looked no more than a few years old. He could see a lot of trees back there, and imagined it was big enough to give Scoot room to run. It was a nice piece of property, carefully maintained.

Curtains and shades were drawn in all the windows that faced the street. There was a small pile of boxes on the porch steps and that made sense. Julia couldn't answer the door. She knew every delivery person who went through Lamb's Corner, after all, and they knew her. Maybe she waited until after dark to take in her mail and packages. He wondered what name she was using.

Dodge thought of Boo Radley, and shrugged the idea away. At this point it would be stupid to jump to conclusions, not when he could just walk up to the door and knock. He could look at her directly and ask questions, reasonable questions that she would have to answer. If not for himself, then for Mayme, who wanted to go to Sweden and was stuck in Lamb's Corner taking care of Julia's business.

For one moment he considered just giving up. Turning around and going back to Lambert Square, putting Scriveners up for sale and moving on. The idea was tempting in a lot of ways, but he couldn't do it. For once he couldn't walk away.

Dodge crossed the street, walked up the porch steps. Under the doorbell a small handwritten label: J. Hamblin. Her maiden name. He rang the bell and inside the house Scoot started barking.

JULIA WAS SITTING AT THE DINING ROOM TABLE IN FRONT OF her laptop when the doorbell rang and Scoot rose straight into the air like an alarmed cartoon dog. It did no good to tell him to stop, and so she focused her attention on the screen and the e-mail she was trying to write to her cell phone company. Striving for the right tone: no-nonsense, professional, pissed as hell. Her cell phone had died on Sunday and she had paid an exorbitant price to have a replacement overnighted to her. A cell phone she should have had yesterday morning, and here it was Wednesday in the afternoon and she was still cut off, out of touch since early Sunday. No way to check her messages and find out what was going on in the shop. And she had got into the habit of listening to Dodge's older messages, the more wordy ones where he was still trying to be amusing, before his patience began to wear thin.

She couldn't blame him for that. If he left Lamb's Corner and never came back, if all her employees quit on her, she'd have no grounds for complaint. She had never meant to stay away so long, but every morning the idea of walking out the door seemed more difficult. She had fled Lambert Square and the prison she had made for herself there and promptly made herself another one.

The thing was, she wanted to go back. Had wanted to go home almost from the second day, but whenever she ran it through in her head she saw herself standing in front of Dodge trying to explain, and coming up empty.

The doorbell again, and now Scoot was in full crazy mode, running back and forth between the dining room and the front door, yipping like his tail was on fire. Julia got up and went into the hall, where she could see the vague shape of a man standing on the porch steps.

Her heart leaped into her throat, because she recognized him. Even like this, through screen and wavy tinted glass, she knew his shape, just as Scoot had picked up his smell.

John Dodge. Finally.

HE WOULDN'T HAVE BEEN SURPRISED IF SHE HAD YELLED AT HIM to go away, but instead Julia just opened the door. Not in the least put out to see him, nothing on her face but a tentative smile. Scoot shot forward and flung himself against the screen door. Dodge was holding the new rescue dog, who was adding his own voice to the commotion.

"Hey." She leaned forward and flicked the hook. "Come on in." Scoot went still quite suddenly, his nose twitching as he took in the strange dog. Dodge was glad of something concrete to do. He handed a surprised Jimmy Dean over to Julia with one hand and picked up Scoot with the other.

Jimmy Dean whined once and then gave Julia a tentative lick on the cheek as Dodge stepped up and over the door swell and into the house.

They stood opposite each other in the dim parlor. Then Julia surprised him again by pulling back the curtains at each window, one by one. Sunlight poured into the room and turned on all the colors: polished wood, the worn green velvet upholstery, Julia's bright blue pullover in contrast to the mahogany of her hair, jeans faded to the palest blue.

She said, "I've been wanting to do that for a while now. Aren't you ever going to talk to me?"

"I've been talking to you every day for three weeks," Dodge said. Words he couldn't call back, as much as he wanted to. She didn't seem to take offense, or even to be surprised at his tone, which was less than the calm he had promised himself.

She sat down abruptly on the edge of the couch. "I looked forward to your messages, Dodge. Every day."

Scoot began to wiggle and Dodge put him down so he could go inspect Jimmy Dean, who let himself be sniffed once or twice and then hopped off Julia's lap to return the favor.

"I thought they might get along," Dodge said. "Maybe we should let them out into the backyard?"

Julia drew in a deep breath. "Good idea. I'll be right back."

He took that minute to get oriented. The house was fully furnished, everything well used and comfortable. No sign of a television or even a stereo, but they would be someplace, probably in the bedroom. A few books on the mantelpiece of the unused fireplace, and against the far wall, two flat wooden packing crates spilling great swaths of bubble wrap. Through the door to the dining room he saw an open suitcase on a table along with a laptop and the remains of a small meal.

Julia came back and stood in the doorway, her arms crossed. She said, "Maybe it would be best if I talked for a bit, would that be okay?" And without waiting she crossed the room to the packing crates and reached into one, pulled out a portrait. An oil painting in a traditional style, three feet square, ornately framed. Dodge recognized it immediately though he had never seen the likeness before.

"Charlie at twenty-one," Julia said. She put it back and pulled out the next one. "Charlie at thirty-one." A good-looking guy with wavy hair, big across the shoulders but a little soft at the jawline.

Dodge didn't know much about fine art, but he had the sense that these were not color-by-number affairs.

Julia said, "Bonnie had his portrait painted every ten years. She had already set up the arrangements for his forty-first when he got sick. These portraits are what Bonnie keeps calling about. This is all she wants. Wait, that's not right. She wants everything, but she'll settle for the portraits. And I wasn't willing to give her anything, not a piece of lint off one of his shirts."

"You had some reason to be angry," Dodge said, but Julia hardly seemed to hear him.

"You remember how I told you that the detective called me just as I was on my way out the door to the funeral? I'm not sure how to describe what happened when I hung up the phone. Do they still talk about nervous breakdowns?"

"Not so much anymore," Dodge said.

"Well, I had some kind of . . . episode. For a half hour I screamed at the walls until the neighbor shouted at me to shut up or he'd call the police. And I woke up, right then. I knew I had to get out, and I knew I couldn't go to the cemetery. I had this absolute certainty that if I saw them put the coffin in the ground I would die. So I left. I sent the limo off to the cemetery with a note for my father, and I packed in a hurry and I got in the car and I drove. I took some clothes, and the important files from Charlie's office, and I took these portraits. At the time I wasn't thinking straight, or at least that's what I told myself afterwards. Now I'm pretty sure I took the portraits because I was angry. I had some idea of burning them. Pouring gas over them and lighting a match."

She sat down heavily and looked at the portraits where she had left them, leaning against the packing crates.

"All I could think about was getting away from the cold and snow, and so I headed south. I was in Tennessee before I could make myself stop. And when I woke up the next morning in a motel room, I remembered this place." She lifted her hands, palms up, and looked around the room.

"Charlie really loved this town. He thought we'd retire here someday, and so he bought the house. He was spending a lot of time down here that last summer and fall, and he oversaw the renovation at the same time he was working at Lambert Square. When I remembered the house it seemed like providence, so I came down here and I made a lot of phone calls. I called my lawyer in Chicago and asked her to arrange to have all my stuff shipped down here, and I called Maude and asked her if the space in Lambert Square she had mentioned to Charlie was still available. I moved into the third floor the next day with nothing more than a sleeping bag and my clothes. When the furniture came from Chicago, I split it up between the apartment and here." She gestured around herself.

"The bedroom furniture?"

"You caught on to that right away, didn't you. I couldn't make myself sleep in that bed, though it took me a long time to admit it to myself."

She studied her folded hands and then raised her head and looked at Dodge. There was something new in her expression, some clarity he hadn't seen there before.

"I really did think that I had people . . ." She paused. "Fooled isn't the right word. I was so sure of what I was doing, that it was logical and reasonable, that I couldn't let myself consider how it must look to everybody else. I just excluded that possibility entirely. Until that morning. How is your head?"

Dodge found himself smiling. "Hard as ever."

She nodded. "Did you think I left because of you? Because I found out about what you used to do?"

"The thought occurred to me."

"That was the smallest part of it. Mostly I went because of the look on Exa's face. She looked at me the way you look at a dog that needs to be put down."

Dodge said, "That's a little strong."

"But it's true," Julia said. "And so I left, and I took Scoot with me. I'm sorry about that, but it was the only way I could think of to let you know that I was coming back. So every day I listened to my messages and every day I told myself, tomorrow I have to go back. But it was so hard, I never could make myself move."

"What did you do about groceries?" Dodge asked.

"It's amazing what you can order off the Internet," Julia said. "Aspirin, canned oysters, a tenderloin of beef, if you're willing to pay the delivery charges. Laundry soap, shampoo, toilet paper, it all came to the door. I think the neighbors are about to bust from curiosity."

Dodge leaned back in his chair. "And now? I see a suitcase on the table in the other room."

"I really did mean to come back two weeks ago," Julia said. "I keep unpacking and repacking. But I would have done it this time. I'd like to tell you I just overcame my fear but that would be a lie."

"So what happened?"

She hesitated. "Two things. I fell asleep on this couch and when I woke up, the first thing I saw were the portraits hanging there over the fireplace." She pointed with her chin. "And a thought went through my head. Bonnie should have the portraits. She was his mother. She'll always be his mother. I don't know what I am anymore when it comes to Charlie, but I'm not his wife. It was like a knot coming loose inside me and everything just . . . falling into place. Bonnie wants the portraits, I'll send them to her, and then I won't have to worry every time the phone rings."

"You think she'll be satisfied with just the portraits?" Dodge asked.

She smiled at him. "You've got this idea that I should call her and work through our differences. Get to the bottom of the anger, is that how you put it? Well, I don't think that's what Bonnie wants, and I'll tell you, I could care less. I've spent enough energy on her and my father, and I'm not going to spend any more. You're making a face like a therapist."

"Am I?" Dodge said. "I don't mean to."

She watched him closely for a moment. "So I'll send the portraits and I'll be free of Chicago once and for all. That's my plan."

"Okay," Dodge said, but he was thinking: stupid plan. Really stupid plan. "You said there were two things."

"The other thing is kind of anticlimactic," Julia said. "My cell phone died, and there's been some problem with the delivery of the replacement. And I realized yesterday that I was living from phone message to phone message, and that it really was time that I came home. Can I ask you a question?"

"Shoot."

"How mad are you at me? Are you here to tell me off and give me the boot?"

Dodge felt himself smiling. "Is that what you want?"

"No," she said. "That's not what I want, but I'm not in a position to be making demands. What do you want? Why did you come find me now? And how?"

He told her about the bill from the property management company, but he didn't have an answer to the more important question. Dodge hadn't asked himself about his own motivations, not in any depth. There was Mayme, of course. He could use Mayme's trip to Sweden as an excuse, protect himself that way. But looking at Julia, he knew it would sound wrong if he tried it.

"Maybe you don't know," Julia said. "I shouldn't push."

"There's one thing," Dodge said. "One thing I'd like. I want you to put on shoes and a coat and finish packing that suitcase, and then I want you to walk back to Lambert Square with me. Right now, in full daylight, we'll walk the dogs back and I'll fill you in on what's been going on since your cell phone died."

Julia closed her eyes for a long moment, and when she opened them they were wet with tears.

This was why he had walked away from therapy. The disappointment pushed up from his gut and sat in his throat like a firebrand. She wanted to think of herself as cured, free of anger, able to move freely through the world, but she was as tied down here as she had been in Lambert Square. If he were her therapist, he would have to point these things out. As somebody attached to her by affection and friendship and love—he could use that word to himself, at least—he could see them, but he couldn't say them. Now he would have to tell her it was okay, he wasn't going to push, she should take the time she needed. But she held up a hand to stop him.

"If you'll help me crate up the portraits, I'll walk back home with you. That's all I really need to do first."

IT WAS DUSK BY THE TIME THEY SET OUT, BUT THEY LEFT THE suitcases and computer bag behind for Dodge to come pick up later with the car. He'd take the crates, too, bring them back to Cocoon so they could be sent from there in the morning. So they ended up walking the dogs back to

Lambert Square as the streetlights came on, the first tentative snowflakes twirling through skirts of light.

Julia was very quiet. He wondered if he should ask her to rate her anxiety, tell him if it was at a manageable three or four and if it started to climb rapidly toward the top of the scale. He was going to ask when her expression cleared and she looked up at him. "I don't know how I'm going to face people."

"Let's worry about right now."

"Spoken like a therapist."

They were quiet for a moment. He said, "Are you going to be able to get past that?"

She didn't answer right away. "I wasn't sure at first. But then I listened to three weeks of messages and I realized it wasn't such a big deal. So you answer questions with questions, everybody's got some kind of quirk."

He laughed so loudly that Scoot turned to look at him.

Julia said, "I'm going to have to figure out a way to make amends to Mayme."

"That's easy enough," Dodge said. "Give her two weeks of paid leave so she can go to Sweden without any worries."

They walked in silence for a while longer. At one point Julia put her hand in Dodge's pocket and his pulse took up a beat. When she spoke again, it was more of a monologue, a discussion with herself about the dogs, and whether she could let Willie and Gloria go, how Boo would adjust to Brooklyn. If Nora would take Boo into the office with her and turn her into a therapy dog.

Dodge said very little to any of this beyond the hums and nods that let her know he was paying attention. Because she did have all his attention, every nerve and fiber was tuned in to Julia. The smell of her, the way her hair lay on her cheek, the noisy little indrawn breaths before she laughed. She was happy, and so he was happy, it was that simple. Tomorrow things might shut down again, but for the moment she believed she had conquered her demons. When they rose up again he would do what he could to help, but if he had learned anything in the past weeks it was that what he could do for her was limited.

They came around a corner and Lambert Square was there, lit up for Christmas.

Julia stopped and looked, her breathing calm and even. She said, "Are you going to Brooklyn?" Meaning Christmas, he knew that without hearing the words.

"Yes," Dodge said. "And to the pen show in Manhattan first. I leave on Monday."

She nodded without looking at him.

He said, "Would you like to come to Brooklyn? Because I want you to know, I'd like to have you there with me for Christmas. If you can. And if not, I'll be back on the evening of the twenty-sixth, and we can have our own celebration."

Now she did raise her head and look at him. A half smile, but nothing unsteady about it. She said, "Maybe. Maybe I can do that. I'd like to."

"Fair enough," Dodge said. "More than fair enough."

43

THE MONDAY BEFORE CHRISTMAS, Dodge wasn't gone more than a couple hours and Julia was in her office still scrambling to catch up when Exa came up from the shop.

She said, "I'm worried about Mayme over there in Sweden. And Bean."

"Not about Pearl?" Julia asked, trying for a smile.

"Better to worry about the Swedes she comes across," Exa said. "You know I'm serious; what if it goes bad?"

It was a conversation they would have every day until Mayme got home, Julia knew that. But Exa's worry was real, and so she responded in kind. "She's got return tickets, and she knows her way home."

"One of the things I like about you best," Exa said, "is the way you put your faith in the people you work with."

At that Julia had to laugh. "Exa. I am not going to Brooklyn, but if I were, I would hand the shop over to you without a moment's doubt. I know you could handle things. But I'm just not ready for that kind of a trip."

Exa grimaced. "You are cutting off your nose to spite your face."

"That's a lovely image," Julia said. "And may I say, one that doesn't make any sense. And now I have to get back to work."

But the phone rang as soon as Exa closed the office door behind herself.

"Cocoon, this is Julia."

"Hey, Jones."

That rush of adrenaline that came along with Dodge's voice, she wondered if that would ever stop.

"Hey. How's the pen show?"

"Crowded. Noisy. I'm learning a lot, I have to admit. I'm starting to think Link knows everybody in the whole world."

"It's that memory thing he's got going," Julia said. "So you're not bored?"

"Strangely, no," Dodge said.

Julia waited for him to go on, and when he didn't she forced herself to let the subject drop. What Dodge did or didn't do with Scriveners was one of those topics that left her tongue-tied and confused and ill at ease.

"Any news on that end?"

"Lots of it," Julia said. "But I'll have to swear you to secrecy."

"Spit it out, Jones."

"All right. I have it on good authority that Nils is going to propose to Mayme."

"This is news? LRoy has been taking bets on this since Thanksgiving."

"On the other end of the spectrum, we've got Carl Durant and Lorna Jean."

"He didn't."

"He didn't, you're right. But he's going to. He said you made him see the error of his ways, and it was time. What did you say to him?"

"Just some home truths about frustrated women. How did you become Miss Marriage Manners?"

"I wish I knew. But wait, there's more. This morning he came to ask me to help him pick out a ring, right? And he's not out of my office ten minutes when Lorna Jean sweeps in, plunks down a Tiffany's catalog and points out the ring she wants. It's my duty to steer Carl to this particular ring."

"Price tag?"

"Twelve thousand."

"Ai ai ai."

"I asked her about it; she said she's putting the bookstore up for sale and she'll pay for the ring herself if she has to."

"She's giving up the bookstore? Where oh where will people go for pictures of kittens and glittery angel figurines?"

Julia heard herself snort. "Your compassion is bottomless."

"My tolerance for kitsch isn't. Does she have any potential buyers?"

"Why?" Julia asked. "Do you want it?" She bit her lip and prayed he would simply pass over that slip of the tongue. It was harder and harder to leave the topic alone. Sometimes she thought the best thing would be to ask straight out, and so she tried to formulate the question: *What's up after Scriveners? How're things going with that Vermont deal?*

She could never manage the right tone, and the reason was clear enough: she didn't know what she was hoping to hear from him.

The list of things she did know was much longer. She was certain that Dodge couldn't make a life's work out of Scriveners. He had gone in and learned everything he wanted to know in record time, turned things around too quickly. Not enough of a challenge. He needed something more difficult to occupy him, something that would take more effort. A cure for cancer. Cold fusion. Peace in the Middle East.

From the beginning he had said he'd be moving on. Hadn't she made him reiterate that promise? And he had done so without hesitation. The bottom line: he would be leaving, and in the not too distant future. He'd go to Vermont or Idaho or Kansas and teach the world the right way to sell shoes, or how to make the perfect banana split, or where the profit was in hula hoops.

He said, "Jones, you okay?" and she started up out of her thoughts.

"One more piece of news. Bean called."

He laughed at that, full-throated. "From Sweden, on a borrowed cell phone?"

"Not this time. I talked to all of them."

"And how's it going?"

"That depends on who you ask. Bean says it's dark and cold, Pearl says it's full of strange people who mean well but don't know how to cook, and Mayme says she's looking forward to coming home."

There was a long pause. "I'm sorry to hear that."

"Yeah," Julia said. "Me too. But there is some good news. When they come home, Nils is coming too. For good. He threatened to quit, and Beate gave in. He's coming back to Lamb's Corner."

"And?"

"I don't know. They seem determined to work it out."

Dodge said, "There's a lot of that going around."

SHE BROUGHT THE SUBJECT OF DODGE'S LONG-TERM PLANS UP with Maude while they went over Lambert Square business at Polly's.

"He's bored," Julia said.

"You think? He strikes me as more driven, and that makes sense after meeting his daddy. There's a man who knows how to wind up his children."

"You told me the Colonel was a perfect southern gentleman."

"I have to work harder on my sarcasm. Or would that be irony?" Maude shrugged.

"You didn't like him."

"Oh, I liked him well enough but I spent a total of twenty minutes with the man when we stopped by that afternoon to visit. He's charming and witty and quick with a story. I just wouldn't want to be his child. You ask me," she said, "John Dodge has got a good dose of Boo Radley to deal with his own self."

Irritation had a taste, acid sharp. Julia didn't need Maude to make her feel guilty, but she did want to know about what she had missed. The truth was, she was sorry about the whole thing. She should have been there on Thanksgiving. It would have been the supportive thing to do. Lately she found herself wondering if she could have been any help to Dodge, if she hadn't been so wound up in the carefully tended garden of her own fears.

"I used to be a thoughtful person," she told Maude. "Someplace along the way I forgot how."

Maude said, "He's a patient man, and he loves you."

Julia put down her spoon. "That's what everybody keeps telling me. Funny, I've never heard it from Dodge."

"So first you run off and hide for a month—"

"Three weeks."

"—and now you're wondering why he's treating you like a horse that's prone to shy."

"So I'm inconsistent. I'm confused. I'm . . ."

Maude raised an eyebrow.

"I'm going to go," Julia said. "To Brooklyn. I think."

"Sugar," Maude said, "nobody will think bad of you if you don't."

"Dodge's grandmother is going to be there," Julia volunteered. "She never comes to Brooklyn for Christmas but she is this year. She's assuming I'll be there, that's my guess."

Maude stirred her soup thoughtfully. "Does that strike you as unusual?"

"Not exactly," Julia said. "But I think mostly she wants to see if she can get me to give up Willie and Gloria."

Maude put both hands flat on the table and leaned forward. "Listen to me now, Jules. If you can't go, you can't go. He's not going to be mad at you. But be honest with yourself, will you, please? If you don't go, it won't be about the dogs."

Julia said, "Do you have a degree in clinical therapy I don't know about?"

"Better than that," Maude said. "I have three little girls, every one of them smarter than me. I have learned to listen for what Mike calls subtext, but really it's just what my granny always told me. The devil is in the details."

"Maude," Julia said, "I am scared out of my head."

For a minute she thought Maude wouldn't respond at all, but then she pushed out a long sigh. "Listen, sugar. Nothing is guaranteed in this life, you know that. But you've got a chance to start over here. A chance to be happy. You can't walk away from that. Now don't start with the what-if's, please. There's no knowing what's going to happen down the line. Maybe Dodge will start some kind of consulting business out of an office on Main Street. Maybe he'll buy some fixer-upper in Houston or Paris or Florence and you'll go along and open up another store of your own. Stranger things have happened."

"Not much stranger," Julia said.

Maude laughed. Then she leaned over and kissed Julia on both cheeks.

"If you don't go to Brooklyn, you can still call the man on the telephone. Tell him you love him, and let things roll on from there."

It was odd, walking out of Lambert Square in the full light of a sunny December afternoon. Odder still was the fact that nobody seemed to notice her. Julia was just another person out running errands the day before Christmas Eve, wearing everyday clothes. Jeans, a sweater and a light jacket, her old converse high-tops, and a pair of gloves she had found when she went through the clothes boxes stacked in the attic of the Armistead Street house. Even the dogs were unimpressed, all five of them much more interested in reading the canine news on every bush, trash can, and patch of grass.

She headed for the river and let them off-leash so they could run along ahead of her. Every once in a while one of them would stop to look back, as if they expected her to suddenly disappear. With the exception of Jimmy Dean, who paid her little notice. He had been in mourning since Dodge left for New York, and showed no interest in making friends with Julia. The only other living creature who interested him was Scoot. But then Scoot was used to Dodge leaving and coming back. As far as Jimmy Dean knew, Dodge was gone for good.

The dogs really were the reason she couldn't go to Brooklyn. Who would take five dogs on short notice, and over the holiday? And poor old Jimmy Dean was just settling in; it would be cruel to uproot him again for a few days. She had an image of buying six plane tickets and what that would look like, if the airlines allowed such a thing. Her five mutts sitting upright, each in his or her own seat, waiting patiently for the flight attendant to begin the meal service. One good thing would be that stewarding all the dogs through crowded airports would keep her focused on something besides her own anxiety.

She would have Christmas the way she always did. She'd sleep late and make herself the things she liked best for the midday meal. There were movies she always watched, because she loved them and knew them so well she could drift in and out of sleep while they played and not miss anything. The dogs would need to be walked. And if she was feeling really energetic and in need of something to do, she could give each of them an overdue bath.

Scoot looked at her nervously, a furry mind reader.

Julia realized she had walked farther than she intended to, and her pulse began to race. She forced herself to start the breathing exercises she had read about in one of Dodge's books. Concentrating on the flow of cold air, the expansion of her lungs, the way colors grew brighter and the world more distinct. Five, she whispered, and continued with her breathing. Four.

Four was pretty darn good, she told herself. Four was excellent when it came to her anxiety level, given where she was.

She would start for home, but not directly. First, Julia promised herself, she would walk around the periphery of Lambert Square, see how far she could get before that all-important number started to climb again. When she hit seven she'd give it up, enough for one day.

An hour later Julia found herself on Main Street, saying hello to the people she passed. As if it were the most common thing in the world to be out, looking in windows, reading signs posted on the bulletin board at the laundromat. Kallsjö was about to start its next round of hiring, the high school drama department was looking for help building sets for *West Side Story*, the bank would be happy to help anybody buy a new car or build an extension, lowest rates guaranteed.

It was a little like waking up out of a long sleep. As though she had been in a self-induced coma without ever realizing it. Had she woken herself up, or was that Dodge's doing? She passed the bank and stopped in front of the cash machine, curious to see if her card still worked after five years.

The machine disgorged five twenty-dollar bills and a receipt, and thanked her for her patronage. She stopped in the drugstore and bought shampoo and toothpaste and a new toothbrush; she went into Wheeler's Consignment Treasures, a place she had heard about often enough over the years, and walked over creaking floorboards to examine chipped wash-basins, boxes of sepia-tinted photos full of anonymous families, brides with arms full of orange blossoms, men in uniform. There was a red-and-white quilt for sale, simple patchwork but carefully done. Julia bought the quilt and an 1890 edition of *Pride and Prejudice* with beautiful endpapers and a silk ribbon place marker.

Now her arms were full, and the dogs had had enough of waiting for her outside shop windows so she headed back home. She felt an odd pang of regret; she was just getting comfortable out in the world, and so she took the longer way, coming up on the far side of Lambert Square and the parking structure, cars swarming like bees, in and out. Business was good this holiday season. People had a little money now, and the promise of steady work. Kallsjö was living up to the promises it made. Big Dove and Trixie went out to the construction site sometimes, just to watch. Like a tailgate party but without the football game, there would be as many as a dozen cars there in the late afternoon as the heavy machines were being shut down for the night, talking about the progress being made. Waving to the workers as they set out for home. Many of them on foot, and that was a pure miracle. Men—and women, too—walking home from work, ready for dinner, satisfied to have done a day's labor and put food on the table.

"It's the little things like that," Trixie said. "That's what was missing in Lamb's Corner. Sometimes I'm afraid I'll wake up in the morning and it'll all be gone, just a dream."

Julia was curious about the Kallsjö site, but enough was enough for one day.

In the alley outside Scriveners she paused, thinking of Dodge's houseplants. His keys were in her pocket, a whole ringful. Alley entrance, apartment front and back, shop front, one house key labeled *Nora* and two car keys. The last time she had seen Dodge's car was in this very alley, caught red-handed with chocolate on her tongue.

She turned and walked back to the parking structure. The dogs followed, radiating doubt.

Each of the shops had two dedicated parking spaces, neatly signed. Cocoon's two spaces were both occupied. The 1962 Ford Fairlane was the only car Exa had ever owned, baby blue and pampered into genteel old age. Big Dove's pickup truck hunkered beside the Fairlane, a patchwork of rust, primer paint, and strategically placed duct tape. A smiley face decal on the bumper, between *Some things are true whether you believe them or not* and *Heritage not Hate*.

The dogs caught sight of Dodge's car and strained toward it, pulling her along. A sturdy BMW with a lot of miles on it, white paint, chrome, leather seats. He had driven this car back and forth across the country innumerable times, long easy drives he had described in loving detail. He stopped when he wanted to, or when traffic got to be a headache. He'd browse stores or walk through a strange town until the roads cleared and then he'd be off again.

"The only civilized way to travel," he had said, and Julia could imagine him cruising along on a sunny day, thinking about where he was headed, what surprises might be ahead.

She used the key to open the door and the dogs piled in without hesitation. Gloria sat in the middle of the backseat where she'd have an unobstructed view of the road, Willie next to her, his head on his paws. Scoot and Jimmy Dean stationed themselves upright at the closed rear windows, tails waving extravagantly. Boo settled in the front passenger seat, looking unusually awake and eager.

Julia got into the driver's seat and started the car.

She drove around town for an hour and found it didn't take long to get back in the habit of shifting gears and using a turn signal. Many of the places she passed were familiar to her simply from everyday talk in the shop. The Food Lion was the subject of many discussions when the Needlework Girls were in attendance. The infamous Huey's Gas Station Emporium, which featured locally smoked hams, pickled pigs feet, Vienna sausages, Moon Pies, RC Cola, Cheerwine, peanuts and pecan brittle, and a couple hundred DVDs to rent, the most scandalous of which Huey kept behind the counter, and would admit to having only if he was sure there was nobody in the station who would sell him out to those most likely to take action in their outrage.

Julia gave in to her curiosity and turned into Huey's; it would be rude to borrow a car and return it with less than a full tank, and beyond that, she found she was thirsty. Once inside it turned out nobody recognized her anyway.

When she got back in the car she had two large bottles of water, a Styrofoam bowl, a bag of beef jerky, cheese strings, popcorn and candy bars, and a half dozen maps. She pulled over to the side and poured water into the bowl until all the dogs had had enough, distributed beef jerky according to appetite and size, and then she opened a map and began to study.

44

"I DO have to admit," Link said, touching a handkerchief to a very red nose, "I have never seen the like." His head swiveled from one side of the street to the other, pendulum-like.

Dodge said, "Watch your step," but Link was too focused on a fully motorized, life-size reinterpretation of Santa's village spread out over the front lawn of a neat brick duplex. He lost his footing on a patch of ice, and Dodge grabbed him by the elbow and held him until he was stable.

They had taken the subway from Manhattan to Brooklyn, a twenty-minute ride in which Link had started a conversation with a conservative Jew by asking about the historical significance of earlocks. Link was educated; he didn't ask stupid or thoughtless questions; he was unfailingly polite. But his curiosity could take him places Dodge preferred not to go, conversations with strangers who reminded Dodge of his internship year right here in Manhattan, and what random violence looked like. But they had survived the discussion of Hassidic clothing and religious practices, just as they had survived an earlier conversation with a woman whose entire face and neck featured an elaborate and quite beautiful tattooed garden, and the Muslim family visiting from Nigeria, the women standing aside, eyes downcast above burqas while the father talked to Link about the World Cup.

Now they walked the three blocks to Nora's place at a crawl so that Link could make a study of Ditmas Park architecture and cultural artifacts. Dodge wouldn't have minded the pace if he had felt comfortable pulling out his cell phone to try Julia one more time, but he really did not want to hear what Link had to say about this newest situation. And really, there was no need. Sooner or later Julia would remember to set up her voice mailbox, and then he could . . .

His train of thought always stopped just there. What was he going to do when he finally got her on the phone?

If he got her on the phone.

That idea sat like a rock in his gut and so he listed for himself the logical reasons Julia might have left Lambert Square (again), without telling him the where and why of it (again), and with no indication of how to reach her. Again. The unfortunate thing was, the list was not very long. Maybe she had yet another house in Lamb's Corner she hadn't mentioned. Maybe Charlie's clothes and personal effects were in that house, and she had been struck by the sudden need to pack it all up and send it off to Bonnie in Chicago.

She had been doing so well, making progress on her own terms and with no help from him. Tuesday afternoon she had walked all the way back to Lambert Square and picked up where she left off, taking over from Mayme, handling co-op business with quiet efficiency, wooing herself back into the good graces of the dogs she had left behind. She had come back to his bed on her own, with a breathlessness that had overwhelmed him.

Sometime between Monday, when he and Link left for the pen show, and Tuesday, something else had happened. He went over their last telephone call once again, wondering if he had missed some note of desperation or panic. They had talked about Mayme, whose introduction to Sweden didn't seem to be going well. They had talked about Leo, about Exa, about Lorna Jean and Carl. About Lorna Jean selling the bookstore. Julia had asked him if he was interested, and then she had changed the subject in a rush. Embarrassed. Maybe even worried. It was a hard topic to back away from once you opened it up, and Dodge had been too unsure of himself to pursue it; he let it go.

Link said, "In't this the street? Sure it is, there's your sister on the porch of that big old Victorian."

Dodge looked up. Nora was standing there, arms wrapped around herself against the cold, rocking back and forth on her heels. She raised a hand in greeting and Dodge waved back.

"It's like one of those old movies, coming home for Christmas, or white Christmas, or something like that." Link pulled out his handkerchief and dabbed his nose again. "Though I was hoping for a reindeer or two on the roof, and one of them big plastic Santas that lights up."

Behind Nora the door opened and the Colonel came out on the porch. He put his arm around his daughter's shoulder and raised a hand in a half salute.

"Yes, sir," Link said. "Just like one of them old movies."

"We came in a little early," Dodge's mother told them, going up on tiptoe even as Dodge leaned down to offer his cheek and kiss hers in turn. Her hands clutched his coat sleeves and she gave him a little shake. "You know how it goes with the transport flights, you take what you can get."

"Sure." Dodge touched his cold hands to his mother's face, an old trick from his boyhood that made her squeak and laugh with pleasure. With his hands on his mother's cheeks he had the strongest urge to mention Julia, to tell his mother about her. At Thanksgiving he had been too distracted and on edge, too unsure of what was going on to talk about her at all. And here he was again, in the same odd place.

"We are going to have a good Christmas, all of us."

"Ma," Dodge said. "Of course we are."

And then he turned and shook his father's hand. Took stock of the evidence that the Colonel was indeed mortal, and growing older. The pale blue eyes just as clear and the gaze just as sharp, but otherwise gravity was doing its work on cheeks and jawline. He still wore his hair in a crew cut, the blond long gone to white. Dodge shook his father's hand. A firm, quick shake, the way he had been taught, and there was even a smile to go along with it.

The Colonel said, "You're looking hale, son. I'm glad to see you."

Dodge felt his mother's gaze on him, and his sister's. He wondered what Julia would make of the Colonel, how she would deal with him when she finally met him one day. If she would look at him and see a stiff old man who had never learned how to let go, and was regretting that inability in himself. If she would find a way to talk to him, so that they would stay on congenial terms.

Nora was answering questions about who was arriving when, Jim and Gigi coming in this evening, T.J. and Sandy first thing in the morning—

"Grandma Lucy?" Dodge asked.

"Freddy will be leaving in an hour to pick her up at the airport," Nora said. "I told her to take an earlier flight but she was worried about Buster Cheney."

"You've got a full house, sounds like," Link said. "I appreciate the invitation to dinner when you've got so much going on. I've been looking forward to it all week, in't that so?"

Dodge agreed that it was so, and then he gave in to the impulse he had been resisting for a couple hours. He retreated to the room Nora had assigned him. To wash up, he told them, and he did wash up and change, too, but he also called Julia's cell phone, which still would not take a message. No luck with her apartment phone or his own. He thought of calling Cocoon to see if Exa had heard anything, but it was five o'clock on the last full shopping day before Christmas, and it was unlikely anybody would pick up. In fact, he doubted he'd be able to get anybody on the phone in all of Lamb's Corner. There was nothing to do but wait.

Freddy and Ben came in with Joe Rocket at their heels and Tom came in from a store run, his arms full of bags, the bags full of bottles. Link and the Colonel were in the parlor with the boys setting up dominoes, and Dodge's mother was tucked away in some corner with Maddie, happy to have her granddaughter to herself until Grandma Lucy showed up and took sole possession.

Dodge went into the kitchen to see if Nora needed any help.

She put him to work cleaning pans and then she closed the door so that the half dozen conversations in the rest of the house were reduced to background noise. She crossed her arms and stood there, waiting to hear what could possibly explain Dodge's willingness to scrub pots.

So he told her. Julia had gone missing again. No luck reaching her by phone.

Nora said, "So where do you think she is?"

"The truth? I don't have any idea."

"Maybe she went to Chicago," Nora said. And: "What, that never occurred to you, that she might want to see the rest of her family?"

Dodge had never told Nora the story of how Julia's father had abandoned her after Charlie's death, and now wasn't the time. He was about to say that when the phone rang and Nora leaned over to pick it up.

"Hello."

He watched her expression go slack with surprise. She said, "I'm glad you called, because Freddy was just about to head out for the airport. Is this because of Buster Cheney?"

Surprise gave way to disquiet. "Okay, Gran. Sure. Will you be careful? The traffic is awful."

She hung up but left her hand on the phone for a moment.

"What?" Dodge said.

"Grandma Lucy is driving," Nora said. "She'll be here in less than an hour, if the traffic holds."

Dodge said, "You're kidding. I thought she gave up her license."

"I wish I were kidding. I thought she gave up her license, too. Let's hope she didn't. She canceled her airline reservation and she's been on the road since early this morning."

"Because of Buster Cheney."

Nora nodded. "'Among other things,'" she said. "Should we tell the Colonel?"

"And spread the terror around? There's nothing he could do, anyway."

"She promised me she wouldn't drive anymore," Nora said, distracted. The timer rang on the stove and she pulled two large casseroles out of the oven and placed them on trivets. Good smells filled the air, and Dodge's stomach grumbled.

Nora said, "I can't remember the last time she broke a promise. Can you?"

GRANDMA LUCY CLOSED THE CELL PHONE WITH A SNAP AND laughed. "It's childish of me, I have to admit it, but I do like getting them riled."

The traffic was heavy and required all of Julia's attention, but she did glance quickly at the old lady in the passenger seat. They had been together in the car since early morning, but despite the traffic and the almost unbroken stream of talk, Julia was feeling more comfortable than she would ever have guessed possible. Especially as she had basically stolen a car and driven it across state lines. Without a valid driver's license, either. In fact, neither of them had a driver's license.

"Never mind that," Lucy had said. "You're only young once."

To Julia's great relief they had not been stopped and thus were spared from trying to make that particular argument stick.

"You sorry you found me and came by?" Lucy asked her now.

"I'm glad to have the company on the drive," Julia said.

Lucy laughed. "You've been in the South too long, honey. You forgot how to answer a question straight on."

"I'll answer," Julia said. "But there's a gas station coming up, and I want to check the map before we get to the Holland Tunnel."

Any detour with six dogs and one old lady with a weak bladder was a major undertaking requiring patience and coordination, but Julia was full of an almost itchy energy and glad of the need to be out, moving through the cold air. The night before when she arrived at Lucy's house, unannounced, she had not got the kind of questions she expected but a lecture about dressing warm and keeping her feet dry. While the dogs surrounded Buster Cheney and examined Lucy's house, Julia was pointed to an old-fashioned bathtub of steaming water, and a cup of equally hot tea was pressed into her hands. Lucy gave Julia some old flannel pajamas that smelled of lavender, slippers too big for her feet, and a worn velvet robe that dragged on the floor but otherwise was heavenly soft.

Finally installed at Lucy's kitchen table, she had been allowed to tell her story, but it turned out she didn't really have one.

"I really did . . . I do really want to go to Brooklyn," Julia said. "But I couldn't face the idea of the airport, and I didn't want to leave the dogs behind, because, because . . ." She hesitated, but there was no help from Lucy, who looked as though she was willing to wait one hour or twenty, whatever it took.

"Because I was gone for three weeks and they are still mad at me about that," she said.

"But driving some seven hundred miles to Brooklyn, that doesn't scare you?"

"Not as much," Julia said. "The truth is, I kept thinking I'd turn around and go back home. Every exit I told myself the next one I'd get off, but then I'd keep my foot on the gas pedal. I left town with nothing but my purse and the dogs, I didn't even stop to get a suitcase, and once I got going . . ." She shrugged.

"What you need," Lucy said, "is a good hot meal, and then a solid night's sleep. Then you'll be ready in the morning."

"Ready for what?" Julia asked.

"Why, ready to go to Brooklyn, in which case I'll be sitting right next to you. Or you'll turn back the way you came."

"I want to go to Brooklyn," Julia said.

"Is that so?" said Lucy. And: "You're in love with my grandson, is that it?"

Julia felt the heat climbing up her neck into her face.

"It's a simple enough question," Lucy said.

"It doesn't feel simple to me."

Lucy sighed and pushed herself up from the table. She went to the refrigerator and pulled out a covered pan, and then she turned to face Julia.

She said, "There are some hard things in this life, and from what I've heard, you've had your share. You had a good husband and he died young, and your own folks failed you when you needed them most. But you survived all that."

"I ran away," Julia said. "I ran away on the day Charlie was buried. I didn't even go to the cemetery, I just got in the car and . . ." She swallowed. "I left."

"And what is it you think you were running from? Was there anything left for you in Chicago?"

Julia wrapped her hands around her empty teacup. "No."

"You think Charlie was looking down from heaven disappointed when he didn't see you by the graveside?"

Julia found herself biting back a smile. "Charlie was a big fan of John Lennon's. He couldn't imagine heaven."

"So it was your daddy and Charlie's mama who had you worried."

"I didn't want to see them," Julia said. "I couldn't bear to look at them."

"Because you took Charlie away from them."

Julia drew in a sharp breath, shocked to the core.

"Because—" She stopped. "Because they held me responsible for his death."

"Ah," Lucy said. The tone a mother uses with a kid who has come up with a transparently flimsy explanation. A mother who was wise enough not to point out the flaw, and willing to stand back while the truth revealed itself without her help.

"You mean they would have been mad at me no matter where he died, or how. They blamed me because I was convenient."

"Grief does strange things to people," Lucy said. "When my husband died, it hit Teddy like a wrecking ball, tore everything out from under him. He never was the same after that, though the other boys all came around in the fullness of time. And then Teddy found the army and the law, and he held on for dear life. All those rules and regulations, to you or me they seem like they'd choke a person to death, but it gave Teddy what he needed. At first I was thankful to see him settled, but then he got married. He nearly buckled under the worry of it, the burden of being a father to those boys. He took to drink, but Sophia would have left him and taken the kids with her, and so Teddy pulled himself together. He is so afraid of himself, so worried about losing control, he can't imagine anybody else living without those rules of his, either. And Dodge wasn't cut from that bolt." She shook her head.

"I didn't know," Julia said. "Dodge never explained it to me like that."

"Because he can't see it," Lucy said. "All that training and studying to help other people and he could never see the simplest things about his own situation." She turned to look at Julia.

"Do you see your daddy for the man he is?"

Another question Julia hadn't ever asked herself, and one she didn't want to think about now.

She said, "I don't want to expend even one more minute thinking about my father."

Lucy smiled. "Well see, honey, that's the problem. Not thinking about somebody takes more energy than you'd imagine. You bust a lot of calories holding him at arm's length. I'd say you'd be better off taking that bull by the horns. Tell him what you think of him for the way he treated you, and see if that wound don't start to heal once you let it drain."

"So you do think I ran away," Julia said, and her tone sounded childish to her own ears.

Lucy didn't seem to notice. She said, "If a house is on fire, you get out right fast or you'll suffocate to death. That's saving yourself, not running away. You needed something else and you went and found it for yourself. Built up a business and made a home, spent some time mourning your husband and then you found a new man."

"It's not that simple," Julia said again. And then, her voice gone hoarse: "Can it be that simple?"

"It can if you let it," Lucy said. She leaned over to read the dial on the oven, her eyes squinted half shut. Gave it a half turn and slid in the pan. Then she came and sat down across from Julia at the kitchen table with its faded cotton tablecloth, olives dancing around martini glasses, using toothpicks as batons.

Lucy said, "Listen to me now. Things are only complicated if you want them to be. You took a couple years to get your feet back under you, drew into your shell while you did it. And while you were in there healing you decided you didn't want another man because you had had enough of hurt. Don't deny it now, just hear me out. And then Dodge came along and you changed your mind. And that's why you got into the car and drove north. Because you couldn't sit around down there in Lamb's Corner waiting to see him, you had to be on the move. So here you are. Now, I ask you, ain't that so?"

The room seemed very bright to Julia, so strongly lit that her eyes didn't want to stay open. They burned with tears, and she squinted them shut against the glare. And then she nodded. "I suppose it is so."

"Well then," Lucy said, slapping the table with one palm. "Let me tell you how this is going to go. We'll eat, and we'll sleep, and tomorrow morning we'll get in that car and drive on up to Brooklyn so you can tell Dodge what he needs to hear. And on the way we'll have a good talk, see what other knots might need untying."

They had done just that. In the morning Julia had come suddenly and absolutely awake at exactly six, eager to be on the road again, headed north. Eager to have Lucy with her in the car, to listen to her stories and tell her own in turn.

They stopped every couple hours to walk the dogs and use the bathrooms and eat some of the food Lucy had packed, pimento cheese sandwiches and slices of pork, boiled eggs and carrot sticks, corn bread muffins and a huge thermos of sweet tea. There were homemade biscuits for the dogs, too. Something Julia might not have attempted, considering the trouble six dogs fighting in one medium-size car might cause. But Lucy was a natural and not one of them acted up with her, not even Jimmy Dean, who lowered his gaze and flicked his tongue in abject apology when she spoke a warning word in his direction.

And now here they were, ready to cross from New Jersey into Manhattan by way of the Holland Tunnel, and all day Julia had held back the one subject she really wanted to talk about.

They got back into the car and she calmly threaded her way into fast-moving traffic, which would have been a plain miracle in any other circumstances but just now she had other things to worry about, and maybe a half hour or forty minutes left in this drive.

The dogs were all asleep, draped companionably on top of one another. Lucy had finally talked herself out, or, more likely, it occurred to Julia, she was waiting.

They drove through the umbilicus that was the Holland Tunnel, sound and light dancing on the walls. Bumper-to-bumper traffic moving fast, people heading home late, thinking of dinner or where to find the money for the phone bill or the tuition, how to spend the bonus that was hopefully coming. She had grown up in a big city and the rhythms were immediately familiar and even welcome, the glow of a million lights as they came up out of the tunnel into lower Manhattan and turned south toward the next tunnel that would take them under the East River to Brooklyn. The very strangest thing of all was the feeling that she was where she should be, that she was headed for home.

She felt Lucy looking at her. Julia said, "Do you think Dodge will buy into the simple view of things?"

"Well sure, honey," Lucy said. "He's just waiting for you to show him how."

45

WHEN THEY WERE all around the table, Nora gave Link one of her widest, most welcoming smiles. She said, "We are so pleased to have you here. Please ask if there's anything you might like that you don't see."

"Mama's southern is busting out," said Maddie with a smile of her own.

Ben put a hand to his heart and fluttered his lashes. "She has always extended every kindness to strangers."

"As God is her witness, you will nevah be hungry again," chimed in Freddy. It was a Bugiardini set piece, but it made Link laugh out loud.

"Because Nora is a southerner," said the Colonel. "And she was well brought up." He sent a meaningful look across the table, one that Dodge purposefully overlooked, but his mother did not.

She said, "Eleanor, whose recipe is this?"

Dodge was determined not to get into any kind of argument. If that meant agreeing when his father declared the sky's natural color to be red, he would do that. As the easiest way to keep himself from talking was to put food in it, he took large helpings of Nora's chicken fricassee, mashed potatoes, roasted carrots, and spinach salad while the discussion turned to Tom's family, the passing down of recipes, and the competition among his aunts and sisters when it came to certain dishes. It seemed for a good while that dinner would go smoothly but then there was a pause in the conversation and Link filled it.

"Colonel, your son has pulled off a miracle, did you know that? I didn't think it could be done, but he has turned Scriveners into a profitable business and in record time."

"Is that so?"

"It is. It certainly is. I have to give credit where it's due. He's got a light but steady touch, knows when to stand back and when to stand up. It's a delicate business, fixing what's broke without causing damage someplace else. Yessir, he's got the knack for fixing things. Businesses and people, too."

Dodge shot Link a warning glance.

"And he's modest," Link added with a wink.

"Sounds like you're done with Lamb's Corner," the Colonel said, looking directly at Dodge. "So what's next?"

And now everyone was looking at him. Link, who had carefully steered the conversation toward this very question because he had never been able to get an answer when he put it to Dodge himself. His mother, holding her breath and hoping for the best. Nora and Tom, poised and ready to jump in if things got out of hand. Fred and Maddie looked worried, and Ben, oblivious at fourteen, asking if somebody could please pass him the mashed potatoes.

Dodge said, "I don't know yet. There are a few possibilities."

"Let me guess," said the Colonel. "There's a firewood concession in Alaska that could use overhauling. Would that be far enough away?"

Dodge's mother put down her fork with a clatter, but Dodge held up a hand to stop whatever she meant to say.

"I might be finished getting Scriveners on its feet," he said. "But that doesn't mean I'm done with Lamb's Corner. I may decide to stay."

"You never stay," his father said. "You make noises like maybe you're going to settle down, and then you run off again. It's the one thing we can count on from you, JD."

Link was looking back and forth between Dodge and his father. He said, "I see I have opened up a painful subject, and I'm sorry for it. For what it's worth, I think it's a shame."

The Colonel turned his head in Link's direction. "That's what I've been trying to impress upon him all these years."

"No, sir," Link said. "You misunderstand me. I think it's a shame that a man like you couldn't see the value of your own son. I would be proud to call him my own, but all you want to do is bad-mouth him in front of family and friends."

A flush appeared high on the Colonel's cheeks. There was dead silence around the table, and Link took that as an invitation.

"I've seen your son extend kindness and generosity to everybody he comes across. I made it hard for him to do his work when he first came to Scriveners, mostly just because I'm an ornery cuss and I didn't like the way things were changing, but he treated me with respect and won me over. He's made friends everyplace he goes, not least because he was the only one who knew how to help Julia. And he did, too. She's woke up out of a long sleep, and that was his doing. Your son's."

The Colonel said, "Do you mean that disturbed young lady who ran off at Thanksgiving? And why isn't she here, if he helped her so much?"

There was a sharply indrawn breath, and then Dodge's mother was standing. She said, "I warned you, Teddy. I told you—"

From the front hall came an explosion of barking, and suddenly everybody was on their feet. Joe Rocket was flinging himself into the air. Dodge couldn't make sense of it, one dog making so much noise, and then Tom was opening the door and an avalanche of dogs was rushing through.

"Merciful heavens," said Link.

"Boo!" said Nora.

Ben yelled, "Buster Cheney!"

"Mama?" said the Colonel.

Dodge would have said something. He would have called out to Julia, who was standing in the doorway, flushed with color and embarrassment. She had Jimmy Dean in her arms, and then Jimmy Dean saw Dodge and he sat up and added his bark to the general confusion.

Julia took a few steps in Dodge's direction, a smile coming up now. Suddenly his own legs started to work and he met her halfway in that seething mass of people and dogs. Jimmy Dean was wiggling with excitement, and so Dodge took him. And then leaned forward and kissed Julia, and she kissed him back.

"I stole your car," she said.

"Best idea you ever had."

"My license isn't even valid anymore."

"And yet, here you are."

"I came away without my suitcase. I don't even have a pair of pajamas. Me, without pajamas."

Dodge grinned down at her. "Second best idea."

Julia glanced around herself and Dodge realized that everyone was looking at them.

"So whose idea was this spontaneous road trip?" Nora asked. "Did Granny Lucy call you, Julia?"

"I wish I had thought of it," Lucy said. "I can't remember the last time I had so much fun. But it was all Julia's idea. She showed up at my door yesterday evening and said she had brought me Gloria and Willie if I still wanted to adopt them, and asked if I wanted a ride."

Dodge's mother said, "Dodge?"

"Oh, sorry." Dodge slipped an arm around Julia's shoulders and turned with her to face the rest of the family. "Mama, this is Julia. Julia, this is—"

"Sophia." She came forward, her curiosity far stronger than any awkwardness she might be feeling, and kissed Julia on both cheeks. "Aren't you the brave one, driving all the way up here in the holiday traffic."

"And my father," Dodge said. "Colonel Theodore Roosevelt Dodge."

"I think you have something to say, Teddy, don't you?" Dodge's mother poked him.

"Welcome," said the Colonel, the knot of muscles in his jaw rolling and clenching. "You're very welcome here, Miss Julia. I admit I had my doubts about you, but it turns out I was wrong. For my son's sake, I'm glad of it."

Link stood back from the crowd, beaming with satisfaction.

MUCH LATER JULIA COLLAPSED, ARMS OUTSPREAD, ON THE BED in a small room on the third floor of his sister's home. Dodge stood with his back against the closed door, looking at her.

"I'm sorry I scared you," Julia said, for at least the fifth time. "I really didn't mean to."

"Where's your cell phone?"

"Huh?"

"Hand over your cell phone, Jones."

She got it out of her purse and then watched while Dodge did things with it. Things she clearly should have done two days ago, but had forgotten about. Or maybe not. Maybe she had needed those two days. Julia got up and peeled herself out of her shoes and socks and jeans, thinking that she'd have to borrow some things from Nora or go out tomorrow—on Christmas Eve, no less—and brave the crowds. There were some shops in Manhattan she had heard interesting things about, places that carried the same kind of stuff she did. Shops she had never thought she'd see, but here she was. She had gotten here on her own, it was that simple.

Dodge sat down next to her on the edge of the bed and put an arm around her waist.

"So how was Lucy on the drive up?"

"Instructive," Julia said.

"A conversation for tomorrow," he said. And: "Arms up."

He pulled her pullover up and off and tossed it aside.

"I like Lucy," Julia said. "She . . . understands things."

He unhooked her bra and it went the way of the sweater. "In a good way or a bad way?"

Julia held on to the front of his shirt and lay back on the bed, drawing him with her.

"Good," she said. "Things are very good. You are very good."

She gave his shirt another yank and he came forward to kiss her, light kisses that he kept breaking off to pull back so he could look at her. As if she might disappear.

"I'm here," she said. "I'm not going anywhere."

"Sure you are," Dodge said, sliding a hand down her back. "You're going with me."

A little tingle then in the base of her spine. Partly to do with the way he was touching her, and partly with those words.

You're going with me.

"Where exactly is it we're going?" She heard the new note in her voice, and he heard it, too. Drew back from his exploration of her neck.

"We'll figure that out together. There's no hurry."

He leaned down over her and kissed her in earnest, and Julia fell into that kiss as she would into a well, sweet-smelling and cool, bottomless. She fumbled at buttons and he helped her, stripping off his clothing without letting go until they were both shivering, naked in the cool air but in too much of a hurry to stop and pull back the quilts and blankets.

"Now," she whispered. "Now now now."

And then her cell phone rang. For the very first time in her hearing, the phone rang and Julia would have gladly pitched it out the window. Dodge leaned back and looked at her.

"You had to set up the phone," she said.

And he grinned and kissed her once, hard and quick before he reached across her—those long bones and muscles and all that lovely skin—and got the phone, flipped it open, and hit the speaker button.

"Julia?" Exa's voice high and tinny. "Is that you, sugar? I'm about worried out of my head about you."

"It's me," Julia said, turning on her stomach to evade Dodge's questing hands. "I'm sorry I worried you, Exa. I'm in Brooklyn, everything's fine."

"Brooklyn! Well, I should've guessed. You put a scare into me," Exa said. And with an edge of suspicion. "You're really in Brooklyn? Is Dodge there?"

"Right here, Exa."

"Well good, because I need to talk to you, too. Leo called me not ten minutes ago to say your car was missing from the parking lot and he thought maybe it had been stole. Do you want me to call the police?"

"The car's here," Dodge said. He was lying on his side next to Julia and he moved closer and ran his bare foot down her leg.

"What's the car doing there?" Exa was saying. And: "Julia Hamblin Darrow, did you drive all the way up there?"

"I did," Julia said, trying to hold Dodge's hands away without making any noise.

"Well, I'll be—" Exa broke off. "What are you two doing?"

"Talking to you on the phone," Dodge said. "How are things down there?" And then he flipped himself in one neat move so he was hovering over Julia's back, suspended on knees and forearms, his skin barely brushing hers and radiating heat like a live bomb.

"We had a real good day today, a record-breaking day if I do say so myself who shouldn't. Oh and there's some good news."

Dodge put his mouth on Julia's shoulder and bit, and then he slid down her back until he was off the bed and his breath was warming the inside of her thighs.

"Lorna Jean," Exa began.

Julia said: "You're breaking up," even as she slapped the phone shut and let out the long breathy moan she had been holding back.

"Dodge. Dodge!"

He raised his head. "Hmmmm?"

Julia turned over, grabbed him by both ears, and pulled him up until they were face-to-face. He was smiling. He was beautiful, and the things she had been wanting from him, very specific things that had to do with penetration and his weight on top of her and lots of sweaty hot thrusting, all that was gone. She still wanted him, but more than that she needed to say something.

"I love you. I drove up here to tell you that. I didn't know at first that's why I was driving up here, but I figured it out. I figured a lot of things out."

"Jones," Dodge said, wiggling a little so that she felt every inch of him, every determined, ready, rock-hard inch. "I love you, too, and I'll tell you all about that in detail. But later, because right now, right now, darling . . ."

"Right now," said Julia.

THEY WOKE TO THE SOUND OF DOGS IN THE HALL, THE FRANTIC click of nails that Dodge recognized even more than the distinctive yips and yaps. He got out of bed and opened the door a crack.

Ben was there, snow on the shoulders of his jacket and on his hair.

He had Scoot and Jimmy Dean on leashes, which he thrust into Dodge's hand.

He whispered, "Mom says breakfast starts in a half hour and an hour after that she's shutting down the kitchen. And Uncle Jim and Aunt Gigi are here with their boys and Gigi brought like, a ton of her chocolate truffles. Oh, and Grandma Lucy invited your friend Link to stay for the whole holiday weekend as he's got no family to go home to."

"Thanks, Ben. That's about all the news I can handle just now."

As he closed the door Ben said, "But I haven't told you yet about this afternoon."

The dogs launched themselves onto the bed dragging their leashes and Dodge climbed in after them. Scoot was sitting on Julia's chest, putting delicate little kisses on her cheek. Jimmy Dean sat at the foot of the bed sending Dodge a look that meant he had some making up to do.

Julia said, "What was that about truffles?"

THEY CROWDED TOGETHER INTO THE TINY BATHROOM, THE IDEA being, Dodge told Julia solemnly, that with so many people in the house it was their duty to shower together to save on the hot water bill.

She said, "I am sore in places I didn't know I had." But she was smiling, nothing of regret there.

"Hot water can work miracles," Dodge said.

She threw him a look. "You just want to get ahold of that adjustable shower head."

"No," Dodge said. "I want to get ahold of you and the adjustable shower head. But I'm saving that for tonight."

He was feeling good. Awake and alert, full of energy and not in the least daunted by the crazy day ahead of them. As he soaped Julia's back and then, more gingerly, her front, they talked about what she should expect, the traditional Bugiardini Christmas Eve afternoon extravaganza when Tom's brothers wrestled the twelve-foot-tall tree into submission and his female relatives crowded into the kitchen to put together a dinner that started with seven different fish dishes and really got going from there.

He heard himself talking, and he realized that Julia wasn't saying much. And it occurred to him that in the bright light of a snowy winter morning she might be having some doubts. In fact, he realized, she must be exhausted, physically and emotionally.

"Jones."

"Hmmmm?"

"We can hide out here all day if you want. Just you and me and the dogs. I'll sneak down for provisions."

She turned to face him and he saw how pale she was. She looked done in, that was the word that came to him. He felt the clutch of it in his gut, but then she raised her eyes to his and managed a small smile.

"I wouldn't miss any of it," she said.

"If you're worried that I'd be disappointed—"

She put her fingers against his mouth. "No, it's not that. I do want to be part of this, but now that I'm here I can't stop thinking about . . ." She paused. "This is so different, I can't begin to explain it to you."

"Christmas with Charlie?"

She didn't flinch at the name, or turn away. She drew in a deep breath. "I haven't let myself think much about my family in the last five years. In fact, I've worked really hard not to think about them at all. But ever since I got on the road with your grandmother, I can't help myself."

Dodge turned off the water and grabbed towels for both of them. Swallowed down the questions that came to mind, because they could only distract her from whatever it was she needed to say.

She took her time drying off, and then wrapped in a towel, she went out to sit on the bed and look out the window. She patted the bed and Dodge went to sit beside her. Behind them both dogs were snoring in a syncopated rhythm.

"Harmonic convergence," Dodge said, and Julia hiccupped a laugh.

"You know the strange thing? Since Charlie died I've dreamed about snow at least three times a week. I turned it into something dark in my mind, but now I remember that I used to love the snow." She turned to look at him. "Would you do me a favor? Go someplace with me?"

"Sure," Dodge said. "What did you have in mind?"

"Vermont. To have a look around, see that movie theater."

"What if I'm not interested in Vermont?"

"Then you could come with me to Chicago."

"Chicago." He cleared his throat.

"It's simple," Julia said. "I need to see my father and tell him some things."

"Is that simple?" Dodge asked.

"It can be. You could try it with your father."

"More wisdom from Lucy."

"I think she's right," Julia said. "I'm going to talk to my father and tell him some simple truths. So I can stop pushing it away all the time. It's too hard, trying to keep them out of my head."

Dodge said, "That's not a bad plan, Jones. If you're sure you want to go, I'll come along for the ride. In fact, we can cross the country every which way from Sunday."

"I'll be Audrey Hepburn, you'll be Albert Finney."

"Remind me which movie we're talking about."

"*Two for the Road.* Set in France, early sixties."

"I remember. We'd have to get a convertible. And didn't that relationship end badly?"

"We'll write our own script." She leaned into him, her gaze still on the snow. "Are you going to sell Scriveners?"

"To Heep and Caro," he said. "In the spring."

"Maybe I'll sell Cocoon," she said, almost dreamily. "Maybe Nils will want to buy it for Mayme."

"Hmmmm," Dodge said. Happy to float along with her as possibilities passed through her mind, pictures of what might be ahead, turned over and examined one by one. There was no urgency in any of this, no need to make decisions right here and now.

Julia's cell phone rang, and they turned their heads in that direction. Dodge leaned over and picked it up, held it so that they could both read the window where the caller ID information pulsed: Truman Hamblin.

She drew in a short, very sharp breath and let it go. "My father. He has never once called me," she said. "Not since I left Chicago. It's always Bonnie who calls."

Dodge said, "Maybe they got the portraits and he wants to thank you."

She looked at him, surprise and understanding in her expression. The phone stopped ringing.

"Or to scream at me."

"Maybe he wants to apologize."

She gave a startled laugh at that idea. That her father might have spent the last five years thinking things through on his own. That he might have come to some conclusions she hadn't anticipated, and discovered some regrets.

"Most likely he's calling to ask about the rest of Charlie's stuff. Bonnie wants it all. She wanted Charlie to herself and now she wants everything he owned. Including me."

"That's an interesting way to look at it," Dodge said.

"It just came to me." Another short laugh. "Welcome to the theater of the obvious."

Before he could think what to say to that, the phone started to ring again and the caller ID winked back into focus.

"He'll leave a message," Dodge said. "You don't have to do this now."

"But I do," Julia said. "I'm going to answer. Maybe it would be best to say those things I need to say right now, get it over with."

"You want me to stay?"

Julia nodded. She held out one hand to Dodge, and with the other she flipped the cell phone open.

In the late afternoon when the tree was up and the younger kids had been put down for naps, Dodge rescued Julia from the kitchen where Nora's mother-in-law and the aunts were teaching her how to cook squid. It had been snowing heavily for a couple hours and a group of the less couch-bound were going sledding, and did she have any interest?

The truth was, Julia couldn't remember the last time she had felt so awake. The idea of walking through an unfamiliar town struck no chords except curiosity and a tingle that might have been the first flush of anxiety but felt at that moment more like excitement.

In a quarter hour she found herself outside, dressed in borrowed winter gear including a silly but warm hat that had pom-poms and earflaps. Someone had stuffed a car full with every surface that could be used to sled, including what Julia recognized as school cafeteria trays, much battered. One of Nora's brothers-in-law—it might have been Jerry or George or Mario—called out to see if they wanted a ride to the park, but Dodge waved him on.

At that moment Julia remembered the dogs.

"They're already on their way," Dodge assured her. "The kids have got them on leashes, don't worry."

Julia found she was almost incapable of worry. She tried to work up some anxiety, but the street they were walking down was beautifully still in the falling snow and the shoveled sidewalks felt solid under her borrowed boots. And Dodge was holding her hand. Even through two sets of gloves she could feel his steady warmth.

"This is nice."

He glanced down at her as if he wasn't quite sure to take that at face value.

Julia said, "I'm really happy to be here."

His expression relaxed. "Me too. I'm glad you're here, too, and most of all I'm glad of a little quiet. I'm kind of surprised you held out as long as you did."

"You thought I might bolt."

"Hey, I almost bolted. I stuck around for you."

"Maybe I was sticking around for you," Julia said. "You don't always have to be the sane one. I can take a turn now and then."

"Good to know." He squeezed her hand. "There is something I'm a little worried about. I should have raised the topic this morning, but given the circumstances . . ." He paused.

To Julia the morning seemed a very long time ago, and that brief phone conversation with her father even longer. A phone conversation that had resolved nothing at all, beyond the fact that the portraits had indeed arrived. Her father's voice had been immediately familiar and still very strange as he hemmed and hawed. Trying to get up the nerve to say something, looking for help. Julia had been utterly calm, and sure of one thing above all others: he would have to find his own words; she would not rescue him. And so she had wished him a merry Christmas and hung up and then cried for ten minutes, tears of frustration but also relief. That she had taken that first step, and survived.

"Look," Julia said, "I know I haven't always been forthcoming about what was on my mind, but I really am feeling alarmingly good. So I may have a relapse or two, okay, I'm aware of that. But I'm not going to borrow trouble, and neither should you."

They had come around a corner and there was a park spread out before them, rolling hills and trees caked in snow, all of it blindingly bright in spite of the cloud cover. From the other side of the park, just out of sight, came the sound of laughter and shouts. People flinging themselves down snowy hillsides as if the idea of broken bones had nothing to do with them. As if the weather and the day had rendered them immune to pain, strangers to the possibility of loss.

Dodge leaned down and pressed his cold cheek to hers, turned his face and kissed her.

"Let's throw caution to the wind, you and me," he said. "Let's see how far we get."

"John Dodge," Julia said, "that's the best idea you've had in a long time."

46

You've reached John Dodge's cell phone. Please leave a message.

Dodge, this is Big Dove calling with Trixie standing right next to me to wish you a Merry Christmas. We wanted to say everything is just fine down here, and to ask about Julia. Exa says she's up there with you in Brooklyn, which I myself am almost afraid to believe but then love is a powerful force for good in this world. You give her a hug from both of us, and take one for yourself.

You've reached John Dodge's cell phone. Please leave a message.

Hey, Dodge, this is Bean. Nils said I could call you so don't worry that I've got in the habit of borrowing phones without permission. I was calling to see how the dogs are and if they miss me, and also to see how Julia's doing because I miss her a whole lot and I hope she's feeling better. And also I've got news Mama said I could tell you. Nils is coming back to stay in Lamb's Corner and they are going to get married. Even Granny Pearl has given her blessing as long as they get married in our church, and I'm going to wear a dress the color of buttercups. And then Mama's going back to college and she's going to study whatever she wants because she won't have to worry about tuition anymore. I think maybe she should be a therapist like you were, because she's good at figuring out what people mean and want even when they won't say it. Like you.

You've reached John Dodge's cell phone. Please leave a message.

John Dodge, this is Bob Lee Cowper calling to say I hope you are enjoying Christmas, and that your new year is a good one, full of welcome surprises and good health. I am having a fine time roaming the world. I recommend it highly. No better way to spend your days.

AUTHOR'S NOTE

To be absolutely clear: There is no Lamb's Corner in South Carolina. There is no Moulton County. Langtree Plantation is a fiction. Likewise, the South Carolina Chicopee River is a product of my imagination. That is to say, I have taken liberties with geography and history both, all in the pursuit of a Story.

I cannot pretend to be a southerner, but I can claim a lifelong interest in southern culture and history. I also have a lot of good friends who are in fact southerners, and who are kind enough to entertain my endless Yankee questions. The usual disclaimers: All errors I claim as my very own. Everything I got right should be credited to the authors of dozens of books, magazines (particularly the *Oxford American*), and helpful friends: Ruth Czirr and Paul Willenborg, Cheryll Kinsley, Bruce Beasley, Penny Chambers, Thor Hansen, and Suzanne Paola.

Finally, I am as ever thankful to Jill Grinberg, agent almighty and voice of reason, and to my editors Rachel Kahan (Putnam) and Jackie Cantor (Berkley Books). Never last nor least: Bill and Elisabeth.